More praise for
LONG RANGE PATROL

"Dennis Foley mastered Ranger-warfare expertise in the cauldron of Vietnam combat, and his authentic *Long Range Patrol* cuts trail, smokes out the enemy, and delivers the reader on target with the same rapid-fire dominance."

—SHELBY L. STANTON
Capt. U.S. Army (Ret.)
Author of *Vietnam Order of Battle*

"[A] sprawling tale of the Army's Rangers operations in the early days of the Vietnam War . . . The combat scenes are so authentic that recruits could study them."

—*Kirkus Reviews*

By Dennis Foley
Published by The Ballantine Publishing Group:

LONG RANGE PATROL
NIGHT WORK
SPECIAL MEN: A LRP's Recollections
TAKE BACK THE NIGHT

Books published by The Ballantine Publishing Group
are available at quantity discounts on bulk purchases
for premium, educational, fund-raising, and special
sales use. For details, please call 1-800-733-3000.

LONG RANGE PATROL

A Novel of Vietnam

Dennis Foley

IVY BOOKS • NEW YORK

An Ivy Book
Published by The Ballantine Publishing Group
Copyright © 1992 by Dennis Foley
Map copyright © 1983 by Random House, Inc.

Map by Alex Jay

http://www.randomhouse.com

Library of Congress Catalog Card Number: 91-90634

ISBN 0-8041-0707-6

Printed in Canada

First Trade Edition: June 1992
First Mass Market Edition: October 1993

10 9 8 7 6

This book is dedicated to Allison, Audra, and Michele.

ACKNOWLEDGMENTS

I wrote this book with the fondest memories and deepest respect for those who gave of themselves to serve valiantly in reconnaissance and long range patrol units in Vietnam.

It would not have been possible without their courage and tenacity. They never complained, never whined, and never gave up.

I must also thank Owen Lock, Chris Bunch, and Allan Cole. Without their help, support, and encouragement these pages never would have been written.

"The people that walked in darkness have seen a great light: they that dwell in the land of the shadow of death, upon them hath the light shined."

ISAIAH 9:2

CHAPTER 1

It had been pelting rain most of the day, but in the break between squalls, the sound of the rain was replaced by the noise of excited insects, which filled the heavy air, blending into a high-pitched shriek. Though the commotion was aggravating, both types of noise covered the movement of the six American soldiers who threaded expertly through the trees in single file. They were thankful to have the overcast and the noise to cover their movement.

In the trees the visibility was so poor that even twenty feet apart each patrol member could feel the man in front far better than he could see him. Still, the patrol made good progress until the third man momentarily lost sight of the man in front of him. Unrattled by the break, he quickly crouched down to silhouette the lost soldier's outline against the only slightly lighter horizon.

Finding the man in front of him, Jim Hollister, a young Infantry first lieutenant, stepped up and tapped three-stripe Sergeant Camacho on the shoulder.

Camacho, in turn, quickened his pace to catch up with Davis, who was walking point. Davis calmly froze and then settled silently into a squat without turning around. He kept his eyes on the black void in front of him and waited for some word to be passed up.

Once Davis had stopped, each man behind him did the same, falling to one knee and facing outward in a ready firing position.

Hollister moved past Camacho, knelt near Davis and whispered in his ear. Before beginning, he exhaled most of his breath to avoid the hissing sounds of whispering that carry great distances in the damp night air. ''Goin' forward to check the ambush site. Hold what you got.''

1

Staff Sergeant Davis, the assistant patrol leader, nodded and looked back to get a feel for where the others were.

"If I'm not here in one five," Hollister said, "hustle back to the last rally point—that burned-out mahogany tree about three hundred meters back. You hear somebody bust caps while I'm out on this rekkie—head straight back to the RP. Don't be a hero. If I make it, I'll find you."

Davis nodded again and replied, "Okay, boss." He watched Hollister as long as his outline was visible and then turned to scan his wedge of the hasty defensive perimeter the team had formed. Satisfied, Davis crawled back to Camacho to pass the word to the others.

Hollister weaved through the brush, his movements silent, slow and fluid, first finding solid footing with his toe, then letting his foot settle while holding his weapon at the ready—high and across his chest. He kept his eyes moving—searching the terrain to the limits of his vision for anything that might be trouble.

Abruptly, the vegetation in front of him ended at the lip of a large bomb crater half filled with brackish rainwater. Before stepping into the clearing, Hollister stopped and dropped to his knee.

For several long seconds he waited and listened. Finally, confident that he could move on safely, Hollister got to his feet and skirted the bomb crater, hugging the tree line to keep from pasting his outline against the skyline.

The Viet Cong platoon leader carried a Tokarev 9mm pistol on his belt. Other members of the nineteen-man platoon carried AK-47 automatic rifles—all except the four who had American M-16s, an RPD machine gunner, and one armed with a B-40 rocket launcher.

Noticing that his men were beginning to tire, the platoon leader poked at some and whispered to others; reminding them to stay alert—American or South Korean patrols could be anywhere in the area.

Detecting motion up in front of him, Davis thumbed his selector lever, ready to drop his rifle off of safe two notches to full automatic. Soon the image took shape—Hollister had returned.

Davis reached back and alerted Camacho, who, in turn, threw a small stick, hitting Specialist 4 Vinson. Eventually the word got back to the last man. The lieutenant was back and they could expect to move out quickly.

Hollister motioned toward the objective. He huddled with Davis and Camacho, then half whispered and half gestured, indicating that he had been to the ambush site and that it was what they expected.

Taking the point, Hollister cautiously moved the patrol forward across the same ground he had just checked out. The order of march was Hollister, Davis, Vinson, Doc Norris, Camacho, and PFC Theodore—the tail gunner.

The closer they got to their destination, the more cautious they became. The last thing they wanted was to be discovered moving into their ambush site. A small patrol was rarely in a position to slug it out with any enemy element while on the move.

They reached the site without delay and held up while Hollister carefully led each man into his firing position. In the darkness it was very easy to get turned around, so he wanted to make sure that everyone knew where the killing zone was and where the other members of the patrol were. Hollister knew of soldiers who had fired on their own patrol members, thinking they were firing on the enemy. He also wanted to make sure he knew *exactly* where each man was.

Once he had positioned the patrol, the final ambush layout was Hollister, Doc Norris, Davis and Vinson in the center, and Camacho and Theodore well out to the flanks. Everyone was facing south but Doc, who faced north to provide their only rear security.

With his compass, Hollister checked their orientation, comparing it to his mental picture of the map that he had memorized earlier in the day, making sure he had his cardinal directions right. Come time to call for supporting fires, there would be no time for him to get oriented.

While Hollister took care of his highest priority tasks, the others laid out grenades and ammunition at arm's length, then— one at a time—moved forward to check out the killing zone and put out their Claymore mines.

Like moving into the ambush site, it was a very vulnerable time for the team. Their fires couldn't be effective or even coordinated if one of them remained forward when they were discovered by someone in the clearing. Instead of returning a heavy volume of fire, they would have to break contact with the enemy and try to make it to the rally point. Even that effort would be compromised by the lack of a coordinated move.

Once everyone was in position for the night, Hollister breathed a little easier. Still, he couldn't resist taking just one more look. One at a time he checked each man's position, fields of fire, ammo, relationship to the others, and their grip on the situation. He had to know that they knew what was going on. Confusion meant disaster—absolutely.

Satisfied the ambush was ready, Hollister settled into the most comfortable waiting position he could find on the uneven ground. He and the others would not move much until they sprang the ambush or until dawn came.

Although he was motionless, Hollister's mind was running. Details kept clicking by—communications, artillery support, medevac radio frequencies and call signs, return routes, escape routes, rally points. He felt his chest tightening and tried to convince himself to relax—to breathe more slowly. No sooner did he start to take his own advice than he felt his fingers absentmindedly reaching out to reconfirm the location of his M-16 magazines and hand grenades.

The VC platoon snaked slowly through the knots of bamboo that defined the transition from the tall trees of the rain forest hills to the paddy fields in the valley below.

The platoon's level of alertness was obvious in their cautious movement. They were anxious as they approached their objective, but were also sloppy, hungry, and weary. No sparkle of humor or hope crossed any of their faces. They walked like men without a future, only a present.

The rain started to fall again. At first it was light and warm, then cold and drenching. A few of the VC pulled out pieces of nylon, makeshift ponchos that afforded little protection from the rain. They all got soaked within minutes.

The platoon leader pulled on a pair of wool knit gloves. He wore them as if they set him off from the others. In the downpour they were far more symbolic than functional.

The hard rain also fell on the ambush site. It made Hollister feel like a real heel for the hell he had raised back at the base camp. Theodore had stuffed a poncho into his rucksack, but Hollister caught it on the patrol inspection and made him leave it behind. He also gave him an ass chewing, reminding him that the rustling of an army poncho could be heard for hundreds of yards in the bush.

It was always cold at night in the field. In the States, journalists wrote about the blistering heat of the midday sun and the smothering heat of the dark jungle. With more than six months in the field behind him, Hollister knew better. He had never been as cold in a German winter as he had been in the rain forest of Vietnam. The season made little difference. When it was warm, huge billowing rain clouds formed late in the day, then it started raining before dark and continued into the evening. Even though it didn't rain all night, each man would still spend the night wet. As the temperature dropped, the wetness became a cold, biting, and draining discomfort that made the night long and miserable. And in the rainy season it was wet all the time. In the dark it was hard for a soldier to tell what season it was. He only knew there were no comfortable nights in the bush in Vietnam.

Cold or not, everyone knew that Hollister was right in making Theodore leave his poncho behind. Ponchos were for base perimeter duty and occasionally taken on patrols for gear that needed to be kept dry. But rolling around in a poncho while sleeping was like putting up a marker in the night to let the VC know where you were.

Phuc, the VC platoon leader, had not been in South Vietnam very long. He was assigned to his platoon after its leader was killed in a B-52 strike three months earlier. Just thirty, he had been a college professor in Haiphong before being drafted and selected for officer training.

Being called to serve his country was expected. He had often wondered what took them so long to get around to him. He had adjusted well to soldiering. But the adjustment to the physical life was not as easy. He had never been very active or physical—as many of his soldiers had been in civilian life. They had been farmers and laborers. He had been a student for as long as he could remember. When he was inducted into the army, he resolved to do his part and not complain. He had convinced himself that if he were to serve well, he might be able to shorten the war and return to his classroom and the students he loved.

But it had bothered him that not much of his training was in the field skills needed in South Vietnam. Instead, it had been heavily weighted toward the political necessities of providing positive leadership for the long struggle facing the North Vietnamese. Phuc had hoped that the study of field operations could be learned on the job. So far, all of his lessons had been hard-learned.

He looked around for some evidence of his ability to motivate his men. He had tried hard, but they all looked tired and un-moved by his pep talk earlier in the day. He rationalized to himself that it was just time to stop for rest and food. They would be better after some rest.

Holding up the column, Phuc went to his three sergeants to coordinate the final plans for the night's operations.

After the platoon established a hasty defensive perimeter, Phuc found a spot in the center. As he dropped his rucksack to the ground, he resisted the urge to groan. He knew that he should lead by example. If he wanted his troops to endure the hard-ships, he must do so cheerfully.

After trying one spot and then another to find a decent piece of ground to sit on, he settled on the exposed roots of a tall tree. At least it was free of the rocks and twigs that had made the first two spots unbearable.

From his wet canvas rucksack he withdrew a small packet wrapped in oilcloth. After weeks in the field he was unaware of its smell; everything he owned smelled. His uniform hadn't been washed in weeks and his few possessions smelled musty, smoky, and moldy. He had even stopped looking at his fingernails. There was no way for him to keep them clean, so he had decided to just ignore them. To Phuc, ignoring personal hygiene was a loss of dignity. But he had no choice, and he hoped that putting the energy into fighting for his country would replace the loss of self-esteem that he suffered for being filthy.

He unwrapped the cloth which held a ball of long-cold cooked rice. As he did at each meal, he routinely picked as many of the small insects as he could see from the grains of rice and moved aside the rice that had been crushed under the pressure of his backpack.

The food smelled of the wood fire that it had been cooked over. From a small tin container Phuc extracted a few pieces of dried fish the size of minnows and mixed them with the cold rice to provide some taste. The meal would never satisfy an American soldier, but for Phuc it was one of the simple plea-sures of his life, and he appreciated it.

Breaking off chunks of the clammy rice ball, Phuc ate his only meal of the day. As he ate he looked around at the outlines of the others. They were lean and wiry. Their hands were cut and callused from carrying their weapons and making their way through the rain forest. It had been days since they had been allowed to dry out their gear, get some sun on their wrinkled skin, and let the platoon barber work his scissors.

A small pain tugged at the center of his chest. Phuc missed his wife, Ly. He put down the ball of rice and took a cheap plastic wallet from his rucksack. Inside it he found his small photo of Ly. He placed it on top of his gear so that he could look at her while he ate. It was so dark under the large tree that he wasn't sure if he could actually see the photo or if he wanted to see it so badly that he could visualize it from memory. He didn't really care. Either way, he could see Ly.

She wore a North Vietnamese uniform and was standing in front of her antiaircraft gun just outside of Haiphong. Her long, straight, black hair was pulled back into a ponytail, revealing strong shoulders and large breasts. Phuc felt a twinge of excitement remembering the last night they spent together. She was a quiet woman, but her demure attitude disappeared when they were intimate. She loved sex and loved Phuc. He missed her. But worse than his longing for her was the feeling in the pit of his stomach that he would die in South Vietnam and never see her or the child she was carrying. Nevertheless, the small picture took him away for a moment from the rain and the cold and the fear. He stared at it.

He felt his eyes starting to flood, and immediately worried that one of his men might discover his loss of control. He quickly wiped his face with the small scrap of camouflage parachute material that he wore around his neck and looked around, but no one was even looking back in his direction.

Phuc took a last look at the photo and carefully tucked it back into its place of safekeeping. Worrying that he could be accused of spending too much time dwelling on himself and his own selfish thoughts, he pulled out a notebook that had seen many trail miles and opened it to look at a detailed diagram of a tiny farming hamlet. He focused on the details—streambeds, footbridges, vegetable gardens. Even the location of the livestock pens was noted. Phuc studied the sketch as he finished his meal. He tested himself by trying to identify the features by their locations on the drawing, since he couldn't read the notations under them.

The hamlet was named My Phu.

"Comrade Phuc, I would like to request extra time for my men to rehearse our actions at the hamlet tonight," said Sergeant Thanh, a man of forty with small, recessed eyes and long, wispy hairs growing from a raisinlike mole on his left cheek. "I am unhappy with the preparations."

Phuc looked at his watch. "Yes. But make sure you work fast," he said, without glancing at Sergeant Thanh. "I want to be back on the march by midnight."

Thanh nodded in acknowledgment and headed back toward his squad. As he walked, one leg dragged slightly from a permanent limp caused by a bomb fragment that he had taken in the hip six years earlier.

But Thanh's general air of fatigue and resignation came from having been at war since his ninth birthday. Phuc shuddered. As a platoon leader he would be repeatedly committed to combat and would most likely be at war until his death. He had never known peace in his life, and in his mind there was no real hope of ever winning the war against the enemy's huge machine.

"Make sure that the American equipment is ready, Sergeant," Phuc said.

Sergeant Thanh looked back at Phuc and grunted affirmatively.

The rain came down harder than before. Phuc wrapped up the scraps of his rice and stuffed the packet back into his rucksack. Rain ran down his face, so he dropped his head to avoid the cold assault. As he did, he wrapped his fingers around his wallet. To him the photo inside it was the only reality in his life that didn't promise death.

Through his burning eyes Hollister looked out at the killing zone. He tried to memorize the details of the small clearing, knowing that even darker hours would surely follow. He picked up the piece of commo wire that had been stretched out to the left of the ambush and yanked on it. He got an immediate response—two tugs. It meant that Camacho was awake and on the job. Camacho was just beyond the turn in the trail leading into the clearing. His job was to give early warning if an enemy patrol approached from the ambush's left.

Picking up the second wire, Hollister tugged again and received two tugs from Theodore, who had the same job on the right flank of the ambush. Hollister dropped the wire, satisfied—for the moment. He had worked quickly to get the ambush set up. There was a long night ahead of him and he felt frustrated that once the ambush was in place there was nothing to do but wait.

He hated being at the mercy of the enemy. He fought the urge to recheck the others or even take a few steps up or down the trail that ran through the center of the clearing. He hoped he wouldn't get sleepy, but he knew better.

Home. That would do it. It always did it. He would think of home. He knew that whenever he thought of home he could keep from falling asleep.

Susan could do it best of all. He wondered how many other American soldiers thought of American women while they were trying to fill the hours on ambushes, guard duty, radio watch, and a thousand other tedious night shifts in the war.

His mind wandered to the night at the Port Authority Bus Terminal on Forty-second Street in Manhattan. He was waiting that night, too. But that night it was good for him to wait.

He had watched her as she walked through the bus terminal. She made eye contact with no one. She was classy, even cocky. It was the first thing he saw about her—her attitude. He then took note of her pleasantly tight Levi's, her boots, and her navy watch coat. Her hair was light brown, long and very straight. Hollister liked the way it flared from her face and flowed behind her when she walked. She said a lot to him by holding her head up and moving with a purpose. She knew exactly where she was going, and Hollister wanted to know too. So did every other man in the Port Authority.

Checking his watch for time till his bus, he picked up his bag and followed her through the terminal.

Trying not to look too eager, Hollister sat down on the stool next to her at the coffee counter. She didn't even look up. She simply kept surveying the plastic-covered menu.

"What'll it be, honey?" the waitress asked, pulling a stubby pencil from her netted hair and tapping the point on her order pad.

Susan made a quick check of her watch and then smiled at the heavyset woman, "How 'bout a piece of blueberry pie and coffee—black?" she replied.

"I'll have the same," Hollister said.

Both women looked at Hollister as if he hadn't been invited. He smiled sheepishly—busted!

The waitress put the pencil back in her hair and stuck the two order slips on the rotating wheel in the window behind her, flipped two coffee mugs onto the counter and filled them.

"Pretty clumsy, huh?" Hollister asked.

"Yes," Susan replied without looking at him.

"Well, maybe I could start with some other clever ice-breaker."

"Don't bother. It isn't likely to work," Susan said as she turned to look at him, making sure that her expression meant business.

He looked into her eyes. They were incredible. Gray, almost metallic. He preferred to think that her gaze was playful flirting. He wasn't going to give up that easily. "My name's Jim—Jim Hollister. And I wasn't really hitting on you."

"Oh?" she replied, not believing him. "Well, it sure felt like you were working up to it."

He smiled broadly. "Well then, in that case, how'm I doing?"

She burst out laughing. "I have to give it to you. You don't come on too strong, but you do make up for it by being persistent and overly optimistic."

"Whew, that's great to hear. I was afraid that I was losing my touch."

"Ohhh, so you do this often?" Susan asked almost playfully.

"No, ah . . . no I don't. I haven't. I meant I haven't had much of a chance lately."

"Too bad. Been in jail, or what?" Susan asked.

The waitress returned and quietly slipped the pie in front of Susan and Hollister. As if on autopilot, she poured more coffee and dropped the checks between the two cups. Susan started eating her pie.

"Worse. Been in the army for the last three years."

Susan made a face. "Hmmm, I was hoping the short hair might mean Olympic swimmer or something."

"We're not going to get into one of those 'I don't date guys in the service' conversations, are we?" Hollister asked.

"No, you won't have to worry about that," Susan answered.

"That mean you do date GIs?"

"No," Susan said flatly. "It means that we aren't going to be talking that long."

"That's too bad. I was hoping we could have dinner together, or something."

Susan pushed the stale pie away from her. "We just did." She got up from the counter.

"Hey, you aren't leaving?" Hollister asked.

"*I* am leaving and *we* have finished this conversation," Susan said.

"Angry?"

"No. I just don't need the aggravation. Anyway, I have to meet a friend whose bus should be here by now."

"So, what are the chances of—" he started to ask.

"Pretty slim," Susan replied, without much conviction. She reached into her coat pocket and pulled out a card. "But don't let that hold you back." She handed him the business card, spun on her boot heel and walked away.

He decided that he loved the way she walked. Her legs looked great in the jeans. He watched until the crowd folded in behind her, then he looked down at the card. It read: SUSAN T. WIL-KERSON, *Editorial Research Assistant, Skyline Magazine—New York.*

The other customers at the coffee counter broke out in cheers and applause for Hollister's partial victory. He blushed, realizing that his efforts had been watched by all. But he smiled and took a mock bow.

A raw burn ran up Hollister's leg. He flinched but stopped himself in mid-response to keep from making noise. It had to be a land leech. The little bastards lived on the floor of the rain forest and found juicy Americans by some kind of radar. When he sat still long enough, they always found him; he'd become conscious of the burning sensation when the raw spot they created made contact with rough clothing or his salty sweat.

There was nothing he could do. He'd just have to wait until daylight to root the little pest out of his boot. The leech wasn't dangerous, but by the time he could get around to removing it, it would probably have some friends with it.

He looked at the luminous dial on his watch and resisted a sigh. It was only midnight. He wrapped his arms across his chest for warmth and tried to think of something else.

It was going to be a very long night—his two hundred seventh night in Vietnam.

Phuc could barely make out Sergeant Thanh in the dark night and driving rain. But he knew that the rain and cloud cover would conceal their movement to the hamlet. Still, the same rain would cause trouble in communications, footing, visibility, and resolve.

"Your squad will lead, Sergeant Thanh."

"Yes. We are ready. May our night be successful," Thanh dutifully replied as he led his squad past Lieutenant Phuc.

Silently, the platoon then took up march interval and slipped back into the tree line. Phuc fell in behind the last man in Sergeant Thanh's squad. He took a deep breath, hoping that he would be up to the task before them.

The people of My Phu had resisted the local Viet Cong and had informed on the VC cadre in the district. The mere fact that they had been disloyal to the Viet Cong was enough for the VC to teach the farmers a lesson. But since they were responsible for the death of three local Communist guerrillas, an example had to be made.

Phuc had been instructed that by dawn there must be nothing but corpses in My Phu.

After more than an hour on the march, Phuc held up his platoon to get his bearings. Without a proper compass or map, he walked off the line of march to the top of a nearby knoll to look out over the valley below them.

As far as he could see through the rain, there were geometric squares of rice. They were like the rice fields near his home in the north. And the rain made it all look so clean and lush.

The valley supplied rice for a large portion of South Vietnam and was named for the largest nearby city—An Hoa. Somewhere in that valley sat Phuc's objective. He looked at his watch. It was nearing two. He would have to move his men faster to get the job done and be able to slip back into the hills before daybreak.

Hollister found himself drawing up into a ball to preserve body heat. To take his mind off the cold, he looked up and down the ambush to check on the others. They were alert and motionless. He wondered what was going through their minds. Were they thinking of sleeping bags? How many of the others had leech problems? How many of them had scooped out a depression in the ground below them to piss without having to get up and leave the site?

He was proud that he would not hear about it until they were back at the base camp. Only then would they bitch and complain and brag. And they would do it in great detail and with much bravado.

The fabric of someone's jungle fatigues made a soft swishing sound as he shifted his position. Hollister looked in the direction of the noise and saw Doc Norris facing to the rear.

Doc was prepared for two jobs. For rear security, his weapon was at the ready. And if they made contact, he would take on his primary job as medic just as soon as the shooting stopped.

While the others had placed ammunition within easy reach, Doc Norris also had the tools of his trade ready. His aid bag was unzipped so he could pull out exactly what he needed. Next to his bag were extra combat dressings, lengths of surgical tubing, a bottle of saline solution, and an open can of blood expander. They rested on a cravat that he could use to scoop up the medical supplies if they had to move in a hurry.

Hollister wanted to occupy his mind with more pleasant thoughts, but he had to resist the temptation to take too many more mental trips. There was nothing easy about being the honcho of an ambush patrol.

The Viet Cong spread out as they approached the hamlet. The lead elements of the platoon had gone ahead to scout the area, then serve as guides for the others to move quietly into firing position without spooking the livestock. Once in place, the platoon was less than ten yards from the nearest farmhouse.

Phuc spotted a small light and some movement near one of the six thatched houses. He raised his hand in alarm. His soldiers froze as a little girl returned from her family's outdoor privy. She could not have been more than nine years old.

At the hard-packed dirt porch of her house, she stopped to put her small kerosene lamp on a shaky wooden bench by the front door. Next to the bench a ceramic crock held drinking water. The girl lifted the lid and dipped an empty soda bottle into the water.

Phuc decided not to wait for her to go into the house. He signaled his squad leaders to continue moving into position.

His plan was simple. Surround the hamlet to prevent anyone from escaping, and then level it with small arms fire and rocket-propelled grenades.

Phuc moved up and down the line of men and silently checked their readiness. Reaching Sergeant Thanh, he pointed at the three water buffalo in the small livestock enclosure. Thanh nodded. He had instructed some of his men to shoot the large beasts first. They were more concerned with the danger of stampeding the water buffalo than about the people they were ready to kill.

Satisfied with the preparations, Phuc raised his pistol. Up and down the line the soldiers took aim. Phuc tried to look confident. Faltering would be taken as a lack of resolve to their cause. The swiftness of his execution must be symbolic of his commitment to victory over the south.

The rain had let up considerably, but the water still dripped down his face and off his nose. He took aim with great care. He couldn't wait. If he did, he might not be able to go through with it.

His pistol jerked back with a crack as Phuc fired a single round. The little girl was knocked off her feet as the report of the pistol began the fusillade of automatic weapons fire.

The pistol bullet passed through her tiny chest and collapsed her lung, leaving her on her back. She couldn't move. All she could see was the thatched roof overhang that had shaded her family's porch for three generations. No one could have heard the gurgling in her throat as the house's wooden beams and thatched walls shattered, splintering and raining down on her.

The sound of rifles firing on full automatic was deafening. First one and then a second structure caught fire. The darkness was pushed back by the flames of the burning hooches and the muzzle flashes of the weapons.

They fired and reloaded as fast as they could. Phuc could smell the offensive mixture of cordite and burning flesh. The pigs squealed but the water buffalo lay dead, no longer a threat to the Viet Cong soldiers.

Phuc looked around to see if there were any civilian witnesses, but he was unable to see anything outside the immediate circle of illumination.

Enough. He pulled a small tin whistle from his shirt pocket and blew it. The firing stopped.

Above the metallic sounds of the soldiers reloading their weapons, he could only hear the crackling of timbers burning and crashing to the ground in showers of sparks.

Phuc reached into his rucksack and pulled out two empty American C-ration cans and held them over his head. The squad leaders passed the word to the soldiers. Each man who had fired Viet Cong weapons bent down to pick up his brass, then dropped expended M-16 cartridges in their place. The ones who had fired M-16s left their brass on the ground, and a couple of them threw down empty M-16 magazines.

Phuc threw the C-ration cans toward the ruins then raised his hand to shade his eyes from the glare of the fire. He looked at the burning huts. The little girl's blackened hand poked through the blanket of debris. Quickly looking away, he signaled the squad leaders to withdraw.

Without a sound the platoon pulled back from what was once a hamlet that was home to six families. Nothing was standing. Chickens, pigs, and fire were the only sounds.

As the platoon slipped back into the tree line surrounding the fields belonging to My Phu, Phuc took one last look. It was gone. There was no more My Phu.

CHAPTER 2

Four A.M. It was the hour that made American soldiers border on self-destructive behavior. Like every other boonie rat, Hollister hated it. It had been bad enough in Ranger School at Fort Benning, but in Vietnam it could be deadly. At that hour Hollister's watch seemed to stop. His reality blurred and nothing registered the same as it did in the light of day.

Once, early in Hollister's tour, he sat bolt upright on another ambush, convinced that a mortar round had just landed within a few meters of his position. But then he couldn't understand why the others didn't notice it. He doubted his senses. He was sure it had happened and that other rounds would soon land. But none of the others showed any sign of alarm. He felt foolish, confused and unsure of his own powers of perception. It made him wary of anyone's perceptions at night after days or weeks of little sleep.

He fought for clarity. His eyes watered and the raw spots on his knees and elbows burned like fire from the hundreds of hours he had spent in the same position on the same kind of gritty, muddy, decaying rain forest floor.

He tried to caution himself not to let the surrealistic perceptions of the night screw up his judgment. It was so easy for the trees to become VC soldiers and the rustling of the brush to be sappers crawling his way.

He had learned one thing about that limbo world between consciousness and sleep—each man has a different reaction to the hallucinations that overtake him. He had seen soldiers try to put imaginary nickels into the trunks of trees, thinking that they were Coke machines. Once while on ambush near the Laotian border, one soldier simply started singing. He wasn't even conscious that he was doing it. The surprise ballad caused the others on the patrol to leap on him to shut him up.

Aching for relief, Hollister shifted his position without success. His muscles were unbelievably stiff. The joints in his fingers ached and the skin across the insteps of his feet hurt from the wrinkled jungle boot tongues and the constant pressure of his bootlaces.

Trying not to focus on how far off dawn was, he yearned for the warm sunlight, still looking back over his shoulder for some hopeful sign of a new day. All he found was the moon, which had started to peek through the fast moving clouds.

The hands on his watch seemed to be frozen. Hollister searched for games to keep focused. In his mind he tried to picture each of the other five scroungy members of his patrol dressed up—formally.

Vinson, a long-legged boy from Tennessee, was more Adam's apple than a tux could ever tolerate. Hollister often wondered how such an awkward softball player could be such a competent field soldier. Vinson was every bit as skilled as he was quiet, and Hollister could always count on him. Quiet, solid, reliable, but never a tux.

Three other soldiers were alive because of Vinson's quick thinking and selfless actions during a patrol that had been hit coming out of a hot landing zone some weeks earlier. Hollister made a mental note to check on a Bronze Star recommendation that he had submitted on Vinson. He didn't want it to get lost in the giant paper-eating machine that was called higher headquarters.

Next to Vinson, Staff Sergeant Davis sat up to make some adjustment to his web gear. Davis was a stocky black soldier from Missouri. Hollister thought that he had probably worn a tux before and would look good in one.

Hollister watched as Davis quietly slipped a brick-sized radio battery out of his rucksack and then silently unfolded a Buck knife with the flick of a finger. He pressed the tip of the blade flat against the battery and slit the plastic bag that covered it. He then slid the new battery into the large cargo pocket on the side of his tiger-striped fatigue trousers.

Davis was merely getting the battery ready for Vinson. And Vinson wouldn't replace the old battery and risk the snapping noises of the locking catches on the battery compartment of the PRC-25 radio. After the sun rose, when the morning rain forest noises would cover the sounds, Hollister would help Vinson do

it. The battery already in the radio was probably strong enough
to last the night, but Davis wanted one ready in case shooting
started and there was a need to replace the old one.

Hollister suddenly realized that there were no sounds. Not
just the end of the rain. Not just night quiet. But no sounds at
all. The normal night rhythms were gone, no insects, no night
birds, and no mosquitoes.

Everyone noticed it. Hollister watched as one by one each
patrol member changed position from almost ready to rock serious.

Hollister's fingers searched out his weapon. The others did
the same, and three of them felt for Claymore mine detonators.
Somewhere out there in the dark someone was coming their
way.

Hollister's mind started to leap from one thing to another—
could be a large cat, or a boar, or even a monkey or two. It
wouldn't be a problem if it was something like that. He shook
himself out of it.

Supporting fires—they had to be alerted. Just as Hollister
turned to his radio operator, Davis pressed the earpiece of Vinson's handset to his cheek to silence it and squeezed the press-
to-talk button four times to alert the base camp radio operator.

Sliding the handset to his ear, Davis heard the patrol base
Operations RTO respond immediately, "Unknown station, this
is Quarterback Three Romeo. We have a contact likely message . . . Please transmit your team number. Over."

Davis clicked the button twice, waited for a second, and then
pressed it three more times.

The base radio operator responded in a serious whisper, "We
copy, Two-three, Team Two-three. If that's an affirm, do not
respond. If incorrect, transmit your number again. Over."

Phuc was glad that the rain had finally stopped, because his
troops might be able to dry out a little before the sun rose. But
it also meant that the veil of concealment that rain had offered
was gone.

The platoon continued moving back up into the hills surrounding the valley. Phuc tried to shift his load to get more
comfortable. His rucksack had not seemed so heavy on the way
down. And climbing back up the same muddy hills through the
wet trees was more difficult.

The others were somber and preoccupied, but Phuc would let
them have a few more moments with their thoughts before cor-

recting them for walking as if on autopilot. Even if there might be ambushes set in the area, the chances were that at that time of the morning all of the would-be ambushers were asleep.

The moon started to throw shafts of light through the double-canopy vegetation as Davis reacted to tugs on the commo wire. It was Camacho giving the signal that enemy troops were moving past his position. Davis made eye contact with Hollister and pointed in the direction of the hidden Camacho.

Hollister looked at the others, who had also seen Davis's signal. He worried that the moonlight might give them away, but even he had difficulty making out his own people in the mottled shadow patterns on their camouflage uniforms and well-camouflaged faces.

Hollister tried to convince himself that they had done all that could be done to ensure their security at that moment. He forced his mind to move on to other things that could influence the outcome of what was sure to be an enemy contact.

As he ran down his mental checklist, Hollister realized that his chest was tightening again and his breathing was getting shallow. Sweat was forming under his arms.

The VC point squad, led by two soldiers and Sergeant Thanh, entered the killing zone of Hollister's ambush.

Phuc, with the second squad, walked immediately behind Sergeant Thanh's squad.

Hollister blinked to make sure that he was really seeing the first two figures in the killing zone. While he was doing that, he anxiously touched his hand grenades for the fourth time in so many minutes, just to make sure that they were still there.

The enemy point man reached the far side of the killing zone—thirteen VC soldiers had followed him into the clearing.

Hollister hoped that the trailing element, which he couldn't see, was no more than a few men. His biggest fear was of executing the ambush only to find that he had fired on the smaller portion of the enemy unit, and that the larger part was still outside the killing zone and able to flank his people.

It was a crapshoot.

Davis was the first to detonate his Claymore mine. The blast ripped through the night, instantly dropping five VC.

The other Americans opened fire. Then the night again lit up with two more Claymore explosions and four grenades that landed in the killing zone fractions of a second apart.

For a few very intense seconds the only sounds Hollister could hear were his patrol's weapons. Seven more VC fell, mortally wounded by the violent bursts of well-aimed American small arms fire.

The other VC realized what had happened and started to return fire in the general direction of the Americans—but they were shaken and forgot their training. For most of them, their aim was much too high.

Soldiers had fallen all around Phuc. He was dazed, confused, and completely disoriented. What could he do? He had allowed them to walk into the middle of the ambush and now he had even lost contact with the squad behind him. "Pull back! Keep firing!" he yelled against the wall of noise that filled the night.

There was no response. He could barely hear the words leaving his mouth; none of his men could hear him. Then the man in front of him seemed to fly apart as he was hit by an M-79 grenade-launcher round. The body kept walking a few steps even though his head, shoulder, and one arm had been blown away.

Phuc wanted to vomit. He thought of death. He thought of Ly. Then he felt something heavy hit him on the leg. Before he could wonder what it was, the night flashed red and yellow with a deafening crack as a hand grenade exploded at his feet. For him there was no pain, no sound. It just ended.

Phuc had been right. He would never see Ly again.

Scrambling on his hands and knees in the brown oatmeal and deadfall of the forest floor, Hollister grabbed the radio handset from Vinson and yelled over the firing, "Quarterback, this is Two-three. We have contact! I say again—we have contact! Launch pickup choppers now. Will break contact and move to the PZ immediately. More to follow. Out!"

Hollister threw the handset back to Vinson. Enemy small arms fire was still passing over his head, cutting through brush, showering him and the others with debris.

Uncertain, Hollister strained to detect any enemy movement. The green and red tracers that had been coming from the killing zone had stopped. He took a chance, shouting, *"Cease fire! Cease fire!"*

The others stopped firing, more from his example than his voice. They were excited and worried that their night vision was shot by the brilliance of the Claymores, grenades, and muzzle flashes.

Davis was the only one who had been cool enough to keep his night vision. He had learned to keep one eye closed so that when the shooting stopped he could open the dilated eye and see as well as he had before the shooting started. Hollister knew the trick, but never remembered to pull it off.

Hollister quickly called out each man's name. One by one they let him know that they were unharmed by replying with a simple Airborne "Okay." Nobody down.

"Stay awake," Hollister cautioned. "They're still out there!" Over his own heavy breathing he turned to Davis. "What d'ya think?"

Davis got up on one knee to get a better look, then whispered, "Looks like maybe a dozen KIA out there." Davis then held his breath to listen some more.

They could hear frantic thrashing noises below their position—down the hillside. Viet Cong soldiers were slipping and falling on the muddy path as they tried to escape.

"Go check out the KIAs. But make it fast. We got to get to the PZ. The whole world knows where we are now."

Snapping his fingers to get their attention, Hollister raised his voice only enough to be heard. "Vinson, you cover Davis. Don't take your eyes off him. If anything moves anywhere near him—blow it away."

Davis put his rifle down and pulled out a .45 pistol. He looked around at the others. "Any more Claymores out there?" The others shook their heads. Satisfied, Davis crawled toward the killing zone.

As Davis started to move, Hollister had a second thought and looked over at Doc Norris. "Go with him. There might still be some wounded."

Hollister looked back at Vinson to make sure that Vinson knew that two of them would be entering the killing zone. Vinson whispered, "I got 'em, sir."

Doc shouldered his aid kit, pulled out his pistol and scrambled after Davis.

Still watching Doc and Davis, Vinson picked up the radio handset and tossed it toward Hollister. "It's already on arty freq, sir."

Hollister smiled at his ever-efficient radioman, took out a green pocket notebook and flipped it open to a page marked by a rubber band. He pulled his right-angle, red-filtered Army flashlight from his web gear and wrapped his fingers across the lens. Turning it on, he allowed a tiny sliver of light to slip through his fingers to illuminate the list of artillery targets he had plotted before the patrol left the base camp. He raised the handset and used his own call sign rather than Team 2-3's. "Saint Barbara, this is Quarterback Two-six, fire mission. Over."

A faint voice responded immediately, "This is Saint Barbara. Send your fire mission. Over."

"Fire targets two niner five, two niner seven, three zero one, and three zero five. Over."

The radio operator at the Artillery Fire Direction Center answered immediately and repeated the target numbers.

Hollister gave the handset back to Vinson. "We gotta move! Choppers are inbound and arty is on the way." He turned back toward the killing zone and whispered loudly, "Goddammit—let's go, Davis! Get it in gear."

Hollister could hear the two men searching the bodies for documents and equipment, but couldn't really see them well. Davis and Norris each finished searching the last bodies and collected weapons from the dead VC. Davis slung his VC's rifle over his shoulder with two others, and Doc Norris hung his around his neck with the length of twine that its dead owner had used. One clunked against another.

The noise made Hollister more anxious. A reorganized squad of VC survivors could pull off a very effective counterattack against his small patrol if he didn't get his men moving.

Policing the battlefield was important, but Hollister didn't want to take more risks for filthy VC ammo pouches or comic books. He split the difference and gave Davis and Doc a bit more time to gather anything of intelligence value.

Finally, unable to wait any longer, Hollister reacted. "Now, Davis! Get back here. We're moving. Leave anything you can't carry and torch it."

"Roger, boss. Just a sec," Davis whispered.

Vinson pulled the handset from his ear. "Sir, redleg sent an 'on-the-way' message."

Hollister nodded. "Davis, get your ass back here. We're moving—now!"

"Look away! Friendly fire!" Davis yelled, warning the others of the threat to their night vision. He dropped an incendiary grenade on the equipment that they couldn't carry. The grenade made a small pop and then hissed as it burned with intense white light. Hot enough to melt through safes, the incendiary grenade would destroy anything it rested on.

Stumbling on the slick muddy ground—enemy rifles clanking—Davis and the Doc jogged back to Hollister's position.

Burdened by half a dozen weapons each and two VC rucksacks filled with captured documents and equipment, they reached Hollister and dropped to their knees. Without saying anything, Davis held out his three M-16s for Hollister to see.

The find was a surprise to Hollister. It was almost unheard of for a Viet Cong unit to have American equipment. It was an important piece of intelligence.

Suddenly, Hollister got a whiff of the repulsive smell that clung to Davis. He had brushed up against the spilled contents of a dead VC's shredded intestines. Hollister tried to suppress the urge to gag.

In the distance he heard the American howitzers firing. Then a second volley. Then Theodore and Camacho ran into the ambush site.

"Okay, we're all here," Hollister said. "That's our covering fire. Split up this VC gear and let's get to the pickup zone. Camacho, you know where we're going?"

"Yessir . . . home. We're going home, sir."

The patrol fell in behind Camacho and was on the run before the first six 105mm howitzer rounds racked the trees along the flanks of the patrol's route to the pickup zone.

Awkwardly, Hollister ran with the others while trying to talk on the radio. His corrections to the artillery were interrupted as he and Vinson dodged the limbs and bushes that seemed to jump between them.

Even with the breaks in commo, Hollister was pleased with the response of the base operations, the artillery and the chopper jocks. Communications helped him control the variables of the night and adjust to the changing situation. And somewhere out in the dark there were the remaining VC who had escaped his ambush, and he had no idea exactly how many got away or how many were still capable of attacking his patrol on the way to the pickup zone.

Over the blackness of the rain forest two Huey slicks and two gunships were racing toward him and his patrol. He hoped that the choppers would find them before the VC did.

Hollister spoke into the handset. "Gladiator, this is Two-six. We are three-zero-zero mikes from the Papa Zulu. Over."

"Mornin', Two-six. This is Gladiator Three-six. We're about zero five out. What's your situation?" the air mission commander asked.

Hollister signaled for the patrol to hold up. Responding to his signal, passed from man to man, they each stopped and fell to one knee. "We've broken contact, but I'm sure enemy stragglers are still in the area. How about a hose-down first?"

"It'd make me a happy man. I'd like to make a marking run across the PZ to make sure I got the right one, if you don't have trouble with that," Gladiator 36 said.

"We haven't had contact since we left the ambush site, but that doesn't mean we weren't followed. Affirm on the dry run. And you can put in the gunship fires anytime you're ready. Over."

"Roger that," Gladiator 36 replied. "Iron Mike's flying gun lead tonight. I'm sure he'd rather shoot 'em into the dirt than hafta unload 'em back at his palatial home. Over."

"Hey—remember who has the gunships, truck driver," Iron Mike broke in.

Hollister smiled. "Okay, Gladiator. Break. Iron Mike, this is Two-six. Over."

"Don't listen to that slick driver, Two-six. Iron Mike here with gun support that'll make your eyes water. Got two Charlie models loaded for bear. Got miniguns, rockets, and a shitload of 40mm grenades. What's your pleasure, Two-six?" Captain Iron Mike Taylor was the leader of the gunship platoon that usually supported the patrols. The playful and reassuring voices of the pilots always had a calming effect on troops on the ground.

Holding the handset against his ear with his shoulder, Hollister dumped the magazine out of his rifle and dropped it down the front of his shirt. He pulled a fresh magazine out of his shirt pocket and tapped Vinson on the shoulder with it before seating it into his rifle.

Vinson nodded, did the same, then signaled the others to load magazines of full tracers into their weapons. All the while, Hollister was mentally recording the inventory of ordnance that Iron Mike listed.

"Once you have a lock on the PZ, I'd like you to burn a ring around it. My lead element will remain three hundred into the tree line on the west side till you've finished your firing runs. Call for a mark if you have any doubt. I have artillery firing west and south of the PZ. So, if you have any movement anywhere else on the perimeter, just consider it bad guys. All of my element will be firing full tracer during the extraction. Adjust your fires accordingly. Over."

"Roger that. We'll punch their tickets for the show. Stand by for a prep. Out," Iron Mike said.

Hollister looked around at the others and raised his voice over the building sounds of the choppers. "The guns are going to make a few hot passes over the PZ."

They waited, trying to keep their eyes on the darkness that encircled them and trying to resist the temptation to watch the choppers go through their preparatory motions.

The pickup chopper was first to reach the edge of the landing zone. It was flanked by the two heavily laden gunships which stayed out over the trees surrounding the landing zone. Behind the guns a second slick, the chase ship, held high and broke short to the right, ready to go in and pick up survivors of any downed ship.

As the pickup slick passed over the center of the landing zone, Hollister yelled into the handset, "Mark-mark-mark."

In response a smoke grenade came flying out of the cargo door tossed by an unseen door gunner. As it fell to the ground the detonator created a spit of sparks followed by a plume of violet smoke. As it hit the ground the small flame at the end illuminated the billowing smoke like a large purple bubble.

Hollister watched the slick as it reached the far end of the PZ. Gladiator sucked it up over the trees and continued to gain altitude as he broke hard right to see where his smoke landed. "How's that, Two-six?" Gladiator asked.

"You got it. Park it on the grape and we'll meet you there. Over."

Iron Mike and his wingman turned toward each other at the end of the PZ, crossed over and started back toward the PZ in the opposite direction.

Through the plastic windscreen of his Huey gunship, Iron Mike could clearly see the margins of the black hole in the stand of trees that Gladiator had just marked. "Okay, Gladiator. I got it. Break. Two-six, put your head down. We're gonna burn 'em a new asshole."

Iron Mike pulled up on the collective and pushed the cyclic forward, picking up airspeed and putting the chopper in a steep nose-down attitude. His wingman mirrored his actions on the far side of the PZ.

Mike squeezed the trigger on his cyclic, and pairs of rockets burst from the pods on either side of his gunship. His wingman fired grenades and miniguns.

While the gunships made their firing runs, Hollister made out the navigation lights of the two pickup ships that had moved to a safe orbit high above the PZ.

More confident of their eventual extraction, Hollister allowed himself a little release.

If things went the way they were supposed to, they would be able to complete the entire extraction under a shield of friendly artillery and gunship fire without a break in the protective umbrella—the pickup sequence would look like ballet. Now Hollister's only job was getting them home in one piece.

In the extraction ballet, every dancer knew that the tiniest screw-up could cause a loss of momentum. And once momentum is lost on a pickup, everything soon falls apart. One delay would lead to another and still another.

Many patrols had been wiped out by delays at the PZ. Hollister's night extraction had the same risks: everyone for miles around knew exactly what was going on and where the American patrol was. Fire support and speed were his only security.

Watching closely, he estimated the flight pass of the gunships and picked a time to move that would put the patrol at the edge of the pickup zone just after the guns had passed by. Confident in his estimate, Hollister joined the ballet. He yelled over the gunships, "Camacho, let's move!"

The gunships pulled up at the end of their firing pass. "Two-six, this is Iron Mike. We're saving the rest of our ordnance for now. Let me know when you're ready and we'll come back to burn more bridges behind you. The PZ is now clear. I say again, the PZ is clear. Guns are safe."

Running, Hollister's voice was a little more excited and short of breath. "Roger, thanks, Mike. Break. Gladiator, Gladiator, this is Two-six. We are at the Papa Zulu, ready for pickup. I will mark my location on your command. Over."

Just then Camacho broke through the trees on the edge of the pickup zone and halted the patrol.

Hollister stopped just behind Camacho and looked over his shoulder out across the PZ. It was getting light. Still, it would stay inky black in the pickup zone until long after they were out.

"Stand by, Two-six. We are zero three out and will call final," Gladiator answered.

Untangling it from under his arm, Hollister passed the handset back to Vinson and looked around at the others. All but Camacho were facing to the rear, to be ready in case they were followed.

Hollister looked back out onto the PZ. Not much bigger than a couple of basketball courts, but it looked huge and threatening. He knew that anyone could be following them. And hundreds of VC could be hiding in the black ribbon of trees that ringed the empty clearing.

But the only way they could ride home was to make that dash to the choppers once they touched down in the clearing—where any VC could drop them from up to five hundred meters away.

Over his own heavy breathing Hollister heard the approaching helicopters getting louder and louder, even though he couldn't see them. Somewhere south of him they had dropped from orbit altitude to the treetops as they screamed toward the pickup zone.

Vinson tugged on Hollister's sleeve. ''Gladiator's on final. He wants a strobe.''

Hollister pulled a handheld strobe light from its pouch, clipped to his harness. He fitted the tubular plastic shield over the business end of the light and turned it on. The high-pitched squealing noise of the charging capacitor could just be heard over the approaching choppers.

Hollister pointed the strobe light where he expected the choppers to break across the tree line.

By the third flash the pickup chopper's red and green position lights broke the blackness.

''We got you . . . let's try an' make this a work of art, folks,'' Gladiator said.

Vinson tugged on Hollister's sleeve again and gave him an exaggerated nod.

Hollister had to get the team to the exact spot where the chopper was to touch down. He didn't want to get them out in the middle of the landing zone one second before they needed to be there. He also had to allow for someone tripping or taking a hit from an unseen sniper in the tree line. There should be no false moves that would cause the chopper to lose forward momentum by landing and having to wait on the ground for the patrol to reach it.

The patrol members readied themselves for the dash to the aircraft, each man pumped to go as he watched his sector of fire. They occasionally stole quick glances over their shoulders to check on the chopper's approach.

Hollister gauged their dash knowing Gladiator would touch down on the nearest possible spot to the leading edge of the clearing, to allow himself maximum takeoff room. The chase ship would pass over the pickup ship, break into a hard turn and come back around ready to drop into the landing zone if the pickup ship was crippled by enemy fire.

"I really hate this shit!" Camacho yelled over the chopper noise. "Who said this was fun anyway?"

"I don't know, but you keep coming to these parties," Hollister answered, trying to cover his own nervousness.

Gladiator cleared the trees, flared nose high to bleed off airspeed, and settled onto the clearing. Its tail rotor clipped some small trees and the popping sounds caused the patrol to react with a start.

Hollister immediately slapped Camacho on the butt and yelled, "Go, go, go!"

Each man fell in line behind Camacho and ran half backward for the first few yards, covering the tree line for enemy fire. Once in the clearing, they turned and sprinted for the chopper doorway.

Camacho leaped and did a belly flop into the chopper. Doc Norris landed next to him, and Theodore landed on top of Norris. Davis threw himself sideways and landed across the three pairs of legs.

Hoping that he had timed it right, Gladiator rolled the Huey forward. As the weight of the aircraft shifted to the front of the skids, Vinson and then Hollister leaped up and in.

The door gunner on the far side was smoking the tree line with six-round bursts of M-60 machine-gun fire, and Camacho started firing out the far side of the ship into the same tree line.

Barely in the chopper, Hollister reached up from behind the armor-plated seat and slapped the co-pilot's helmet, yelling, "Go, go, go!"

Vinson and Theodore began firing out the near side of the chopper at the spot they just left.

From above Iron Mike saw the tracers as he heard the *coming-up* call from the pickup ship. It was clear for the guns to roll in again.

Hollister raised his head just as the pickup ship lifted its skids off the clearing and started forward and up. At that same moment the tree lines on either side of the chopper exploded in matching ribbons of rocket, minigun, and grenade fire from the gunships.

Relieved, but not even close to being safe, the entire patrol started yelling encouragement to the chopper and gunships' crews—none of whom could hear them.

As the pickup chopper skimmed the top of the tree line on the far end of the landing zone, Hollister and Vinson looked out and back behind them at the black hole they had just left. It was ablaze with ordnance raining down from the two gunships.

Gladiator pulled them out of range of any enemy small arms fire.

As the chopper climbed, the temperature dropped considerably. "I'm freezing my goddamn ass off. You fuckers can have this job!" Theodore yelled to the door gunner who huddled in the corner of his cut-out seat compartment to shield himself from the ninety-knot wind that was making his lips slightly blue.

He smiled at Theodore and pointed down at the Vietnamese countryside. "I'll take it, my man. You won't get me down there with nothin' faster than my feet to get me out of trouble."

The two soldiers smiled at each other. Grunts never understood the bravery of chopper crews, and vice versa.

"Clear your weapons! Clear your weapons!" Davis yelled over the chopper noise.

After dumping his magazine into his hand, Hollister yanked back the charging handle on his rifle to eject the round that was in the chamber, then scooted to a sitting position in the doorway of the chopper. He threw the selector switch on the left side of the rifle to the safe position, took his first deep breath, and looked out past the foothills, across the glasslike rice fields, at the huge orange ball coming up out of the South China Sea. He looked back inside at the team members. They were all there in one piece. He couldn't help but look back out at the sunrise and whisper, "Thank you . . ."

CHAPTER 3

The four choppers crossed over the barbed wire surrounding the sprawling American Airborne brigade base camp. Only then did Hollister start to feel a release from tensions that had knotted his gut when they lifted off six days before.

The gunships peeled off and went to a different landing pad, where they could reload their weapons systems if another patrol called in a contact.

The two slicks began to settle down on a large asphalt pad with a three-by-ten-foot yellow and black arc painted on it. Inside the arc an amateur had painted the words LONG RANGE PATROL.

Just off the pad a jeep and trailer were waiting. The trailer was filled with chunks of dirty Vietnamese ice, cans and bottles of beer and soft drinks.

The driver got out of the jeep and stood next to it, looking up at the landing choppers. It was Easy. Hollister smiled. Easy could always be counted on to take care of his troops.

The pickup chopper touched down and the team wasted no time getting out.

"Listen up, you dickheads. I want you to ground your weapons, make sure they're cleared. Pile the captured equipment next to the vehicle before you touch any'a that beer. And I don't want any shit about it," Davis yelled.

The team members hastily dropped everything in one huge pile and headed for the trailer cooler.

Hollister got out of the chopper and stepped up on its skid to get closer to Captain Peter Shelton—Gladiator 36.

"That was pretty smooth. Will you thank your people for us, sir?" Hollister asked through the window in the pilot's door.

Captain Shelton flipped the lip mike away from his face and

30

smiled at Hollister without looking at him. Preoccupied with shutdown procedures, he answered, "It's all in a day's work there, young lieutenant. Hell, derring-do is our specialty . . . the really hard stuff takes us a bit longer, but I'll pass the word. Glad to help."

The others were already telling war stories about the ambush as they sloshed beer all over themselves trying to drink it. Hollister moved to the cargo bay, leaned against the chopper and pulled out a cigarette. Putting it to his lips, he lit it and watched Easy's beaming face as he listened to the excited soldiers tell and embellish their tale.

Hollister met Easy on his very first day in South Vietnam. After hitching a ride on a cargo plane from Saigon, Hollister found himself standing outside the airfield at An Hoa.

The smell was like nothing he had ever experienced. It was a strange mixture of dust, mildew, rotting fruit, sewage, charcoal ashes from unseen cook fires, and exhaust fumes.

He had expected things to look a little more like World War II newsreels. But it was the summer of 1965, and American troop units had only been in country for a few months.

As Hollister stood there he felt vulnerable, wondering if it would be a year that would leave him proud, ashamed, or dead. In that moment of anticipation he said a little prayer that he would not embarrass himself or his family.

Suddenly, a jeep careened around the concertina-wire fence surrounding the airfield and stopped. The jeep's untuned engine drowned out the noise of the Vietnamese civilians scurrying along the roadside. It, in turn, was eclipsed by the bellowing of an enormous NCO who wrestled the jeep through the throng.

"Get the fuck off the damn road, you slant-eyed motherfuckers!" screamed First Sergeant Horace P. Evan-Clark.

The driver had a large, round, whiskey-reddened face punctuated with a thick rope of rust-colored handlebar mustache. His forearms were damn near as large as Hollister's thighs. Each bore a faded tattoo that had lost its proportions in the years since they were injected under his leathery skin.

The jeep had spooked two older Vietnamese women who were pushing a load of scavenged cardboard on a twenty-year-old bicycle. They lost their grip, and the load turned the bike over into a roadside sewage ditch.

"For Chrissakes, if you hadn't been stealin' that shit you

wouldn't be pickin' it out of the fucking sewer. You the dumbest bunch of sons'a bitches I ever seen!''

Hollister had seen loudmouthed NCOs before, but Evan-Clark had added a special insensitivity to this common trait.

Evan-Clark turned his attention away from the shaken women and looked over the hood of the jeep at Hollister. Throwing something that looked like a well-worn version of an old army salute, he automatically shifted into a more deferential tone. "Sir, you Lieutenant Hollister?" he bellowed.

From Evan-Clark's tone of voice, Hollister knew that he was being tested. He just wasn't sure how. Something from his training back at Fort Benning told him that he had to take the initiative from this crusty old relic. Hollister quickly ran through a couple of options in his head and only concluded that a rank-pulling showdown wouldn't settle anything. A new second lieutenant, Hollister was sure of one thing—no lieutenant could operate in a vacuum in an infantry unit. The NCO contingent in an Airborne brigade was a tight network. And Evan-Clark was obviously a charter member.

"I just dropped off a young soldier on his way back to the World and got a message that I should be lookin' for a new lieutenant just in from Camp Alpha," Evan-Clark explained.

"That's me, First Sergeant." Hollister threw his duffel bag into the back of the jeep and immediately turned to the two old women. He assumed that Evan-Clark was wondering if Hollister was going to call him on his stupid driving stunt.

"Give me a hand. These old gals need somebody your size to get their load back upright again," Hollister said without looking at the first sergeant.

Hollister heard him mumble a muted "Yessir" as he climbed out from behind the steering wheel and helped get the old ladies and their bicycle upright.

They didn't talk much as they threaded through the streets of An Hoa headed for the base camp. Hollister was trying to size up the mountain of a man. Evan-Clark's right sleeve bore the 82nd Airborne Division shoulder patch—either he saw combat with the all-American division in WWII or the recent action in the Dominican Republic. One was a real paratrooper's war, Normandy invasion and all. The other was a schoolyard fistfight.

The master parachutist's badge on Evan-Clark's baseball cap was a clue. The tiny bronze star attached to the wings meant he had made a combat jump. That meant WWII. Hollister was impressed.

After some preliminary conversation that served to position the two, Hollister found out that Evan-Clark was the senior non-commissioned officer of the brigade's forty-man provisional Long Range Patrol detachment. Discussion about the LRP unit came so easily to Evan-Clark's lips that Hollister got the sense that the first sergeant was feeling him out as a possible candidate for the unit.

"Did the lieutenant go through ROTC?" Evan-Clark asked in the archaic third person, which was still commonly used by NCOs over forty.

"Nope. I'm still trying to finish college. I was a staff sergeant before I went through OCS. Actually, I was drafted and spent a couple years in a mechanized infantry battalion in Germany till my platoon sergeant talked me into applying for Officer Candidate School," Hollister said, only telling Evan-Clark a half-truth.

The whole truth was that Hollister had to fight with his platoon sergeant to apply for OCS; but he wanted Evan-Clark to feel that he was a lieutenant because of an NCO somewhere.

It worked. Evan-Clark straightened his back, taking some little pride in a fellow sergeant's perception, professionalism, and devotion to the development of leaders.

"There's two majors and a lieutenant colonel struttin' their stuff back in the States 'cause I did the very same with them when they was young soldiers."

"I'm sure they're pleased you did," Hollister replied.

The first sergeant looked quickly at the large blue-and-red-rimmed face of his Rolex GMT Master watch that would dwarf a normal man's wrist. "If the lieutenant isn't in too much of a hurry, we could stop off at Bell's," Evan-Clark suggested.

"What's Bell's?"

"Well sir, it's a cross between a car wash, a bar, a cathouse, and a laundry." Evan-Clark spoke as if it were a fact of the war that they were forced, even expected, to go to places like Bell's to take care of some of the understandable necessities of soldiering in a foreign war zone—like laundry and jeep washing.

Hollister felt that Evan-Clark was waiting for him to become squeamish and object. Searching for a no-loss solution to the situation, Hollister recalled the hours of leadership classes that covered the taboo of overfamiliarity leading to contempt. But he didn't want to start off on the wrong foot with an NCO who would soon be spreading word about the new lieutenant, so he tried to reply without giving approval.

"I've got a whole year, Top," Hollister said, using the more informal, unofficial title.

Evan-Clark jumped on Hollister's response. "That's good, sir! 'Cause we ought to get Mamasan at Bell's to sew up some name tapes for the lieutenant's uniforms, and I gotta pick up my laundry, and . . ."

Bell's was a large shack sitting alongside the road on the outskirts of An Hoa. The ground around it was wet and muddy from the bevy of young boys who moved quickly from jeep to jeep washing them.

The building contained a bar and whorehouse. It was covered with flattened Carling's Black Label beer cans recycled as a Viet version of aluminum siding. Rock music escaped through the entrance, which was decorated with shocking pink strips of tubular plastic hung from the top of the doorway. Mixed with the music were the high-pitched giggles of the Vietnamese girls inside.

A cute little bar girl, appropriately named Toy, brought the first two Bier 33s Hollister would see. She quickly ran back to the bar and returned with a glass of ice chunks covered with several rice husks. Putting the glass down in front of the first sergeant, she jumped into his lap.

"Ice for you, Sergean' Easy. You want V'namee whiskey?" Toy asked.

Evan-Clark laughed like a department store Santa Claus. Reaching into the cargo pocket on the side of his jungle fatigue trousers, he retrieved a small, well-worn flask engraved with the outline of a green beret and a dagger.

Evan-Clark poured himself a few fingers of rye from his private stock and waved the flask in Hollister's direction. "Would the lieutenant like to sweeten his beer a bit?"

The thought of a Vietnamese boilermaker at eleven in the morning made Hollister's stomach tighten. "No, Top. I think this beer will be about all I can handle until I get used to this heat."

Evan-Clark shrugged, dropped the flask on the table, and turned his attention back to Toy.

She giggled girlishly as he groped her tiny but unmistakably feminine body. She broke into a pidgin Vietnamese bar girl courting ritual that was common play with Americans. "Easy, I love you too much."

"I know. You love me too much, and you love every GI with a piaster in his pocket that comes through those doors."

She playfully struck Evan-Clark on the shoulder, making him laugh at her. "You numba ten, Cheap Charlie."

Still laughing, Evan-Clark ran his large hand over her little bottom and up under her breast. "Let's go into the back, girl."

She recoiled in mock horror. "No! No can do. Toy very good girl. Toy no can do!"

The first sergeant reached into his shirt pocket. He pulled out two hundred piasters and dropped the bills on the table. "So, what do you say, girl? Do you suppose that for two hundred P you can do? Or do I have you confused with a real business-woman?"

Toy thought for a fake beat and countered, "No, three hun'red P."

Evan-Clark took a long pull of his drink and swallowed with a grimace. "Okay, okay. But you better make the top of my head cave in, little girl."

Hollister tried not to show his discomfort when Evan-Clark turned to him for some sort of approval.

"The lieutenant wouldn't mind if I get myself a little Viet-namese blow job?" Before Hollister had a chance to answer, Evan-Clark got to his feet, threw Toy over his shoulder and headed to the back rooms.

Pleased that he hadn't had to reply, Hollister watched Evan-Clark pat Toy on the ass and disappear through the doorway. As soon as they were out of sight, he looked around the room, but was relieved to see that no one was looking back at him.

With no alternative, Hollister waited, trying to finish the awful-tasting French-Vietnamese beer. While sitting there, he declined several invitations from a parade of other prostitute bar girls who tried to entice him into one of the other back rooms.

Dragging Toy behind him, Evan-Clark returned. His face was flushed and the veins on his nose were bright red.

Toy babbled. "Easy, you numba one GI. You my super sweet-heart. But why you sweat so much? Toy do all the work and you sweat."

"Hush, girl. Go get us a couple'a beers," Evan-Clark said as he dropped back into his chair and lightly tapped her on the behind.

After taking a deep breath, he turned back to Hollister.

"Goddamn, it's hot in them fuckin' little rooms, Lieutenant."
He leaned back in his chair to straighten his leg enough to pull
an olive-drab handkerchief out of his pocket and mop his forehead. His size and weight almost crushed the flimsy wrought-
iron and plastic chair.

Toy returned with one beer. "Mamasan say she no hab no
mo' beer. She say mo' beer come abou' one hour."

Making a disapproving face, Evan-Clark killed the beer in
one long drink. While he was drinking, Toy picked up Hollister's beer, pulled it to her lips and took a long drink.

By the way Evan-Clark put his empty down on the table, and
his reluctance to paw Toy, Hollister could tell that he felt a little
self-conscious about his condition and behavior. The sergeant
quickly tried to divert attention from himself by looking fur-
tively at his watch. He feigned the sudden onset of punctuality.
"Lieutenant, we had better get on the road; I 'spect that the
brigade adjutant's waiting to sign you in and ship you right out
to a line battalion."

Pleased that they were back on the business of soldiering,
Hollister got to his feet without any objection. As he started
toward the door, Evan-Clark stopped him. "How 'bout the rest
of your beer, sir?"

Hollister simply shook his head and avoided making eye contact with Evan-Clark. He was not going to tell him that he didn't
want to drink the rest of his beer after Toy had just quenched
her thirst with it.

Looking off to the west, Hollister and Evan-Clark saw the yellow-
gray weather front moving in from the inland valley. As it got
closer, the temperature dropped over thirty degrees in minutes.
The rain began to fall, immediately drenching them. Hollister
tried to take his mind off the sudden cold. "Why did the girls
at the bar call you Easy?"

"Ya see, Lieutenant, I was born in South Africa. My parents
are British. That's where I got the hyphenated last name. When
I joined the American Army, my buddies started calling me
E.C. for short. But when I got to Vietnam, the bar girls thought
the guys were calling me Easy, and that's been my new nickname since my first week in this shithole."

"How 'bout the young soldiers?" Hollister asked. "What do
they call you?"

"Oh, they call me First Sergeant Evan-Clark to my face, all

right, but I'm sure they love calling me old Easy behind my back.'' He chuckled and looked at his watch.

"We gonna be able to get to Brigade in this rain or is it gonna get worse?'' Hollister asked.

"Can do, easy, Lieutenant.'' Easy put his foot into the accelerator and the jeep lurched forward with painful engine-revving sounds as the aging clutch slipped. "We'll get to Brigade rear soon enough, but you're gonna have to hold on.''

Recalling it, Hollister was glad he met Easy that first day in country. It was through Easy that he found out about the LRP Detachment. Over the months that Hollister served as a platoon leader in a rifle company, he listened to all of the stories and fables about the mysterious, elite, and experimental Long Range Patrol unit.

When he had finished six months in the field as a platoon leader, he started getting feelers from Brigade Headquarters about his interest in possibly being reassigned to a staff job as Civic Actions officer.

The headaches associated with Civic Actions programs hardly appealed to him. And Hollister had absolutely no interest in a staff job. So he applied for the LRPs. He was surprised and terrified at the possibilities when he was told that he would be going to the LRP Detachment for an interview.

He and a half-dozen soldiers assembled at the detachment for a briefing and an interview. Captain Shaw, Operations officer, moved the group to a small outdoor classroom. He explained that the LRPs were new, experimental, and constantly changing. In the few months they had been in existence, there had been several changes of mission and a number of reorganizations. All he could promise was more of the same until they figured out the best way to use the LRPs and the most effective organizational setup.

They were called LRPs because they often worked beyond the range of the supporting fires that normally covered the local patrolling of infantry units.

Their missions were varied, but fell into raid, ambush, and prisoner-snatch categories. They had tried reconnaissance only, but found it to be too costly in resources for the limited amount of useful information that they could bring in. So reconnaissance became a secondary mission for LRP patrols.

Captain Shaw went on to explain that every man in the unit was a volunteer from other combat units and they were all hand-picked. Anyone who fucked up was immediately sent back to an infantry battalion.

The detachment was small, only two platoons of three teams of five men each. Functionally, the headquarters was set up like a small battalion. And the turnover of personnel was a constant problem.

The LRPs' biggest problem was support. They had no choppers of their own but had to rely on them to get in and out of the bush. The uncertainty about how many choppers they needed and how often they got chopper support was a problem they hoped to work out.

Each man accepted into the unit would go through intensive training on patrolling techniques. If he made it through, he would go out on patrols with a few different teams to see how he got along with them. If he didn't become a problem, he would be accepted as a permanent member of the LRPs.

Shaw cautioned them that most of the applicants washed out or quit.

Hollister wasn't sure why, but the setup sounded good, and it was with troops. He had just about talked himself out of a staff job—it would be too far away from troops. He started out as a line soldier and felt most comfortable among them. If pressed, he might have admitted that he was somewhat intimidated by the thought of having to operate in the more sophisticated environment of experienced staff officers who had a wider grasp of the big picture and proper staff procedures. No, Hollister knew his place was with the troops, and if he didn't fight to stay with them, he would end up behind a podium briefing visitors or handing out fertilizer to Vietnamese farmers. He put his bid in to join.

Easy spotted Hollister at the chopper. He said, "You better get on over here and get some of this beer before your sorry excuses for Airborne soldiers drink it all up, Lieutenant."

Hollister finished his cigarette, crushed it on the cargo deck of the helicopter, and field stripped it without even thinking about it.

"Okay, Top. Hold on. I'll be there in a sec, just save me a beer and don't let anyone have a second one. We still have a debriefing."

Watching for Easy's wave of acknowledgment, Hollister rolled the shredded paper from his field-stripped cigarette into a ball and automatically slipped it into his pocket.

Remembering one task still undone, Hollister lifted his aching leg up to the deck of the chopper, ripped the laces on his boot loose and slipped his foot out of it. His naked foot was pale, wrinkled, and traced with the reverse impression of every fold, crease, and seam of his boot. He had stopped wearing socks with his jungle boots after his first week in the field. It beat wrestling with slipping woolen socks.

An instructor in Ranger School had once told him, "A Ranger's feet are like an odometer. You can take a look at them and tell how far a Ranger's gone and how hard the drivin's been." Hollister saw that he was starting to stack up some hard mileage from the looks of his feet.

He searched around for his passenger and found him up under the hemmed edge of his pant leg. The leech was only about an inch and a half long, but he was fully gorged on Hollister's blood.

"Need a leech wrench?"

Looking up, Hollister found Captain Grady Michaelson, his detachment commander, standing next to him holding out the stub of a lit cigar.

"I been carrying this little fucker around with me all night, sir."

"They have a pretty good deal . . . food, transportation, and free heat all at once."

Hollister took the cigar stump from Michaelson, knocked off the ash and then blew on it to stoke the burning end. He then brought it to the tail of the bloodsucker. Before the bright red tip of the cigar ever touched it, the leech curled up toward its head and simply dropped onto the floor of the chopper.

Remembering that the door gunner would have to clean out the chopper, Hollister swept the leech out onto the landing pad.

Captain Michaelson stuck his jungle-booted toe out and stepped on it. It gave out a weak pop and squirted Hollister's blood in three directions, making a star-shaped stain on the pad the size of a man's hand.

Blood ran freely from the perfect circle of raw flesh that the leech had left behind on Hollister's leg. Captain Michaelson checked his watch. "Better get something on that. You know that those things take forever to stop bleeding. And we got to get the debriefing over soon. Anyway, I've got two more teams to brief before lunch." Not waiting for a reply, he patted Hollister on the shoulder, turned and walked toward Operations.

Hollister liked Michaelson. But it hadn't always been that

way. Michaelson had been at the Ranger School in Florida when he went through the Ranger course.

The swamps along Florida's Yellow River were the most disgusting combination of water, mud, decaying plant life, and sheer mystery. That was where he had first harvested a leech.

Michaelson was a Ranger senior instructor, just back from his second tour of duty in Vietnam, where he'd been an advisor in an Airborne battalion, then a Special Forces detachment commander in the Mekong Delta. It was very rare to find an infantry officer with that much combat experience in the Vietnam War. There was still a large number of Korean War veterans, but the size of the U.S. contingent in Vietnam from 1961 to 1964 was very small.

Over time, Hollister's opinion of Michaelson had warmed up considerably. As he watched him walk across the area, he wondered if he would ever be like Michaelson.

Michaelson was the first soldier who really taught him anything about war. Up until that point he had only learned about tactics, techniques, field expedients, equipment, and a long list of memorized firing rates and maximum effective ranges of weapons. But with Michaelson he learned his first hard lesson about being a troop commander when his forty-man Ranger training patrol was struck by lightning during a freak Florida storm.

It was the most frightening and chaotic thing that Hollister had ever experienced. The lightning struck without warning, killing two Ranger students outright. It then struck a second and a third time in an area not much larger than a football field.

Bodies were tossed about by the violent discharge that flashed through them. The air was filled with the smell of ozone and flying tree branches. Leaves and bits of sphagnum moss were hammered from the cypress trees that dotted the narrow sandbar they were on. But there was no way to get away from the repeated lightning strikes. The students panicked and ran, screaming and begging for someone, anyone, to help them.

When it did stop, the patrol had been reduced by three dead, six maimed, and four others seriously injured.

Michaelson radioed for medevac choppers, but insisted that the patrol members remain *tactical* and follow Ranger procedure in preparing the wounded for evacuation. He wanted them to secure a perimeter as if they were still in an enemy-held area.

Many of the students, Hollister included, thought that they should have suspended the training because of the deaths and injuries. Michaelson was not sympathetic. Picking up on Hollister's negative attitude, Michaelson grabbed him by the fatigue shirt and stuck his face close. "Ranger, in combat there will be no time for your people to sit around and feel sorry for themselves. No one will let them drop their guard just because they've taken a few casualties. What you do here you will do on the battlefield. Now, get tough or get out!"

He let Hollister go, looked at his watch, and raised his voice for the others to hear. "Ranger Hollister, assume that your patrol has taken casualties as a result of an enemy mortar attack. Your patrol leader and assistant patrol leader are among the casualties. Now, take charge of this patrol, get them organized, and move them out. The longer you let them think about it, the more sorry they're going to feel for themselves. Soldiers who feel sorry for themselves get to be dead men real soon. Now get 'em going, Ranger!"

Since then Hollister had needed to use what he had learned from Michaelson, and he was sure that his soldiers were alive because of it. But it didn't make him any more popular than it had made Captain Michaelson on that night in the Florida swamps.

A little foggy, leaning up against the side of the chopper, and almost out on his feet from lack of sleep, Hollister was happy that Michaelson had decided to accept him into the detachment. His opinion of the man had changed so much that if he were asked, the one thing he would say about Michaelson was that he was a good man. And in their business that was as good as it got.

Michaelson reached the Operations tent, turned to look at Hollister and tapped his wristwatch.

Hollister got the message. He looked back to Easy and the troops. "Okay. We're due in Ops in zero five!"

CHAPTER 4

Detachment Operations was housed in a large utility tent stretched over a wooden frame, surrounded by crotch-high sandbag parapets. Inside, the plywood floor sagged in places and showed the wear from constant use. Still, it served the purpose. It was the heart and center of all things tactical within the detachment.

The tent was divided in half by a row of beaten-up file cabinets. At one end of the tent a bank of radios, resting on a bench made out of plywood and two-by-fours, was flanked by situation maps and folding field tables that belonged to the Operations officer, the Operations/Intelligence sergeant, the Fire Support officer, the Artillery Liaison officer, and the Intelligence officer.

The opposite end of the tent was used as a briefing and debriefing area. A large easel held the map of the local area, covered by an acetate overlay. It was positioned next to a wobbly pedestal podium to which an amateurish set of parachute wings made out of Masonite and painted with a very cheap brush had been nailed. In front of the easel ten rusted folding metal chairs were arranged in two concentric semicircles.

In the briefing area Hollister sat in the front row with Team 2-3. Behind them sat Easy, Operations officer Captain Ken Shaw, Captain Michaelson, and Intelligence officer Lieutenant Skip Perry.

At the podium Sergeant First Class Hector Marrietta, Operations/Intelligence NCO, guided them through the debriefing. Those in the front row read from their notebooks. The back row took notes.

Marrietta was an American Indian from Arizona. He had been in the army for seventeen years and knew his business. He wore master parachute wings, was a Pathfinder, a Ranger, and a Jungle Expert. On his right shoulder he wore the combat patch of the 187th Regimental Combat Team. As a corporal in the Korean War, Marrietta served under a young colonel who had become his top general—William C. Westmoreland.

"All right . . . we ready?" he asked deferentially, glancing to Captain Michaelson. Michaelson nodded. "Lieutenant Hollister, before you start with your part of the debriefing, I thought you'd want to know that we've sent the captured weapons and equipment up to Brigade S-2 already. So, they won't be available for the debrief," Marrietta added.

"What's the hurry?" Sergeant Davis asked.

"Seems that this is the first time we've captured American weapons that weren't antiques," Lieutenant Shaw said from behind Davis.

"That mean something, Lieutenant?"

"Don't know. There've been reports of VC units with newer American weapons, but we haven't seen it around here before. We don't know if there's a different supply channel or if there are new VC priorities in our AO or if it's just a unit we aren't carrying on our Order of Battle. We'll see what the super spooks at Brigade have to say about it."

"Mind if we get on with this, Sergeant Davis?" Marrietta asked, a little irritated.

"Guess not. Just wondered. We never been in that much of a hurry to do anything before," Davis offered, slightly under his breath.

Eager to get finished, Hollister looked over at Davis disapprovingly. Catching his boss's look, Davis reined in his urge to playfully parry with Marrietta.

While Marrietta looked at his notes on the podium and reread the patrol's mission, Hollister wondered himself about why the VC would suddenly have the newer American equipment. He tried to refocus on Marrietta.

After the adrenaline pumping the team members had just experienced, debriefings were usually boring. As Marrietta droned on—rereading for corrections, the time schedule, and the mission that took the patrol out to that spot on the ground—patrol members searched through crumpled cigarette packs for dry cigarettes, and finished off the cans of beer and soft drinks they had brought in with them.

Wanting to get a head start on the postoperations activities, Doc Norris slipped a combat dressing out of his trousers pocket and began rubbing the remaining camouflage grease from his face.

"Sir, would you start?" Marrietta asked.

Hollister put his soda can down on the floor and swapped hands with his notebook before speaking. "I'm going to let Sergeant Davis handle most of this since I was only acting as patrol leader with his team. So I'll try to confine my comments to things that were mission specific and let Davis handle the rest.

"Okay, we were running late on the morning of the insert. Our schedule called for First Call at 0415 and breakfast from 0430 to 0500. But at the mess hall the spoons were running late. The cook stoves were not fired up and the coffee wasn't done."

"A man can't be his best without a good breakfast," Vinson joked.

Hollister shot Vinson a hard look. "We ate C rations, which we had to get from supply. This made us ten minutes late arriving at the chopper pad."

Wanting to know if he was being listened to, Hollister looked up and caught Marrietta making a note of the problem.

"The ride was uneventful and the insert went off like we had rehearsed it. Oh, I might say that we need to check the choppers better before lift-off. The insert ship had some kind of fuel, like diesel, on the skids that a couple of us got on our boots. The smell stayed with us for most of the first day. I'd hate to lose a team just because some of us smelled like a motor pool."

The smell was especially irritating because they routinely stopped using soap, shaving cream, toothpaste, deodorant, or any other cosmetics days before a patrol so that they wouldn't give themselves away in the bush.

"*Contact! Contact!* This is Quarterback One-one. We have contact!" The words blasted through the speakers on the radio bench at the other end of the tent.

"Sergeant Marrietta, why don't we break this off, send these people to chow, and get some weapons cleaned?" Captain Michaelson said. "We can pick it up after we see what One-one's got."

The second row reassembled around the radios without waiting for Marrietta to answer. By then a runner had dashed out of the tent to the mess hall, where he passed the word and sent coffee-drinking pilots racing to their choppers.

Even though Michaelson had offered early chow, none of the members of Hollister's patrol wanted to leave. They were rarely in the Operations tent when enemy contact was made. Each man wanted to watch how smoothly the complicated dance went. They wanted to know that when they called in their own enemy contact the next time, the Operations and Fire Support staff would work like a finely crafted Swiss watch. And they also hoped that their friends on 1-1 were okay. Trying to stay out of the way, they hugged the far wall of the tent and watched, hardly breathing.

The radio crackled again with a situation report from the twenty-two-year-old sergeant who was in charge of Team 1-1. "I have two friendly WIA! Estimated ten Victor Charlie fired on us zero three ago. Small arms, a couple of B-40 rockets, and some ChiCom grenades. They have broken contact. I have requested indirect fire into their location. I think they followed us from the LZ. We are compromised—request *immediate* extraction. I say again—request immediate extraction. Will keep you posted . . . Stand by. Out."

Still seated on a folding chair, Davis held his head in his hands, his elbows resting on his knees as he listened. "Jackson's got his shit together," he said. "If they ain't blowed 'em away by now, they ain't gonna stay around in the daylight for us to pound their dicks in the dirt."

Every radio and field telephone was pressed into service. The tent was buzzing—radio speakers hissed and popped with message traffic, responses, and confirming readbacks. And Team 2-3 didn't miss any of it.

Captain Michaelson ran out of the tent to go with the launching pickup ships. A third chopper had arrived earlier to allow Michaelson to use Gladiator's ship as a command-and-control chopper. One would be a pickup, and another a chase ship. All three slicks would rendezvous with Iron Mike's gunships en route.

To protect 1-1 while it waited for the pickup choppers, the Artillery NCO directed fires onto the coordinates of the last VC sighting. Captain Shaw, Operations officer, ordered a close air-support mission which diverted a pair of Air Force F-4 Phantom jets to the contact site from an air base sixty-five miles away.

At a nearby field table SFC Tillotson, the senior medic, gave the receiving hospital a complete report on the wounded and the estimated arrival time. To reduce possible delays in treatment, he read out the names of all the soldiers on the patrol, their blood types, and any allergies.

Anxious, Hollister walked to the map behind the podium.

The location of the 1-1's last report was marked with a grease-penciled blue box with its team number. He estimated the flight time to be less than twenty minutes.

Quickly, the radio traffic picked up considerably as the choppers got closer to the team. Everyone in the tent could hear Gladiator and Captain Michaelson as they calmly went through the routine of identifying the team. The team leader spoke hurriedly, but with precision. No one missed the sounds of the gunships raining fire around the team, which could be heard in the background of the radio traffic.

Using C-4 plastic explosives, the team dropped two trees to prepare an emergency landing zone. That gave away their exact location, but it was better than trying to make it to the nearest landing zone while four men tried to carry two.

Michaelson's voice crackled over the small speaker again, confirming the team's location. "I've got you. The slicks are on final. Get those two wounded cowboys on board. We're going to hold as long as you need. So don't worry. We're not going to leave anybody behind."

The radios went silent while the pickup took place. Hollister tried to picture the pickup ship and guess how long it would take to touch down, pick up the team, and report coming out. The radio silence seemed to go on much too long. He looked around the tent. Nobody moved. It was the critical moment.

Iron Mike's was the first voice. "They're out! Let's roll in hot for one more pass and then follow Gladiator back to Quarterback base." Mike Taylor's message was meant for his wingman, but the Operations tent burst into a scream of triumph. They were out! Coming home.

Easy spoke up. "This calls for a beer." He went to the Coleman picnic cooler in the corner, only to find it filled with water from ice that had melted during the night.

"Sergeant Marrietta, you think you could keep this cooler stocked? A man could get heat stroke from a shortage of body fluids!"

Marrietta played the game. "Right, First Sergeant. I'll get right on it." He turned to Specialist 4 Bernard, the captain's driver. "What's wrong with you, Bernard? You want the first sergeant to die here in my Ops tent? 'Cause if he does, you are going to have to haul his ugly butt outa here!" He turned back to Easy. "Ah, no offense, Top."

* * *

Dog tired, Hollister carried his rucksack by the top of the frame and his rifle by its carrying handle as he walked across the LRP compound.

Weathered ridges in the weed-covered ground suggested the strict regimentation of paddy dikes and irrigation ditches, but they had long since been replaced by GP Small tents, a weapons testing area, a vehicle maintenance area, a chopper pad, and a forty-foot-tall wooden wall supported by telephone poles.

The wall was used to train newcomers in rappeling skills, but it actually served as a recruiting device. There was hardly a spot in the sprawling base camp from which you couldn't see the brightly colored yellow letters LRP painted on the rappeling wall. It didn't just announce the location of the LRP compound. It was a challenge to some to try to become a LRP. No soldier could see the large letters emblazoned on the wall without wondering if he could hack it.

His eyes had to adjust to the relative darkness of the hooch, but he knew where everything was, and moved automatically as they made the change.

The inside of the hooch always smelled musty. But even that stink was almost covered by the scents of weapons-cleaning solvents, oils, and camouflage sticks. Hollister didn't care. It smelled much better than the mud spot where he had spent the night, and much better than he did. He just wanted to drop his gear and get cleaned up.

He hung his rucksack on a large spike a previous tenant had sunk into the four-by-four upright supporting the tent's horizontal ridgepole. He then placed his rifle on a field table and looked around the hooch. He was happy to have a real canvas cot with a clean poncho liner and a small but reasonable excuse for a pillow that he'd bought in a roadside shop. He really didn't want to know what it was stuffed with. But he did know that whenever it got damp from the rain, it smelled of rice husks.

On his cot the mail clerk had left three envelopes. After a beer, a debriefing, and cleaning his weapon, the first two things every man wanted were his mail and a shower. Everything else could wait.

In addition to the envelopes, there were three daily editions of the *Kansas City Star*. He picked them up and threw them across the hooch to a pile of others—all still rolled up tightly for mailing from the States.

His parents didn't understand that to read the *Star* was a reminder of how far away from home he was. Besides, the news was twelve days to two weeks old, usually out of order, and the papers refused to unroll.

He had tried to read them at first, but his interest in the sports section had simply waned since he had arrived in Vietnam. Still, he didn't have the heart to tell his mother that he didn't want to read them.

He picked up the envelopes. One was from Susan, one from Phillips 66 with a printed message across the front: *Ease your travels. Put a Phillips 66 credit card in your wallet and a smile on your face.*

The absurdity of the offer tickled Hollister. He smiled and mumbled to himself, ''Right. That'll sure ease my travels a lot.''

The return address on the third envelope was from the IRS. Hollister opened it quickly and found a form letter stating that they could not find his 1964 income tax return. Could he advise them? Hollister laughed out loud. Troops in Vietnam were exempt from filing income taxes until they returned to the U.S. His best guess was that he might owe something just over seventy-five dollars. Hell, he only made three hundred dollars a month before taxes.

He dropped the IRS letter on the shaky field table that served as his desk and flipped the Phillips letter into the metal machine-gun ammunition box that was his trash can.

He raised Susan's letter to his face and searched for a scent of her on the envelope. There was none. It smelled like the rest of the hooch—musty. The letter would be a treat for him after he cleaned his weapon and took a shower. He wanted to open it right up and read each of Susan's words. But he knew from experience that if he read it right away, he might not get around to the necessities of life before some other crisis came up. And that could be costly.

Resigned to prioritizing his actions, Hollister stripped off his boots and fatigue uniform. He separated his belt from the loops on the trousers and threw the uniform into a pile in the corner.

Wearing no underwear or socks, he inspected himself for damage. Both of his hipbones were raw. One was lacerated by the constant weight and rubbing of his field gear. These spots were on top of sores that had healed many times before. Every patrol marked him.

Someone had fabricated two wardrobe-style lockers out of plywood and ammunition boxes for his hooch. One was his and one was his roommate's, Lieutenant Lucas—the platoon leader of the first LRP platoon.

Lucas's half of the hooch was almost a mirror image of Hollister's. The letters and rolled-up hometown newspapers on the cot meant that Lucas was either out on a patrol or on the R&R he had been waiting for when Hollister left.

It was a team from Lucas's platoon that had just made the enemy contact. Hollister didn't envy Lucas. Either Lucas was on R&R and would feel bad about one of his teams getting shot up, or he was out with another patrol and would be pissed that he missed the contact.

Well, that was Lucas's problem. Hollister stepped over to his locker, flicked a long-legged spider off the shelf with his index finger, and pulled out an olive-drab towel, his shaving kit, and a bar of soap. He searched out his shower shoes under his cot and slipped into them while he wrapped the towel around his waist.

Hollister turned back to the empty half of the hooch and felt a little lonely. He had kind of hoped that Lucas would be there. Lucas was always good for a laugh. A smile crossed his face as he recalled the night just after Christmas, when he and Lucas got stinking drunk at the Brigade Officers Club. So drunk that they had to pay the Vietnamese bartender to lead them back to the LRP compound only a thousand meters from the club.

The next morning, they tried to disguise their hangovers. Captain Michaelson spotted their pain and ordered them to give the demolitions class for the newly assigned LRPs. The blasts from the quarter-pound blocks of C-4 made them think seriously about never drinking again.

Lucas and Hollister always had lots of fun together. Hollister liked being able to talk to someone the same age and rank. They were the only two platoon leaders in the detachment, and shared many of the same problems. Hollister always felt comfortable with Lucas.

Outside his hooch, Hollister felt a little silly walking to the showers with a towel and his shaving gear. He was somewhat self-conscious about his color, pasty-white except for his forearms, neck, and face. Even the tan on his face stopped just above his eyebrows. A sergeant at Officer Candidate School called it a 1542 tan, after the number used to designate the officer speciality of Infantry Small Unit Commander—a platoon leader.

For twenty yards around the showers the ground was muddy

and very slippery. In the dry season the excess water evaporated quickly as the day's sun baked it away. During the wet season it hardly mattered since everything stayed soggy all day.

The showers consisted of a sturdy wooden scaffolding made out of four-by-fours supporting three salvaged fifty-five-gallon fuel drums painted black to absorb as much heat as possible. At the top of each drum a rifle-cleaning rod attached to a wooden float indicated the water level. Hollister picked one that was almost full and stepped under the simple garden faucet that was the closest they could come to a shower head.

Hollister turned on the spigot and tried to avoid the water, but it came out at a strange angle and quickly ran down his wrist to his armpit. It felt like someone had slapped a cold crowbar against his skin. Determined to overcome the cold, he splashed some water on himself, then a little more. Eventually it got bearable.

Getting the soap out of his close-cropped hair made him wish for some legitimate shampoo instead of a bar of Palmolive. Even without real shampoo he was happy to be able to get the field grime off his skin.

He looked at the distorted image of himself in the tin mirror nailed to one of the uprights. Traces of camouflage stick clung to his ears, nose, and mouth, and the clean areas were reddened from the scrubbing. He lathered again and scrubbed harder.

While he showered, choppers settled on the LRP pad, having returned from picking up Team 1-1.

He pulled down a cheap cherry-colored plastic bowl that someone had left there to be used as a washbasin. Putting the bowl on the wooden pallet between his feet, he gave himself a final rinse. The runoff partially filled the bowl with soapy water.

His face a little cleaner, Hollister looked across the compound toward the chopper pad as he tried to wipe the soapy water from his eyes. Only the two slicks had landed. Four LRPs got out and went through the same arrival ritual that his men had undergone earlier. But for them it was almost without words. They lacked the excitement and spontaneity of his team. Even Easy passed up the chance to badger the troops with his bluster. Hollister guessed that they had taken the wounded to the Brigade hospital on the other side of the base camp before returning to the LRP compound.

Feeling a little guilty about the time he was spending in the shower, Hollister wrapped the towel around his waist and picked up the bowl, placing it on a chest-high shelf nailed onto the scaffolding. He fished around in his shaving kit and pulled out a toothbrush, a tube of Colgate, and a shaving brush.

While working up a lather, he looked back up at 1-1. They hadn't even dropped their gear. They had picked up something to drink and were walking slowly across the grassy margin of the landing pad toward Operations. He knew how they felt. There was a terrible feeling of loss, vulnerability, and mortality every time a team took casualties.

As he shaved, the C&C chopper spiraled out of the sky at a high rate of speed and made a hotdog landing.

Hollister watched Gladiator dump the pitch off the blades, causing the chopper to settle its full weight onto the skids. As it did, Captain Michaelson jumped out of the chopper and ran over to Operations.

As Hollister got down to the short and painful strokes on his chin, he noticed Easy approaching. Something was wrong.

"Sir," Easy said.

"What is it, First Sergeant?" Hollister asked.

"Ah, the Old Man radioed ahead and asked me to round you up. He wants you to get up to the hospital. Lieutenant Lucas's been hit bad."

"Lucas?" Confused, Hollister looked back at Easy and then over toward the choppers. "He was out with One-one? I thought he was on R and R or out with another team."

"Yessir—he was with One-one. You want me to go with you?"

Easy's offer was a sure sign that Lucas was in a bad way. Hollister scooped up the water in the bowl and made a hurried attempt at rinsing the soap off his face. "No. I'm sure the Old Man and One-one need you back here for the debrief. How's the other guy? You hear?"

"He's okay. Word is that he's only got a couple'a frag wounds and'll be back to duty in no time at all."

Hollister stepped quickly through the muddy shower area and then broke into a run back to his hooch. He yelled over his shoulder, "Get me a vehicle, will you?"

In a clean uniform, Hollister stood in front of his hooch buttoning his pockets when Specialist 4 Bernard pulled up in Captain Michaelson's quarter-ton, the best-kept jeep in the detachment.

It was Bernard's baby, and he took pride in its appearance and condition. Unlike other jeeps, it was spotless, well-painted, and always well-tuned. The vertically mounted spare tire rim was covered by a circle of plywood that had the LRP insignia painted in the center between the words DETACHMENT COMMANDER. Two whip antennas marked the rear quarters of the vehicle and provided Michaelson with long distance communications capability over two FM radios. Even from a distance it was clearly a commander's jeep.

"I'm ready if you are, Lieutenant," Bernard said.

Hollister jumped into the jeep and braced his floppy LRP hat for the wind. "Let's go."

They made a wide U-turn, heading for the front gate.

"So what's the deal with Lieutenant Lucas? What do you know about it?" Hollister asked.

"I didn't even know he was out with One-one until I looked at the status board after the contact," Bernard said as he raced down the dirt roadway of the base camp.

"Wasn't that the team leader's voice on the net during the contact?"

"Yessir. But the Old Man tol' me that Lieutenant Lucas went along as an observer. Seems he had an assistant patrol leader in One-one he wanted to check out to put into One-three when One-three's team leader rotates next month." Bernard shook his head. "Y'know, I can't believe that anyone would want to go on any more patrols than they absolutely have to. But that's Lieutenant Lucas for you. He's short. Ain't he?"

"Yeah, I think so. Couple of months at most. What d'ya know about his wounds?"

"I heard half a the conversation that Doc Tillotson had with the Clearing Station. It sounded like multiple frag wounds and boocoup serious, sir."

They rode the rest of the way to the hospital in silence. Hollister was thinking about the very real possibility of getting wounded himself. Over his months in Vietnam he had formed a very definite attitude about it happening to him.

It all started that night in Ranger School when the lightning struck. He had never seen people killed or so severely injured before. His reaction surprised him. The dead didn't bother him that much. They were gone. Something about their death and its finality wasn't as painful to him as seeing those who were terribly disfigured by the violent trauma, and the burns that some of the students had suffered. It was the first time he ever really understood what the word *maimed* meant.

One of the students had been under a tree when the lightning struck. It hit the tree, then leaped to the soldier, striking him in the side of the face. The charge then found the fastest path to the ground through his body. The boy's left ear, most of his jawbone, and part of his tongue were ripped from his face. As the charge passed out of his body, the bottom of his right boot was blown away from the vulcanized seam which held it to the upper part of the leather and canvas. It took most of the meaty portion of his heel and arch with it and looked like the foot had exploded from the inside. To Hollister that man was maimed. He would never be normal again.

As a platoon leader in an Airborne battalion and in the LRPs, he had seen even worse. Each time, Hollister was reminded of his feeling of dread of the life-altering impact of being maimed—not dead, but maimed.

That night in the Florida swamps he said a quick and sincere prayer that he be allowed to die rather than live like that. It wasn't the last time he said that prayer.

"Sir, we going in?" Bernard asked.

Hollister looked up from the stopped jeep at the entrance to the Evac Hospital. He hoped that Lucas would not be maimed.

CHAPTER 5

Hollister and Bernard walked up the dirt path marked off by whitewashed rocks which led to the emergency entrance. The hospital was a mix of tropical buildings with half-screened and half-louvered walls, tents, and a new Quonset hut that served as the hospital's Clearing Station.

Inside the Clearing Station a male nurse stopped Hollister and Bernard. "Can I help you?"

Before responding to the voice, Hollister peered over the head of the seated nurse into the triage area behind him, where several stretchers rested on tall sawhorses. Four of them held soldiers being attended to by small clusters of medical personnel. "We're from the LRPs. You have two WIAs that were just evac'd?"

"Yessir, but we haven't even got their names yet. Can you recognize them?" the nurse asked.

"Yes, how are they? Can we see them?"

"One of them's in pretty rough shape. Lemme go see if you can go in." The nurse walked back to the treatment area.

Hollister looked at the normally talkative Bernard. He was silent and slightly pale.

The size of the LRP Detachment and the vulnerability of the small patrols made every man compensate for the danger by acting as if he feared nothing. Easy liked to remind Hollister that "you have to watch out for them, Lieutenant. They all think that their asses are made out of bumpers."

But when they did face the worst, it was with the brutal realization of how truly fragile they were. The bravado was gone from Bernard's face.

"You can come back into the treatment area, but try to stay out of the way. Okay?" the nurse said as he returned to the pair. "Your guys are on the right."

Reaching the first soldier's stretcher, Hollister recognized a twenty-year-old LRP from Perth Amboy, New Jersey.

"Zanger, you okay?" Hollister asked from behind the two medics.

"Hey, sir! I'm cool. Ain' no fuckin' gook good enough to get me! The doc tells me that I might have to go to Japan for a while, but I'll be back," Zanger said, pumping to the adrenaline firing up his system.

Bernard stepped around and took Zanger's hand, which was entangled in an IV line, to reassure him.

Zanger made a head gesture to a stretcher surrounded by doctors, medics, and nurses attending to the patient. He lowered his voice. "The lieutenant's fucked up bad, sir. He took most of the shit."

Hollister started to work himself around Zanger's stretcher and toward Lucas. Zanger realized what Hollister was doing. "He's gotta be okay. He saved my ass out there. Goddamn gooks fucked him up . . . but he ain't never gonna be back, sir."

A surgical smock moved aside, revealing Lucas's upper body. Hollister resisted the sudden urge to show the horror he felt. The last thing Lucas needed was to see a friend reel back in shock at his wounds.

Lucas was an off-white color just short of death. His upper chest was chewed up by several fragment wounds. It looked to Hollister like he had been hit by a ChiCom hand grenade or RPG frag.

The smock moved again and Hollister saw the ragged saffron splinters of bone that ended Lucas's arm just below the shoulder.

"Luke, it's me, man—Hollister. I'm here. Can you hear me?"

One of the doctors on the far side of Lucas looked up and pointed a bloody surgical instrument at a spot where Hollister could stand without being in the way.

Oh Jesus! Hollister thought when he finally saw Lucas's face. A tube up his nose was filled with sections of blood spaced by air breaks its entire length. Lucas's face was pockmarked with more frag wounds, and it looked like Lucas's cheekbone had been crushed. Blood was dripping slowly out of his ear, and his dry lips were beginning to crack.

A medic leaning over Lucas's remaining arm yanked loose a rubber tourniquet in frustration. "His veins are collapsing. I can't start a new line in his arm."

Without looking up, a doctor probing the damage to Lucas's chest said, "Get over here and do a cut down on this leg."

The medic moved around the stretcher and dropped the cold stainless steel instrument tray in the narrow space between Lucas's knees. He pulled a small swab from the tray and wiped some of the field grime from Lucas's ankle. Without waiting for it to dry, he picked out a small surgical blade and cut into Lucas's leg. With an instrument that looked like a crochet needle, he fished inside the incision and came out with a small vein. "I got it," he said to the doctor at his elbow.

The doctor looked down at the vein. "You do it. You've seen it done enough times. Make the cut as small as you can and force the line into the vein. Let the vein hold the line in. Okay?"

The medic nodded and cut a small nick in the vein. Blood shot nearly two feet into the air. The bleeding stopped quickly when the medic inserted the small plastic intravenous tube into the vein. Immediately, blood ran into the tube. The medic followed the line to make sure it wasn't kinked, and reached for the plastic bag of blood expander at the other end. As soon as he raised the bag in the air, the blood left the tube and reentered Lucas's body along with the fluid from the bag.

The scene was controlled chaos. The doctors fired instructions and cold medical observations back and forth across Lucas's body. The clanking of the surgical instruments made its own music, almost drowning out the gurgling and choking noises coming from Lucas's face.

From the condition of his head and shoulders, Hollister could only guess that there was a lot of collected fluid and damaged tissue inside his friend's head. He tried to think of something to do or say. He raised his hand to touch Lucas, but he couldn't reach Lucas's remaining hand. So he grabbed on to Lucas's cold and trembling foot.

The doctor who had placed Hollister gave a sign of approval with his eyes as he pushed on a large drain tube he was trying to force into an incision he had made in Lucas's chest.

"Luke, you're going to be okay, man," Hollister said.

Though one of his eyes was dilated and the other was normal, Lucas seemed to respond to Hollister's voice. The dilation wasn't from drugs—there was a strict medical rule about not giving morphine to head-wound patients. So the abnormal iris meant a very serious head injury.

As he watched Lucas, Hollister noticed that the stretcher beneath Lucas's head was pooling with heavy blood coming from an unseen head wound. And while all this was happening, Lucas's eyes searched for something; maybe him, Hollister thought.

Guessing what it was, Hollister tried to soothe him. "Everyone else is okay, Luke. They got out okay. Zanger has some minor scrapes, but everyone else is okay."

Lucas relaxed his clenched fist and tried to raise his fingertips, as if giving some sign of recognition.

"These folks are going to take good care of you. Just try and relax and let them help you," Hollister said, on the verge of rambling—searching for the right thing to say. He felt so helpless, and even though no one said so, he felt in the way.

Lucas began to squirm as the doctors probed the wounds in his face. The squirming turned to thrashing and he started making loud choking noises.

One of the doctors threw the probe across the room and grabbed a small scalpel off a tray at his elbow. He moved up to Lucas's head, slipped one hand under his neck and raised it. Lucas's head tilted back, exposing the curved length of his throat. The doctor drew one finger down the front of the throat until he found the right spot, and then plunged the scalpel into a point near Lucas's Adam's apple and pulled the flesh back. The small wound filled with pink bubbles and hissed as Lucas began to breathe freely through it. A second set of hands fed a small section of tubing through the wound and taped it to Lucas's neck.

The doctor finally spoke to Hollister. "We have some more work to do here with this young man. You suppose you could come back?"

Hollister nodded. "Luke, I'm getting in the way." He squeezed and slightly shook Lucas's foot for emphasis. "I'll be back later. You just hang in there, man. We need you—"

The doctor was getting impatient. "Please!"

Hollister let go of Lucas and stepped away from the stretcher. He knew that he would never see Lucas again. Even if he lived, Lucas would quickly be evacuated to Japan or Okinawa.

At the other end of the Quonset hut the nurse who had met them handed Hollister two plastic bags of personal effects, an M-79 grenade launcher, a .45-caliber pistol, and an M-16 rifle. "You want these now or do you want to wait for them to find you guys?" he asked.

The weapons and gear had to be returned to the unit to reconcile the property books, and the personal effects had to be safeguarded. "I'll take 'em," Hollister said. He grabbed the bags and awkwardly scooped up the weapons with his free hand, careful to keep the muzzles pointed away from anyone. He had to assume that no one on the medical staff had cleared the weapons. He was sure that Zanger and Lucas hadn't taken the time to clear them.

Outside, Bernard sat in the jeep with his hands crossed on top of the steering wheel and his forehead resting on his wrists. Pale and sweaty, he looked like he was going to lose his breakfast at any moment. Spotting Hollister coming through the doorway, he tried to pull himself together.

Seeing Bernard's condition, Hollister shook his head. "Move over. I'll drive."

"But sir . . . I'm okay. I guess I just ate something that—"

"Whatever it was you ate, I don't want it to turn the jeep over with me in it. So I'll drive. Now get over in the shotgun seat."

After dumping the bags and the weapons in the back of the jeep, Hollister popped the empty magazine from Zanger's rifle and yanked the charging handle back. An unexpended round flew out of the chamber and fell on the jeep floor. He then pointed the .45 at the ground, pressed the release button to allow the magazine to slide out, and then jerked back the slide—ejecting still another unexpended round.

Leaving the .45 locked and cleared, Hollister then picked up Lucas's M-79. It had a bullet hole through the barrel and another fragmentation hole in the wide part of the wooden stock. Thumbing the break release on the top of the weapon, the hinge worked and the grenade launcher broke open, shotgun style, at the midpoint. An expended grenade shell casing was still seated in the chamber. Hollister pulled it out and looked at it. It was what was left of one of the experimental rounds that Lucas had taken on the patrol.

From the markings on the casing, Hollister could tell that it was a new shotgun round which contained several large ball-bearinglike fragments designed for wide coverage of a target over a limited range. Hollister wondered if some VC was carrying any of the frags. He dropped the weapon next to the others on the backseat and got behind the wheel.

They neared the LRP compound before either one spoke. Bernard seemed to get himself together, and felt like talking about Lucas. "He was my first platoon leader when I was a cherry. We went on a lot of humps together. I sure liked him, even if he was a little hard on us."

"He's not dead yet."

Bernard looked directly at Hollister. "He's gonna be. Isn't he? He looked like shit. I've seen that color before. And his arm's gone, he took a head shot. Hell, sir, it even looked like he had some brain damage!"

"So now you're a surgeon?"

"No, sir. You know what I mean. Lieutenant Lucas is pretty close to buyin' it."

Hollister didn't argue with him; no point to it.

Bernard turned slightly in his seat and looked back in the direction of the hospital. "He was who I wanted to have around when the shit started, sir. There was no fuckin' with Lieutenant Lucas. VC screw with him and he'd level 'em."

Back in his hooch, Hollister picked up the letter from Susan. He wanted to read it, but couldn't get Lucas out of his mind.

Bernard would probably be the first one to hear about it. The call would come in to the orderly room. Hollister absentmindedly tapped the letter on the field table and looked over at Lucas's half of the hooch. He dreaded the inventory. It was customary for an officer, preferably one who knew the casualty, to inventory his personal effects and prepare them for shipment back to the States. He was sure to be tagged to do it.

Hollister lit a cigarette and unbuttoned his shirt to get some air. To get the image of Lucas lying on that stretcher out of his mind, he turned back to the letter. But it didn't work, so he decided to go with it, and forced himself to remember Lucas—the way he was—as a loud, confident, Airborne Ranger. Hollister looked over at the Teac tape deck that was Lucas's joy. An old college classmate in the States had made him reel-to-reel tapes of Petula Clark, the Righteous Brothers, the Stones, and Sonny & Cher. Lucas played them at all hours, making their tent a little piece of home.

Eager to hear it again, Hollister stepped over to the tape deck and flipped it on. The Beatles spilled from the two speakers positioned on top of the wall lockers. It was the mid-chorus of "Eight Days a Week." Hollister sat down on Lucas's cot. For that minute he was alone. He missed his friend. He wondered who would fill Lucas's slot in the first platoon. Who would move into the hooch?

The irritating, dull rattle of the field phone on his desk snapped Hollister back to the moment. He picked up the handset.

"Lieutenant Hollister, sir."

"Sir, this is Specialist Bernard," the voice on the other end said.

"Is it Lucas?"

"No, sir, no word on him yet. I was told to call you. Captain Shaw wants to finish your patrol's debriefing now. He needs to get it done right away."

"Okay, I'll be right there. Oh, Bernard?"

"Yessir."

"That banged up M-79, you still got it?"

"Yessir, it's in the orderly room with the .45 and the M-16."

"Go ahead and turn the other weapons back in to Supply, but hold on to the M-79. I want to see if I can salvage it."

"Hell, sir, that thing's a mess," Bernard said.

"Might be useful if I can get an armorer to tinker with it."

"You got it, sir."

"Thanks, Bernard."

By the time Team 2-3 returned to the debriefing, the equipment they had captured was back. Brigade had returned what they no longer needed, the usual items: rucksacks, eating utensils, loose ammunition, ballpoint pens, Ho Chi Minh sandals, weapons cleaning rags, a few cleaning rods, rifle magazines, homemade and ChiCom ammo pouches, and lots of unrecognizable medicines.

The gear was filthy and smelled of cook fires. Much of it bore holes made by the Claymore frags. All of it was still wet from blood, rain, and mud.

SFC Marrietta stood at his podium. The captured weapons leaned against the wall behind him. On the podium he had the Tokarev pistol, a small stack of unimportant papers, a few pieces of American web gear, and two wallets—one of them Phuc's.

The men from 2-3 had all had a chance to scrape off the grime and get some food. And each man proudly wore fresh tiger-stripe fatigues. The uniforms were clean, starched, and pressed, but they had a shine that came from the hot irons that scorched the rice starch the laundry girls used.

Except for Hollister, everyone had their trouser cuffs turned up and wore shower shoes without socks. It was Detachment SOP for the field troops to take every chance to dry out their feet in order to prevent foot problems. It was the one policy that none of the NCOs had to encourage.

"Brigade has no idea what to make of the U.S. gear you all captured. They took the serial numbers and they're gonna try to find out where the M-16s came from. The other stuff will be harder to track down. It coulda come from Americans, South Viets, or Aussies,'' SFC Marrietta said.

"Did we get the notebook with the diagrams in it back?'' Hollister asked.

"No sir. They want to look at it some more.''

"When it does come back, I want to go over it with Duc. Okay?''

"You mean Sergeant Lam,'' Marrietta corrected.

"Lam?''

"He's the new interpreter—Duc's replacement,'' Marrietta said.

"We gonna get Duc back?''

Marrietta shrugged his shoulders and made a face. "Lieutenant, yer guess is as good as mine. We screwed up when we let Brigade know what a good job Duc was doing. My guess is that's the last we'll see of Duc. Next time we should complain.''

"You're right. So, how's this new guy?''

"He seems to be okay. I think we can get him up to speed.''

Satisfied, Hollister pulled out his notebook. "So where'd we leave off?''

"You were finishing your part of the debrief when we got interrupted by One-one's contact, sir.''

"Oh, yeah—choppers. I think I made my point on the fuel smell. We ought to put that on the assistant patrol leader's checklist.''

Davis looked up from his notes then shrugged slightly, letting Hollister know that he didn't want the additional work but knew that it had to be done. The added work could save lives.

"Sergeant Marrietta, will you include that in the debriefing notes and remind me to add it to the patrol briefing checklist?'' Captain Shaw said.

Marrietta nodded. "Yessir.'' He then turned back to Hollister. "Go ahead, sir.''

Hollister looked up from his notes, "While I'm on the subject, let me say that the slick and gun support was absolutely flawless. If all the mission inserts and extractions could go like that, we'd be able to take lots of the pucker factor out of what we do.''

Captain Michaelson smiled from the back row. "I'll pass that on to the chopper jocks, but it'll probably cost you a round of drinks.''

Hollister waited for the laughter to die down, then continued.

"I think we have to talk about radios some more. If we could just get a small radio that would allow the team to talk to nearby stations, like the choppers and listening posts, it would make life a lot easier out there. I know that I'd much rather have some kind of walkie-talkie in my hand than run through the bush with the handset in my fist and the radio on Vinson's back. We are beating the shit out of the handsets, cords, and sockets. It's just a matter of time before we rip the cord out of the handset or the backpack again."

"I've passed that up the chain. They tell me at Brigade Signal that they are trying to find an off-the-shelf civilian radio that will fill the requirement," Captain Shaw said.

Hollister looked back down at his notes and then over his shoulder. "I want to take a look at the captured equipment after we finish here. I think we should all know what produced the most casualties. If I find that most of the hits came from the Claymores, I want us all on the firing range again for some more practice."

There was a general shuffling and a little grumbling. Nobody wanted to hear that they were bad shots—not in their business.

"That's about all I have. I think that we were lucky, though. We could have run into a much larger unit and they could have wrapped themselves around us and blown us away. If I had to do it over," Hollister added, "I would have made a better recon of the ambush site and laid out some more early warning devices."

"Sergeant Davis, I already have your notes," Marrietta said. He looked up to Captain Michaelson. "We went over his stuff over coffee earlier, sir. It'll be in the After Action Report."

Michaelson nodded.

"Okay then—Brother Camacho, your notes?" Marrietta said.

Always a bit nervous speaking in front of others, Sergeant Camacho cleared his throat. "I agree with the lieutenant. If we could get some smaller radios, we could get a lot more done. I had a better view of the enemy patrol and could have told the others what to expect, but there was no way without a radio. If I'da had a radio, I would have told them not to trigger the ambush."

"What are you talking about, man?" Davis asked in surprise.

"I counted more than sixteen that I could see, and I didn't know how many more there were in the column that I couldn't see. I had to guess that they had us outnumbered at least four to one. From where I was sittin' it looked like we coulda got our asses waxed. We just got lucky. If those gooks knew that we were such a small ambush patrol, they would have done a job on us."

There was a moment of silence.

"Goddamn, man!" Davis said, not knowing what else to say.

"That sure says something about needing those radios," Hollister said.

"You have anything more?" Marrietta asked Camacho.

"No, other than I'm glad to be here bitchin' about it."

The room broke out in laughter. It was an especially funny comment coming from Camacho, who rarely had much to say.

"Doc?" Marrietta asked.

"I'm still havin' a problem with priorities on ambushes. I only had mortally wounded zips out there last night. But if I'd had one of us shot up, there's no way I would have worried about any VC wounded . . . even if they were wounded more seriously than the American."

"You keep doing what you are doing. You're the man on the ground, and we can't give you a hard and fast rule beyond checking out the Americans first and then deciding who needs your help second," Captain Michaelson said.

"Yessir. I roger that. Thank you, sir."

"You patch up some zipperhead before you do me and I'll give *you* a wound, Jack!" Theodore said.

The others laughed. But the moral issue was clear to each of them, and none of them envied Doc's dilemma.

"Okay, comedian, what you got?" Marrietta said as he stepped forward from the podium and bent down into Theodore's face.

"Me? Ah, nothing. It was okay. I mean nobody likes an ambush, but I walked away. Y'know what I mean?" Theodore said nervously, trying to be funny.

"I'm glad you're happy, Mr. Theodore. I'd lose sleep if I thought you were out there in the bush not having a good time. Now, let's get back to this debriefing, if Theodore is finished," Marrietta said.

"I'm through, Sarge," Theodore said.

But Marrietta kept a steely lock on him.

"Really, Sarge. I'm through . . . you can go ahead," Theodore added nervously.

"Thank you. Okay, that leaves Vinson."

"Of course, I second the small radio request. But I had some trouble from the time we got off the chopper. At our first ambush site, on the first night, I had lots of trouble establishing commo with the net control. It cleared up the second and third days, but the last two days it was a problem again. I had lots of static and sometimes there was no commo at all," Vinson said.

Marrietta looked at his notes, "Your commo problems matched the rain pattern. You must have some built-up moisture in the radio or the handset. You change handsets?"

"Yep, and it didn't make any difference."

"Turn your radio in and we'll send it over to Signal for a checkup," Marrietta said.

"That's all I have unless I can put in a suggestion that we get some different uniforms. I just can't seem to get these tigers to ever dry out."

"We're already on it, Vinson. You aren't the first to bitch about the uniforms," Marrietta said. He then turned his attention to the officers in the second row. "Sir, you have anything?"

"No. I just want to say that you did a good job," Captain Michaelson said. "I think we might have something important in the fact that the bad guys are using U.S. weapons. If it turns out to be something, you were the ones to discover it."

Captain Michaelson turned to Hollister. "I think that you ought to give these folks the next seventy-two hours off—no details, no extra duty. I'll see what I can do about getting them to Nha Trang."

There was a unanimous "All right!" from the patrol members. Nha Trang was a plum for them—a beautiful coastal city that had every delight the Orient could hold for an American male.

His cap in hand, Captain Michaelson stood to leave. "Good work, Two-three."

The team members all stood while their commander left the room. Their voices meshed as they all said their thank-yous while saluting Michaelson. Michaelson returned the salute with a simple "Carry on."

"Who gets the Tokarev?" Marrietta asked, holding the prize of captured equipment.

The team members looked to Hollister for a reply.

"Anybody want it?" he asked.

All five looked at each other. No one wanted to be the first to speak.

"Since no one is credited with the kill, it's not actually anyone's. What'dya say we give it to the pilots?"

Davis, sour-faced, spoke up. "I don't mind givin' it to the

chopper jocks. I just wouldn't want it to go to some rear echelon motherfuckers up at Brigade, sir. You know those chopper crews—they'd trade their mothers in for a case of steaks or some good imported booze."

The others mumbled in agreement. "And if we do give it to them, who do we give it to—the guns or the slicks?" Theodore asked.

"Let's let luck decide. If the last digit on the serial number is even, it goes to the slicks; odd, the pistol goes to the gun platoon. Fair 'nough?" Hollister asked.

"Fair as you need to be with helicopter jocks," Theodore said.

"Sergeant Marrietta?" Hollister said, gesturing for him to check the number.

Marrietta turned the pistol over to read the serial number. "Zero eight two niner niner—guns."

Marrietta handed the pistol over to Lieutenant Hollister. "You wanna do the honors, sir?"

"Okay. What do you all think about having it mounted on a plaque with the date and Team Two-three, and the names of everyone involved engraved on it?"

"Good idea," Doc said. "But who is gonna pay for it?"

"Since it's the lieutenant's idea, and since he is makin' all that big-time officer money and officer jump pay, he ought to pop for the plaque," Theodore said.

"Okay, I'll pay for it," Hollister said above the laughter. "But you run into the ville and have it made up, Theodore."

They all burst out laughing again. Theodore had let his mouth get him into more work again.

"Okay, okay . . . fair enough. I'll do it. But I get to pick what order we list the names, and I think that reverse alphabetical order ought to put me right on top."

Vinson looked up from his soft drink. "Where'd you learn how to spell, asshole?"

Doc threw his patrol cap at Theodore. "Yer so full of shit, Theodore. Let's go get a beer and figure out what we're gonna do in Nha Trang."

The team whistled, applauded, and cheered at the sound of the words Nha Trang.

"Sir, we're going over to the Fish House for a cold one. You comin'?" Davis asked.

"I'll be over. You guys save me a beer."

"Yessir," Davis said as he turned to the other four. "Last man there is on my detail list."

The team exploded from the briefing area and through the doorway.

Hollister took a second to enjoy their enthusiasm, and then stepped over to the captured equipment. One of the wallets caught his eye. He opened it. The first thing he found was an ID card. But it was the kind of fake South Vietnamese ID card that was all over Vietnam. He had often wondered why the Americans even bothered to check civilians for ID. It was more likely that if a Viet had an ID, it was a fake.

He looked through the compartments of the wallet. It had only one other thing in it—Ly's photo. He looked at it for a long moment. Like Hollister, the dead man who had owned it had someone waiting back home.

"You want that, sir?" Marrietta asked. "We're through with it."

"Yeah. I'd like to keep it," Hollister said as he tucked the photo into his shirt pocket. He didn't know why.

He just wanted to keep it.

CHAPTER 6

Preoccupied with thoughts of Lucas, Hollister sat on his cot. He wondered if there was even a remote chance that Lucas would live, or if he would ever be the same even if he did live. And if he wasn't the same, would people pity him?

A painful thought stabbed Hollister—Lucas's girlfriend, Cindy. Did she know yet? They'd notify his family first. Then his family would surely tell Lucas's Cindy.

He didn't want to think about Lucas anymore. He kept seeing his friend on that gurney with his life oozing out of him.

Looking for something to distract him, he remembered that he still had a letter from Susan. He was sitting on it. Picking it up, he went over to the field table.

Ripping it open with a ballpoint, he checked the ten-day-old postmark on the envelope and then began reading.

> *Dear Jimmy,*

He loved that Susan was one of the very few people who had ever called him Jimmy.

> *It's been so hot here. The weather forecast is for some rain, but I don't think we will get any. I just want it to get to something normal.*
> *How are you, my love? I miss you so much. I keep looking at the calendar on my desk and nothing happens. When you left, I told myself that I would keep busy, but that hasn't helped me at all. I find that I just miss you while I'm busy.*

He felt the same way. Knowing he had less time left in country than he had already put in helped a lot.

I never know what to say in these damn letters. There is something so disjointed about you being halfway around the world and in the dark while it's daylight here. And the differences between your world and mine make me feel like what I write is very petty. If it sounds that way, just know that I'm doing what I can to not make your life any more complicated or make you more homesick. That sure rules out plenty of topics for me.

The letter you wrote last Sunday got here before the one you wrote on the previous Friday. It doesn't make much sense to read them out of order. But I just try to rearrange things in my head. And it sure beats not getting mail from you.

Things at work are the same. I have been staying at work much later than usual. I keep trying to tell myself that it is because I want to stay busy. But the truth is that I'm avoiding the television news. They seem to be covering Vietnam a lot more each night. I wonder if the Korean War would have been much different with television coverage. It's getting to be all that people talk about. So, I avoid television and people who want to talk about it.

He wasn't really sure what she was talking about. There hadn't been much Vietnam on TV when he left.

I'm not trying to avoid people, just conversations about Vietnam. The people who seem to have the most to say about it are talking out of their hats. It makes me so angry that they pretend to be so concerned about our presence in Vietnam and what our national policy is or should be. Crap, most of them are just worried that they'll get sucked into it. I could take it if they would just say that outright. But no, they have to run on with crap that pisses me off.

He liked it that she spoke her mind.

From here it's all so confusing. But there doesn't seem to be a complete picture anywhere that you can use to form an opinion. I hope you don't get upset with me for questioning this. It's just getting to me—because it's personal for me.

Hollister thought about telling her how confusing it was for him in Vietnam when he wrote back.

*Enough about that. It's not what you need to hear about
either. Are you okay? Do you miss me? I am crawling the
walls without you! Have you heard anything about meeting
on R&R? Is it really possible? It would be so great. I don't
even care where it is. I just want so much to be with you.*

He made a mental note to check on his R&R again.

*If you can find someone with a camera, would you send
me a photo or two? I'm wearing out the ones I have just
looking at them.*

*Okay, honey, I want to get some sleep and get this in the
mail the first thing in the morning. I love you.*

Good night, my darling.

Susan

Even though it was midday for him, he whispered ''Good
night'' and carefully refolded Susan's letter.

As he slipped it into his pocket to read again later, his fingers
brushed the photograph of Ly. He pulled it out and leaned it up
against the canvas case on his field telephone. *Her* darling would
never come home. Hollister felt a twinge of guilt. He wanted to
apologize to the woman. He felt himself getting depressed by
the photo, by missing Susan, by Lucas.

The sound of an engine snapped Hollister out of it. He looked
through the screen. Just outside, a gaudy Vietnamese jeep with
two passengers pulled up and stopped. Supplied by the Americans, it was painted with a darker gloss enamel version of an
olive-drab. The facing around the instrument panel had been
chromed, and the canvas seats had been replaced with more
comfortable ones, covered with red fabric.

Captain Michaelson stepped out of the Operations tent, approached the jeep from the far side and greeted the two visitors.

In the front seat sat a fat Vietnamese Army colonel, his Vietnamese rank insignia pinned on the placard of his shirt between
his pockets. He carried a walking stick, wore brown riding boots
and a black baseball cap with a Vietnamese parachute badge
pinned to it. Under the fatigue shirt and around his neck he wore
a violet silk scarf. Finally, he wore the most unmilitary-looking
wraparound mirrored sunglasses.

Hollister immediately disliked the fat colonel.

An unusually tall American Army colonel jumped from the
backseat of the jeep and landed in front of Captain Michaelson.

"Captain, have you met Colonel Le Van Minh, the province chief? I'm John Baird, his new senior advisor." They saluted and shook hands all around.

Michaelson looked directly at the American colonel. "I think Colonel Minh and I met some months ago at an Operations briefing on an ARVN sweep, but didn't get to talk. And I'm pleased to meet you, Colonel," he said to the American. "Is there something I can help you two with?"

"Actually, I'm new in my job and Colonel Minh has been taking me to visit all of the district headquarters in his province. We went by Brigade Headquarters to visit your general. While we were there, we heard a lot about this long range patrol business you folks got down here. I'm not familiar with it and neither is Colonel Minh. So, we thought we'd drop by to find out just what it's all about. You suppose, Captain, that you could take a few minutes and brief us?"

Captain Michaelson agreed to take the two to Operations for a briefing, but Hollister knew Michaelson well enough to tell that he was just going through the motions, being courteous to the two colonels.

Lighting a cigarette, Hollister watched them cross the compound. He was bothered by how he'd instantly formed a dislike for the pair. He passed it off to his mood. He had a bad attitude toward all advisors. He wasn't sure if he was jealous of their rear-area attitude, their bungalows, refrigerators, cold beer, television and movies every night—or if it was because they siphoned off so much of the supplies that were destined for the troops. He had seen all the goodies in his few visits to their advisory team houses.

"You shit!" Theodore said, throwing an empty beer can at Vinson. "You can't sit there and tell us that shit."

"I can. I have a special sense. I know when we are going to find a VC. I can smell 'em and I can feel 'em moving in the bush," Vinson said, placing his fingers to his temples.

Davis, Camacho, and the Doc hooted and whistled at Vinson's claims.

Two-three's hooch was similar to Hollister's, but was larger. It was made from an adapted GP Medium, was encircled by a parapet of sandbags, and was erected on a hard stand remaining from a long-demolished civilian structure. No one knew what the old concrete floor had been used for, but it always smelled of fish. Around the margin of the slab, bits of ceramic tile hinted that it had been built during the French occupation of Vietnam. Now it was their home, and they had turned it into a little piece of America. Still, everyone called Team 2-3's hooch the Fish House.

The Fish House's comfortable rectangular interior held six cots, wall lockers, footlockers, and two folding field tables. The cots and lockers were crowded together at one end of the hooch to allow for a lounging area. There they had a card table made out of a large wooden cable spool, and a fragile-looking Vietnamese wrought-iron and plastic-weave couch.

A large ammo box lined with two issue ponchos and filled with dirty ice from the village served as the beer cooler.

The team members were passing around a quart of Jim Beam. Each man took a drink, washed it down with some beer, then passed the bottle to the next man.

There was an awkward lull in the laughing and fun-poking. Norris walked to the screened window and looked across the company street at 1-1's empty hooch. The team was in Operations getting debriefed. "How do you s'pose Lieutenant Lucas is doing?"

"I hear he ain't gonna make it. They say he took a head shot," Camacho said without looking up from the Jim Beam bottle. He peeled away at the label with his thumbnail. "I heard that they didn't even know what hit them."

"He's not dead yet," Hollister said as he entered the Fish House.

" 'Tench-hut!" Davis yelled.

The others scrambled up but were stopped when Hollister said, "As you were. I didn't come over here to break up your party."

They all fell back to their lounging postures. Doc Norris asked, "You saw him this afternoon, sir. Did they say anything about his chances?"

"No. They were too busy trying to keep him alive."

"You want a beer, Lieutenant?" Davis asked.

"Sure. Fire one my way."

Davis pulled a rusty can of Ballantine beer from the cold, murky water and threw it in a high arc to Hollister.

Ready, Hollister caught it in one hand while sidestepping the water that flew along with the can. He reached over to the nearby tent pole, grabbed the end of a boot string tied to a church key, and pierced the can top.

The beer was not great, but it was wet and cold. Hollister

sipped it, cautious to avoid rice husks left from the ice and the rust that had formed on the rim of the can. As he did, he watched the team playfully spool down from the excitement of the previous night. It was their calm between storms. They had been back from the ambush patrol just long enough to slow down, but not long enough to start worrying about the next patrol. Patrols were relieved of housekeeping and guard duties for the twenty-four hours after they returned—even if they weren't as successful as 2-3 had been.

Eventually they found themselves back on the duty rosters pulling details, taking training, training the new guys, or out in the company street doing PT, still terribly hung over. But this time they were going to Nha Trang.

Happy they were all alive and home, Hollister raised the beer to his lips again. It was bitter. The troops thought that the beer was exposed to extremely high temperatures in the holds of cargo ships while in transit to Vietnam, and that accounted for the less-than-fresh-brewed taste. Hollister couldn't do much about the taste, so he just ignored it and drank.

Wearing fatigue trousers, an olive-drab T-shirt, and shower shoes, Theodore stepped over to a small mirror nailed to his crude wooden wall locker. He looked at himself vainly. "You going to Nha Trang with us, sir?"

Hollister wiped the beer from his lips and reached in his pocket for a cigarette. "I'd like to. But the time off was given to you all, not me. I'll have to check with the Old Man."

"Hell, sir, the captain can get along without you for a couple of days. I'm guessin' that the biggest part of the war will still be here when we get back."

"It isn't that, Theodore. You have to understand the politics of being the junior officer in a detachment with only two captains and three, ah . . . two lieutenants," Hollister said.

Davis jumped in to distract him. "Well, we can send Ho Chi Minh a message and tell him that he'll have to hold up the fucking war while we go to Nha Trang and get our ashes hauled with some of his slant-eyed beauties."

The hooch erupted in catcalls and whistles. "Come on, Lieutenant. Tell the Old Man it ain't good to send us to Nha Trang without no officer. How we gonna get over? We'll be in the shit with the leg MP's the minute we get there without you to take the point," Theodore added.

"Theodore, I have every confidence that you can confuse the system with very little effort."

"He could fuckin' derail a concrete train," Vinson added.

Theodore quickly killed his beer and hurled his empty can at Vinson.

"Incoming!" Vinson yelled as he rolled off his cot, dodging the can.

Hollister liked being included in the grab ass. Too many officers were so stiff that they couldn't relax, and the troops wouldn't invite them to. He had always been comfortable with troops, and they with him. He had decided that he could take less credit for personality than being an NCO before he was commissioned. That piece of his background rarely escaped the troops.

The question about Nha Trang was actually a veiled invitation to join the team while they had as much fun as they could pack into their passes. For Hollister to avoid the invitation would work once or maybe twice. But after that, he knew it would sour the feelings that they had for him. They would think that he felt he was too good for them or that he disapproved of their off-duty conduct. "The first sergeant working on the passes?" Hollister asked.

"I already talked to him. He's gonna have 'em typed up for us tonight. We can skate in the morning if we want," Davis said.

"You wanna leave then?"

"I'd think that we got the best chance of scrounging transportation if we get an early start. I already called over to the slick company to see if they got any aircraft going in for maintenance. They said that they would—"

The crude screen door opened and a newly assigned PFC stepped in. " 'Scuse me, y'all. I'm lookin' for Lieutenant Hollister."

"You found him. What is it?" Hollister said.

"Oh, yessir," the round-faced boy said, his eyes adjusting to the dim light in the hooch. "The first sergeant sent me to get you. Seems the Ol' Man—I mean the Detachment Commander—wants to see you right away, sir."

"Okay. I'll be right there."

The PFC just stood there, not knowing if he would be dismissed or if he should just go on his own.

"Well? Anything else?" Hollister asked.

"Ah . . . no. No sir."

"Okay, then. You can go," Hollister said flatly.

The PFC self-consciously backed to the doorway and exited without turning his back.

Theodore burst out laughing. "Jeezus Christ! I hope that fucking cherry doesn't end up on any patrol with me."

Sergeant Camacho took a long sip of the Jim Beam, then some beer, and wiped his mouth with his tattooed forearm. "Why? He's a better soldier now than you're ever gonna be, Theodore."

Hoots and jeers followed Camacho's comment. Someone threw an empty beer can at Theodore. Hollister spoke up over the racket. "Sergeant Davis, you make the arrangements. Let me know what you decide. And try to leave part of Nha Trang standing for the REMFs."

Davis stood up and assumed something near a position of attention, although his left hand held a beer. "Sir, you can count on me. I will take care of everything. I consider it my responsibility to take these youngsters under my wing and show them around the big city."

"I'm not sure if that's supposed to make me feel any better," Hollister said.

Detachment Headquarters was the back half of an old school-house. It was a relic of the French era that had been abandoned some years earlier when the small stream nearby had undercut one end of the school's foundation. Army Engineers had provided support for the foundation by placing old railroad ties in the space that once was earth. It was the only real building in the LRP compound, and the best thing about it was that it also served as the mess hall. The two functions were divided by a crumbling plaster wall, and Hollister could count on there being something to eat or a cup of hot coffee there.

Captain Michaelson's office was a small corner room with windows that were simply square holes in the masonry. He looked up when Hollister entered. "Jim, we got some shit in the wind. Brigade wants you to go to Nha Trang and meet with the CID spooks."

"Me? We screw something up?"

"It's got something to do with the gooks your patrol greased. But I've never in all my time in the army ever heard of a corps headquarters wanting to talk to a platoon leader."

"You think it has something to do with the captured American weapons, sir?"

"Could be. CID might have found out they were stolen, but

why they would want to talk to you is beyond me. There's a chopper laid on to pick you up at 0515 tomorrow."

"Yessir. Will that be all?"

"Yes, about that. But I want you to inventory Lucas's gear for shipment."

"Oh, no. Did he die? Did you get word?"

"No, not yet. I just left him a half hour ago. He didn't look any better to me." Michaelson looked at his watch and gauged the time. "They should be evac'ing him right now. So, let's get his gear together to get it headed for the States."

"I'll take care of it right away, sir."

In the outer office Easy was hunched over some paperwork on his desk.

"You think you can arrange for someone to pick up Lieutenant Lucas's gear from my hooch in the morning, Top?"

The first sergeant looked up with a pained expression. "I don't want to, but I'll do it." He took a sip from a coffee mug with a first sergeant's chevron decal on one side and master parachutist wings on the other. "He was a good man. His platoon's going to miss him."

Hollister knew that in spite of all of his bluster, Easy was going to miss Lucas too. They had become close friends, but Easy just didn't know how to show his loss. "Yeah, I know what you mean. Anyway, I'll get it inventoried and his stuff will be ready before I leave for Nha Trang in the morning."

"Airborne, Lieutenant."

Hollister passed by a team hooch belonging to the first platoon. He could hear Johnny Cash singing "Ring of Fire" on a scratchy portable record player inside. He hadn't liked country music much as a teenager, but while he was an NCO in Germany, one of his senior sergeants used to drag him to the NCO Club to have someone to drink with. Every night a different country-western band played at the club, and it was always packed. Hollister soon learned to like country music, but rarely had a chance to listen to it much since he had started OCS. Candidates thought it wasn't sophisticated enough for their self-image.

Lucas had loved teasing Hollister about his shit-kickin' music.

It was still dark when the field phone rang in Hollister's hooch. He stumbled out of his rack and pressed the cold receiver to his face. "Hollister, sir."

"Good morning, sir," Specialist Bernard said. "You asked me to call. It's 0400 and the start of another wonderful day in the Republic of Vietnam."

"Right . . . Thanks, Bernard." Hollister dropped the receiver in the carrier and tried to focus. He found his trousers in the dark and slipped them on. His clothes were cold, wet, and clammy from the high humidity and the night dew.

Buckling his belt, he stepped through the door, opening it with a shoulder.

The smell of mess hall coffee mixed with the ever-present odor of field cook stoves. The portable stoves were all metal, so they were routinely oiled after cleaning. And each time they were fired up, the burning oil overpowered the aromas of breakfast.

"At ease!" yelled Sergeant Kendrick, a large, thirty-year-old career mess sergeant.

"Carry on," Hollister responded.

"I got some hot coffee over here," Kendrick said.

"Good. I need something to get my blood moving this morning."

The sergeant grabbed a coffee mug off the stacks of them near the coffee urn and poured a cup for Hollister. "You want something in it, sir?"

Hollister took the steaming cup from Kendrick and shook his head. He smiled at the handiwork on Kendrick's paper cook's cap, which had a ballpoint pen copy of the LRP scroll drawn with the words AIRBORNE MESS SERGEANT in the middle.

Kendrick was one of those men destined to be a cook. He was slightly overweight, gregarious, possessive, and his manhood was not threatened by the job. He took pride in his work, even though it was sometimes awful.

The coffee burned Hollister's lips, but it was coffee.

"You want some breakfast, sir?"

"No. I'm not sure I can take it this morning—"

"It'd be no trouble. I got two teams coming in in thirty minutes for chow. We got bacon and potatoes cooking now. How 'bout some eggs with it?"

"No, I have a chopper ride to Nha Trang. It'll be all I can do to keep this coffee down this early. Thanks, anyway, Sergeant K."

* * *

Hollister looked at his watch. It was five. Time to head over to the pad. He made one final check. He had decided to put on his regular jungle fatigues. It was commonly held among the LRPs that the REMFs at higher headquarters were crazed with petty jealousy at the sight of soldiers wearing any type of not-completely-authorized uniforms. The fact that the tiger-stripe fatigues had been okayed by Hollister's Brigade Commander wouldn't mean much in Nha Trang. Wearing them was asking for a hassle from MP's, staff clerks, and senior officers who would object to the *special* status of the LRPs.

But even in his regular olive-drab jungle fatigues Hollister stood out. His brigade shoulder patch was topped with two distinctive arcs—one reading AIRBORNE, the other a hard-earned Ranger tab. On his chest was an embroidered Combat Infantryman's Badge and a Senior Parachutist's Badge. These insignia alone set him apart as one in five thousand soldiers.

The true discriminator was the Ranger-style LRP scroll patch that was sewn to his right pocket. In 1965 there were only three provisional Long Range Patrol units in Vietnam. New as LRPs were in Vietnam, exaggerated tales of danger and skilled guerrilla fighting were already widespread among the troops. Hollister was just getting used to soldiers staring at him or whispering among themselves when they spotted the insignia. He liked the distinction.

He patted his shirt pocket to check for his notebook with the patrol notes and the address of the officer he was to see in Nha Trang.

He looked at the gear that he had packed and stacked on Lucas's stripped cot. Everything Lucas owned fit into a B-4 bag and a footlocker. The issued uniforms, bedding, and combat gear were segregated to the side for the supply clerk to pick up. Easy would take care of the rest. Hollister knew when he got back there would be no sign that Lucas had ever existed, and that bothered him.

Just to keep something around that was Lucas's, Hollister grabbed the corner of an embroidered name tape that simply read LUCAS and ripped it off a shirt.

There was hardly a faint glow on the horizon as Hollister walked to the chopper pad, but he could make out a slick parked on it, a standby chopper that was always available in the event a patrol made contact during the night. The crew members slept in the chopper for speed.

"Gooooood morning, Vietnam," a door gunner said from within the chopper.

Closer, Hollister made out the outline of the gunner leaning up against the transmission hump. "Know anything about a chopper going to Nha Trang?" Hollister asked.

"We're it."

The other door gunner slammed the door on the far side of the chopper and walked around to Hollister's side as he adjusted the one-piece flight suit that he had been sleeping in. "We gotta make a run to Nha Trang for parts, so we're gonna take you there on your way back to our flight line, Lieutenant."

"Great. How soon are we ready?"

"Just as soon as we load the rest of the passengers."

"And here we are," another voice said out of the dark.

Hollister turned around. Davis, Doc Norris, Camacho, Theodore, and Vinson were approaching the chopper, shoulder to shoulder.

"This looks like trouble," Hollister kidded.

They stopped at the chopper, still on line. Davis saluted, half seriously announcing, "Sir, Team Two-three prepared for movement to the objective area."

Hollister returned the salute and laughed. "D'you suppose that Nha Trang is ready for Two-three?"

"Let's surprise 'em, sir. That way we can get 'em with their pants down," Theodore said.

"You talkin' about the boys or the girls?" Vinson asked.

Theodore took off his cap and made a playful swipe at Vinson.

CHAPTER 7

Belted tightly into the co-pilot's seat, Hollister looked over his shoulder at the other LRPs. They were all asleep in the cargo compartment.

Turning back around, Hollister looked over the instrument panel at the sunrise. Through the headset in his flight helmet he heard the click of the intercom transmit button. "If you are going to be my co-pilot, you are going to have to quit gazing off at the view. That's for passengers, not pilots." The voice was Captain Pete Shelton's—Gladiator 36.

Although they were seated only eighteen inches apart, the chopper noise made it necessary for them to talk over the intercom.

Shelton pointed at a small button on the deck near Hollister's boot. "Step on that when you want to talk."

Hollister followed Shelton's instructions and spoke into the lip mike. "I can see why you guys love this business. It's gotta be the best view of this war."

Shelton laughed. "Yeah, it's great cruisin' along at fifteen hundred feet. But when you get down to treetop level it starts getting pretty nasty."

"Sure smells a whole lot cleaner up here."

"Hmmmm, and a whole lot cooler when folks aren't shooting at you. So, what d'ya say? You want to fly it for a while?"

"Me? Fly? Ah . . . sure. What do I do?"

"Easy. Put your feet on the pedals. That'll turn the nose left and right. Take the cyclic—the stick between your knees—in your right hand. That'll tilt the rotor disk, letting you go where you want to. Just push or pull it. You'll catch on real quick."

Hollister gingerly followed Shelton's instructions. "What now?"

"The collective is along the left side of your seat. It controls the basic up and down of the chopper. Since we aren't going up or down, just don't fuck with it till your next lesson. The most important thing is who is in control of this beast. If we get into a world of shit, I'll take control of the ship by saying, *'I got it.'* When you hear that, pull your hands and feet away from the controls and just let me have it. Okay?"

"Okay."

"Then *you got it*." Gladiator let go of the controls, reached into the calf pocket of his flight suit and pulled out a pack of Camels.

Surprised by how quickly Shelton released control of the chopper, Hollister tightened his grip on the cyclic and applied pressure to one pedal and then the next with a series of over-corrections. His jerky motions made the chopper fishtail, tilt forward and then back; raising the nose to the sky, then more or less straight and level. Hollister heard the door gunner kidding him over the intercom, "Oh my God . . . we're all gonna die in Vietnam!"

Overwhelmed by the responsiveness of the aircraft, Hollister tried to ignore the door gunner and get used to the controls.

"Give it a little slack," Shelton said. "Easy, man! You've got a death grip on the cyclic. Loosen up."

Hollister relaxed his grip and the chopper leveled out and continued on a straight ahead course.

"Okay, now—try to make some slow and easy moves. Give it a right turn."

Hollister pressed the pedal and jerked the cyclic to the right. The chopper took a violent turn with the nose oversteering to the right, the tail coming around to the left. Then the chopper started losing altitude. He quickly pulled back on the cyclic and pressed the left pedal. Overcontrolling—the chopper rocked over to its left and continued to fall off its cushion of air and pick up descending airspeed.

"Easy, easy," Shelton said. "Don't move the controls—think them."

"What?" Hollister asked, not understanding Shelton's instructions. "Think them?"

"Yeah, just think about pulling back on the cyclic. Just think it."

Hollister did what he was told. The nose of the chopper slowly came up. The airspeed fell off slightly and the chopper leveled out.

"See. This baby will do what you want it to do with a minimum of input. You don't have to beat the shit out of it."

The sudden feeling of control excited Hollister. "Man, is this great!" Hollister whispered, forgetting to step on the intercom button.

Shelton reached over and pointed at a small button among a cluster of other controls on the contoured handgrip of the cyclic. "If your feet are busy, you can press this to talk."

Hollister nodded, looked at the button and then pressed it. "This is really, really something terrific."

"If you want the truth, we don't fly for the terrific. We fly to keep from getting assigned to mud-sucking grunt jobs like yours."

"Don't knock it. At least I don't have to worry much about gravity."

"You do now. So . . . be gentle with it. It's a powerful machine, but it don't take a sledgehammer to fly it."

Getting used to the feel of the nearly five thousand pounds of flying machine, Hollister made his corrections more subtle and watched the chopper smooth out.

"That's better. With some serious work we could probably make a real aviator out of you. But we'd have to get on the job before all your time on the ground causes permanent brain damage," Shelton said, kidding Hollister.

"I could get to like this," Hollister said as he gently rolled the chopper, heading back toward the coastline. As he did, he noticed that the sun had turned into a large orange ball rising out of the near black water.

"So, you going to Nha Trang to rape and pillage with your guys?"

"No, sir, I got a command performance. I've been called up to Field Force Headquarters to talk to some CID people about the ambush the other night. I haven't got a clue why."

"I'll bet it has something to do with that ville that got leveled."

"What ville?" Hollister asked, surprised.

"Hell, didn't you hear it happen? Bad guys walked into the valley and wiped out an entire hamlet and everyone in it a couple hours before you guys waxed those gooks. Might even be the same VC."

"Hear it? Hell, I couldn't hear anything in that rain. This is all news to me."

"Well, I didn't get the whole story, but there's some bad shit in the wind," Shelton said. "So, keep your head down."

"My experience tells me to dodge everything in country."

"Amen on that," said one of the door gunners over the intercom.

The airfield at Nha Trang cut diagonally through the center of the coastal city. Rows of choppers dotted its apron, and vintage Vietnamese Air Force prop-driven A1-E fighter bombers were lined up in front of their hangars.

The two well-used runways were rice paddies that had been graded and covered with pierced steel planking to make serviceable landing surfaces. The amount of airplane traffic was evident in the absence of grass or weeds growing through the three-inch holes in the PSP.

Somewhat cramped, Hollister sat in the front seat of the pedal-powdered cyclo as it threaded along the outside of the airfield's barbed wire.

The aging Vietnamese cyclo driver wore only threadbare shorts and a scrap of filthy cloth around his neck, which he used to wipe the road grime from his face. Hollister watched the old man as he held his chin up and pumped the pedals with a labored pace, trying not to lose the forward momentum that he had gained. To Hollister, the man was one of the images of Vietnam that he would long remember. He represented the thousands of poor Vietnamese who were trying to hold things together by sheer determination in face of the growing war.

Children played along the roadside, stopping long enough to pelt the passing Americans with pleas for money and candy and offers of prostitution, soft drinks, and fresh fruit.

Put out by their behavior, the old man spoke harshly to the children. They hurled insults at him and quickly returned to their play. Hollister assumed that he was really unhappy with what the war and the Americans had done to all of them.

Nha Trang could have been a city in France if the temperature were cooler. Much of the architecture was French, and the streets frequently converged in traffic circles rather than blunt intersections. The roads were clogged with bicycles, cyclos, motorbikes, three-wheel minitrucks, and endless convoys of military vehicles.

Standing on a box in the center of one circle was a Vietnamese traffic policeman wearing a splendid khaki uniform with white

leggings, gloves, and a hat that was large for his small head.
Though he took his job very seriously, not one driver paid attention to the policeman's whistle blasts or exaggerated hand
signals.

As the cyclo turned onto the beach road, Hollister motioned
for the old man to pull over. Then he got out of the cyclo and
paid up.

Straightening the skirt of his jungle fatigue shirt, Hollister
automatically checked to see that all his buttons were fastened.
It was a habit learned at the Seventh Army NCO Academy in
Germany that had become automatic.

Fairly confident, he started toward the headquarters building
entrance. Walking past two sentries, Hollister returned the salutes of the starched, pressed, and spit-shined American soldiers
in the sandbagged shack outside what had once been a fine
French hotel.

As he climbed the steep flight of steps, Hollister looked back
across the boulevard at the narrow ribbon of blinding white sand
that edged the blue-green waters of the coastline less than fifty
yards away. As beautiful as the town was, no one living there
had ever seen it without troops. Before the Americans, there had
been the French, the Japanese, the Chinese, the Cambodians,
and on and on back into the history of the country. He realized
how lucky Americans were to have spent a hundred years since
the last bloody battles of their own civil war.

The words GRAND HOTEL had been carved into the masonry
over the large entrance, but the freshly painted wooden sign that
hung above it read: HEADQUARTERS, I FIELD FORCE, VIETNAM.

Hollister entered.

"Can I help you, Lieutenant?" asked a sharply dressed MP
standing at a reception desk.

"Yes, I'm looking for, ah . . ." Hollister pulled his notebook
from his pocket and checked. "Captain Wasco."

"Yessir. Captain Wasco is down in the basement—Room
Eleven." The MP pointed to the stairs and Hollister took them.

Just inside the doorway to Room 11 a pretty Vietnamese
woman in her early thirties sat at a desk in her tightly fitted
traditional ao dai. "Good morning, Trung-Uy," she said as she
stood up.

"Oh, hi . . . good morning." Hollister smiled and snatched
his hat from his head. "I'm Lieutenant Hollis—"

"Trung-Uy Hollister. I know. Captain Wasco is expecting

you. You will wait, please?'' She stepped away from her desk
and went into another room. Hollister tried to be subtle about
watching her trim little behind as she shifted around the typing
table next to her desk and walked away.

Wasco was a truck of a man. In his late thirties, he was balding
and addicted to cheap White Owl cigars. His uniform was heavily starched, but with none of the fading that a field soldier's
gets. The branch insignia on his collar indicated that he was a
Military Intelligence officer—a spook. He sat across the table
from Hollister while another American in cotton slacks and a
short-sleeved shirt flipped through several pieces of paper in a
folder that had a classified document cover sheet on it. The
warning on the cover read: SECRET—NOFORN. He placed the
folder on the table and opened the maroon book next to it to a
marked passage.

"Lieutenant, my name is Mr. Elliott. I'm from Criminal Investigation Division. Let me start by telling you that it is my
duty to read you your rights under the provisions of Article 31
of the Uniform Code of Military Justice.''

Hollister straightened in shock.

Elliott continued, "Article 31 of the UCMJ specifies that no
person subject to this code shall compel any person to make any
statement or answer any questions without first being advised
that any statement made by him can and will be used against
him in a trial by courts-martial—''

"Hold it! Just what's going on here?''

"Sit down, Hollister,'' Wasco said. "You're not being
charged with anything, but we have to advise you of your rights
before we question you.''

"Question me about what? I know my rights. I know them
by heart. You don't need to read them to me.'' He sat back
down. "Just tell me what's going on. I'll tell you both right now
that I have nothing to hide.''

Wasco and Elliott exchanged glances. Elliott closed the red
book and leaned forward on the desk. "Six South Viet families
were executed in the An Hoa valley only a few miles from where
you had an ambush set up.

"Vietnamese Army units searched the area next morning and
found that the people were killed with American weapons. And
U.S. equipment was found at the site. They're suggesting that
an American unit did it, and they're pissed.''

Hollister was baffled. "Is this a supporting-fires thing? Somebody think I dropped artillery on those people or rolled gunships in on them? 'Cause if that's what you're getting to—''

"Wait, hold it. Just relax, Lieutenant," Wasco said. "Let's go through this by the numbers. Elliott and I want to get to the bottom of this. We have to give Saigon some answers, and right away. Now, you are the closest thing we have to any information about the incident, and we want to hear everything you know."

"Me?"

Wasco slid a map out from under a pile of papers and tapped it with his fingers. The map had U.S. and Vietnamese unit locations marked on it. "You just about owned the valley that night. The nearest allied unit was over thirteen klicks away."

"Okay . . . what do you want to know?"

"We want you to tell us the whole story from the time you got the patrol warning order till you got back."

"Sure, yessir. I can do that. But I don't know anything about—''

"Just tell us what you do know," Wasco said. "We'll try not to ask you what you don't know."

Using his notebook, for the next two hours Hollister recounted the minute details of the ambush patrol. The questioning went on an additional hour after that. They stopped only to read back dates, times, and grid coordinates for accuracy.

While they did, Hollister pulled the stack of black and white photographs they had been looking at to his side of the table and spread them out. Each photo was marked with the date, time, and compass direction of the photo. He was horrified by what he saw. Children were burned and crushed by the weight of their collapsing houses. Several of the old people were photographed in death with their arms around each other and around what Hollister assumed had been their grandchildren. And the remains of assorted livestock littered what was left of My Phu.

He flipped through more close-ups of spent American rifle cartridges, American web gear, C-ration cans and plastic wrappers, spoons and empty cigarette packages.

"Some sick fucks, huh?" Wasco asked.

Hollister took the question to mean that Wasco believed his story. "I can't think of any reason for this. These people weren't VC, they weren't a threat to the South Viets or the Americans. They were old people and children—not soldiers. They were just simple farmers."

"Look at the casualty figures sometime and find out how many 'simple farmers' are getting dead in the middle of this,"

Elliott said. "If you ask the South Viets, they'll tell you that
they were VC sympathizers. If you ask the farmers, they'll tell
you that they just want to be left alone."

"That's what this war is all about. Isn't it?" Hollister asked.

"What's that?" Wasco replied.

"About just being left alone," Hollister said, sliding the photos back across the table.

Wasco stood up, lit another cigar and blew smoke toward the
ceiling. "Well, we know a lot more now. We really appreciate
your cooperation, Hollister. You got to understand we're under
a lot of pressure to get some answers to Saigon before this gets
to the press. We better be able to account for every swinging
dick that night or take the heat for not knowing what the fuck's
going on."

Wasco closed the folder that contained his notes and looked
to Elliott. "You need anything else?"

Elliott shook his head no. "Lieutenant, now that I've heard
about what you guys do out in the field, I have a renewed respect
for how you guys spend your nights." He stuck out his hand.

Relieved, Hollister accepted the compliment and the hand-
shake. "If you're through with me, I, ah . . . I have to . . ."
Hollister stumbled.

"You have to take advantage of being in Nha Trang," Wasco
said.

"Yessir. And my team is in town. So I have to make sure that
they leave something standing." Hollister stood and started for
the door.

"Oh, one thing, Hollister," Wasco said.

"What's that, sir?"

"Don't leave Dodge."

They all laughed.

It was much hotter when Hollister got back out on the street.
He walked north, toward the point where it was rumored that
Madame Nhu had her winter villa.

It had only been four months since Hollister had been in Nha
Trang. But in that short span things had changed. He was amazed
at the increased traffic, the large number of troops on the streets,
and the black market stalls set up along the sidewalks. He avoided
as many of the street hawkers as he could and kept on walking.

At the next intersection he spotted the screened-in porch front
of The Nautique—a French restaurant that had the best food in
Nha Trang.

The inside of The Nautique was nothing special, but all fifteen tables were filled. And every customer was an American serviceman. Loud and raucous, they were all support, supply, headquarters, and logistics troops—REMFs.

"Do you have a reservation, Lieutenant?"

The man who had asked him, Mr. Valle, was a Frenchman in his fifties. He carried a plastic-covered menu and wore a clean apron around his waist.

"A reservation? Ah, no. I don't, but I just came in from the field and I sure would like to—"

Valle studied Hollister's uniform, noted the combat badges and parachute wings. "Airborne! For you, I can find a table. Wait here a moment, monsieur."

Valle walked to a table piled with dishes and empty beer bottles and had two of his Vietnamese busboys quickly clear the table. He waved Hollister over and handed him the menu, first wiping it with his sleeve.

It was in French, one of many languages that Hollister had not mastered. He put the menu down. "I know what I want. I want a steak—medium rare—and a beer."

"Pommes frites? Potatoes?"

"Sure," Hollister said.

A waiter brought the beer and poured it. Valle stood there and watched Hollister raise the glass to his lips. Hollister made a surprised face.

"It is French beer. You have had it before?"

Hollister reached for the bottle, jockeyed it in his hand to read the label.

"Bier LaRue? No, I haven't. It's different, but it's cold and it's wet. And that is all it takes for me to like it."

"It is a good beer, monsieur. I 'ave been drinking it since I was your age. It won't kill you, but these will," Valle said as he reached out and tapped the wings on Hollister's shirt. "Wait." Valle went to the back of the restaurant and returned quickly.

"Lieutenant, look at this." He thrust a framed and yellowed photograph at Hollister.

It took Hollister a second to focus and realize that Valle was showing him a photograph of rows of French paratroopers proudly wearing their berets and the oversized French parachutist badges.

"Most of my regiment was killed in Cao Bang—up north. I was wounded," Valle said. He raised his left hand, revealing the scars. "I was a machine gunner. But more importantly, my friend, I was a paratroop soldier."

Hollister knew of the battle that nearly destroyed the entire regiment during the French war with the Communist Viet Minh. "I see what you mean. Well, I promise to take care."

"*Bon.* Men who jump are men who fight. If you fight long enough, you will die. You take much care. I know what it is like out there. Now, enjoy your meal," Valle said sincerely as he took the photograph and walked away.

It was obvious that Valle had his fill of the rear echelon soldiers who frequented his restaurant. It's a kind of fraternity, Hollister thought. There are soldiers and there are the Airborne soldiers. Hollister sipped his beer and remembered his own induction into the Airborne brotherhood.

That morning the noise inside the cargo compartment of the huge C-130 was deafening. Hollister's heart raced when the red lights came on near the two open troop doors in the back of the aircraft. He could only distinguish parts of words spoken in certain frequencies over the roar of the four giant engines as the jumpmaster began his precise jump commands.

Hollister wasn't comfortable with the idea of being in an airplane, any airplane, for the first time in his twenty years. Yet there he was, cinched into the webbing of a T-10 parachute, getting ready to hurl himself out of that same airplane. The jumpmaster yelled out again.

"Get ready!"

Sixty-four Airborne students responded instantly by slamming one foot down on the metal flooring in unison.

"Outboard personnel—stand up!" the jumpmaster screamed with an upward gesture of his palms.

Hollister and the other jumpers seated against the airplane's outer skin struggled to their feet and faced the rear of the aircraft.

Like the others, Hollister was thinking, Will I chicken out in the door? Can I do this?

The jumpmaster yelled, "Inboard personnel stand up!" even before the outboard jumpers were fully standing.

"Hook up!" was the first command that Hollister really heard. He fastened the static-line connector to the taut, overhead anchor-line cable that ran the length of the aircraft just above his ear.

The safety pin in place, Hollister carefully traced the path of the yellow static line from the cable to where it disappeared over his shoulder into the back-mounted parachute pack tray. The Airborne School instructors' stories of jumpers repeatedly slamming against the fuselage at the end of hung-up and misrouted static lines ran through his mind.

"Check equipment!"

He looked at and touched every part of his gear the same way he had a thousand times before in the training area at Eubanks Field.

"Sound off for equipment check!"

The last jumper started the report, and it carried forward until the jumper behind Hollister hit him on the ass and screamed, "Okay!" Hollister reached forward with his free hand and did the same to the man in front of him, then yelled, "Okay!"

The okays continued up the line until the first man pointed at the jumpmaster and yelled, "All okay!"

"Stand in the door!" The jumpmaster grabbed the first man in line and jerked him into the open doorway.

All eyes were on the first man. Beyond his face was the red light. When it changed to green, they would disgorge from the aircraft as if attached to one another.

The jumpmaster dropped to his knee, stuck his head out into the prop blast, looked down and made one last check of the drop zone a half a mile ahead and 1,250 feet below. Satisfied that it was clear and safe for him to put the jumpers out, he returned to his feet. He took a solid grip on the first jumper's lift web just over his hip and shoved the soldier's flapping static line to a point along the anchor-line cable where it wouldn't foul.

The red light went out. The green one went on.

"Go!" the jumpmaster screamed as he slapped the first jumper on the butt, shoving him out the door. Then, as fast as he could turn back to the second jumper, he reached up and tapped him out the door behind the first man.

Very quickly Hollister found himself standing in the door, knees bent, outboard foot forward, both hands on the outside of the door, looking down. His heart pounded as the wind first dried and then teared up his eyes.

He started to pull back a bit before hurling himself out into the blast of air that was passing his face at breathtaking speed. Just as he started forward and out, he felt the jumpmaster crack him on the butt with the palm of his hand.

Hollister exited the door in an out-of-control posture that was nothing like the tight exit position he had practiced hundreds of times on the ground in the mock-ups.

Just as he realized he was in the wrong body position, he felt his feet being snapped toward the rear of the aircraft and then felt a sinking sensation as his forward momentum was overcome by gravity. The hot, dry blast of the props swept up his back and across the stubble of the Airborne crew cut under his tightly fastened helmet.

Suddenly, Hollister realized that he hadn't been counting. And his eyes were closed! He tried to catch up with the critical timing by rushing the count, "One thousand, two thousand, three thousand, four thousand!" as he opened his eyes.

He was turning on a vertical axis, and the noise of the aircraft had almost disappeared. Then a forceful tug pulled the parachute out of the pack tray, snapping him into a facedown, feet-toward-the-departing-aircraft attitude.

Remembering his training, he tried to look up to check the deployment of the parachute. He remembered to ask himself, Do I have a full parachute? Is it a malfunction, a partial inversion, a cigarette roll?

But something was really wrong. He couldn't raise his head. He looked down. The drop zone was directly below him, but he had no idea how high he was. He had never been in a plane before—how could he be expected to know? He didn't even know if he had a parachute above him or how fast he was falling.

Reaching up above his helmet, he found that the two sets of risers attached to the suspension lines were twisted. *Start running*. That's what they said in training. *If you are twisted—start running*. The motion will start to untwist you under your parachute so that you can control the landing.

Hollister felt silly pumping his legs, but it worked. Slowly at first, but soon he was spinning until he was free and the twisting stopped. Finally he was able to look up.

He remembered to check for holes in the canopy. *If you spot a hole or a tear larger than your helmet, return to a good tight body position and deploy your reserve chute!*

Thank God! It was a full parachute. It looked so big. Hollister suddenly remembered the ground. Why the hell was he looking up?

Voices. He could hear the voices of instructors on the ground.

"Jumpers. Place your feet and knees together. Look around and below you. Slip clear of jumpers below you. Then check the horizon. Tuck your chin into the hollow of your neck and pull your elbows into your sides. Feet and knees together. Make good parachute-landing falls,'' they kept repeating.

"Do not, I say again, do not attempt to make a standing landing!" yelled a particularly ugly Drop Zone Safety NCO.

"If you make a standing landing, I will make your sorry ass do push-ups until your dick falls off!"

The trees! Hollister's eyes were now at the same level as the trees! Okay, okay, he kept telling himself. Be calm, prepare to land, look out below for—

Whoomp! He hit the ground like a sack full of rocks. Nothing hurt.

Nothing hurt! Yeah, he was sure—nothing hurt. He moved a leg and then the other. Still no pain!

He was okay. He did it!

"You takin' a nap over there, fuck stick?" a Drop Zone Safety NCO yelled.

He was talking to Hollister. There was no one else near him. The twists in Hollister's chute had broken him out of the cluster of the other jumpers. Now he was in a world of hurt because the NCO would be focused on him.

Once standing, Hollister realized that his suspension lines were draped all over him. He started to extract himself from the lines when the sergeant reached him.

"What the fuck are you doin', boy?" he bellowed.

"Ah, gathering up my parachute, Sergeant."

"Well, get out of the goddamn harness first, you dickhead. You try that shit in any kind of wind and you'll be scooping up gravel with your lower lip."

Hollister was so excited over what he had just done that there was no way he was going to do anything right.

The Drop Zone NCO kept yelling at Hollister while he found the quick release assembly on his chest and unfastened the buckle that held the reserve chute in place. Releasing one of the fasteners on his reserve, he then made one quick hit on the large release button, but nothing happened.

"Where the fuck have you been the last three weeks, dickhead?" the NCO screamed.

He realized that he had not pulled free the safety clip, nor had he twisted the large release button off of the locked position. Trying not to let the NCO rattle him, he snatched the clip free, made the necessary quarter turn on the button, and slammed the heel of his hand into the button. The entire parachute rig dropped to the ground.

"Give me twenty-five push-ups, dickhead, and then figure-eight that chute," the sergeant yelled with his face pushed into Hollister's. "And when we get back to the company area I want you to report to me for some remedial training. If I'm not satisfied with your performance then, you won't be on the jump manifest tomorrow! Miss that jump and you get recycled back to the first week'a training. Got that?"

"Clear, Sergeant. Airborne," Hollister screamed just before falling to the front-leaning rest position to start knocking out the push-ups.

"Your steak, Lieutenant," Valle said.

Hollister looked up and smiled. "Real fresh meat. God, it's been a while." He cut into the steak and took a bite. It was just right. But there was a very slight trace of something that he couldn't place.

"It is not cow. It is water buffalo," Valle said. "But it is the same thing."

Valle was right. Except for the very slight taste difference and the slightly tougher consistency, it was a filet mignon.

"It's perfect," Hollister said as he pushed a forkful of European-style potatoes into his mouth. What heaven for a grunt!

CHAPTER 8

The cyclo pulled up in front of Marie Kim's. Hollister paid the cyclo driver, tipped him, and entered a Vietnamese bar that was becoming well known throughout Vietnam as a bar for combat soldiers and only *Airborne* combat soldiers.

It hadn't been the bar's policy to exclude all the leg REMFs. Nha Trang had a large Airborne population because Fifth Special Forces Group Headquarters was located there and much of the associated in-country training took place there. So the Airborne soldiers stationed in Nha Trang frequented Marie Kim's, and those who came there for training were quick to find the bar.

Heckling legs who dropped in until they were either forced to leave or provoked to fight became a favorite sport of the Airborne customers. Those poor legs who did stumble in the front door by chance were immediately met by a wall of screaming, catcalls, and flying beer cans and bottles.

The owners of Marie Kim's were pleased at how the exclusivity had worked out. The bar's reputation spread, and every Airborne soldier in Vietnam made an effort to get to Marie Kim's as if it were some sort of paratrooper's Mecca. Of course, the popularity allowed the owners to up their prices. Over time, the management added prettier girls, live bands, and more atmosphere. But for the Airborne troops, Marie Kim's was legendary for the fraternity and the girls—not the interior decorating.

Hollister stepped from the city traffic and bright sunlight into Marie Kim's. The interior was hot. He was immediately struck by the smell of beer, stale cigarette smoke, and perspiring soldiers. The traffic noise outside was immediately drowned out by the very amateur Korean rock band at the far end of the long, narrow room.

Before he could see in the darkened room, Hollister found himself guiding on a loud, synchronized chant from a table near the bar. The words *"Two-six, Two-six, Two-six"* filled the room, louder even than the bad band. Team 2-3 stood in alcoholic glory, chanting loudly. Vinson, Camacho, Davis, Doc Norris, and Theodore enthusiastically repeated Hollister's radio call sign as they waved their beers in the air.

Hollister weaved through the crowded room to their table. A chair appeared from somewhere and two bar girls stepped up to take his drink order.

"American beer? You have American beer?"

A bar girl of no more than thirteen shook her head. "No hab."

"Okay, how 'bout thirty-three?"

She wrinkled up her face, confused—her English was lacking.

"Ba mui ba . . . thirty-three?"

"Okay. Can do. *Ba mui ba.* We hab," she said as she wheeled to place the order.

"Goddamn, sir. We thought they fuckin' court-martialed your ass," Davis said.

"No . . . but I thought I'd never get out of there."

"The waiting hasn't been that bad, sir," Theodore said.

Theodore was smugly stroking the bare leg of the little bar girl on his lap. She was not yet in her twenties, wore a miniskirt and a tube top that she kept fighting to keep up while Theodore was trying to slip it down.

"Oh, this is Tuyet, sir. She loves me too much."

Hollister saw that Theodore was on the verge of getting shit-faced.

"Trung-Uy, you wan' girl? I can do. Get you pretty V'namee girl. Cherry girl. You wan'?" Tuyet asked.

Hollister spotted the half-empty champagne glass of Saigon Tea on the table. It was the toll exacted by the management for Tuyet's presence on Theodore's lap. The glass had been refilled several times. Though varying widely in content throughout bars in Vietnam, Saigon Tea was universally overpriced and under-strength.

To prevent a barrage of arguments and charges against Hollister's manhood and spending practices, he said, "Let me have a beer first. Okay?"

Before Tuyet could begin her second round of sales pitching, she was interrupted by Davis, who leaned as far across the table as he could to be heard. "So what's the deal with the spooks? They fuckin' with you, Lieutenant?"

"Something's going on that I don't understand at all. The other night, when we hit that VC patrol, someone wiped out a whole hamlet down on the valley—just below our ambush site."

"Same patrol we ambushed?" Davis yelled.

"Don't know, but whoever fired up those civilians was using American weapons. And we did police up some U.S. gear."

"Goddamn slope motherfuckers! I told you, sir. This shit is 'cause of the lazy-ass South Viets. If they'd get their lazy asses outa their fuckin' hammocks at night and patrol the valley, there'd be more rice to eat and more civilians alive there in the goddamn mornings."

"You talk too much, Davis. Be nice. Don' be ugly," Tuyet said, reacting to his anger.

Davis gave Tuyet a glare. "Why don't you just let babysan over there buy you more Saigon Tea? Okay?"

"Hey, Sarge. Some slack here. This is my one love in the world. Do what she says, be nice," Theodore said, using the excuse to embrace and fondle Tuyet some more.

Davis leaned back in his chair, threw his hands in the air, and howled like a wolf. "Yeah, she's yours, man—and every other stiff dick with two hundred piasters."

The others laughed at Theodore. "Lemme tell you something, young soldier. You don't leave those zips alone, you gonna end up broke and dead from dick rot," Davis said.

More laughter.

"Hey! It's my money—"

"And your dick," Davis added.

"Right. So let me do what I want with it, Sarge."

Davis leaned forward, took a sip of beer, and spoke just above the noise level. "Lis'en here. You end up on one of my patrols with a sneezin' peter and it's gonna fall off out there. I ain't compromisin' no patrol to call a Dust-Off in for your dick."

Vinson had been quiet up to that point. "Here, Theodore, this ought to sterilize it for you." He picked up a beer, pulled open the front of Theodore's shirt and poured a full beer down the front of his chest.

The others laughed hysterically as Tuyet jumped to her feet swearing in Vietnamese. Theodore just sat there shocked.

Suddenly the room started to pick up the words the band was singing. It was to become one of many Vietnam anthems. One, then another, soldier stood and sang along with Bobby Bare's

"Detroit City." Most of them didn't know all the words, but they all sang loudest at the lyrics "I wanna go home. I wanna go home. Oh Lord I wanna go home."

The Annam Hotel, a single-story building, had a large central room that served as a makeshift lobby, with several guest rooms off of it. In recent years more tiny rooms had been added onto the back of the hotel, over what had once been a laundry area and livestock yard.

As they entered, Hollister spotted a group of Vietnamese prostitutes waiting to be picked over by the arriving guests.

They ranged in age from eleven to fifty. All smoked harsh Vietnamese cigarettes or Salems, and their dress was less than provocative. Those few who had made some attempt at makeup were miserable failures. The older ones had terrible teeth and put their hands to their mouths each time they laughed.

The team stopped in the center of the checkerboard-blocked linoleum floor, discovering the cluster of available women before any other feature in the hotel lobby.

Davis pointed to a numbered door. "That's mine, Camacho's is next to it, and Doc, Vinson, and Theodore are in the back. You can bunk in with me if you want, Lieutenant. There are two half-assed racks in my room."

Hollister looked at the hookers. "I'm sure you'd like a little more privacy. You know, in case you want to *entertain*?"

Davis nodded. "Oh, yessir—entertain. I may just have to do that. I think that I need to work on improving relations with our little zipperheaded allies."

"I'll see if the papasan here has anything left." Hollister walked over to the old man sitting behind what served as the hotel desk, smoking a homemade cigarette stuffed into an L-shaped wooden cigarette holder.

Navigating with great difficulty, but with some care for his own dignity, Camacho quietly moved to his room and entered, unnoticed by the others.

Hollister thanked the old man, who got up to lead him to his room. He turned to let the others know that he had been successful. But by then they'd all disappeared. So had the prostitutes. Hollister knew that they wouldn't miss him.

While he waited for the old man, he had to shake his head in amazement at the range of emotions they had all been through in the previous forty-eight hours. He was suddenly very tired and ready for bed.

Hollister turned and followed the old man toward the back of the hotel. As he walked out the back door, Hollister heard Theodore trying to convince two of the hookers to try out a threesome. He smiled at Theodore's approach. Smooth it wasn't.

The deuce-and-a-half truck stopped outside the LRP compound. Hollister and Team 2-3 leaped from its bed. A couple of the team members hollered thank-yous to the driver for giving them a lift. But their voices were lost in the trumpeting of the exhaust stack, which left a plume of black diesel smoke.

As the truck pulled away Sergeant Davis said, "Whoa! What the hell . . . ? Bar-bee-cue!" breaking into a wide grin.

The others ran around the truck and looked into the LRP compound. There, outside the mess hall, stood most of the detachment, spread out around three half-barrel barbecue grills made of old oil drums.

Easy, Doc Tillotson, and Sergeant Kendrick were manning the three fires, cooking steaks and chicken over soft Vietnamese charcoal. There was lots of loud talk, and not one hand was without a beer or drink in it.

Many were working on soft drinks because one patrol per platoon had to remain on alert at all times—sober, gear packed, each man in the compound and ready to go on fifteen minutes' notice. It was one policy that no one complained about.

Stuffed, Hollister dropped the last of his chicken bones on a paper plate. With no napkins, he licked the remainder of the grease on his trousers. The stains would blend in with the old traces of rifle-cleaning solvents and oils he had used to clean and lube his weapons.

"Pretty good shit, huh?" Easy asked, standing in front of Hollister with a T-bone steak held out for him.

"Right. But I can't eat another thing, Top. Where the hell did you get this, anyway?"

"Lieutenant . . . you know better than to ask a first sergeant where he got something. 'Cause if you ask, I have to tell you. And if I tell you, you'll have to do something about the logistical channels that I used. You were an NCO long enough."

"Well, Top, sometimes I forget my place. I just hope it won't go hard on me when I get invited to that big NCO Club in the sky," Hollister said.

"Lieutenant, there'll be a standing invite for you there—it's policy. You'll be forgiven for accepting a commission."

Hollister raised his hands in surrender. "Okay, okay. Wherever it came from, I loved it. Please give my regards to the nameless and faceless who were responsible for the first Class A rations I have had since yesterday."

"Yesterday?" Easy said with surprise.

"Yeah . . . I slipped into The Nautique yesterday and had a steak. Water buffalo steak, but it was still steak."

"Valle tell you his war stories?"

"Yeah . . . and warned me, too," Hollister said.

Easy put the steak back down on the mess hall tray. "I been knowin' Valle nearly fifteen years. We went to the Jungle Warfare School together in Singapore. He was one helluva Airborne trooper. You shoulda seen him the night we were in a whorehouse in Penang and this dumb fuck from—"

Bernard ran out of the Operations tent yelling, "Top, where's Cap'n Michaelson?"

Easy pointed toward a cluster of troops. Bernard made a quick turn and ran to the captain.

"Contact?" Hollister asked.

Easy looked around at the others in the compound. There was no sign of activity at the Operations tent or near the chopper. "I'd guess not."

Bernard excitedly explained something to Captain Michaelson. They could tell that something hot was happening; judging by Bernard's gestures, it was somewhere north and west of the LRP compound.

Captain Michaelson looked around, caught Hollister's eye and signaled for him and Easy to meet him in Operations ASAP.

Inside Operations, Hollister, Davis, Sergeant Allard—team leader of 2-1—and Easy quickly took notes while listening to Captain Shaw. Captain Michaelson, Lieutenant Perry, Gladiator, and Iron Mike stood nearby.

Shaw pointed out a spot on the easel-mounted map. "This is where the chopper crew spotted the downed aircraft. And, because of the dense foliage, they were only able to ID the birddog crash site. They saw no signs of life, but that doesn't mean anything at this point."

Shaw looked up at Captain Michaelson, who gave him a hurry-up gesture as he tapped the face of his watch. "So, even though this is a little loose and doesn't give you a lot of time to prepare, we have to go with what we have, and fast.

"Lieutenant Hollister will take two teams from his platoon

in to find and evacuate any Americans from the crash site. If there are any critical items or any onboard ordnance, it will be evac'd or destroyed at his discretion.''

Shaw pulled a chrome collapsing pointer from his shirt pocket, extended it and pointed to a clearing on the map a few inches from the grease-penciled crash site on the map overlay. ''Movement will be by chopper to an area up the ridge line from the downed aircraft.

''The heavy team will take only one day's rations and the basic load of ammunition. Extra demo will be necessary to blow trees if you find any survivors who need immediate evac.''

Hollister listened to the operations order. His mind clicked on to a thousand little things that he had to remember and make sure got taken care of before the team lifted off. He knew that the first thing he had to do was to assume that the single-engine two-seater had been shot down—even if it had only gone down from engine failure. And based on that assumption, he could organize the rescue force and prepare for the worst.

He hated short-fused missions. LRP teams didn't have the mass or firepower to overcome a lack of planning and rehearsal. And on a recovery mission they would go in like noisy elephants and be anchored to a spot on the ground until the evacuation was completed.

VC in the area could move at their own speed to screw with the Americans. A downed aircraft was great bait for an ambush. And Hollister couldn't prep the area with gunship runs and artillery because there might be a couple of pilots wandering around. He told himself to forget how he hated rescue missions and just get on with getting the job done. He looked at his watch. It was getting late and it was getting dark.

At dusk the four slicks stood at flight idle on the LRP pad. Near them the eleven-man team was outlined by the strange strobing of the flashing red running lights of the helicopters. Each man was hunched over by a heavy rucksack.

Hollister hurriedly inspected each man's gear by looking at and touching everything—a variation of an Airborne jumpmaster's inspection. Touching what he looked at kept the inspector's eyes on the equipment. There was time to be saved by looking at some things while touching others. But that made the inspection incomplete and could cost lives. So, Hollister's eyes followed his fingers.

After he slapped the last man on the back, Hollister was satisfied that there had been no equipment compromise in the short warning time. But he was out of time. Only a faint red line on the horizon separated the night from the setting sun.

After some last minute coordination between the pilots, Michaelson gave them all the go. He got into the right seat of the command-and-control chopper, Hollister and Team 2-3 moved to the first insert chopper, Allard and Team 2-1 moved to the second insert chopper, and Easy moved to the cargo compartment of the fourth ship.

Easy would be belly man in the chase ship. The belly man was a senior sergeant or one of the more experienced officers not otherwise busy during inserts and extractions. The job required being an extra set of hands and eyes to help make sure that if the chase ship was pressed into service, things happened fast. The belly man helped each man into the chopper and was responsible for accounting for all of the bodies—dead and alive.

Once the chase ship had picked up a team or chopper crew, it was the belly man's job to sort out who needed medical attention, apply first aid, and advise the pilot on the needs of the wounded while the crew focused on getting the chopper out.

Easy had used his rank to pull more than his share of belly rides. He was lots of bullshit and bluster, but there wasn't a man in the heavy team that evening who wasn't happy to know that First Sergeant Evan-Clark was belly man in their chase ship.

For a change, the members of the teams were relatively silent. Conversation was confined to business. The mission was foremost in everyone's mind, and no one was in a playful mood.

One of the first things Hollister had noticed after joining the detachment was that there was something about the anxiety of night helicopter insertions that always took the normal level of bravado down several notches. They didn't do night airmobile assaults in infantry battalions.

The chase ship followed a few rotor disks behind the two insert ships. Slightly behind the chase and a few feet above was the command-and-control ship. Flying in staggered trail, the four slicks were flanked on the left and right by two Charlie-model gunships.

Charlie-model gunships were a recent addition to the Airborne Brigade's support. They looked like the B models, but had a greater lift capacity and had earned a reputation for accuracy and overwhelming firepower. They could also loiter in the area longer and carry more ordnance than the older choppers. Very few of the lethal choppers were in country yet.

The flight of six leveled off at 2,500 feet and settled into a coordinated race to the landing zone.

In Hollister's chopper he, Vinson, and Camacho sat in the right door. Davis, Doc Norris, and Theodore did the same in the left. At eighty knots their fatigue trousers flapped violently and their legs trailed to the rear from the wind.

Hollister jockeyed for a comfortable spot just inside the door, where there was a small pocket of not-so-turbulent air. In that narrow corridor he could have all of the visibility he wanted while avoiding the strongest eye-watering wind.

Hollister remembered the first time he rode in the door of a chopper over enemy-held terrain. Logic told him that he was easier to see and more likely to get hit by ground fire sitting there. He soon found that even if an enemy gunner got lucky enough to hit the chopper, there was no safe place. An AK-47 round was just as likely to pass through the thin skin and fuel cell of the chopper before striking him as hit him in the door. The only advantage of being hit in the door was that the round would not be distorted by striking the chopper first.

Where to be when a chopper was going down was another matter. Pilots and crews felt that they were more likely to survive a crash belted into their seats, wearing their chicken plates—slabs of fabric-covered metal made to fit over crew members' chests. Most wore them strapped across their chests. But many opted to sit on them. Hollister guessed it was all a matter of personal priorities.

But for grunts, going down in a chopper brought on only one thought—be as close to the doors as possible. The last thing they wanted was to be inside when a chopper crashed. It was fraught with peril. If the blades struck anything, the mounts could give way, causing the engine and transmission to come through the cargo compartment and destroy anything in their path. At least that was the myth.

The second big fear was fire. Fire was the aviator's nightmare. Hollister suspected that there was not a pilot flying in Vietnam who had not seen a friend burned into what they laughingly called crispy critters. There were no small fires in chopper crashes. So, all this considered, Hollister sat in the door.

He got comfortable and looked around the chopper. The others were in a kind of twilight sleep. Few would drop off on such a short flight, but they were all deep in thought. Hollister guessed that none were thinking about anything closer than ten thousand miles.

CHAPTER 9

Hollister looked straight out at the gunship flying alongside. The position lights on its side glowed brightly and the beacon on top rotated. The two pilots were silhouetted in the red light given off by the instrument panel.

Iron Mike Taylor was flying left seat. He must have looked over and spotted Hollister looking at him because he raised his fireproof glove in a thumbs-up. Hollister returned the signal and smiled. He had a healthy respect for Iron Mike, who had saved his ass more than once.

Mike had often asked Hollister to come along on a gun run to test-fire weapons systems. But Hollister had repeatedly dodged the invitation, from a need to stay ignorant about how accurate or inaccurate the gunships were; not wanting to know if the gunships were not surgically accurate.

Hollister had called on Iron Mike on several occasions to walk minigun and 40mm grenade fire to within twenty meters of his position. Iron Mike never hesitated and he never missed. Hollister wanted to keep thinking that Iron Mike was just that good and that the high-speed gun platforms were just that stable.

The six choppers started to bleed off altitude as they approached the landing zone. The door gunner looked over to see if Hollister knew they were approaching the crash site. Hollister nodded, refolded his map in its plastic map case and shoved it down into the cargo pocket on the side of his trouser leg. He then grabbed onto the door frame, leaned out and looked forward and down.

The objective area was covered with two-story-high nipa palms and thick bamboo surrounding a crescent-shaped landing zone just a hundred meters long. The LZ was covered with chest-high elephant grass and small clumps of new tree growth. It looked frightening at night.

No one needed to pass the word to the others. They were aware of the slight change in altitude that told them they were on final approach. They watched as the gunships peeled off to line up on the two long sides of the dogleg LZ.

The patrol members moved left and right, up to the edge of the doors. And each man made a final equipment check.

To help conceal the aircraft in the jet-black sky, the pilot had turned off all nonessential navigation lights.

Hollister looked around to see if everyone was ready, tapping a few to make sure that he had eye contact. Distinguishing the team members was hampered by the stripes of green, black, and loam camouflage stick that covered their hands, faces, and necks.

Everyone was ready except Theodore, who was asleep against the bulkhead, his weapon across his lap. It wasn't uncommon for fear to show itself in drowsiness.

Reaching out, Hollister touched Theodore on the knee. He instantly awoke, pretending that he had not been dozing.

"We're almost at the office. Time to go to work," Hollister yelled.

Theodore smiled back at Hollister. It was his first rescue mission; he was cotton-mouthed and had difficulty swallowing. Topping it off, the fading pain and dullness of his hangover didn't improve things.

Hollister reminded himself to keep an eye on Theodore before he made one last check of the others. He knew Theodore suffered from a lack of confidence and that he would have to work on him.

They were getting close. Hollister leaned back out and got a fix on Allard's chopper. He then looked down again—for any sign of ground activity—then leaned back in and looked at the instruments. The compass direction was zero eight five—just what he thought it was. He wanted a feel for his orientation once he got out of the chopper. And the chopper's compass was much better than pulling out his own and trying to read it.

The door gunners picked out likely enemy positions, aimed at them until they were sure that they were dry holes, and then picked out newer, more threatening ones to aim at.

Hollister looked out again. If there was any small arms fire coming from the ground, it would be the door gunners who would be first to see it and return fire. If the machine guns were silent, then they were probably not being fired upon. That was momentarily reassuring. Then Hollister remembered that the Viet Cong might be holding their fire until the choppers dropped off the patrol. Then they could put more accurate grazing fire across the landing zone to cut the patrol down before they got to the trees.

Getting closer, Hollister raised his rifle, pulled the charging handle back, then let it slam forward to chamber a round. He yelled, "Lock and load!" as the treetops reached up to skid level.

The others flipped their safety selectors off safe and raised their weapons to a ready position.

"Remember, move steady, but fast!" Hollister cautioned them. "But don't kill yourself tripping up in the grass!"

Not everyone got every word over the shrill screaming of the chopper, but they got enough to smile back at Hollister and give him a nod of acknowledgment or a thumbs-up.

The two gunships circled the troop ships in opposing directions while the three Hueys descended in trail formation on short final approach. As the slicks broke over the leading edge of the LZ, the C&C chopper slowed, holding high and short of the LZ, and the chase ship pulled up short behind the two insert ships.

By the time the lead ship crossed over the margin from trees to grass, the team members were all standing on the skids.

The choppers kept losing altitude. Finally they flared—nose high to burn off forward airspeed. Inside, every man stopped breathing. It wasn't intentional, just some primal defense mechanism triggering the reaction.

A decisive moment was coming up, a window of time when Hollister and the others no longer had any control over their destiny. If they were going to get blown away on landing—well, it was just going to happen. That was totally out of their control. They were completely vulnerable, and nothing would change that.

LRPs felt that when they ran across the landing zone after touching down, there was always a chance to cheat death if they made the right zigs and zags. But they didn't feel the same way when they were passengers in a slowing helicopter that quickly becomes an easy and defenseless target.

The sensation always gave way to a *What the fuck?* attitude and a very strong desire to get out of the chopper onto the landing zone and back on the ground, where each man felt he had some control.

The team members watched the tree lines and stole frequent glances at Hollister. If he went, they went. If he signaled to wave off, the chopper would abort the landing, pull out and go around.

It put a lot of pressure on Hollister to size up the ground situation based on a quick look out into the black, without his sense of sound to help him. He had to rely on a seat-of-the-pants feeling he had for things that he couldn't see.

They all waited for Hollister to make the move. No one wanted to get out of the chopper only to find out that the LZ was crawling with VC and that Hollister had aborted, leaving the eager soldier on the LZ alone.

Suddenly, time and events seemed to speed up to a surrealistic pace. The relative peace and quiet of the flight to the LZ was behind them. The ground seemed to leap up at them. The insert ship hit the grassy field, bounced, rocked a bit while overcoming its own momentum, and slid forward on its skids.

Hollister had seen nothing to stop them and couldn't wait any longer to make the decision. He jumped from the chopper, leading some, and yelled out to the others, "Go! Go! Go!"

As soon as he was on the ground, he took two long strides and looked back to the right rear of his chopper. Allard's ship had landed and his team started to spill out.

The chase ship crept up above the insert choppers, kept going, passing over the top of the two on the ground. It then corkscrewed up and to the right to clear the gunships that were still low-level prowling the tree lines.

In less than a second the first man was out from under the main rotor blades of Hollister's ship and the C&C ship passed over the LZ, broke right shuddering and popping, and joined the orbiting track of the chase ship.

With the last man out of each insert ship, all four pilots pushed forward on their cyclics and sucked the matching collectives up under their sweat-stained armpits as they snapped the choppers forward, up and out of the landing zone.

Having both pilots, in each ship, handle the controls provided a safety redundancy. If the aircraft commander took a hit, the co-pilot would already be on the controls and could take command of the ship.

From a distance it appeared as if the choppers only touched the grass, spit out the patrol, and rocketed back into the sky. Every move was coordinated to eliminate any delays. Making it smooth was what the pilots, LRPs, and air crews practiced over and over again. The actual LZ was no place for on-the-job training.

Bent over as they ran, most of the team members lost contact with each other as soon as they stepped out into the head-high grass and darkness. The only noise they made was their labored breathing and the zipping sounds from the canvas tops on their jungle boots and the fabric of their trousers rubbing against the elephant grass.

The choppers gone, the patrol moved to a predesignated point in the tree line. Without the screaming turbine engines, they could finally hear if they were being fired upon or not.

Hollister looked around at the edge of the landing zone and tried to pick out the ten other members of the patrol. Closing on Hollister, each patrol member dropped to the ground, orienting on his sector of responsibility. They held their breath, scanned the darkness and listened as they searched for any threat.

There was a distant sound, they thought. They all listened for it again. But there was nothing. They strained to hear something—anything that would confirm the identity of the noise. If it was a noise—but it wasn't followed by another one.

For them any noise was important. It could be a villager, an animal, a Viet Cong soldier, or a wooden ox bell. Even the absence of noise in an area where they should hear something was a critical bit of information. But squatting on the edge of the LZ, there was only the sound of the night creatures in blended harmony.

Hollister was finally convinced that the landing zone was cold. He snapped his fingers and made an exaggerated gesture in the direction of movement. The flanking soldiers passed on the signal and the patrol moved out at a crouch, deeper into the margins of the dense tree line.

Once inside a large stand of tall bamboo, they stopped again, dropped to one knee and alternately faced out. Again they froze. Again they waited for a sound. And again—nothing.

Hollister didn't want to linger. He picked up a small pebble and pitched it over Davis's body, where it struck Camacho on the leg.

Camacho looked back, made out Hollister—understood his message and gave a thumbs-up. He pulled his compass off the loop on his web gear, near his neck, and leveled it. The dial settled, he found the azimuth he had marked with the luminous line on the rotating bezel and followed it to a point on the horizon with his eyes. Satisfied that he had a unique reference point, he stood up and moved out. Each member, in turn, got to his feet and followed the man in front of him.

As they moved, Hollister looked around to make a quick check on the interval between soldiers. They walked silently and efficiently through the random pattern of trees, bushes, and impenetrable clumps of bamboo. Their footing was sure, steady and silent. It was obvious to Hollister that not one of the men was thinking about anything but what he was doing. It was the only reassuring thing about the patrol for him.

It wasn't that way in the rifle platoon that he had spent the first half of his tour with. In a rifle platoon there was always a mistaken sense of security in numbers. Anytime a maneuver unit reached over twenty-five, there was an increase in daydreaming which was accompanied by a drop in security. Somehow, they felt that whatever needed to be done to secure the movement of the platoon was being taken care of by the others.

Hollister's gaze moved back up to the front of the file. Camacho was the most skilled point man in the detachment. Newly assigned LRPs would be sent by their team leaders to spend time with Camacho. Except for the medics, everyone on a team walked point at one time or another. In some teams the job of walking point stayed with one man; a permanent volunteer point man was rarely a cause of complaints within the teams.

Camacho and Hollister had talked over the route to the downed Air Force spotter plane back in Operations—giving Camacho his lead on the move from the LZ. There was no time for them to stop and talk about the little decisions that had to be made on the move. It was up to Camacho to decide which route to take when the brush demanded decisions and offered him options. Time was so important that they would sacrifice some of the security that normally came with cautious movement. So, Camacho would pick the faster route over the safer one. That was one of the reasons that the patrol went out heavy—reinforced by Allard's team.

Camacho made his decisions based on what he could see—and his instinct. He wouldn't cross open space that would silhouette the patrol against the skyline, making it an easy target. So, he had to make a call each time he found one—left or right? He wouldn't choose a route that would take the patrol down to lower ground or one that had water or serious mud along the way. He wanted a path that would place the patrol on equal or higher ground than any potential attacker—a route that was dry, level, clear enough to walk through, and covered with enough growth to conceal their movement. And if he was real lucky, it wouldn't be covered with dead bamboo.

Bamboo was always a problem. New, live bamboo was fairly easy to deal with. It gave way with little resistance, was quiet and felt smooth to the touch. Old, dead bamboo was the problem. It was brittle, rigid, and still strong.

Most dead bamboo seemed to be on the diagonal—requiring a decision. To go over it was to risk making noise by pressing down on it. To go under it was to risk having equipment catch up on it and hang you up while the man behind freed it.

Sergeant Camacho was an expert at sizing up bamboo that he couldn't even see. His fingers, toes, and shins would tell him what move would make the least noise and hold him up for the least amount of time. A smart slack man, second in line, would watch Camacho's moves and copy him. Camacho always said that there were only two serious ways of breaking bush—he preferred the easy way.

Hollister checked his compass while on the move. He knew from the footing that they were heading down the ridge line toward the crash site. Camacho was dead on the route of march they had selected.

As they moved down the hill toward the downed aircraft, Hollister hoped the information they had received was accurate. The chopper crew had seen the aircraft, but there was still a possibility that their coordinates were wrong or it could have been just a piece of the plane that had broken off. If that were the case, they could end up hundreds of meters away from the actual site of the fuselage and any survivors.

What Hollister didn't want was just to be close. He had to find the exact location. Wandering around in heavy vegetation looking for it could be a world of trouble for his patrol and could mean the life of a surviving pilot.

As Hollister stepped into a small spot, open to the sky, he noticed that his shadow stretched out for several feet. Over his shoulder he saw the full moon climbing out of the horizon—a mixed blessing. The extra illumination would make it a little easier for them to move and, ultimately, to identify the crash site, but it would also make them more visible to the VC. He knew that Camacho would adjust his route of march to take the patrol through more vegetation to break up their outline and help conceal their movement.

Regardless of the moon's phase, the VC would take advantage of the patrol's destination to hit them en route. Hollister had to assume that there were VC in the area, that they knew as much as the Americans about the available landing zones and the location of the downed aircraft. And that they had everything near the crash site under observation.

If that wasn't enough to worry about, if either of the pilots had survived the crash and mistook them for VC, they could be shot by the survivors they were trying to rescue. Of course, there was also the possibility that his own people could mistake the survivors for VC and fire on them.

After about thirty minutes Camacho held up the patrol and called Hollister forward. Camacho pointed ahead and down off the top of the finger they had been contouring. He was pointing to where they had estimated the crash site to be.

Without discussion, Hollister motioned to Doc Norris, walking slack, that he and Camacho were going forward for a quick recon and would be back in five minutes. Doc Norris nodded that he understood and gave a raised-hand, crossed-fingers signal of hope.

Hollister led Camacho through the stand of bamboo that marked the steep drop-off to the shallow valley sixty feet below. At the far side of the bamboo Hollister saw that it opened up into a small clearing covered by a twenty-five to thirty-foot canopy. He crawled a little closer and then went completely flat to reduce the likelihood of being seen or hit if shooting started. Satisfied with his observation point, he motioned for Camacho to come forward.

Both of them pulled out binoculars and scanned the open area in front of and below them. Field glasses were useful at night because they weighed little, didn't require batteries, and concentrated the available light—allowing them a better view of the area.

They scanned the area for several moments, looking carefully for any color, texture, or outline in the dark and mottled clearing that might look like something man-made. To be able to detect even the slightest movement, they moved their points of focus very slowly.

Camacho spotted something. Below them, on the opposite side of the clearing, was the exposed tip of the vertical stabilizer on the crumpled fuselage of the light plane. The aircraft's outline was completely distorted by the shadows falling on it and the fact that the wings had been sheared off in the crash. They couldn't see the wings, nor could they tell if there was anyone in the hidden cockpit.

They listened for any sign of life. While they did, Hollister sized up the immediate situation. The plane could be booby-trapped or used as bait. Since the fuselage could only be approached from the clearing, there was no way to conceal the movement of his soldiers approaching it. He would have to set up a security element that could place accurate fire across the clearing in order to protect the others who would move to and search the aircraft.

He knew that it would be tricky and that a long night lay before them. A few more minutes of listening, and then he signaled to Camacho to return to the patrol.

Hollister and Camacho rejoined the patrol, explained the situation and made sure that every man knew what was going on and what was expected of him. But even with the situation clear to all, it still took eighteen minutes to move the patrol into position.

At the crash site Hollister placed Allard's team on the high side of the clearing to cover the area with observation and, if necessary, small arms fire. Once they were in place and ready, he and Team 2-3 moved to the aircraft to try to determine what had happened to the pilots and what needed to be done.

On the move, Hollister and Team 2-3 used traditional infantry maneuver techniques. Half of the six would move while the other half covered their movement. After a few long steps the moving element took up hasty covering positions and the second half moved. While they were moving, Allard's team stayed above and behind, covering everyone. Using this technique got the entire patrol to within twenty feet of the tail of the fuselage without being fired upon.

Hollister held up 2-3 and then motioned for Camacho to move forward so they could both look into the cockpit while Davis kept the rest of 2-3 at the ready.

Hollister's heart was pounding in his temples as he and Camacho moved. He prayed that neither the plane nor the area around it had been mined or booby-trapped.

Behind them the rest of 2-3 watched as Hollister and Camacho edged forward, reaching out with their fingers to feel for trip wires as they kept their eyes on the cockpit.

After a few well-placed steps, Hollister reached a point where he could see what had happened—the plane had simply crash-landed in the trees. The pilot had skillfully slipped the plane between most of the trees, stripping off the wings while doing it, only to hit one fifteen-inch tree trunk dead on the end of the prop shaft. The tree didn't give and the plane crumbled.

Looking at the amount of damage to the wing tanks, Hollister was surprised that there had been no fire. He assumed that the ripping away of the wings had somehow prevented that.

Edging forward, he stopped at the cockpit door. He turned back to see if the others were in position before he made another move. They were.

Vinson held up the handset and pointed off and up into the night—he was in contact with the choppers Hollister could hear orbiting in the distance.

Hollister motioned for Camacho to hold back in case the door was booby-trapped. He then ran his fingers around the edge of the door and peered into the cockpit to see if anything was connected to it.

He considered pulling out his flashlight and making a more detailed search. The red-filtered light wouldn't do much more to give away their position, but the extra time it would take made him decide just to take a chance. He took a deep breath and yanked the door open.

Nothing happened.

He let out the air trapped in his lungs and leaned over to look into the cockpit, only to find the small piece of Hell.

The tandem-seated pilots were trapped in the crash. The engine had been pushed into the lap of the command pilot, killing him instantly. The force of impact and weight of the engine collapsed the front pilot's seat onto the ankles of the co-pilot in the rear seat. He was still alive, unconscious and pinned by his broken ankles to the floor of the plane.

Hollister turned and motioned for Doc Norris to hurry to his position—following his path. He then looked back into the cockpit. The co-pilot must have suffered a great deal of pain, as plenty of thickened blood covered the floor of the cockpit. From what Hollister could see, the injured pilot had torn off the legs of his flight suit and made them into hasty tourniquets before losing consciousness.

Looking up, Hollister could see more signs of the co-pilot's earlier agony. Above him on the bulkhead was a first aid kit; on the other side and also out of his reach was a universal, multi-purpose cutting tool designed for crash survival. The co-pilot had clawed the quilted plastic insulation material from both sides of the plane, trying to reach the two rescue items. They were still in place just beyond the bloodstains he left on the shredded insulation.

The patrol members moved from a posture of caution, security, and noise discipline to noise, speed, and effort at the expense of security. Hollister called the gunships in to circle the crash site and be their eyes from above, and told them to assume that the only friendlies in the area were in or near the downed plane.

The patrol's security was or would very soon be busted by the medical evacuation that was coming up. So the choppers prowled the crash site with their searchlights on even though it took any doubt away from where the Americans were working.

Eerie shafts of light illuminated the margins of the clearing, cutting through the windblown vegetation but making it that much easier for the team at the aircraft to work.

After giving Doc Norris a chance to look at the unconscious co-pilot, Hollister decided that there was no way to take the wounded man back to the insert LZ or to the pickup zone that they would use later. He would never survive the move. So, he instructed Davis to have half of his team clear a small hole in the cover for a chopper to medevac the injured flyer out on a cable. The other half went to work trying to free the lone casualty.

And as they did, he came to, screaming. His cries could be heard for thousands of meters in the night as they pulled his broken legs from the grip of the dead man's seat.

Anxious that time was against them, Hollister made a quick look around the perimeter and tried to anticipate any problems. Not seeing anything, he moved over to Vinson.

Vinson held the handset away from Hollister and gave him an update. "I've called for the medevac and asked for a ship with a winch—but I told them if they didn't have one available, we would do with a slick with a McGuire rig.

"Iron Mike told me that his guns are running low on fuel so he's gonna be replaced on station by a pair of B models in two zero. Gladiator has two more ships on standby back at the base camp to replace his when needed."

Vinson took a breath and smiled. "So, what's left? Who do you need to talk to?"

Hollister took the handset. "Is it okay with you if I tell the Old Man what the situation is?"

Vinson felt a little foolish. "Oh, yeah. I knew there was someone else. Sure, sir. Go ahead and tell Cap'n Michaelson. But I'd bet that he knows what's going on from the radio traffic."

"Don't assume anything when it comes to radios—especially when he's in a chopper." He raised the handset to his face.

"Six, this is Two-six. Over," Hollister yelled into the mouthpiece over the sounds of the circling choppers.

Captain Michaelson answered promptly, "This is Six. Go."

"This is Two-six. We are getting the whiskey india alpha out of the bird dog, and as soon as we can evac him we'll get the KIA out. If we can get the wounded pilot out without much sweat, I'd like to evac the body the same way. I'm not sure I want to tie up half of my element carrying the KIA while we work our way back to our LZ. Over."

"This is Six. Yeah, go ahead and try that. Gladiator just advised me that the Dust-Off is inbound and it *does* have a winch. Go 'head and use it with the WIA and we'll use our chase for the KIA. Over."

"Has Gladiator got an ETA on the Dust-Off? Over."

"Stand by."

Waiting, Hollister looked around. They'd removed the co-pilot from the plane and moved him clear of the fuel tanks. Doc Norris was working on him by the light of a red-filtered flashlight, making Norris and his patient an easy sniper target.

Hollister watched Norris while he waited for Michaelson to come back up. He hated that Norris had to use the light, but he had to see what he was doing.

Norris didn't seem to be as concerned as Hollister was. He pinned two empty morphine Syrettes through the pilot's flight suit collar and bent the needles over so that the receiving medics would know what drugs had been administered to the injured flyer at the crash site.

Davis and Theodore had fabricated splints out of split bamboo poles and held them in place while Doc Norris tied them snugly against the man's shattered ankles.

Hollister looked at the others. While the living pilot was being prepared for the trip out, Camacho worked at removing the front pilot's seat to pull the dead man out from under the plane's engine.

"Two-six, this is Six. The Dust-Off is zero two out. You ready for him?"

Before answering Michaelson's question, Hollister turned to Doc Norris. "You ready for the Dust-Off or what?"

Doc Norris didn't even turn around. He simply raised his bloody hand and held up three fingers.

"We need about three more mikes. Can you have the Dust-Off come up on my freq and I'll vector him in?" Hollister asked. "Over."

"Roger that. Stand by."

Hollister looked around again. He knew that this was the time when soldiers got too interested in what was going on inside their circle and not in what they were supposed to be doing—providing security.

Two of Allard's men were looking back toward the crash site. He wasn't sure if his voice would carry that far over the chopper noises. So, he picked up a rock and threw it at the duo.

It worked. As soon as they realized who threw the rock, they turned their attention back to their slices of the patrol's uneven perimeter.

"Two-six, this is Dust-Off Five-niner. Over."

Hollister looked up through the treetops and tried to distinguish the medevac chopper from the others. He had no luck. "Five-niner, this is Two-six. Will you give me a visual? Over."

"Rog. Watch my nav lights."

Hollister looked up through the hole in the tree cover chopped out for the medevac. All he could see was the faint outline of two gunships and two slicks. Then one of the ships flashed all of its lights on and off twice. Hollister noted the relative location of the red and green lights on the sides of the chopper, so he could determine the direction of flight.

"Got it, Five-niner. My location is out your left door. Watch for my mark. Over." Hollister motioned for Vinson to turn on the strobe light.

"I got it," the pilot said. "I'm going to make a pass and take a look. Watch my ass for ground fire . . . okay?"

Hollister simply clicked the press-to-talk button twice—to tell the pilot that he understood and would comply.

The chopper made a high pass over Hollister, a hard right turn away from the crash site, and kept in the bank until he was heading back toward the site again. As he did, he quickly bled off altitude and picked up airspeed to come across the opening in the canopy at high speed—reducing his exposure.

The chopper crossed the treetops in an exaggerated, nose-down attitude. Suddenly the chopper broke right and up and the pilot's voice came back over the radio. "Okay, my man. I got you. What's the condition of the WIA? Can he take me reeling him in? Over.''

''No choice. He's lost lots of blood and looks plenty shocky. It would take us a couple more hours to clear an LZ large enough to get you in here. Don't think he has that kind of time. Over.''

''Okay. It's yer call. I'm going to lower a horse collar. Can you strap him in it and send him up to me?''

''Roger that.''

''We're inbound now. Watch for my wire,'' the pilot said.

''Standing by,'' Hollister said. He dropped the handset to the crook of his neck, put two fingers in his mouth and let out an ear-piercing whistle to get everyone to look his way.

''Dust-Off's inbound. Let's make this fast!''

CHAPTER 10

The Dust-Off chopper got louder and louder, but no one could see it through the tree cover. Then its chin-mounted searchlight dimly penetrated the canopy two hundred meters north of the patrol and small sparkles of light flickered through the trees as the pilot eased the chopper toward the evacuation site.

Suddenly the light moved directly over the patrol and flooded the tiny clearing, painting everyone with such intense light that it washed the color from their uniforms and equipment. It looked liked they'd been dusted with white powder.

Though Hollister was more optimistic about the chances of getting the injured pilot out okay, there were plenty of negatives. Once the Dust-Off chopper stopped its forward crawl over the hole, it was like placing a pin in the map and telling every VC in the area exactly where the evacuation was taking place. It also told them that every American was working without benefit of hearing or night vision. So, all enemy eyes in the area would be focused on the chopper marking the patrol's location.

The pilot brought the chopper to a steady hover only fifty feet above the rescuers. If he took ground fire and lost power, it would most likely mean the lives of those waiting below the chopper for the cable. They all watched anxiously as the violently whipping branches thrashed the skids while the pilot settled into the treetops.

Doc Norris and Davis carried the injured pilot to a spot directly below the chopper as the medic in the Huey's open door threw the switch lowering the winch line with the horse collar.

Wanting to reassure the chopper crew, Hollister raised the handset to his lips and cupped the mouthpiece with his hand to cut down on the feedback of chopper sounds. "You're looking good, Five-niner. Just keep it coming. You're right on the mark. Fifteen more feet.''

The tension in the back of Hollister's neck turned into a knot as he impatiently watched the steel cable slowly unwind, lowering the rescue device.

Davis stood on his tiptoes and reached up to grab the spinning strap. Once he got a firm grip on it, he guided it down to the injured pilot.

Doc Norris moved to the pilot's head and lifted him to a sitting position. Without wasting a second, Davis slipped the horse collar down over the pilot's shoulders and began to buckle it under his arms.

Suddenly Allard's security team started firing across the top of the rescuers at something on the other side of the downed aircraft.

The Dust-Off pilot broke in on the radio. ''Shit! We're takin' fire man! How close are you to hookin' that guy up?''

Hollister tried to shake off the sinking feeling that came over him knowing that they had been busted by the VC. ''Shit!'' he said to himself. He heard his people firing but couldn't hear the VC. He looked up only to see green AK-47 tracers slicing by the Dust-Off chopper. Pumping his raised fist, he gave Davis an unnecessary hurry-up hand signal.

''They're strapping his arms down now . . . maybe fifteen seconds. Stay with us, man. This guy's only got one chance. If you have to go around, he might be a KIA by the time you get back!''

''I'm going to try to hold what I got, but those fuckers have my number. For Chrissakes . . . put some heat on that VC fire, will ya?'' the medevac pilot said without a quiver in his voice.

''You get this guy out and let me work on the ground fire.'' In spite of the vulnerability of the hovering chopper, Hollister was amazed at how pilots always seemed to keep their voices so matter-of-fact.

And Five-niner was no different. ''Okay, you keep those fuckers off my back and I'll get him out,'' the pilot said as calmly as if he were asking Hollister to pass the salt.

Hollister heard enemy rounds cracking over the pilot's mike. This pilot had balls.

Since there was no one between him and the VC firing positions, Hollister pressed his rifle to his hip, careful to point the muzzle toward the ground twenty yards in front of him, and started firing three-round bursts in the direction of the enemy fire. His hope was that the rounds would strike the ground between him and the VC and skip low through the VC firing position. He knew he wouldn't get lucky enough to hit anyone, but he wanted to do something to reduce the accuracy of the enemy fire. At his side, Theodore took the cue and did the same.

"Iron Mike, this is Two-six. Did you monitor mine with Five-niner? Over," Hollister yelled into the handset over the noise on the ground.

Iron Mike broke in. "Hold your fire. I've got the little fuckers spotted. We're rolling in on them now. I'm gonna be very low and very close to keep from hitting your people, and I don't want to eat any of your fire. So, hold what you got till I make a pass and see what I can do."

Hollister raised his rifle horizontally over his head and started yelling, "Cease fire! Cease fire! Hold your fire!"

Everyone quickly realized that the gunships were on a firing run and stopped firing while they made their passes.

Davis had tied the wounded man's arms to his waist with a pistol belt to keep the unconscious pilot's arms from rising, which would allow him to slide through the horse collar and fall free. Satisfied with the rigging, Davis turned to Hollister and gave him a take-him-up signal.

"Iron Mike, we're holding up on the fire. Break. Five-niner, you can take him up now. He is strapped into the collar but cannot help himself. We are clear."

Iron Mike clicked twice and the medevac chopper pilot replied, "That's good, pal, 'cause I'm running out of rabbits' feet up here."

The gunships crossed within yards of the hovering Dust-Off chopper, firing into an area on the far side of the downed plane. They fired full bursts of minigun and rocket fire into the tight bamboo thicket. From the ground it looked like a red-hot string of metal squirting out of the minigun muzzles while small explosions flashed at the backs of the rocket pods as the rocket motors ignited. As the ordnance impacted in the target areas, tree branches, dirt, rocks, and debris were thrown everywhere.

In the center of the circle the cable slowly reeled in the pilot through the hole in the treetops. All around, the patrol members held their breath, alternately watching the pilot disappear through the canopy and searching the darkness outside the pool of light for any more VC firing.

Hollister looked around while he had the chopper lights to get a better picture of the situation. From where he stood, he could see the gunships making more firing runs while the flier got closer to the evac chopper's skids.

Between gun runs Davis's team fired into the suspected enemy positions and Allard's team was still securing the high ground.

Then the medic on board the chopper reached out and grabbed the injured pilot's flight suit.

Without waiting, Camacho and Davis dragged the dead pilot over to the spot his co-pilot had been just moments before.

With so much going on at once, the noise level was almost painful. For a thousand years nothing important had happened in that little depression, but that night an event of violence and mercy was taking place. Soon the first chopper would move out and the dead man would be pulled up through the same hole in the thrashing trees.

The medevac pilot broke the squelch as the chopper's nose disappeared from the hole in the sky. It immediately went dark again, instantly disorienting patrol members who had lost their night vision. "Two-six, we got him. We're getting out of here. My doc says he made the trip up okay. We'll give you a status later. Keep your heads down. You guys do good work."

Hollister let out a breath. "Thanks, we owe you a beer. Break. Iron Mike, you still taking any fire? Over."

Iron Mike came back over the radio. "I don't think there's anything left down there to shoot at us, partner. Anyway, we're dead out of fuel and have to go home and rearm. I've got a pair of hogs loitering at three thousand just west of here, if you need them. I'm gettin' outa here before I have to push this chopper home."

"Roger, thanks. Break. Six, this is Two-six. You copy? We finished the evac and still have the KIA to get out."

"This is Six. Roger. I'm going back to refuel. Gladiator One-five and Place Kicker are going to McGuire your KIA out. Any problems with that?"

"Negative. Holding our own. We're ready any time," Hollister said.

"Stand by . . . they're on the way in."

Davis and Camacho had taken a sling rope, carried by every LRP, and fastened a harness for the dead man. As Davis made final checks for strength and good knots, Camacho hooked a strobe light to the dead man's boots.

"Two-six, this is Place Kicker. Over."

Hollister smiled at the gravel sounds of Easy's voice. "Go ahead, Kick."

"I'm still ridin' belly on the chase. We're going to ease into the same spot the Dust-Off used and drop you a rig. That okay with you? Over."

"You and Gladiator One-five know that the Dust-Off took ground fire in that same spot?"

"We ate our Wheaties this morning."

"Okay, then. I'm ready when you are, Top."

"Stand by . . . we're inbound to your location," Easy said.

The chase slick followed the same approach that the Dust-Off had. Soon the belly of the new ship filled the hole in the canopy and began thrashing those below with the downwash of the rotors and blinding them with the searchlight.

A dark object flew out of the left door and then another from the right. Easy had thrown the two 120-foot climbing ropes out of the chopper. The running ends of the ropes played out while the other ends were anchored to metal tie-down rings on the floor of the helicopter.

Davis reached for the ends of the two snaking nylon ropes. He found the two mountain climbers' snap links at the end of each rope and double-hooked them to the dead man's harness.

While they rigged up the dead pilot, Hollister kept looking for any signs of enemy fire. He was sure that at any moment the VC would start firing again. Even if they had killed the ones who did the earlier firing, others wouldn't be able to pass up the chance to pop a few rounds at the second hovering chopper. He scanned the entire perimeter for any signs of the enemy, but it was silent outside the circle.

Davis finished rigging the body, then gave Hollister the thumbs-up to pass on to the hovering chopper crew. While he waited for the chopper to lift, he and Camacho held tension down on the lines to keep the slack from whipping them into the surrounding trees and getting entangled.

Hollister pressed the mike to his mouth, cupping his hand around the mouthpiece again to be heard over the noise. "Okay, Kick. Take him up. Watch the trees on the south side of the hole. A couple of them are big enough to eat your lines."

"Roger that. Stand clear, we're coming up," Easy said flatly as the chopper started to rise, quieting the vibrating ropes.

As the ropes stretched and began to lift the dead man, Sergeant Camacho reached over and turned on the strobe light. It started flashing repeatedly, enabling the pilot to see his load and helping him judge clearances during his takeoff and landing. But for the LRPs the strobe meant something more.

It meant that they got the Americans out. It meant that every VC for miles could see that they didn't sneak out at night. They went out with a strobe flashing—thumbing their noses at the VC.

As the chopper kept gaining altitude, the body slowly raised off the ground and cleared the hole in the canopy. Once Easy saw the strobe light reflecting off the top of the trees instead of through them, he called Hollister. "We're clear, Two-six. We're going on home now. You be careful," Easy said as the light and the sounds of the chopper faded.

"Rog, Kick. Break. Six, this is Two-six. Evac complete. We're going to finish up here and move to the Papa Zulu. I'll call for the aircraft four zero minutes out. Over."

"Roger that," Michaelson said from a point in the sky far from Hollister's team. "Good job. I got one more thing for you to do. But *you* make the call. If you have the time, work through the VC firing position and see if you can find anything. If you get hung up or have any problem with that, just pass on it. Understand that it has the lowest priority. Over."

"I understand. Let me check it out and I'll see what we can do. Over."

"Bring 'em all home," Michaelson said.

"Wilco, boss. Out." Hollister passed the handset back to Vinson. He spoke up, trying to gain time, instead of whispering to regain noise discipline in the tiny perimeter. "Davis, you, Allard, and Camacho come over here. And the rest of you—look sharp out there. The zips would have to be blind not to know where we are. Do I have to say more?"

He expected no answer, but simply wanted to jerk them back into some sense of security.

The chopper gone, Hollister had difficulty making his eyes readjust to the darkness. After getting used to the searchlights and strobes, their absence made the night even blacker for him. While he squinted to make out things around him, he heard the rustling as Allard slipped down through the saplings on the hillside. He was also aware that someone else had moved silently to a point just outside of arm's reach.

"Sir . . . it's me and Camacho," Davis said.

"Okay, Sergeant Davis. Wait a sec till Allard gets here."

"I'm here," Allard said out of the dark.

"Good. Here's the deal. I want to tie in the gaps in our security and get a couple of things done before we head out. Sergeant Davis, you take your folks and move them to the far side of the bird dog. Leave me with one man and the thermite grenades.''

Before Davis could answer, Hollister added, ''Make it Theodore. Okay?''

''Okay, sir,'' Davis said. ''Anything else?''

''No, you just worry about anything outside, and Theodore and I'll take care of the aircraft.

''Sergeant Allard?''

''Yessir.''

''Keep your people up on the hillside, but tie in with Davis's new positions.

''All of you . . . once we are through trashing the radios and equipment on the bird dog, I'm going to call Allard's team to close on Davis's and we're going to check out the enemy position.

''Now, if we don't find something right off, we'll forget it. I don't want to spend the rest of the night groping around in the bush looking for Charlie while he's watching from the bamboo. Questions?''

There were three no's.

''Davis, you and Allard take off. I want to go over the route of march to the PZ with Camacho.''

''Yessir,'' both team leaders said.

As soon as they left, Hollister snapped his fingers to get his radio operator's attention. ''Get out your poncho, Vinson.''

Vinson took the loosely rolled poncho off the frame of his rucksack and spread it out. He ducked his head under it, taking his radio with him.

''Okay, sir,'' Vinson said.

Camacho and Hollister got under the poncho so that all three heads were just inches apart. Hollister spread his map case out on the ground and turned on his red-filtered flashlight. Every VC in the province knew their general location, but he didn't want to create another good target for some sniper while making a map check.

The trio took a few seconds to adjust to the light under the poncho while Hollister turned the map case around to orient the map. He then tapped a point on the side of a ridge line with the tip of his mechanical grease pencil. ''Okay. Here we are.''

He drew a short line, stopped it with a small dot, then drew the line around and up the ridge line and to a different clearing than the one they landed on earlier. ''We'll go to this point, set up, and check out the VC firing positions. From there we'll follow this route to the PZ. If you need to take some detours to get us around what looks to me like fairly thick shit—do it. Just get us to the PZ, Camacho.''

Camacho took a long look at the route before he spoke. ''Yessir,'' he said, copying the route onto the small section of his own map that he had pulled out of his shirt pocket. ''But we're going to play hell trying to fool 'em. They'll be selling tickets along our line of march. They know that we need to go home sometime.''

''That's why I want to get us to that PZ and the hell out of here before folks get too comfy in the bleachers,'' Hollister said.

Camacho tapped three points on his map with his pencil. ''And there are only a few LZs near here. They got at least a one-in-three chance of picking the one we have in mind.''

''I know. That's why I picked the shittiest one. So, let's try to be back at the base camp by the time they figure it all out.''

''I'll get us there just as fast as it can be done, sir. Let's hope nobody gets dinged up on the way. Carrying a wounded man'll slow us down plenty.''

''I hear you. Now, I'm planning on having the guns circle a PZ we're *not* going to use to draw them off, and then come over to the actual PZ at the last possible minute. That might just confuse them a little,'' Hollister said.

''I hope it works, sir.''

''You ready?'' Hollister asked as he fastened the igniter to the end of the fuse.

''Yessir. I got everything packed up,'' Theodore said.

''Okay, get in here and check out my setup.''

''Me?'' Theodore said, surprised.

''Yes you. How you ever going to become a team leader if you don't get on top of every detail?'' Hollister asked.

''Uh . . . I guess I . . . I mean I'm not sure I . . .''

''Just get in here and double-check me. You've been through this in demo training until you can do it by heart. Now it's the real deal.''

Hollister carefully slipped out of the collapsed front seat section of the airplane and Theodore squeezed in.

With his flashlight, Theodore traced the igniter up the length of fuse to the thermite grenade on the top of the instrument panel, across to the second and third thermite grenades spaced along the full width of the panel. With his fingers he traced the fuse down the far side of the instrument panel through a wide loop, which would add burning time, and finally to a block of plastic C-4 explosive.

"If this works, the grenades'll ignite and burn down through the instruments," Hollister said. "After they're pretty much destroyed, the C-4 will scatter what's left of this bucket over about an acre of prime Viet real estate."

"Looks good to me, sir," Theodore said.

"Well, light the fuse."

Theodore looked back at his platoon leader. "You want me to do it?"

"That's right. If you checked it—it should work. Right?"

Theodore looked at the fuse path one more time. "Yessir." He took the igniter in his hands and yanked it forcefully. A tiny flame worked its way along the fuse toward the thermite grenades. Theodore quickly stepped back out of the aircraft. "We better get moving, sir!"

Hollister grabbed Theodore by the sleeve. "More guys've been hurt hurrying away from demo than just walking away. Now, you just take a breath and relax. I cut that fuse for twelve minutes before it even reaches the first thermite grenade."

Camacho held up the patrol and walked back to Hollister. "If I'm right, the VC position is just ahead of us by about fifty meters," he whispered.

Patting Camacho on the shoulder and nodding his head to show that he understood, Hollister reached back and motioned to Davis that he was going forward with Camacho.

"Don't go doin' nothin' crazy now, Lieutenant," Davis whispered.

Hollister and Camacho edged forward on their stomachs. The area was very faintly lit by the light from the crash-site fire that had grown to a football-game bonfire size. They stopped frequently to try to detect any movement. Dancing shadows and light from the flames made it difficult to distinguish real motion; it was doubly hard when they too were moving.

After a few minutes they came on a narrow corridor that had been cut into the trees by the repeated passes of the gunships. Open to the sky, it was littered with bits and pieces of trees, palm fronds, and branches. They stopped again and watched, looking up and down the channel. Nothing was moving.

Then Camacho tapped Hollister on the arm and pointed off to their right front.

Squinting against the harsh light, Hollister saw something. There, in the fallen branches, was a foot—a man's sandal-clad foot. Camacho started to move forward. Hollister grabbed his arm. "No, my turn. You just watch my ass."

Just then the C-4 in the bird dog detonated with a ground-shaking crack. The debris rained down around them for several seconds.

Hollister waited for the wreckage to stop falling and then crawled forward to the foot. It was still in the same position. As he got closer, his mind started to work on him. Was this a live VC playing possum? Was he just unconscious? Was he likely to wake up and freak out? Did he have a grenade in his hand? Had his buddies booby-trapped him and left him for Hollister to find? Hollister decided to just focus on what he was doing and stop running all the wild possibilities through his mind.

The safe thing would be to shoot first and check out the body later. But if the VC was really just unconscious, that would be murder. He finally decided to just keep the muzzle of his rifle trained on the area where he presumed the rest of the body to be—beneath the vegetation. That way he'd be ready to fire a burst of well-aimed M-16 fire if he had to. It meant that he had to give up the initiative.

He got closer. Nothing happened. Still no movement. The VC *had* to hear his uniform scraping across the ground cover and deadfall. He was close enough that he could smell the sickening sweet smell of heavy organ blood. *He was dead!* Hollister thought. No, it *could* be from another soldier nearby. The odor didn't mean that the guy attached to the foot was seriously wounded or dead.

Finally, Hollister was within arm's reach. No movement, no sounds, no signs of life. He poked at the foot with his rifle muzzle. Nothing. He did it a second time and the foot flipped over, revealing the splintered stock and part of a blown-apart receiver of an AK-47 rifle beneath it. Hollister reached up, hooked the stock with the front-sight blade of his rifle and yanked it backward—away from the foot.

The rifle remnant came away freely and the leaves slid off the top of the foot, revealing that the foot was not connected to a leg or a soldier or anything. Just a foot.

Enough! That was all he needed. A probable KIA and a

weapon. If there were more bodies around, someone else could find them. Not him. Not his LRPs. He grabbed the AK-47 stock in his left hand and crawled backward to Camacho's position.

CHAPTER 11

Tired and hungry, Hollister was still in his field uniform, dirty and smelling of aviation fuel from the downed bird dog, when he arrived at the orderly room. Bernard was sitting behind the first sergeant's desk reading a *Playboy* magazine.

"The Old Man want to see me?"

"Yessir," Bernard said, getting to his feet. "Let me check." He hurried over to Captain Michaelson's office and tapped on the door frame. "Sir, Lieutenant Hollister's here."

Captain Michaelson must have motioned to Bernard to send him in because Hollister could hear no response in the outer office. He also knew whatever it was the detachment commander wanted to talk to him about was not good news. He could feel it in Bernard's tone.

Inside Michaelson's office Hollister stopped in front of the captain's desk.

Captain Michaelson stood facing out the window into the night. "Sit down, Jim."

Hollister took a chair and sat upright. His mind ran quickly over the recent events. He tried to discover a mistake he might have made or a missed step during the rescue operation that might be the topic of Michaelson's meeting.

Captain Michaelson turned around and grabbed the pack of Pall Malls on his desk. He popped one out and offered the pack to Hollister, who waved him off.

Michaelson pulled a well-worn Zippo out of his pocket, lit the cigarette, threw the lighter on his desk, and exhaled, deliberately gaining time. "There's no easy way to tell you this. Lucas died last night at Camp Zama."

The words jarred Hollister but didn't surprise him. The loss was something he had thought about several times since seeing

Lucas at the hospital. The announcement of his death pushed several buttons at once for Hollister. The loss of a good friend, the loss of a fellow platoon leader, the reminder of their mortality, the random nature of who gets hit and who doesn't—all of it clicked through his mind.

"Oh, there's something else. His parents want you to escort his body home."

"Me? I don't even know his parents."

"I guess they must know you from Lucas's letters," Michaelson said as he pulled out his chair and sat behind his desk. He leaned back in his chair to be able to see the far side of the outer office. "Bernard, bring that paperwork in here on Lieutenant Lucas."

Bernard entered Michaelson's office with a folder containing odd pieces of paper. He handed it to Michaelson and left, hardly making a sound as he walked.

Michaelson quickly handed the folder to Hollister without opening it. "Everything you need to know is in there."

Somewhere out in the darkness, through the open window, one of the LRP teams had a radio on. It was playing "The House of the Rising Sun." Hollister scanned the paperwork—words jumped out at him: Lucas, Died of Wounds suffered in RVN; NOK: Margaret and Ellis Lucas, New Canaan, Connecticut; Marital Status: Single; Dependents: None . . .

He closed the folder and listened to The Animals for a moment, not aware that Michaelson had opened the footlocker next to his desk, pulled out a bottle of Jack Daniels and a couple of mess hall cups.

Michaelson poured a long shot in each cup and pushed one in front of Hollister. "Here," he said, gesturing to the cup. "Have yourself two fingers of R and R."

Hollister lifted the cup and took a good-sized sip of the liquor. It assaulted his parched mouth and burned down his throat. He immediately felt the flush that it always gave him.

"You leave in the morning," Michaelson said. "You have any questions?"

"Yessir. What about my platoon?"

"I'm pretty sure that Sergeant Davis can fill in for you while you are gone. The question is, who will fill in for Davis?"

"Camacho. He's been ready for a team for a long while, sir."

"Okay. Don't worry about anything. Go help Lucas's family. I'll have a letter ready for you to take with you in the morning. You can tell them that I am recommending him for the Silver

Star. From what I've been able to find out from the others on the team, he deserves it.''

After killing the rest of the booze, Hollister got to his feet and stared out the window at the dark night. A chopper was flying across the far side of the base perimeter. Its flashing lights triggered Hollister's memory of Easy's chopper carrying the dead body of the Air Force pilot—the strobe flashing.

"What's the story on the Air Force flier we evac'd?"

"He's alive. But that's about as good as it's going to be. Doc Tillotson talked to the hospital about an hour ago. He'll keep the legs, for all that's worth. They found out that he's got some spinal damage, too," Michaelson said.

Hollister dropped his head to think of the pilot. It seemed to him that the bad news was running ahead of all other news. "Oh" was all that he could muster. He raised the folder and changed the subject. "I'll get my gear packed. I'm not sure about this. But I guess someone ought to go who knew him."

"Try to squeeze some time for yourself out of whatever time Brigade gives you back in the World."

"Hey, Lieutenant!"

He heard someone yelling, but Hollister wasn't even sure what time it was. He had fallen asleep on his cot trying to read *Doctor No*. He had been trying to read it for weeks, but that night the exercise was just to distract him from Lucas and the rescue operation and Vietnam in general without using booze to dull the noise in his head.

It bothered him that he hadn't finished a book since he'd been in country. He had always loved to read for pleasure when he was in high school and during his first years in the Army. Vietnam had cut into his Ian Fleming novels.

"Hey, Lieutenant," two voices yelled from outside.

Hollister looked at his watch. It was almost two. The voices were clearly Doc Norris's and Theodore's. He got to his feet and stuck his head out the door of his hooch. There they stood, in all their drunken glory, each gripping a bottle of Jim Beam by the neck.

They managed two unsteady salutes and became very formal. Theodore spoke for both of them. "Sir, Team Two-three and Two-one are having a—a . . . a meeting. Yeah, a meeting. And we were sent by Allard and Davis. Oops! *Sergeant* Allard and *Sergeant* Davis, to invite you to the meeting."

Hollister smiled. "Okay, if it's an important meeting I'll get over there in zero five."

Theodore straightened up with an unsteady swaying. "No sir. We were instructed to escort you and to protect your flanks from any hostile fire in the area. We'll wait here till you're ready . . . sir."

Having been to late night *meetings* before, Hollister knew that there would be no rational conversations for the next few hours.

The two teams had taken over the mess hall dining area. The building was everything they needed for their meeting. It had light, chairs, tables, and some ice.

Kendrick's night shift was working in the kitchen area and wasn't worried about the two teams getting stinko. It was becoming a ritual. Hollister entered, flanked by the two trying-too-hard-to-look-official LRPs.

Camacho was the first to spot the trio. He jumped to his feet, accidentally collapsing his folding chair behind him with a loud metallic clunk as he screamed, "Attench-hut!"

The ten LRPs and four spoons in the background snapped to a wide variety of positions of attention.

"Carry on. Please, as you were," Hollister said.

They all immediately returned to what they were doing. Davis, Allard, and Camacho stood against one wall drinking while trying to maintain some faint vestige of dignity. The other, younger and more junior soldiers were carrying on the way young soldiers have done for centuries. War stories were picked up where they had left off. And topics like women and cars were reevaluated in the haze of beer and bourbon.

Vinson stepped up to Hollister as Theodore and Doc Norris broke for the beer cooler. "Sir, what's yer poison? We got us Jim Beam and San Miguel. Davis has some buddy over at the PX that got us the sierra mike. It's great to drink something out of a bottle instead of those rusty cans."

"Beer'll be good for me," Hollister said.

Vinson started to walk toward the beer cooler when Hollister reached out and stopped him with a touch on his sleeve. "No. You finish yours. I can get my own."

The gesture didn't go unnoticed. Vinson caught another LRP's eye as Hollister walked over to the iced beer and reached down into the elbow-deep ice water.

"Hey! Listen up! Hey! Shut the fuck up, you assholes!" Theodore yelled. The others quieted down and looked over.

Suddenly realizing his error, Theodore shot a glance at Hollister and said, "I, ah, I meant you . . . uh, us junior enlisted assholes."

The room erupted in laughter and cheers. Then Theodore raised his hands again. "With the lieutenant here now, we have an impartial judge. He can do the job. Right? With him here we can move the tables around, act like stupid squids and start doing—"

"Carrier landings!" the others all chimed in at the tops of their voices.

Wiping beer from his lips, Hollister rolled his eyes. He had been through carrier landings as a young soldier.

Three of the more sober LRPs grabbed two of the long mess tables, moved them to the center of the room and placed them end to end. The others cleared the scattered chairs and other tables out of the way while Doc Norris poured beer on the tabletops.

"Hey! You guys fuck up my mess hall and you'll be spending all morning cleanin' it!" yelled the assistant mess sergeant from the kitchen area. His announcement was met with a barrage of hisses and boos.

As the booze was turning the setup into an uncoordinated effort, Davis, being the second ranking man in the room, took over. "Okay, most of you guys know the rules. You fuckin' newbies just *shut* up and *listen* up.

"The deal is—each man starts his flight approach from the other end of the room. With your arms extending out to the side, shoulder high to increase your aerodynamics. In that posture, you *will* simulate a navy airplane coming in for an aircraft carrier landing.

"The tables will serve as the carrier deck. You must approach the deck at full speed, using your arms to stabilize your descent. At a point to be selected by you, you will vigorously leap into the air and make a belly-down landing on the beer-soaked tabletop.

"The object of the drill is to slide to the far end of the table and come to a complete stop with your nose exactly over the far edge of the second table. And I mean exactly! During your landing you must not touch the table with your hands or arms or hook your toes or legs over the sides to slow your landing. Got that?"

The others yelled out, "Clear, Sergeant! Airborne!"

Davis finished. "Any man here who fails to come to the

correct stop or touches the table with his hands or feet will be expected to immediately hit the floor, knock out ten good Airborne push-ups, get back to his feet, kill one cold San Miguel, and come around and do it again. *And* any arguments will be decided by the lieutenant. He has final say! Okay, Theodore. Yer first.''

Theodore handed another LRP what was left of his beer and a half-eaten can of Vienna sausages and backed up against the far wall. Once in position, he leaned forward, started making engine noises, and thrust out his arms. The others started clapping in unison and yelled "Go, go, go" as Theodore ran, full speed, toward the table, reached it, leaped into the air and belly flopped on a veneer of foamy beer.

They cheered loudly as Theodore slid freely down the length of the first table, overshot the end of the second table and crashed, face first, into a pile on the concrete floor beyond and below it.

Laughing hysterically, the others started screaming, "Knock 'em out! Go around! Kill that beer!"

Theodore did all three and joined the line that had formed near the back wall.

The landings continued for the better part of an hour. As they got drunker, they got worse at it and no one was able to stop. They looked like bums in their beer-soaked uniforms, but there was a smile on every face. They were simply stealing the moment from the war to have fun and blow off some of the tension.

Hollister was pleased to be included. But after a few beers laced with bourbon shooters, it was getting too late for him—remembering that he had to get an early start for Japan.

Japan. The word rang some bells in his head. He would be able to go to Japan, but he wouldn't get a chance to enjoy any of it. He wondered if he'd have time to get something for Susan. *Susan!* He hadn't let her know that he would be coming home. That would have to wait until he got to Japan. There was no way he could get a call through to her from Vietnam before he left.

The LRPs were getting drunker and louder. Hollister looked over at Davis and made a silent gesture. Davis motioned as if he were going to announce the lieutenant's departure.

Hollister shook his head, pointed at his watch, then pressed the tip of his index finger to his lips.

Davis knew of his early morning mission, so he gave his boss a somber salute.

* * *

Someone knocked on the frame of Hollister's hooch. "Sir, it's 0430 hours, and you said that you wanted someone to wake you up."

Feeling the chill in the damp morning air, Hollister slowly came out of his fog. Then he remembered—Japan. His head hurt. He sat up and grumbled, "Oh, yeah. Okay. Thanks. I'm up." Hollister stood and immediately felt the uneasiness in his stomach.

Ten minutes later, Hollister was shielding his eyes from the bright lights inside the mess hall. As he started toward the thirty-gallon coffeepot on the field range, he looked around. The damage to the mess hall was moderate.

The floor was a limp goo of beer and gravy-colored mud. A chair was broken, a tabletop was delaminating before his eyes, and the area was littered with empties. That wasn't going to go down well with several people in the chain of command. Before he could run through the available options to prevent his people from getting heat, he was interrupted.

"Don't worry about it, sir," Sergeant Kendrick said as he stepped up to the coffee urn and poured a cup for Hollister. "I sent one of my boys over to wake up Allard and Davis to invite them over here before we serve breakfast. I want to give them an opportunity to disappear all of this before it becomes a real problem."

"I appreciate it, Sergeant Kendrick. They were just blowing off a little steam."

"Oh, I have no problem with that, sir. I just want them to take their steam outa my mess hall now.

"Would you like some eggs, sir?" Kendrick asked.

Hollister tried to shake off the repulsive thought of the greasy offering. "No, I think that right 'bout now coffee is all I can handle. Thanks."

Kendrick looked at Hollister and realized how hung over he was. He poked his thumb over his shoulder at the trashed dining area. "You part of all this carryin' on last night, Lieutenant?"

"Let's just say that I was in the cheering section when I should have been getting some rack time. Now, I'm paying for it. Big-time."

Hollister felt the chill through the soles of his Corcoran jump boots. The metal floor of the C-130 was very cold after flying for three hours over the Sea of Japan. He tried getting up and walking around the cavernous interior of the plane to get some feeling back into his toes.

At the front of the aircraft he found a double-pot coffee maker that was held in place against the bulkhead by an ingenious combination of cargo strapping. There, a tired-looking load-master—an Air Force sergeant with an uncountable number of stripes—was pouring himself a cup. "You think that you might want some'a this shit, Lieutenant?"

"Yeah, anything dark and warm will do."

Wrapping his hands around the sides of the cup for warmth, Hollister tried to ignore the smell and taste of coffee that had been on the burner far too long. He threw some of it back, gritted his teeth, and swallowed.

"Humpf," grumbled the loadmaster. "You must be a desperate man. Going home? Your year over?"

"I'm going back TDY. I've got to pick up a friend's body in Japan and escort it home."

"Yeah, I see lots of that," the loadmaster said matter-of-factly as he topped off his coffee mug, then climbed the short ladder into the cockpit—without saying another word to Hollister.

Hollister wandered over to the forward window. Bored, he bent down and looked out into the night. He could faintly see the outline of the horizon. It was purple above a crimson line that fell off to black. He looked at his watch. It was nine P.M. Vietnam time, but he had no idea what time it was in Japan. All he knew was that crossing open water in C-130s seemed to take forever.

It felt like it was well below freezing when Hollister walked down the tail ramp of the C-130 at Tachikawa Air Force Base. The roar of the four huge prop engines running down kept him from being able to talk to the loadmaster. But the loadmaster knew what the question would be anyway, and pointed to a small building between two of the maintenance hangars. Hollister smiled and thanked the rumpled airman.

"There'll be a shuttle bus leaving from the front of this building in fifteen minutes that'll take you to Camp Zama, sir," an Air Force tech sergeant told Hollister as he pointed in the direction of the army hospital compound that was less than an hour away.

Hollister looked at the clock on the wall to get a fix on the local time and pulled the stem out on his watch to make the adjustment. He was not sure if he was ahead or behind on his sleep, but no matter what, he had never liked being awake at quarter of four in the morning—even in Japan.

Outside, the sky was overcast and snowflakes spat at Hollister. The field jacket in his B-4 bag would be a little bit warmer, but it looked like crap from months of being folded up in his duffel bag back in Vietnam. He decided to tough it out. The fresh air was crisp, and he figured that he needed to clear his head anyway. He was happy that the major pain of his dull hangover was almost gone as the shuttle bus pulled up.

Camp Zama was a small army post, well outside of Tokyo, that also housed a hospital. The hospital was an intermediate step on the way back to the States. Such hospitals were scattered throughout the Pacific, in Okinawa, the Philippines, Guam, and Hawaii. Some of the wounded were patched up and sent back to Vietnam. Most were given a breather, some additional treatment, and then shipped to hospitals in the States as soon as they were fully stabilized.

Expecting the Graves Registration building to be filled with the dead soldiers' bodies, Hollister was surprised when he found that it was only a small office next to the baseball diamond.

"Lieutenant, here are your flight orders, customs forms, and transportation vouchers for air movement on commercial carriers once you reach CONUS," the clerk said, handing Hollister the paperwork without looking up from behind the customer counter.

Hollister was just as happy. He really didn't feel in any mood to discuss his task.

The clerk read from a typed-up briefing that took up several pages in a notebook and was protected by cracking plastic covers surrounding each yellowing page. He continued to read until he reached a blank line that had to be filled in according to the topic.

"You will have to contact . . . ah." The clerk looked from the briefing book to the paperwork and found the exact entry he was looking for to finish his statement. "Callestone, Captain Callestone in New York City. He is the Survivor's Assistance Officer appointed to take care of the deceased's family needs.

"He will fill you in on what has been done for the family

and give you the details of the family's wishes for the remains.''

The clerk slapped the last of the paperwork on the countertop. ''And here are your personal travel vouchers. You will be paid per diem and mileage for any official travel not covered by a military travel voucher.

''You will be leaving tomorrow by bus at 1620 hours. Please be here in time to get checked off by the driver.''

The clerk took a breath, but didn't change his flat delivery. Hollister wondered how many hundreds of times he had done this.

''You will be expected to travel in Class A uniform during the performance of your escort duties. If you are missing any uniform items, the Quartermaster Sales Store is directly behind this building and is open during normal duty hours. Since you are an officer, you will be expected to pay for all missing items yourself.

''You will check in with our detachment at the airfield, in Building T-1542, to sign for the remains. You can stay at the BOQ that is down four buildings to your right as you get outside.

''The maid service in your BOQ will launder any clothing you need if you get it turned in by 1900 hours tonight.''

Hollister was amazed that the clerk made it through the entire briefing without ever looking at him. As he reached the end of the briefing book, the phone rang and the clerk matter-of-factly got involved in a dispute over a number relating to a body that had been shipped earlier in the week.

Hollister stuffed all the paperwork in the larger of the envelopes that came with the packet, shook his head, and quietly left the building.

The inside of the BOQ was something out of an infantryman's dreams. Small, efficient, and clean, it had a Hollywood bed with real sheets, a tightly tucked-in army blanket, and a full feather pillow. In the corner of the room there was a sink with a mirror, and terry-cloth towels hanging on metal bars on either side of the mirrored medicine cabinet.

The furniture was quartermaster-issue, dark red-purple-looking mahogany, and was spotted against the two-toned, white over light green walls. The floor lamp and the table lamp on the nightstand completed the room. It was warm, clean, and private—even if government sterile.

A check of his watch told him that he had time to get a shower and a short nap in to make up for the sleep he had lost in the past several days.

Outside the BOQ, Hollister noticed that it was already getting dark. He remembered that he was getting hungry and that he only had to walk across the street to find the small Officers Club. He could certainly get something to eat there.

Inside the club, Hollister had to walk around the fish pond built in the lobby. Dozens of orange and white Japanese *coi* played in the warm pool. He suddenly felt a world away from the crash site that had filled his mind only scant hours before.

The club officer, in civilian clothes, stopped Hollister at the door. "Evening, Lieutenant. Your first time here?"

"Yes . . . I'm TDY from Vietnam—escort duty."

The officer made a face in response to the unpleasant duty and gestured Hollister to the inner doorway. "The bar is this way, and the dining area will be serving in about a half hour. . . . Hope you enjoy your stay. Sorry about the duty."

Hollister walked into the bar, grabbed one of the tall stools and sat down. Behind the bar an array of bottled liquor was displayed on mirrored levels lit by invisible lights.

The bartender was a Japanese civilian wearing a crisp white shirt and a bow tie. He dropped a cocktail napkin in front of Hollister and raised his eyebrows.

No longer feeling any of the ill effects of the carrier-landing drinking ceremony, he ordered without fear. "Johnnie Walker—black, over ice."

The bartender spun on his heel, snatched a glass from a stack on the back bar, scooped up ice with the glass and poured the drink in one smooth motion.

Placing his cigarettes on the bar, Hollister centered his lighter on the pack. He picked up his drink and felt the sweat forming on the glass. Pressing the rim to his lips, he took a tentative sip of the scotch, fully intending to savor the creature comforts of glass, clear ice, and a real polished bar, when he felt a slap on his back.

"Hollister, you snake-eatin', low-life motherfucker!"

The voice was unmistakable—Kerry French, Hollister's roommate at Officer Candidate School. He pulled a bar stool back and jumped up onto it.

"What the fuck are you doing here, H-man?"

"Kerry, king of sick call! What are *you* doing here? I thought you were holed up somewhere at Fort Gordon."

"Oh, man. That came to a screeching halt after I got orders for Vietnam. Hell, I really thought that they would forget about me and I'd be able to slide."

"Well, I told you that you wouldn't be able to get out of this like you did all that field training at Benning."

Kerry blushed a little and gestured to the bartender to refill Hollister's drink and give him one of the same. "I had a great time while it lasted though, man."

"So where you going?"

"The Cav."

Hollister flinched. "The Cav? Shit, man, you're in a world of hurt."

Kerry took a sip, made a face, and then raised his index finger to make a point. "Oh, no. I got it all figured out. While I was at Fort Gordon I was an instructor on antitank weapons. I checked around and a couple'a guys I talked to, just back from the Cav, tell me that they hardly ever use their 106-recoilless rifles—anywhere."

"What's that mean?"

"I did some more checking. Found out that the biggest problem that they have at the An Khe base camp is getting rocketed and mortared. Well, there's a tit of a mountain right in the center of the base camp. I guess there must be at least a couple'a dozen serviceable 106s in the division. And, if I talk them into putting all of those useless 106s up on top of the mountain in a circle, they could be effective countermortar fire.

"My guess is that they'd see the brilliance of my idea and make me the officer in charge. I could spend the whole year on that hilltop and I'd never have to leave the base camp. Great idea! Huh?"

"Man, there are people over there that have got your number. You'll be humpin' the hills so fast you won't even get a chance to say the word 'recoilless,' " Hollister said, laughing at his friend.

Kerry saw the bartender opening a new bottle of bar scotch and wrapping it in aluminum foil. "All right. Let me show you I haven't lost my touch."

French tapped his glass on the bar. "Hey, Mr. Barkeep. How 'bout giving my friend and me some free scotch out of the mystery bottle?"

"Whoa! I was drinking Jack-black!" Hollister said.

Kerry motioned for the bartender to pour anyway. "Listen, Mr. Hollister. This is free, F-R-E-E booze. We get to drink all we want to drink here for free."

"What the hell are you talking about?"

"Pal, I've been here for three days waiting for a flight to Saigon. They keep a sporting man's bottle of scotch, bourbon, and vodka on the bar—all wrapped in tin foil so you can't see what's in them. You can order as many drinks as you want and they are all free—unless."

"Unless what?"

"Unless you get the last shot in the bottle. Then you pay for the whole bottle and they open another bottle and wrap it up."

"So, how do you suggest we keep from paying for the bottle?"

"If we stay here long enough and keep count of all the freebies that are given out, we can estimate when we are approaching the danger point."

French made two marks on a cocktail napkin. "Now, all we have to do is wait until the count gets close to twenty and we'll know to let someone else finish off the bottle."

Hollister raised his glass to salute enterprise. "You haven't changed a bit, Kerry. I've missed your shit, you rascal."

French took a long sip of his drink and finally got serious. "So . . . how bad is it, Jim? Bad as we guessed it might be?"

Hollister's smile faded. "It's a lot worse . . . a whole lot worse."

Kerry killed his drink and then pushed the glass toward the bartender for a refill from the tin-foiled bottle. "Aren't you scared?"

"I'm petrified every day that I'm there."

"So how can you face it?"

"I don't know, Ker. All I know is that if I don't let myself think about it too much, I get so busy getting ready for the next patrol that I'm getting out of a helicopter before I know it. Hell, then I'm there," Hollister said, finishing his drink. "But let's talk about something else. Is the World still back there?"

"I don't know anymore. I did my damnedest to soak up the best parts before I left. But my plane landed here and my connecting flight was canceled. So . . . I have to continue my pre-Vietnam party here for however long I have. Wanna join me?"

"No, I've got to get back to the States with my friend's

body. . . . I'm escort officer for a lieutenant from my unit.'' He looked at the expression of surprise and anxiety on Kerry's face. "No, it's nobody you know.''

French and Hollister caught up on some old friends and some not-so-happy stories about others who'd been unlucky in Vietnam. They kept drinking, kept counting, and the bartender kept pouring.

The after-work crowd arrived, filled the bar, and ordered from the tin-foil-wrapped bottles. When the count got dangerously close to the maximum, Kerry suggested that they wait out the deadly last shot.

An Air Force captain sitting near French and Hollister asked what the deal was with the wrapped bottles that everyone was ordering from. Kerry explained, encouraging the captain to get his free drinks. He ordered—and made it. Kerry made another mark on the napkin.

A warrant officer on the other side of the bar ordered a drink from the wrapped bottle and made it. Then the confident Air Force captain thought he could do it again. He ordered another refill from the bottle and got the fatal last shot.

Cheering, whooping, and hollering filled the bar as the captain paid for all the shots in the bottle at the going bar price.

Kerry leaned back and grinned at Hollister while he balled up his fist and playfully tapped him on the shoulder. By then Hollister was starting to feel the scotches. "Hey, where do we get something to eat around here?''

Kerry's eyes brightened. "Have I got a surprise for you, man. I know this place in town that you will just love.''

Hollister looked suspiciously at the expression on Kerry French's face. "What are you getting me into, man?''

"Hey, just trust yer old buddy Ker. I won't let you down.''

The cab let them out in front of a one-story building that looked much like the rest of the homes on the narrow Japanese street. Hardly any traffic passed, save a few bicycle riders coming home from work.

Inside the fenced-in yard, a beautiful rock garden flanked the stone path leading to the front door. Kerry and Hollister entered and stopped in the Asian version of a foyer, a ground-level room that allowed the visitor to take off his shoes before he entered the real front door.

The sliding shoji doors opened. Kerry and Hollister were greeted by two very pretty Japanese women dressed in ornate kimonos. Kerry turned to his friend for some sign of appreciation. "Huh? What'd I tell you? Stick with me. It gets lots better."

CHAPTER 12

It wasn't much consolation that Hollister was going to be making the trip across the Pacific in a C-141, the closest thing that the Air Force had to a commercial passenger jet.

He stood on the ramp of the airfield with the other three escorts—a sergeant and two captains. Shoulders hunched against the damp winter cold, they all squinted as the Japanese wind cut across their faces, killing time by talking about the usual topics—Vietnam, women, and home. As they waited, the door to a huge hangar rattled open, revealing a large stack of metal caskets. The conversation came to an abrupt halt.

Under the watchful eye of an Air Force sergeant, twenty of the caskets were loaded onto baggage carts and moved to the gaping rear ramp of the C-141 by Japanese civilian ground handlers.

The inside of the C-141 was a government solution to moving passengers as well as cargo. Both went into the huge compartment. As a concession to the living cargo, the jet was temporarily fitted with passenger seats. Still, what comfort they provided was offset by the fact that the seats faced to the rear, facing the cargo, the baggage, and the caskets.

The caskets were arranged in stacks, three high and end to end. Even soldiers who were going home had difficulty showing their joy while seated only a few feet from the containers.

Hollister woke with a start. After a few seconds his head cleared and he realized where he was. The shrill pitch of the jet engines was getting monotonous, and his head was still a little foggy from the long night with Kerry French and his pretty Japanese friends.

Unsure how long he had been asleep, Hollister looked around

the jet. He was the only one of the eleven passengers who was awake. Unbuckling his seat belt, he walked back to the coffeepot and poured himself a cup. It would be hours before they landed in Anchorage to refuel. He walked back through the passenger area to the cargo area near the tail ramp.

Passing the first stack of caskets, Hollister checked out the cards attached to each metal container. He found Lucas's on the top of the second stack. Finding a small jump seat next to Lucas's casket, he sat down. It would probably be the last chance he would have to be alone with his friend.

For a long while Hollister could only look at the box. Visions of the last time he saw Lucas tried to creep into Hollister's mind, but he forced them out. He wanted only to remember the good times. He remembered how much help Lucas had been to him when he was new in the LRP detachment. Lucas was a good officer and a good friend, and Hollister knew he would not soon forget him.

He reached out, touched the casket, and whispered, "I'm really going to miss you, buddy." As he did, he felt his throat choke up. He took a sip of the coffee to try to force himself to swallow. Leaning back in the jump seat, he decided to ride the rest of the way with his dead friend.

Red Cross volunteers met the plane and served coffee and doughnuts to the jet passengers while they refueled in Alaska. Hollister understood the safety reasons for having all the passengers debark the jet during refueling, but that didn't help him with the weather. He rubbed his hands up and down his arms to try to get some blood pumping. Even stamping his feet didn't help ward off the cold.

It occurred to him that his body had been exposed to a temperature differential of over 120 degrees in the past seventy-two hours. He laughed to himself at how much he missed the same heat that he hated in Vietnam.

Someone spoke to him over the scream of the 141's engines, but he couldn't make out who or what. He turned and found a hand thrust out toward him. One of the Red Cross volunteers was holding out a paper cup filled with steaming coffee. He smiled and nodded at the woman. She smiled back and patted him on the shoulder in an appreciative, motherly way.

His fingers felt the warmth of the coffee in the paper cup emblazoned with a simple red cross, but the fluid had cooled by the time it hit his lips. The same woman then handed him a doughnut.

A ground vehicle behind him swung around, throwing its headlights on her face, which was surrounded by a circle of fur attached to her jacket hood. In her forties, her smile was genuine, and Hollister couldn't argue with her dedication. After all, it was three in the morning—Alaskan time—and cold.

Almost inaudibly, she screamed, exaggerating her words. "You going home?"

Reading her lips and body language, Hollister took his free hand out of his pocket and pointed at the caskets that were visible through the open tailgate of the C-141. He tried to make himself understood. "No, I'm escorting a friend's body home."

The Red Cross worker sighed. "I'm sorry, hon. We meet boys like you every flight, and it really makes us start to wonder."

Another passenger interrupted the Red Cross woman as he reached for one of her doughnuts. She and Hollister never finished their conversation. But he'd heard her message of heartfelt sorrow. He had never been pitied before.

With the side of his hand Hollister wiped the condensation from the window to see Fort Dix, New Jersey. It had not changed much since he was an infantry trainee there.

He pulled the collar to his field jacket closed, more out of the memory of Fort Dix in the winter than the reality. Even so, the bus taking him to the Transportation Office was cold and the plastic seats were stiff. No matter. He didn't care. He was back in the World, away from the shooting and the helicopters and the constant nagging fear that gripped his gut.

He decided to act as if the change were permanent. As the rows of double-roofed World War II vintage barracks slipped by with their interior lights off and their single fire lights on, he made a deal with himself. He promised himself not to worry about Vietnam until the night before he had to return. Then, as he rethought the promise, Hollister let out a little laugh. *Forget about Vietnam*—that was easy to say.

He wiped the fogged window again and peered out onto the manicured grounds of the sprawling training post. Through the spitting snow he saw the huge parade field where his first physical training classes had been taught by NCOs whose faces and names were blurred in his memory.

Still, Hollister clearly recalled the hours of pain and soreness that they inflicted on him and his classmates. Those mornings always started out in the dark with a formation run from the company area to the parade field. There, the field first sergeant screamed instructions from a five-foot-high PT platform in the cold black morning air. As he yelled, two hundred trainees moved from a column of fours to a huge square at double-arm interval to begin the grueling and repetitious Army Daily Dozen exercises. He didn't know then that physical training would be a necessary part of soldiering that he wouldn't ever learn to enjoy.

Keys, logbook, map, and trip ticket in hand, Hollister crossed the motor pool to the vehicle assigned to him.

Closing the door to keep out the cold, Hollister sat in the front seat of the olive-drab sedan. He stuck the keys in the ignition and started the car.

He quickly surveyed his paperwork. The pile contained orders, transportation vouchers, payroll paperwork, and endless addresses and phone numbers. On the back of one of the manila envelopes, he had started a list of things to do.

One item had been on his list since just after arriving in Japan: *Call Susan.* He had tried twice from Japan, only to get a busy signal once and no answer the second time. He quickly made some additions to the list and crossed out others.

He checked the time. It was only four. It was too early to call Susan, who would still be at work. He didn't want to bother her there. Stuffing all the paperwork into a large envelope, he decided to get on the road. His hope was to get the jump on as much of the rush hour traffic as he could. He threw the aging sedan into gear and headed out of the huge motor pool.

Gas. Hollister looked up from the instrument panel of the vintage Dodge sedan. The last thing he wanted was to run out of gas on the road a long way between gas stations.

As he topped the next gentle rise his eyes found a gas station on the New Jersey Turnpike. He was tired of sitting in the broken-down seat. And he was hungry. He had lost track of how many hours he had been in transit, how much sleep he had missed, and how little he had eaten. But whatever he was suffering from jet lag was overcompensated for by his excitement to see Susan. Still, he needed gas, cigarettes, and a phone. He tried the turn indicator, which didn't work, and pulled in.

Getting out of the sedan, he buttoned his blouse. The army-green uniform had not been designed to sit in or to ward off cold, wet, winter wind. He thought about wearing his hat and then opted not to since he only had to cross a few yards of concrete before he was inside.

As Hollister walked into the station manager's office he could hear Sergeant Barry Sadler singing "The Ballad of the Green Beret" over a radio in the grease-rack area. He smiled at the lyrics. "One hundred men will test today, but only three win the green beret." He looked around for whoever had selected the radio station.

Out front the pumps were busy with homebound commuters. Hollister busied himself looking at the road map taped to the wall. In ballpoint pen someone had marked an X and written U ARE HERE at the service area on the turnpike.

From the X his eyes followed the turnpike past New Brunswick, up through New York and on to New Canaan. The drive wasn't that long in actual miles, but even if he tried to make it, he wouldn't get there until nearly midnight. Anyway, he didn't have to be in New Canaan until the funeral.

A young mechanic came into the office, wiping the grease off his hands with a shop rag.

"Hi. Say, do you have change for a dollar?" Hollister asked.

The mechanic recognized the uniform and smiled. He hit the No Sale button on the register and deposited a few bills from his grease-ringed shirt pocket. "Vietnam, huh? I got a brother over there in Quang Tri. Been there?"

Hollister shook his head. "Nope. I never got that far north. He's a Marine?"

There was not enough correct change in the register. Slamming the drawer shut, the mechanic reached into his pants pockets and pulled out change from each. Holding his dirty palms up, he scanned the change. There still wasn't enough to make a dollar.

"Yeah. He's a MP. Little shithead. I told him not to join the Marines. But he had to go an' be Mr. Big Shot Marine. Ya know, I don't have enough ohange. People come in here and wipe me out for the damn candy machines. I could open one of them. Wait a sec."

He leaned back and yelled out the open doorway to the pump area, "Hey, Larry. C'mere a minute."

A long-haired pump jockey bounded into the office. The smile on his face quickly cooled when he spotted Hollister's uniform. "What d'ya need, man?"

The mechanic jabbed his thumb at Hollister. "The lieutenant here needs change of a buck."

The pump jockey reached into his pocket and came out with a huge handful of coins. Poking through it with a blackened finger he found the correct change. He handed it to Hollister and took the dollar without looking at him. "I got customers," the pump jockey said, looking at the mechanic, and left. It was clear that he wasn't happy.

"What's that all about?" Hollister asked.

"He's one of those peace pussies that think we ought to love the fucking commies into submission. Don't pay no attention to him. He's jus' afraid of getting drafted." The mechanic laughed. "Hell, guess that he don't want it to interrupt his meteoric career in the petroleum business."

Hollister thanked the mechanic and walked outside the station to the doorless phone booth next to the rest rooms.

The phone rang forever, and Hollister was afraid that Susan wouldn't be home. He was thinking about the next opportunity to call when a voice on the other end said, "Hello?"

Hollister's heart beat faster. "Susan. Honey. It's Jim."

"What? Jimmy, are you okay? Where are you? Have you been hurt? Oh my God!" she said.

"Calm down. I'm okay. Really—everything is fine. I'm in New Jersey, near exit nine on the turnpike. I can be at your place in an hour or so, if I don't get lost or the traffic and the weather don't kill me."

"Jimmy, oh Jimmy! This is so great. Yes . . . yes, please hurry. Oh, I can't believe that it's really you. Are you sure you're okay? You're not hurt? What are you doing home? What's going on? Is it over? I mean, do you have to go back to that awful place?"

"Susan. Susan, relax, honey. I'm fine. I'll explain it all to you when I get there. Now let me get back on the road. Okay?"

"Okay. Hurry. I can't wait to see you. I've missed you so much, honey."

"I'll be there as soon as I can. Oh, and Susan . . . I love you."

Her voice got softer and more serious. "I love you too, baby."

Hollister hung up and waited for the operator to call him with the toll charges. As he waited, he looked over at the third pump island. The long-haired pump jockey was leaning up against an oil can display rack, staring at him.

Hollister had never felt hate before, but he was sure that was what he saw in the boy's gaze.

Finding a spot, Hollister maneuvered the army sedan into a parking place half a block down from the Café Wha in Greenwich Village. He felt a twinge of guilt knowing he was on the gray side of authorized use of an official sedan to go see his girlfriend. He rationalized, telling himself that the stop at Susan's was on the way to Lucas's home in Connecticut. Anyway, he had to stay somewhere. And wherever he stayed, he would have to get there in the sedan.

The Village had changed a bit. When he was last there, everyone dressed in coffeehouse black or looked like the Kingston Trio. Clearly, the prep school look was gone and there was a shift taking place. More Levi's, and the hairstyles were longer on the men and straighter on the women.

His feet hurried him around the car to the trunk to get his bag and then across the sidewalk and to the walk-up that was Susan's place.

Susan looked through the peephole in her door and then screamed, "Jimmy!" The door burst open and she was standing there, trying to keep from hopping up and down. She was every bit as beautiful as he had remembered. Her hair was clean and shiny, and the faded jeans she wore told him that she hadn't gained a pound.

He stepped in and took her in his arms. She smelled so good. She was warm and soft. They held each other tightly, trying to convince themselves that they were really together again.

Susan pulled her head back to kiss him. It was wonderful. That moment with Susan was something he had thought about for months. Now it was happening.

Suddenly, Susan pulled away. "You're so skinny! What happened? Are you okay, Jimmy? Really okay? Don't lie to me."

He held her by the waist, their hips pressed together. "I swear. I'm okay. It's just that Vietnam is the best diet in the world."

"What is all this about? Why are you home? Tell me . . . Tell me . . ."

Stepping back, Hollister reached up and pulled off his necktie. He then undid the four large brass buttons on his uniform blouse. "Later."

Susan smiled devilishly. She started helping him with the buttons on his shirt. They picked up the pace, hurriedly undressing each other, leaving a trail of clothes from the front door to the bedroom.

Finally Susan stood naked before Hollister. She was delicious. He took off his watch and his dog tags and walked over to her. Without speaking, he lifted Susan in his arms and placed her on the bed. As he straightened up, she grabbed his wrists and placed his hands on her bare breasts.

They sat in her kitchen—Susan in a large terry-cloth bathrobe, Hollister in his boxer shorts and a T-shirt. He moaned with pleasure as he devoured a BLT that Susan had made for him. It was after two in the morning.

"This is so good. Food is the second thing I missed in Vietnam."

"What was the first?"

He nodded toward the bedroom.

Susan giggled playfully and swatted the air near his shoulder. "Ohhh. Well, I hope you aren't caught up on that yet."

He wiped the corner of his mouth with a napkin. "This sure is a good sandwich."

She reached over to the side sink and turned the clock around. "Well, if you're all caught up on the other . . ."

He laughed. "I might get caught up if we get back in that bedroom."

"Well, just how soon do you think you'd like to do that?"

He put down his sandwich, scooted his chair back from the table, and stood up.

They exchanged looks, and both bolted for the bedroom laughing, in a mock race.

Hollister woke before dawn. He quickly realized where he was and rolled over to face Susan. He couldn't resist the urge to slowly slide the sheet down off her shoulder to a point below her naked hips. He watched her breasts gently rise and fall as she breathed. She was as beautiful as he had remembered her in the long dark nights on so many patrols.

He took his index finger and placed it gently on her neck just below her ear, then traced the outline of her figure down over her shoulder, down her arm to her waist and over the curve of her hip.

Suddenly her eyes fluttered. She woke gently, smiling at Hollister. "Hi, honey."

"Hi yourself. I didn't mean to wake you."

Susan smiled in disbelief. "Oh yeah?"

"Okay, okay. I confess. I couldn't wait for you to wake up."

"I'm glad."

He reached out to embrace her, hoping to make love again. She let him fondle her for a moment and then put her palm on his chest, pushing him away. "You promised."

Hollister looked at her, puzzled. "What did I promise? Not to touch you?"

"You promised to tell me why you were home. Is it over? I mean, are you finished over there?"

Hollister fell back onto his pillow, remembering his mission. "No. It's not like that. I'm home on escort duty."

"What's that?"

He told her. And she listened quietly, recognizing the pain that he was in even though he was trying to disguise it.

When he finished, she made love to him. It wasn't hurried and passionate like the night before. It was warming, healing, loving and caring.

Later Hollister sat at the kitchen table drinking freshly brewed coffee. "I can't remember the last real cup of coffee I had. I've been drinking powdered C-ration coffee and overboiled mess hall coffee so long that this is heaven."

As he talked he watched Susan flit from the bedroom to the bathroom, getting dressed for work. Hollister could see her standing at the mirror in her bathroom from where he sat. She leaned over the sink to put the final touches on her eye makeup wearing her bra, panties, nylons, and a garter belt.

The sight of Susan's perfectly toned body so provocatively clad tempted him to interrupt her. But she caught his eye in the mirror and gently shook her head from side to side; she had to go to work and couldn't be late.

He quietly watched her as she kept dressing, checking her watch every couple of minutes. It reminded him that he too had things to do. "I'll be back the day after tomorrow—Friday. But I have to leave the next day to head back to Vietnam."

There was a moment of silence as she looked at him in the mirror. "I'll be back from work early this evening. Will you still be here?"

Hollister got up and poured another cup of coffee. "Yes. I think so. The funeral is tomorrow, and all I have to do today is make sure that Lucas's remains get to the funeral home." He turned back around and she was standing in front of him fully dressed in a conservative wool dress and moderately high heels. She looked wonderful. "I'll be here. Count on me."

"I will. I'll give you a call during the day. Just make yourself at home. Relax. There are a couple of books in the front room that I have to review. You might be interested in them." She reached up and touched his cheek. "I'm so happy to see you, honey. Even if it is such a terrible job you have to do."

She kissed him lightly on the lips, picked up her purse, and opened the front door. She turned back and looked at him. "I really loved last night. 'Bye," she said as she closed the door behind her.

Hollister finished calling the Survivor's Assistance officer, Captain Callestone, and the Transportation Office at Fort Hamilton, to tie up some loose ends for the army. He ran down the checklist again to be sure that he hadn't skipped something. Every item was lined through except the entry that said *Lucas family*, and had the home address next to it.

He knew they had been notified by Captain Callestone that he was coming. He also knew that he wanted to put it off just as long as he could. He wasn't sure what he would tell them. What if they asked about Lucas? Would he be forced to tell them the awful details of his pain and wounds?

He got up and crossed the room, pulled the curtain back and looked out the window. None of the people out in the street seemed to know about the Lucases of the war, men who were proud to serve in Vietnam. He decided that even though he didn't know Lucas's parents, he would hold back as much of the painful details as he could. He just couldn't see passing on the pain to them.

He got another cup of coffee, put some real cream in it as a treat, and wandered into the bathroom to clean up. The room smelled of Susan's soaps and perfume. He decided that before he got into the shower he would just spend a few moments savoring the scents and remembering what she looked like standing in front of her mirror putting on her makeup. It filled his chest with a warm and exciting feeling.

After a shave and shower, he made another pot of coffee, found some clean underwear in his B-4 bag, and wandered into the small front room of Susan's apartment. On the coffee table he found the books that she had mentioned. He picked them up and shuffled them to look at the titles.

One was a book on interior decorating that didn't interest

him, one was a murder mystery, and the third was a review copy of a novel entitled *The Confessions of Nat Turner* by someone named William Styron.

He put the other two down and began to leaf through the novel. He read a paragraph or two and then moved several chapters and did the same. He couldn't generate any interest in the book and wondered if anyone else would be able to. He couldn't tell if he wasn't interested or if he just wasn't in the mood to read.

Hollister checked his watch. It was only a few minutes to one. It would be hours before Susan would be home. He needed a drink and something to take his mind off the Lucas family.

It was a small neighborhood bar like hundreds of others that dotted the street corners of New York. This one had seen plenty of changes since it was built in the 1930s. Nevertheless, Hollister thought it odd for a place called Paddy's Irish Isle to have a new neon sign over the door that announced "Go-Go Dancing."

Hollister assumed that the owner had opted to put money into updating the atmosphere inside the bar rather than into replacing the missing asbestos siding that skirted the building.

His eyes quickly adjusted to the dark as he stepped through the double doors into a short hallway that was flanked by two cigarette machines.

He felt a little conspicuous coming to a bar in the early afternoon, and then realized that his uniform would tell people that he was a soldier in transit just taking a minute out for a short one. That was never unusual for New York.

The inside was a single room with an L-shaped bar. In the two front corners of the room little platforms had been built to serve as stages for the go-go dancers. Only one of the dancers was working. She wore bell-bottom hip huggers, a bare waist, and a fringed bikini top.

The dancer couldn't have been more than twenty, but she looked older—tired. As the jukebox pounded out Wilson Pickett's "In the Midnight Hour," the dancer ground her hips in a pattern that would keep her in the smallest amount of floor space and expend the least amount of energy.

The bartender had started at the far end of the bar, gauged Hollister's choice of stools, and met him on the other side of the bar. "What's yours?"

Unsure, Hollister scanned the stoppered bottles, then looked down the length of the bar where two large wooden pegs pointed skyward from a hidden keg. "Draft. I'll have a draft."

The bartender poured Hollister a tall beer, spilled off the head, topped it off and then placed it on the bar in front of him. He then dropped a stiff cocktail napkin next to the drink. "Enjoy," he said as he went back to a stack of dirty glasses.

Silently, Hollister nodded and raised the beer to his lips. It went down smoothly. He tried to remember when he had last had a draft. Beer in Vietnam was always in bottles and cans and never tasted as good.

After a second sip Hollister put the beer down and turned around on the off-level rotating stool. The go-go dancer had found a better groove in "Going to a Go-Go" by the Miracles, and moved a bit more. Hollister watched her more closely. He realized that in spite of her lack of energy, she certainly had a great figure and a flat, tight stomach. It made him think of Susan's.

"So, what's your story, General?"

Hollister turned around. A second dancer had taken the stool behind him. "Mine? Same as everyone else's. Just trying to get by."

She pulled out a cigarette and started looking around the bar for matches. Hollister pulled out his lighter and lit the cigarette for her. The flame allowed him to see her face. She couldn't have been more than thirty, but she looked forty. Her makeup looked like it was layered on top of old makeup.

"Thanks, hon," she said, taking the cigarette from her lips and exhaling the first long drag. She looked up and made eye contact with him. "So, really—what's the story here? You just another GI lookin' to get lucky or what?"

He laughed and shook his head. "No. I'm just killing a little time and having a beer."

She laughed and took a sip from her drink. "Man, you *are* different. You aren't crawlin' up my leg, you don't smell, and you ain't one o' them longhairs."

Hollister quickly realized what her life must be like. He felt sorry for her, knowing that every night was a constant battle for her to retain some fragment of her dignity. "Can I buy you a drink?" he asked.

"Sure . . . why not? I only have to dance, not drive," she said as she waved at the bartender for another round.

Hollister caught the expression of disgust in the eyes of a young, collegiate-looking customer sitting on the short end of the L. He seemed to be in the middle of trying to grow long hair and a beard. The beard was spotty and the long hair was at that awkward in-between length. It also looked as if it hadn't been washed in several days. From his expression it was clear that he had no use for Hollister.

Hollister wasn't sure what the guy's attitude problem was, but decided to keep an eye on him. The dancer followed Hollister's eye line and spotted the other customer. She turned back to Hollister.

"Ignore him. He's one of those college fucks that come in here, get drunk, pat us all on the ass, and then leave without thinkin' about leaving a tip."

"He doesn't seem to like me."

"None of those peace fucks like guys like you, General."

He chuckled. "Well, I just came back from where folks really don't like me. Wonder what I did to him?"

She flipped the ash from her cigarette and looked down at the other guy. "You didn't whine, man. That's what pisses him off the most, I guess."

The guy got up and pushed his glass away from him in disgust. Turning, he walked out the door without looking back. On the bar he had left the correct change for the drink.

Walking up the manicured path made Hollister feel uncomfortable. He was anticipating meeting Lucas's grieving family. He had to guess that they'd try to be pleasant to him since they had asked that he escort their son's body home. Still, he knew that meeting them would be very awkward.

Looking up from the path, he finally took in the house itself, a new and very expensive A-frame. He had never pictured Lucas living in anything like it. A layer of new snow barely covered the great carpet of leaves that had fallen from trees that some landscape architect had deliberately spaced across the gently rolling estate.

On one side of the house the driveway looped through a section of the lawn. Hollister could see that there were several visitors, from the number of expensive cars parked in the driveway. He stopped at the front door, rang the doorbell and swallowed to clear his throat. Remembering that he still had his overseas cap on, he pulled it off and folded it in one hand.

There was no answer. He rang the doorbell again. Waiting for someone to answer, he suddenly felt self-conscious. He smoothed the skirt on his blouse and reached up to check the centering of his necktie. He had rehearsed his words of condolence twenty times in the car on the way up from the city. He quickly went over it again in his head.

"Who is it?" a man's voice asked from behind the door. It opened before Hollister had a chance to reply. The man was a twenty-five-year-older twin of Lucas. He had the same face, eyes, and strong jawline. At one time he had probably had his son's smile too.

"Sir, I'm Jim Hollister . . . I . . ."

"Hollister, oh yes, Lieutenant Hollister. Please, come in."

Mr. Lucas didn't look directly at Hollister. He only turned and led him into the foyer.

Inside, several grieving members of the family were fussing around Mrs. Lucas. She turned to see who had arrived. Spotting Hollister, she stopped talking and stared at him.

Hollister was not sure if she was upset by her loss or somehow disturbed by his arrival. He just waited for someone else to make the first move.

"Margaret, this is Lieutenant Hollister from—"

Mrs. Lucas stood up, dropping her Kleenex. She reached out to take his hand, still staring into Hollister's eyes. "I know. Thank you for coming, Lieutenant."

"Jim, ma'am. It's just Jim, please," Hollister said.

"Of course it is. We have heard so much about you."

Not sure what to do with his hands, Hollister awkwardly fumbled with his cap. "Ah, ma'am . . . I'm terribly sorry about your loss. We were good friends and I, ah . . . I—"

She helped him through the moment. "Please sit down here, next to me."

Mrs. Lucas moved over and sat back down. He shuffled sideways around the low coffee table and sat next to her. There was not another sound in the room, even though twelve mourners were there with the Lucas family. All of them looked at Hollister as if he were from another planet.

"Will you have a drink?" Mr. Lucas asked.

Hollister nodded, feeling that every word was being recorded.

A pinch-nosed woman wearing black clacked her china coffee cup into its saucer and broke the silence. "Did you go to West Point, too, dear?"

"No, no ma'am, I didn't go there."

When he didn't offer some reasonable alternative, such as

having gone through ROTC at Harvard, the woman wrinkled up her nose as if she smelled something offensive. "Oh. I see."

Mrs. Lucas abruptly shifted the subject. "Were you with him when it happened?"

He'd been afraid of that kind of question. "No, ma'am. I wasn't."

"He was our only son, you know. We had very big plans for him after he got this army thing out of his system."

There was a note of disapproval in the woman's voice. Lucas had never mentioned to Hollister that his mother disapproved of him being an Airborne-Ranger infantry officer.

She fumbled for another tissue to wipe the tears from her eyes. "I'll never understand why this country ever got into such a mess in Vietnam. If Jack Kennedy were still alive . . ."

Mr. Lucas handed Hollister a bourbon. The diversion made it possible to avoid commenting on her remark. He raised the drink to his lips and tasted the expensive liquor.

All around him the conversations touched on every topic except Lucas's death. He was not included in any of the discussions and felt very awkward. So he simply tried to smile and be polite. Time moved very slowly.

At the grave, Hollister braced himself against the cold air and listened to the minister who stood at the head of the polished coffin. He spoke as if he were in a large church, projecting his voice against the spitting snow and constant wind.

As he listened, Hollister thought it was odd that the minister didn't mention Lucas's sacrifice or his unselfishness to volunteer to go to Vietnam. It was as if he was just dead and Vietnam had nothing to do with it. It seemed to Hollister that the minister was using an invocation that fit almost all of his funerals, with Lucas's name plugged in at the appropriate place.

The family had refused a military burial detail. And it didn't seem right to Hollister that a soldier like Lucas would be buried in a Connecticut cemetery with no recognition of his service or how he had died. Standing there in the cold, he wondered why they even asked for him to escort the body.

He looked over the coffin at Lucas's parents. They were meticulously dressed, ramrod stiff, and very reserved. They had treated him politely, but without warmth or any recognition that he and Lucas had been very close friends. He'd never known people with money. They weren't anything like their son. They were cold.

* * *

Later there was a reception at the Briarwood Country Club. It was a larger version of the family get-together at the Lucas house before the burial.

That was the first time he got to talk to Cindy—Lucas's girl-friend. At the grave she had stood apart from the Lucas family.

Cindy was every bit as pretty as Lucas had described her. Blond, petite, and a shade on the brassy side—she wasn't cut from the same cloth as the people at the country club. There was no stiffness or distance in her voice. Hollister thought she was perfect for Lucas.

"We had lots of plans. I guess they're all up for grabs now," Cindy said as she let Hollister light the cigarette she had pulled from her purse.

He tried to avoid anything painful for her. "Have you had time to decide?"

Cindy took another glass of champagne from the tray a waiter was carrying around. "I'm still going to Africa."

"Africa?" Hollister asked.

"Yeah, Luke and I were going to join the Peace Corps after he got out."

"Peace Corps? I didn't have any idea that he was even plan-ning on getting out of the army."

"He thought that people in the army might hold it against him if he let them know that he was not going to extend. He still had a year and a half before he was even eligible to get out, so we just kept the plans in the family."

"Looking forward to it, huh?" Hollister asked.

"Sure, we were, but his folks were dead set against it. They blamed me for putting the idea in his head. They still weren't over being angry about Luke volunteering to go to Vietnam when they found out about our Peace Corps plans."

Hollister looked at her, surprised.

"Vietnam was a huge *inconvenience* to them. Now it's killed their son and they are white-hot about it."

"I got a feeling that they were unhappy. They didn't say that much to me," Hollister said.

"You? Didn't you get the picture about you?"

"Me? What about me? I thought they wanted me to escort his body back because we were friends."

Cindy laughed. Her third champagne was starting to take effect. "They had to look for your name in his letters. They asked for you because the old man was in the navy during World War Two and he figured that Luke's body would get special treatment if there was an officer escort with it.''

CHAPTER 13

Susan returned from work to find Hollister sitting in the near dark on her doorstep with a bouquet of red roses in his hand. It had been a long day for her and she appreciated his gesture. Seeing him, she ran up and kissed him several times on the nose and lips. Then, looping her arm through his, they walked up the three flights to her place.

"Is it over?" she asked.

"Over?"

"With your friend? Do you have to do anything more with the family?" Susan asked.

Hollister was about to tell Susan about Lucas's family but he stopped himself. What good would it do? "Yeah, it's over. I don't have to go back there. Mind if we just don't talk about it anymore?"

Susan studied his face for some sign of what was bothering him, but couldn't find it. "So, what's next? And don't tell me that you have to leave right away. I'd rather not hear it, if that's all you have to tell me."

As they reached her landing, Hollister took her keys and opened the door to her apartment. "I told you that I have to go back."

She closed the door and looked at him expectantly. "Well?"

"I have to leave tomorrow night on a late flight out of La Guardia." He looked at his watch and quickly calculated. "But we still have about twenty-six hours before I have to go."

"And then it's straight back to Vietnam?"

"No, I get a one-day layover in Kansas City. I'll be able to see my family."

"That's good, Jimmy. I'm sure they'll be so excited." She

thought for a second. "So . . . what do you want to do with our time?"

"Can you take tomorrow off?"

"Count on it! . . . So, what do you want to do?"

With a lecherous grin on his face, Hollister reached up and slipped his tie to one side, loosening the knot.

Susan smiled and teased. "You are really an animal. Just like something out of the wild."

"That mean you aren't interested in what I have in mind?"

Susan stepped closer to Hollister and reached up to unbutton his shirt. He dropped his tie and started on her blouse.

"You hungry?"

Susan rolled over on her side to look at Hollister. Sweat pooled in the hollow of his throat. She took her hand and ran it over his chest, wiping the perspiration off. "James Hollister, Vietnam has knocked some weight off of you, but it sure hasn't slowed you down."

They laughed as he pulled her to his side.

"Is that yes or is that no?" Hollister teased.

Susan slipped from his grasp and jumped up from the bed. She stood naked, her hands on her hips. She let him look at her for a long time.

He couldn't take his eyes off of her. She was young and fresh and beautiful. He wanted to burn her picture into his memory for the times that he would again spend thinking about her—his remaining nights in Vietnam.

"We're going out. Get your lazy butt up, Hollister!"

"Where? Where are we going? I want to know before I make any move that stops me from soaking you up."

Susan playfully grabbed a pillow and hit him with it. She fell across his body and they embraced. He held her—it was a different embrace. It was filled with the fear that he would lose her, or that he would not be able to come home and pick up where they would leave off, or that he would come home like Lucas. He tried not to let her feel his fears, but he couldn't conceal his anxieties from her.

They held hands as they walked down the streets of Greenwich Village. Dinner was simple—Italian food and lots of cheap Chianti at the Grand Ticino. For dessert they went to Thirty-fourth Street to the Tivoli restaurant for coffee and New York cheesecake. They laughed and played like teenagers. By the early morning hours they were finally comfortable again.

Neither of them had admitted that they'd been awkward with one another for the first two days Hollister was home. In spite of their intimacy and sleeping together, it wasn't until the third day that the distance their separation created had contracted. But the hours were growing short for them.

Susan went along to sit with him while he waited to board his plane. She was sad that he was leaving her again, angry that he had to go, and worried about what might happen to him back in Vietnam. She was also conscious of her self-centered emotions, and that bothered her too. But the one emotion she was not uncomfortable with was her desire to never let him go.

She looked up and saw Hollister returning from somewhere in the crowd with coffee in flimsy paper cups.

Susan took a sip. "It's hot, but hardly coffee," she said, striking out at the coffee rather than at him.

He understood. He too was confused and angry at the parting. For a moment he wondered how many times they would have to do this. He hadn't decided about staying in the army, and he hadn't made a move to make their relationship anything more permanent than the unspoken commitment that they had. He put his cup down and took hers from her hands.

Susan wasn't sure what he was doing, but she didn't object.

"I've been trying to find the right time, and there just isn't one." Hollister couldn't seem to form his thoughts into the right words.

"Go on, Jimmy."

"Okay, here goes. I don't have any idea what the future holds for me. I just know that I want you to be part of it. I haven't decided a lot of things, and I'm not even sure if you would even consider—"

"Yes, Jimmy. Yes," Susan said, trying to rush the moment and not let him talk himself out of it.

"Yes?!"

She smiled and reached up, taking his face in her hands. "Yes, I will marry you."

All of a sudden twenty people in the waiting area cheered and applauded.

Susan and Hollister realized where they were and laughed at the onlookers who were eavesdropping and cheering them on.

"There's one thing, though."

"What's that?"

"You have to promise me that we'll stop living our lives in airports and bus terminals."

Hollister laughed and took her in his arms. As he stood up, he pulled her to her feet and then lifted her off the floor. The crowd cheered louder.

Hollister boarded the plane with the sinking feeling that only comes when a man leaves the woman he loves. It weighed on him.

The stewardess was perky and a bit too much like a cheerleader. But he needed a drink. So when she came by, Hollister ordered a scotch and some ice.

He had picked a seat adjacent to the tiny jet galley. It was a trick that most soldiers quickly learned. The proximity made them the first and last stop for stewardesses going to and from the galley. And it also gave them a chance to chat and flirt with the pretty stewardesses who usually killed time there when not occupied with the other passengers' needs.

Her chrome name tag read *Tammy*. Hollister watched her as she made the drinks. She was tiny and very pretty. She had a terrific ass, even though the airline had tried to conceal it in a rather matronly-looking uniform.

Hollister thought he'd been discovered when she turned around with the drink tray and caught his eye. If she had noticed that he was looking at her, she didn't say anything. But she had that something in her eye—that flirty twinkle women get when they know they're being appreciated and aren't upset about it.

"Vietnam?"

"What?" Hollister asked as she placed the drink on his tray table.

"Going to Vietnam?"

"Oh, yes. Going back. I was just home for a few days," Hollister said. He saw no reason to go into details.

"In that case you just let me know when you need a refill. It's on the house."

"This airline policy?"

"Nope, just mine," she said. She smiled at him, then walked down the aisle to serve the others.

He watched her walk away as he sipped his drink. Her great legs pulled his thoughts back to Susan. Months of longing to be with her had only been partially satisfied by the hours that they stole from his escort duty. He hadn't thought to tell her, but he appreciated how hard she tried to take his mind away from Lucas and his platoon and Vietnam.

She had said little about it when he awoke bathed in sweat from a particularly horrible dream about a night patrol that went wrong. As they sat in the dark talking about it, Susan tried to console him by telling him that she considered his preoccupation with Vietnam a sign of his responsibility.

She told Hollister that she would think less of him if he could simply clear his mind of Vietnam and his platoon just because he was in New York with her. She held him in her arms for the longest time that night. Neither of them knew how many more nights like that were ahead of them.

The stewardess brought Hollister a second drink and took away the little bottle from the first one. He was glad that she did; it had always bothered him to see businessmen on flights with several empties scattered on their trays. To Hollister that was a certain sign of a problem.

Hollister looked out the window into the black night. Susan would still be in a cold, damp cab somewhere on her way back to her apartment. It would be a very long day for her. For her the sun would be up in a little over three hours.

He would get to Kansas City in time for the morning traffic, but it would be nothing like New York's. His folks had never been to New York. They would never understand how people could live there. They were just simple farm people, and he was eager to see them.

Uncomfortable, Hollister got up, took off his blouse and folded it neatly. Satisfied that his efforts would minimize wrinkling, he placed it in the overhead bin. As he did, Tammy moved up the aisle behind him. She lightly placed her hands on either side of his waist as if to let him know that she was behind him and not to back up. He thought he heard her say something like excuse me, but couldn't be sure over the sounds of the jet engines.

Turning, Hollister saw her move up the aisle and stop at a couple with a small child. She bent over to help the child with something, revealing more of her great legs. At the same time she quickly glanced back down the aisle to see if he was looking and caught his eye.

Hollister appreciated the attention. It helped his mood. But as he looked back toward his seat he noticed a passenger sitting in the row behind his, staring at him with the same look he had seen in the bar in Greenwich Village. The young man wore a colorful wool serape, had long straight Prince Valiant hair and a leather thong wrapped around his head.

Suddenly Hollister wanted the guy to say something to him. He felt an urge to confront him with whatever the hell was bothering him. But it didn't happen. The passenger finally broke eye contact and raised the book in his lap to continue reading.

Fuckin' pussy, Hollister thought. He tried to picture the guy in a rifle platoon for a day in Vietnam and then wondered why the hell he was so angry with the guy. He was embarrassed by his attitude.

Sitting back down, he picked up his empty plastic drink glass from the seat next to his and placed it on the tray table for when Tammy returned to ask him if he wanted another. He did.

Losing interest in what was going on in the cabin, and tired, Hollister didn't get to the drink before sleep overtook him.

On the ground, Hollister's parents were standing next to the airport terminal with their collars up to shield them from the cold Kansas wind. He waved at them from the top of the truck-mounted ladder that the ground crew had driven up to the jet's doorway.

As he walked down the steps, Hollister felt the early sun against his back. He had a normal infantryman's reaction to the sun at his back. He was aware that it blinded his parents' view and prevented them from seeing him. He laughed at himself. He had never been so conscious of the sunrise and its affects on visibility before he went through Ranger School. He wondered if he would ever turn it off.

"There he is!" his mother yelled as he reached one of the tar-rimmed concrete squares of the airfield apron.

His parents hurriedly encircled him with firm hugs, his mother's breaking first, so she could take his face in her hands and kiss him just below the eye.

He had forgotten how much he missed them. At that moment, all his cares seemed to fade, and the tension that had built up between his shoulders just melted into the hugs.

"Oh, baby. You're so skinny! Are you okay? Is there anything wrong?" Mrs. Hollister asked.

"Here, here. Leave the boy alone," Mr. Hollister said. "For Chrissakes, Louise, he's been in a damn war, not at a cupcake factory!"

"How's Susan?"

"She's fine, Mom. She sends her love to you both."

"I'm glad. She's such a nice girl."

Hollister's father took his AWOL bag from his son, and the trio turned into the air terminal. Just then the passenger who had been seated behind Hollister passed on his way in. He gave the family a disapproving look.

Mrs. Hollister spotted her son's reaction. "Never mind, James. There's lots of those beatniks around here since you left."

"Beatniks?" Mr. Hollister said.

"You know what I mean."

The Hollister men laughed.

The station wagon turned out of the airport property that always seemed to Hollister to be under some construction and headed west on the airport road, out of Missouri. Mr. Hollister chose to use the farm roads, never having become comfortable with I-70, the interstate that would speed up a short leg of the trip.

As they rumbled along the roads, a hissing sound told Hollister there was a hole or two in the muffler, letting exhaust pressure escape.

"Doesn't sound good, Dad," Hollister said.

"Drove over a chunk'a ice yesterday that musta had some rocks in it. Punctured the damn thing like it was an eggshell," Mr. Hollister replied.

"Maybe I can fix it for you—"

"Oh no you don't, mister," Mrs. Hollister responded. "You ain't gonna be home long enough to be doin' chores. I want you to get some rest and some good food in you."

Hollister was amazed at how little the countryside had changed since he had been a boy. He loved Kansas. There was something solid about his part of the country. It was simply home.

He sat back and looked at his folks. They were getting older. Both had just had their fifty-eighth birthdays. Hollister wondered if the work around the farm was getting to be too much for his father. His color was good, but he was getting leaner and seemed much more weathered than he had remembered him.

"Looks like we might get a little more snow soon," Mr. Hollister said as he leaned over the steering wheel to look up under the sun visor.

"Had much, Dad?"

"Nope, it's been a good winter. Not like two years ago—" the old man said, as if he were going to rehash it.

"Jimmy doesn't need to be worryin' about the weather. Sakes, he's visitin'—not here to plant corn," Mrs. Hollister said.

The exchange tickled Hollister. His whole life he had listened to his parents correct each other's topics or choice of words.

The path from the driveway to the front steps of the old farmhouse was clear of the snow that had fallen the night before. His father had been up early to shovel the walkway for his mother.

Hollister looked around the aging farm. Kansas was not pretty in the winter. The level fields were brown patches of frozen mud with blotches of blown snow in the low spots. The stumps of ragged brown cornstalks extended in rows to the margins of the Hollister property, and the livestock huddled in the enclosure near the large barn.

Worried she might slip, Hollister helped his mother up the front stairs. Her walk had not been too steady since she had injured her hip in a fall three years earlier.

While he was preoccupied with his mother, his father opened the front door.

There was a strange silence as they entered the simple gray and green fifty-year-old farmhouse.

Hollister closed the door behind them and walked into the gaping archway that led to the parlor.

Suddenly the room erupted in a chorus of "Surprise!"

Startled, Hollister was caught completely off guard. Hugging the far wall of the parlor were twenty-five of his friends and relatives.

They all broke from hiding and gathered around him, hugging and kissing him, shaking his hand and patting him on the back.

Hollister looked through the crowd and caught sight of his parents standing by the door to the kitchen. They were beaming at having pulled off the little surprise.

By midnight the crowd had thinned and Hollister went out onto the back porch to clear his head. He had had far too much to drink.

Leaning on the dried-out railing around the porch, he heard the animals moving out back and became conscious of similarities with the smells in Vietnam. Missing was the decaying smell of rotting vegetation and the ever-present odor of wood and charcoal cook fires.

He looked up at the moon and wondered if his teams were on the ground somewhere, looking at the same moon. Had they holed up for the night in a thicket that would hide them until dawn? Had they put out their Claymores? Was the commo with the base station good?

"Thinking about going back?"

Turning around, he found his cousin Janet leaning against the doorjamb with two bottles of beer in her hand. She offered one to Hollister.

"Thanks."

"Well," Janet said. "Are you?"

He nodded, not knowing why he should feel apologetic about thinking about his teams and Vietnam. "It's all I ever think about anymore."

"You know how much we worry about you?"

"I'm sorry."

"Jimmy, it's not like when we were in high school. We all worried about you getting hurt playing ball. But this is different. We just reached a population of thirty-one hundred last year, and we've already had two boys killed in Vietnam. It's crazy, Jimmy. Your mama won't let you see it, but she worries herself sick. Your dad is just as worried, but he's proud of you, too."

He had no reply.

"It's not like it used to be around here. We don't all have the fun we used to. Everyone was trying to put on their best face in there tonight. It's just not fun here in Lansing anymore. Boys are worried about Vietnam. But they all had fathers in World War Two or Korea, and they can't tell them they're afraid. Kids are running off and getting married just to keep from being drafted."

Her words sank in. Janet's husband was a pilot in the air force in Germany. They didn't need to talk about where he'd be reassigned after he left there. He knew.

Hollister took a sip of his beer and lit a cigarette. "So everyone's scared?"

"No," Janet replied. "I think they're more than just scared. They're pretty damn confused—there's so much argument about us being over there. That—that . . . I don't know, Jimmy. We just don't want to lose any more kids from here."

He reached out and hugged her. She couldn't hold back any longer and broke into tears.

"How long you been holding this in?"

Janet sniffled and rummaged through her sweater pocket for

a Kleenex. "Since last month. Paul got orders for Vietnam. Oh, Jimmy, we haven't told his parents or mine or even yours. They're worried enough." She kept crying, and he held her without speaking.

As on so many mornings in his childhood, Hollister was awakened by the sound of his father outside beginning his chores. He looked at the clock. It was five, and he realized that his mother was cooking something delicious, the coffee was brewing, and he had a terrible hangover.

In the bathroom he balanced his shaving kit on the corner of the old sink and found his razor. He looked in the mirror at the dark circles under his eyes and realized that he had really been screwing off since he was told he had to take Lucas's body home. Too many long hours, too much to eat and drink, and absolutely no exercise.

He found his B-4 bag, pulled a pair of woolen socks from a side pocket and put them on. In another compartment he found the tiger-stripe PT shorts that he had made in the village outside the base camp in Vietnam.

He knew that it would be cold out until the sun came up, so he went to his dresser and pulled out a pair of cotton work gloves and an old sweatshirt with the sleeves cut off.

He stopped on the way out and looked around his room. He had not really taken it in since he'd returned. He reached out to touch his old dresser. There was a knob missing and the top was a mass of scars, water rings, and orange peel varnish. It had been handed down in the family and showed the damage from years of service in a boy's room. Still, it was as clean as Hollister had remembered it.

On the desk in the corner were his high school books, still covered with brown paper bags. The effort proved necessary to protect them. The covers were torn—a couple had deep grass stains from the many times that he had dumped them on the football field before practice.

Even standing there, home seemed so far away since he had been in Vietnam.

Hollister tried not to make too much noise as he walked down the back stairs that led to the kitchen, because his aunt and uncle from Topeka had stayed over rather than try to make the drive late the night before.

When he reached the bottom of the stairs, his mother turned and looked at him. "Where do you think you're going, mister?"

"I've got to go run off some of your good food."

She wiped her hand on her apron and gave him a look. "Now don't you go tryin' to butter me up. You can't go out dressed like that."

"Mom, I'm going out to run. I'll be fine."

His jump boots clumped against the crumbling edge of the asphalt, and the sun warmed his face as he turned onto the short stretch of U.S. 73 leading into town. The air was brisk and clean, reminding Hollister of high school track practice before school. It was held in the mornings because of harvest season, and freed up the boys to be home in the afternoons to work on their farms.

He passed the WELCOME TO LANSING sign rimmed with Rotary, Toastmasters, and VFW insignias. Hollister hated running. He had always hated it. But his decision to do things that required running, like track in school and Airborne units in the Army, weren't swayed by his dislike for the boredom and discomfort that he always associated with running. To him running was essential, part of trying to ward off the ill effects of his bad habits—smoking and drinking. Like so many others, he felt that if he did enough running, he would be able to continue to drink and smoke without their having a negative impact on his health. Deep down, he knew what a crock that was. But it was what men did. It's what paratroopers did. It's what he would continue to do.

Lansing had the same red brick buildings that its founders built after the turn of the century. The only new structures were warehouses and storage areas with metal frames and corrugated siding. Most of what they held used to be down at the railhead, a few blocks over. But there wasn't as much rail commerce anymore; harvested goods still left to feed the country, but on diesel eighteen wheelers. Even that early in the day tractor trailers were blowing by.

"Jimbo! Hey, Jim!"

Hearing his name, Hollister looked back over his shoulder and saw Beeler Andrews, the neighborhood barber, unlocking his door and waving at him. Jim waved back and kept on running to the center of town.

He reached the sidewalk on Main, in front of the feed store, and stepped up on it without breaking his stride. Mr. Kessell was setting out display items and saw Hollister approaching. He

took the pipe from his mouth and raised it as Hollister passed.
" 'Lo boy. Good ta see ya home."

Reaching the end of the sidewalk, Hollister looked both ways at Eisenhower Street and crossed at a jog. As he did, a new Ford Mustang turned the corner in front of him. Hollister looked at it longingly. He had never owned a new car. He wondered if he would ever be somewhere long enough and have enough money to buy a Mustang. Thoughts of a normal life brought back Vietnam. Before he could think about normalcy, he had to get Vietnam behind him.

As he looked up from the sidewalk, a car from his past stood at curbside near the end of the block. Petey Nellis was standing at the driver's door of his '49 Mercury. They had done a beautiful job chopping, channeling, and lowering the two-door sedan. It had no remaining chrome on it except the bumpers, two teardrop spotlights flanking the windshield, and baby moon hubcaps.

As Hollister got closer he adjusted his stride to stop to say hello to Petey. Hollister raised one hand to signal Petey that he saw him. But Petey turned away, got in the car, and quickly drove off.

Confused, Hollister stopped and turned around to watch him drive away. He could see Petey looking in the rearview mirror at him. There'd been no mistake.

As he continued through town, Hollister thought about what Janet had said the night before. Things had changed. When he left for Vietnam, hardly anyone even knew where it was, much less had any opinion about it. He was discovering the extent of the polarization. It hurt a little to think that he and the others in Vietnam were not being supported.

Sucking in a deep breath, he decided that he couldn't think about it. It would only depress him if he tried to focus on the growing antiwar attitude.

His mother made him shower before she let him into the kitchen. Everyone else had eaten, but she kept some biscuits and gravy warm for him in the aging oven. He had worked up an appetite on the run and felt a little self-righteous about running with a hangover.

"Saw Petey Nellis this morning and he avoided me like he owed me money, Mom. You know what that's about?"

"Story goin' around is that his father has pulled some strings to get him by the draft board, and it slipped out at the VFW.

Now his father's claimin' it wasn't his doing, and Petey's avoiding everyone—ain't just you.''

Hollister's father came in, wearing bib overalls and a cap that read FOSTER'S FEED STORE. He had some small part of something in his dirty fingers and mumbled something about needing his glasses.

His mother poured herself a glass of milk and sat down to watch her son eat, just enjoying the few moments together.

"Your father and I are going to church before we take you to the airport. You plannin' on going with us?"

Hollister hesitated for a long time and shook his head no.

"Don't you go to church in Vietnam, honey?" his mother asked.

Without looking at her, Hollister answered, "All the time and none of the time, Mom."

She looked around at his father. "Well, what does that mean?" she asked.

Before he could reply, Hollister's father looked over the top of his reading glasses as if to say, Enough . . . let him be.

Finished with breakfast, Hollister poured himself another cup of coffee and walked over to the half-windowed kitchen door. Through the steamed-up glass he could see that the light was on in the work shed; his father was back out there. Hollister filled a second cup and went out the back door.

Without turning away from the bench-mounted grinder, Hollister's father spoke over his shoulder. "Son, you better close that door b'hind you. I'm afraid that the wind might get it and pull a hinge a'loose."

Hollister kicked the door closed and stepped to his father's side. "Some coffee, Dad?"

His father kept working on the ragged edge of a well-worn chisel. "Thanks. Just put it down."

After a couple more passes of the tool over the rotating stone, Hollister's father stopped, raised his glasses and looked critically at the new edge. Without taking his eyes off of it, he picked up the coffee mug and took a sip.

He put the mug down and let the glasses fall from his brow back to the bridge of his nose. He peered over the top of the glasses, searching out an oily rag that hung on a nail near the grinder. Feeling the rag for the presence of oil, he dipped it in the oil dripping under the grinder and then passed the rag over the bright new edge to keep it from rusting. "How is it?"

Hollister understood that his father was asking about Vietnam and how he was making out. "All I can tell you, Dad, is that it's nothing like what I expected."

His father turned around and looked at him for the first time. "You okay?"

Hollister looked down into the black of his coffee, cupped between his hands, nodded affirmatively and shrugged.

"My war wasn't at all what I expected, either," his father said as he put the tattered and stained canvas cover back in its place over the grinder motor. He paused for a minute to think back and then pulled his glasses from his face, folded them up and slipped them into the top pocket in his overalls.

Those were the first words his father had ever really said to him about war and its effect on him.

His father put the newly sharpened chisel in its place on a pegboard nailed up behind the workbench. "You know that your mama cries at night?"

Leaving again came all too fast for Hollister. He had barely enough time to tell his family about asking Susan to marry him. They were happy for him. They had liked her from the moment they first met her. Hollister thought that it must have been because they thought she was smarter and classier than they were—that she would be good for their son.

His mother came into his room while he was dressing to go to the airport. She quietly sat on his bed and watched him pack while she fidgeted with the hem on the apron between her knees. "Honey, you gonna be careful, aren't you?"

"Sure, Mom. Don't worry about me. I'll be okay. Anyway, my tour is almost over. I'll be back before you know it. And you'll have grandchildren to fuss over."

Her lip quivered slightly. "That Lucas boy didn't have much time left over there, did he?"

Tears were silently painting lines down her cheeks before dripping onto her dress. He knelt down in front of her. "Mama, I'm gonna be okay. I'll be back soon."

She reached out and touched his cheek. "I read the papers, honey. I'm terribly afraid. Your daddy and I pray for you every night."

He couldn't say anything. He just gathered her to his chest and held her while she quietly cried for him.

* * *

There wasn't much to do in the terminal at the Kansas City airport. Hollister had told his folks not to wait. They would have argued with him but his mother had a doctor's appointment that she couldn't postpone.

At the ticket counter Hollister stuck his hand inside his blouse to get his tickets. As he handed the agent the envelope, a folded scrap of paper fell out. The agent picked it up from the countertop and handed it to him.

He opened it. The note was on TWA stationery. It was from Tammy, the stewardess on the flight to Kansas City. She gave him her address and phone number and invited him to call her when he returned from Vietnam.

She must have noticed his reaction to the longhair behind him because she added a PS that read: "Some of us appreciate what you are doing."

CHAPTER 14

Hollister was still in a fog as he rode through the dirt roadways of the brigade base camp. He had slept through the whole flight from Seattle to Saigon, only waking up for the refueling stops.

The deuce-and-a-half pulled up to the LRP detachment area and slowed to a jerky stop. Hollister stepped out of the elevated cab onto the muddy roadway and thanked the driver for the ride. The driver nervously pumped the accelerator, killing time while he waited for Hollister to walk around to the back of the truck to get his gear.

One of the soldiers riding in the rear threw Hollister's bags down for him and then banged on the tailgate to let the driver know they were ready to continue.

The truck drove off belching diesel smoke from its oversized exhaust pipe, and Hollister entered the detachment area. It had hardly been three days since he had seen Susan and he already missed her. He reminded himself to finish the last few lines of the letter he had started in SeaTac airport and send it to her.

Suddenly Hollister noticed something was very wrong. There was no activity in the LRP area—none. The standby choppers were all on the ground with the blades tied down. None of the crew members were even in the ships. And only a couple of soldiers were crossing the compound. They seemed to have no hustle. They moved with some sense of sadness.

Hollister dropped his gear at the step to his hooch and ran over to Operations.

Inside, the entire leadership of the detachment was seated in the briefing area, the overflow standing behind those seated in the few available chairs.

Captain Michaelson was speaking. He looked up, spotted

Hollister and stopped. "Welcome back, Jim. Got some very bad news. We've lost a team."

The words felt like a sledgehammer slamming into Hollister. It was every LRP's nightmare—being overrun.

He quickly searched the faces in the room to determine who was missing. He found Camacho, then Allard, but no Davis. Where was Davis?

Michaelson interrupted the search. "No, it wasn't one of your teams. It was One-three from Lucas's old platoon—Smith's team. Sergeant Davis is over at the mess hall with Marrietta, debriefing the pilots."

Camacho and Allard looked like hell. They were dirty and muddy and their uniforms were torn. Camacho had a dressing on one of his hands.

The debriefing continued with the details of the actions after the team got hit and after Operations lost radio communication with it.

Hollister would have to get filled in on the earlier details. Much of it was self-explanatory. Patting his pockets for something to write on and with, he realized that he had dropped all that with his bags.

Camacho ripped a few pages from the steno pad balanced on his knee and handed it to Hollister. Grabbing a GI-issue ballpoint from the counter that held the radios, Hollister began taking notes. America never happened. Susan didn't happen. He was back.

Michaelson had finished the debriefing, getting as much as he could from those who had prepped the team to go and evacuated the bodies afterward. Before dismissing the group, the captain scheduled a meeting for the following afternoon to brief everyone on his conclusions and lessons learned, and what adjustments had to be taken to prevent such catastrophies in the future.

Once the crowd had cleared the briefing area, Michaelson motioned for Hollister to sit. He took out a pack of cigarettes and offered one.

Lighting the Pall Mall, Hollister took a drag and pinched off a bit of tobacco stuck to the tip of his tongue while he waited for Captain Michaelson to speak.

Michaelson clenched his fists and then relaxed them, letting emotion slip through his usual reserve. "This was fucked! A whole team dead! No goddamn reason for it. It shouldn't have happened."

"How'd it happen, sir?"

Michaelson took his foot off the folding chair and turned to the map. He shifted his cigarette to his other hand and stabbed a small hamlet on the map with his finger. "There's an ARVN outpost here. Night before last they started taking incoming small-caliber mortar fire—sixties. They didn't have any targets to shoot at and they were only guessing how far out the VC were, so they called for the VNAF to come in with close air support.

"We put up a flare ship and the Viets launched two flights of A1-Es from An Hoa. They dropped a shitload of HE into the area where the ARVNs suspected that the mortar fire was coming from. They say that the aircraft took ground fire, but there were no hits."

Michaelson stopped and looked at Hollister. "I really doubt that they took any fire. Probably a face-saving thing for the ARVNs who picked the grid coordinates for the zoomies to bomb."

Hollister nodded. It was not the first time he had heard of manufactured Vietnamese combat.

Michaelson continued, "So, sometime during the night there was a pissing match between the ARVNs and MACV over the truth. It got to the point that by dawn the Province Chief's honor was at stake and he demanded a BDA to prove that his guys weren't totally incompetent."

Hollister knew what Michaelson was going to say. He sighed and put out his half-smoked cigarette on the sole of his boot. He started to put the butt into his pocket, but he was still in his khakis. Bernard, on radio watch at the other end of the tent, reached over, grabbed a small trash can and held it up for Hollister, who flipped the balled-up butt and made a basket.

Michaelson kept on without pausing for the two-pointer. "So the shit rolled downhill and we got a call from Brigade to divert a team to do the bomb damage assessment."

Hollister knew that a BDA was one of the worst missions possible—nothing clandestine about it. The VC knew that when an air strike went in, they could count on someone showing up sometime later to evaluate the damage—either by air or walking the ground.

"I tried to talk Brigade into getting someone else—like a rifle company—to go count bomb craters and shredded trees. I was told that if we waited to move a slower unit into the area, the

ARVNs would claim that the Americans waited too long, allowing the VC to drag off their casualties."

Hollister shook his head. "That's bullshit."

"It gets worse," Michaelson said. "They said that all they wanted was for the team to go in right on top of the craters, do a body count, pick up anything of intelligence value, and then we'd yank 'em."

"They land on top of the bad guys? That how it happened?"

Michaelson pitched his own cigarette butt over to the trash can and shook his head. "No. Put 'em down within five hundred meters of the bomb craters. The LZ was stone cold. Which, I guess, is the worst thing that coulda happened."

"How's that, sir?" Hollister asked.

"I still had a team to extract and another one to put in before dark. Brigade told me to use up the blade time on our choppers—they'd send other Brigade ships to pick up Smith's team if it had to be pulled before I finished with the other sorties."

"I don't like the sound of that," Hollister said.

"I didn't, either. Well, things got boring at the BDA site and they found nothing to indicate that there had even been mortars set up there. Smith reported that he didn't think there had been anyone there since the Stone Age.

"Then it started to go real sour. Things got backed up. Brigade choppers got diverted to a rifle company contact on the other side of Brigade AO and—"

"Lemme guess," Hollister said. "They decided to leave the team in till first light."

"Bingo. But by 2100 hours last night the team was reporting movement around them. They called for illumination and it stopped for a while. Then it started up around 0300 again. They reported movement, then called in contact—then nothing.

"We thought we got a short transmission over an URC-10, but we couldn't be sure. Could have been one of the VC fuckin' with the thing."

"My people go in?"

"Yeah," Michaelson answered. "Since we didn't have commo, we orbited over the location with all the flares and illumination we could muster looking for them. It didn't take long to find the team.

"Davis took Camacho's and Allard's teams in heavy to set up a perimeter and evac the bodies. They were all KIA and stripped of weapons and gear."

Hollister tried to conceal the shudder that went through his body as he sat looking at the map.

"Get over to your hooch and change. I want you to go with me to ID the bodies."

Michaelson and Hollister arrived at the Graves Registration Unit near Brigade Headquarters. They hadn't said much on the ride up, and for a change Bernard confined himself to simply driving.

They arrived just as the bodies were being moved from a crackerbox ambulance and into the far side of the GP large tent that served as the GRU. Michaelson and Hollister left Bernard with the jeep and entered from the street side.

The tent had a small office in the near end improved by scrounged ammo-box planking used to create a wobbly floor. Two desks flanked the room, and the tent was cut in half by a bank of beat-up wall lockers.

A clerk sat at one desk typing on a filthy Underwood typewriter—unaware that the two officers had entered.

A figure slipped through the split in the wall lockers—an older soldier who had probably been assigned to the unit as some type of light duty. Too old for his rank, which was Specialist 6, he coughed uncomfortably before speaking. "Mornin', sir. I'm Specialist Olsen. You must be from the LRPs."

Michaelson nodded.

"Well, sir, we are off-loading the remains now. I'll need you to ID the bodies. If it's all right with you, we'll send the personal effects down to your unit tomorrow afternoon after we get everything inventoried."

Michaelson nodded. "That'll be fine." He gestured toward the back of the tent. "Let's get it done."

Hollister was not prepared for the undignified way the bodies were arrayed. They had been placed on ankle-high wooden cargo pallets that were laid out on the floor. Each body took up two pallets and there were square Sears window fans at the head and foot of each pallet. There was also a large floor-model mess hall fan that was tilted down to blow across the bodies.

When Hollister looked at the arrangement with a puzzled expression, Olsen caught his eye, sprayed a mist of GI DDT into the backs of the fans and explained, "Keeps the flies from lighting on 'em and laying eggs."

Hollister's stomach heaved at what he saw and what he smelled, but he forced himself to tough it out. He pulled out his notepad and fished for a pen, then turned to Captain Michaelson. "Where do you want to start?"

Michaelson looked down at the body nearest his feet. "I don't think there is any good place. Let's start here."

Hollister nodded and watched while Olsen and Michaelson squatted down and turned the face toward them. Michaelson quietly spoke the soldier's name—Smith.

Hollister liked that about Michaelson, that he knew the name of every soldier in his command. Even the new ones didn't escape his memory. He even took the time to find out about each man. He knew who was married, who was going back to school after Vietnam, and who had kids. Of course, that made the identification much harder for Michaelson.

"Look at his fatigue shirt," Michaelson said.

Hollister looked at the body. The lifeless form was a mass of wounds. A bullet had ripped through the side of the soldier's neck and severed his spine. His torso had what looked like two large fragmentation wounds and his right hand was missing. Hollister fought to keep his stomach calm.

"It looks like the neck wound killed him, but he had all these other hits too," Michaelson said, fingering the many smaller holes in his shirt. The fragments had ripped the fabric and left the ragged edges of the material stuck in the wounds. "These are Claymore wounds. Damn!"

"Claymores turned around on them?" Hollister asked.

"That's my guess. They must have put them out so far that they couldn't see them in the dark, and the VC slipped up and reversed them."

Hollister scribbled a reminder as Captain Michaelson stood up and moved to the next body. It was worse than the first. The contents of the soldier's lower abdomen were missing. His lower intestines were still back in the bush somewhere, and his lower abdominal cavity had filled up with expanding organs and debris from the field.

Suddenly Hollister felt a little light-headed and the tent seemed hotter. His footing was starting to feel unsteady.

"Cap'n, Lieutenant—I gotta spray some more of this shit," Olsen said as he shook a GI DDT can and sprayed the bug killer into the fan to distribute it across the bodies. "Sorry, if we don't use this and keep the fans going, the bodies are a mess of maggots by the time they get to Saigon."

Hollister was happy to have an excuse to leave the tent for some air.

Outside, Hollister refused the cigarette that Captain Michaelson offered him. He leaned against the tent rope and looked down at the ground. With the tip of his jungle boot he moved a small pebble around. "This is really fuckin' hard, sir."

"It's not going to get easier as long as you wear that uniform. It's your job. If it didn't hurt and if it didn't make you sick, I wouldn't want you running a platoon, and kids like those in there wouldn't want you for a boss."

"But it's so goddamn senseless. There's no reason for them to be laid out in there," Hollister said.

"You and I have to figure out why they're in there. I've got to take responsibility for not fighting hard enough to get out of the mission. But beyond that, we have to figure out why the fuck they were jumped and how the Claymores got turned around."

Hollister didn't want to have to come to the GRU again—ever.

Hollister sat in the dark collecting his thoughts. It was only a little after nine, but it was pretty quiet for Vietnam. He might have stopped at the second drink, but all the teams were in and the detachment was on a stand down. He poured himself a third from the bottle of Johnnie Walker Red Label that rested on his footlocker.

The booze was room temperature and bit his tongue, but it dulled his senses enough to put some distance between him and the unsettling experience at Graves Registration.

He couldn't understand why the deaths of LRPs had hit him so hard. He'd experienced KIAs while he was running a rifle platoon, and there was Lucas. But the loss of a team felt like a weight resting on his chest. He rolled the remaining scotch around in the bottom of the cup and tried to shake off the feeling. It wouldn't go. He lit a cigarette and put out the one that was in his C-ration can ashtray. Exhaling, he decided to move on to something productive—something to take his mind off the bodies on the pallets and the revolting smell of the DDT.

He remembered the letter that he had started in the States. He turned on the light and found it in his AWOL bag. Spreading it out on the desk, he moved his drink and the bottle to a convenient place on the desk and picked up where the letter ended.

He had already written about how he felt about the visit and their marriage plans, so he added how lucky he felt to have her in his life and said he couldn't wait to see her again. He told her lots, but he told her nothing. He didn't tell her about the bodies of the dead LRPs that he had helped identify. He didn't tell her about the bloody, stinking personal effects that he had to help inventory. He didn't tell her that he had pains in his gut that wouldn't go away—even with the scotch.

By not telling her the whole truth, he knew he was lying to her. It had been that way with every letter he had written to her and his parents. So, writing was something he kept putting off because he felt so uncomfortable about lying—by omission—all the time. Then he felt guilty about not writing enough. He poured another drink and thought about writing something else— also harmless. But even that made him feel worse. Taking another drink, he tried to rationalize that bad news was not going to help Susan feel any better about anything. Lying to her was in her best interest and not his. He didn't have a choice. He wanted to protect her. He finished the drink and poured still another.

Finally, feeling the booze, he sat up straight and told himself to shape up. Write something bright, something positive, he told himself.

Picking up his pen, he added that he was sorry that they had not gotten around to discussing the particulars. He would probably be getting alert orders soon, letting him know where he was going when he returned to the States. The rumor mill had it that all returning infantry officers were being sent to training assignments—rather than combat units.

He worried about what that would mean to her career. Did she still want to be a writer? He was sorry that he had not asked her.

There was a knock at the door. "Sir, you in there?" Theodore said from outside.

"Yo, come in," Hollister answered.

Theodore stepped in, snatched his hat from his head and saluted. "Sir, I'm CQ runner tonight. I was sent over here to get you. The Old Man wants to talk to you."

Hollister looked at him, a little puzzled.

Theodore picked up on it. "Oh, they tried to call you from the orderly room but your Lima-Lima is out. I'm supposed to check it at this end and then follow the WD-1 back to the switch if the phone looks okay."

Hollister turned over his letter to Susan and moved away from the desk to give Theodore room to fuss with the field phone.

"Know what it's about?"

Theodore moved over to the phone and replied, "No sir, I

don't. I just came back from getting some coffee and was told to come get you. Didn't seem to be any kind of flap, just said, 'Ask him to come see me.' "

Theodore spotted the picture of Ly, the dead VC lieutenant's wife, leaning up against the canvas carrier of the phone. "Hey, sir! Where'd you get this picture of this good-lookin' gook honey with the big tits?"

Hollister was just putting on his shirt, and suddenly his blood pressure spiked. "What?! Put that down! What in hell's wrong with you, Theodore?"

Startled, Theodore spun around. He wasn't sure what he had done, but he automatically snapped to attention.

"That came off a VC that *we* killed. Probably somebody's wife, and now somebody's widow, and you come in here and talk shit about her like she's somebody's whore! How'd you like it if someone found your girlfriend's picture on your dead-ass body and started talking shit about it? Huh?"

Theodore started to sputter with no answer.

"Goddammit, Theodore—why is it you have to be running your fucking mouth all the time?" He caught himself getting far too angry and knew that he had to cut it right there before he went too far. "Get your sorry ass out of here, soldier."

Theodore mumbled yessir, saluted, and bolted through the door, not waiting for a return.

Hollister picked up Ly's photo and held it in his hand. He thought of Susan, and Lucas's Cindy, and the photos of the girlfriends and wives in the wallets of the dead LRPs at the GRU.

He realized that he had had too much to drink and had over-reacted to Theodore. He threw the picture across the room, sat down on his cot, and dropped his face into his hands. He wanted to make the pain go away, but had no idea how. After a minute he whispered to himself, "Nice, Hollister. Really fucking nice. What an asshole!"

Then he remembered that he had to go see Captain Michaelson. Getting to his feet, he buttoned his shirt and looked for his hat. It was on the field table next to the letter and the almost empty bottle of Johnnie Walker.

He picked up the letter and tried to decide what to do with it. There wasn't time to finish it, but he wanted to get it off. He pulled out his pen and added, *Honey, got to run. Boss needs to see me. Can't finish now. Want to mail. Know that I love you, Jim.*

He stuffed the letter into the envelope and licked the flap. Like most envelopes, it wouldn't stay closed in the humid weather. He put it in his pocket till he could get some tape. Then his eyes fell on the bottle. He thought about having a short one. No, he wouldn't.

He walked out into the night.

Hollister passed through the mess hall on the way to the orderly room. Sergeant Kendrick saw him coming and was about to holler "at ease," but Hollister raised his palm to stop him. He then turned to the pot of simmering coffee and poured a cupful. "Thanks—needed a cup." He wondered if Kendrick could tell that he'd had one too many scotches. He wondered if the Old Man would.

In the orderly room Hollister saw Easy hunched over a stack of paperwork. "Midnight oil, Top?"

Easy looked up and quickly snatched his glasses from his face. He was vain about wearing them, but they weren't an option when he was trying to read. He got up, dropping the glasses on the paperwork. "Casualty Feeder Reports on the KIAs. I'd rather have my ass kicked in a rock fight, Lieutenant!"

"I know what you mean. The boss in? He wanted to see me."

Easy stepped around his desk, slipped into Michaelson's office, and then stepped back out. "Yessir, he's free. Go right on in."

Hollister realized that he still had the coffee cup in his hand. He quickly put it down on top of a file cabinet and entered Michaelson's office.

The captain was leaning on the window ledge, looking out into the dark, when Hollister entered. "You wanted to see me, sir?"

"Yeah, sit down, Jim. We have to talk about a few things. You want some coffee?"

Hollister wondered if he had slurred his words. Did the Old Man know he had had too much to drink? "Yessir . . . I'd like that."

Captain Michaelson turned around and yelled, "Bernard!"

"I know—coffee, sir," Bernard yelled back, having just walked into the orderly room.

Michaelson looked over to Hollister. "So . . . how ya doing, Ranger?"

"I have to admit it got to me, sir. Hell, I just now ripped

Theodore's head off and shoved it down his throat over nothing.''

Michaelson sat down and leaned back in his chair. "Well, you'll have plenty of time to make up with young Mr. Theodore."

Hollister looked up for a sign of the real purpose of the meeting.

"Jim, we have to make some assignment changes around here and we have some big training holes that we have to fill."

Bernard slipped in, put down the two cups of coffee, and silently stepped back out.

Michaelson thanked Bernard, took a sip, put the cup down, and picked up a piece of lined paper with notes on it. "We've been hurt bad in the last couple of weeks. The hardest part after the losses is the realization that we are at fault for some of the KIAs. We have either not trained these folks well enough or we are overestimating our own survivability. Either way, we have to get on it, and now!"

"Agreed," Hollister said.

"I'm hurting for junior officers. I'm not long for this job, and you'll be getting seriously short in no time. First platoon has no officer and is missing a team and a half. It's gonna call for some buckling down and some heartbreakin' reassignments."

"Where do we start, sir?"

"I'm going to have to peel away some of the most experienced people to rebuild the first platoon. I need to find a replacement for Lucas and one for you."

Hollister pressed his ballpoint against his notebook to jot down details. "Okay, sir. What'll it take?"

"Until further notice we will consolidate the first and second platoons for training. Eventually, you'll be getting two new lieutenants to break in. And I want to spread you around to cover for Captain Shaw."

"Is Captain Shaw going somewhere?"

"No, I'm grooming him to replace me. That means he needs you to cover for him now and then. So, you'll be running a larger platoon and helping Shaw. It'll be good for you."

Raising his eyebrows, Hollister jotted down a few notes to himself.

"Tomorrow morning I want you to come to me with an accelerated training plan and recommendations on how to cover our leadership losses."

Standing to stretch, Michaelson absentmindedly unsnapped

the clasp on his Rolex and rubbed the skin under it. "Questions?"

Hollister got to his feet and shook his head. "No sir. I don't think I'll have any until I get into this. But when I do, I'll bring 'em to you."

"Count on it. Now, go get some chow and some rest."

Hollister saluted, "I will, sir. But first I've got some things to do. Good night, sir."

"Theodore!" someone yelled, waking the sleeping soldier.

"What? Who's that?" Theodore said, pulling the poncho liner from his face.

Bernard closed the screen door to the hooch behind him. "Hey, man. Lieutenant Hollister wants to see you over t'his hooch—right fuckin' now!"

CHAPTER 15

Hollister flipped his footlocker open; the lid came to rest in an upright position against his cot. A photo of Susan on the inside of the lid caught his attention long enough for him to steal a moment just to drink her in. He was angry that he was rattled and acting unlike himself. He had always thought that there were other junior officers who were better at many of the skills demanded of a platoon leader, but his best accomplishment was his ability to control himself, his emotions and behavior. Reserve and control were two of the features of the NCO trainers at the Seventh Army NCO Academy that most characterized them as professionals. They could rip a soldier apart without raising their voices or resorting to bullying. They never seemed to sweat, worry, or rattle.

He recognized the trait in a leader, but hadn't mastered it. If he wanted to lie to himself, he would blame his outburst at Theodore on the deaths or the visit back home or the scotch. But he wouldn't do that. He blamed himself.

He remembered how quickly he understood the value of self-control while he was in OCS. His experience with the NCOs in Germany helped it all come together for him while he was a candidate. Many of his classmates just didn't get it. And it was a cause for dismissal for several of them.

But while Hollister recognized the importance, the tactical officers in OCS gave him a hard time about controlling his emotions. They often did things to get under his skin—to make him lose control. After plenty of practice, he changed self-control from a problem to a small success. Hollister agreed with his tac officer when he'd been asked, "What good are you to anyone if you can't be counted on to be consistent?"

Enough, he told himself as he reached out and touched the

tips of his fingers to Susan's picture. Then he looked for another ballpoint pen. His had started to skip earlier in Captain Michaelson's office.

The tray was filled with the odds and ends that collect in a soldier's footlocker—insignia, soap, grease pencils, stationery, bootlaces, the pen he was looking for, and name tapes. Name tapes! He remembered the name tape that he had taken from Lucas's uniform. He closed the footlocker and went to Lucas's old wall locker.

Inside, he found the curled and faded name tape lying on the shelf. Picking it up, he picked the short bits of thread that extended from its border as he looked around for some way to nail it up in the hooch. On the locker door he found two different color thumbtacks that still had the corner scraps from some long discarded calendar under them.

He tacked the name tape to a horizontal two-by-four on the hooch frame so he could see it every time he sat at the desk. Then he looked across the room and found Ly's picture on the floor. He picked it up, walked back to the upright and tucked the bottom edge of it behind Lucas's name tape.

He had found the place and the purpose for Lucas's name tape. He would use it to prod himself. He wanted to make sure that when he got tired and felt that he had done enough—enough training, checking, and rechecking—he would remember Lucas. He wanted others to know that Lucas had once lived in that hooch, and he wanted to think that Lucas's death would help him remember his job.

But Ly's photo was the other side of the same notion. Something told him that it would be easy to get so angry and so vindictive that almost anything could be justified in the name of payback. Ly's photo would keep him from confusing his motivation to train his people to prevent any more useless deaths with revenge. There were plenty of things that Hollister was unsure about, but his gut told him that revenge would be a dangerous and very seductive motivation to give in to. The name tape and the picture would help keep things in perspective.

There was a knock on the hooch frame. "Lieutenant Hollister? You wanted to see me, sir?"

"Come in."

Obviously unsure about how to act after getting his heels locked earlier, Theodore entered. He stopped just inside the hooch and waited for Hollister to set the tone.

"Spin that footlocker around and sit. I want to talk to you."

Recognizing that he still had it on, Theodore snatched his floppy LRP hat from his head and sat down.

"I wanted to tell you that I was out of line earlier," Hollister said. "I jumped on you for no reason. I'm not saying what I felt was wrong. I just did it wrong. I overreacted, and you were in the impact area."

"That's okay, sir. We all get, you know . . . off days," Theodore said, bunching his hat up and releasing it.

"I wanted you to know that I'm not angry with you, and I wanted to talk to you about tomorrow."

"Tomorrow?"

"Yes, we're going to have to make some serious changes in the platoon, and I have to lean on all the old-timers. You've been here long enough to be one. I'm going to be recommending some personnel changes to the Old Man and I need some details.

"First thing after chow tomorrow, I want you to get over to the orderly room and get me the DEROS dates on everyone in first platoon."

He pulled out his notebook and flipped it open. Tearing out two pages, he handed them to Theodore. "And combine the list with this one from our platoon. I'd normally ask the first sergeant or Bernard to do this, but they're going to be asshole deep in paperwork for days. So, try to get the info without getting in their way."

"No problem, sir. I'll get on it first thing."

Pleased, Hollister stood up. "Good, and I'm going to be leaning on you to help out on training. We're going to turn up the heat, and I want you to be one of the demolitions instructors. So, break the books before we get to it. Okay?"

"Yessir. Airborne!" He waited for Hollister to return his salute and then quickly stepped through the doorway. Just outside he stopped and turned back. "Ah, sir. About the picture thing—"

"I know. G'night, Theodore."

"Good night, sir."

The scotch and the cigarettes hurt Hollister's body as he ran alongside the combined platoon made up of his teams and the remaining members of Lucas's platoon. It was policy that teams took physical training every morning when they were back at the base camp and not preparing for a mission. There had always been an energetic competition between the two platoons to see which one could do the most PT, make the most noise running, and turn out the largest number of LRPs for morning runs. Those days were over until the decimated first platoon could be rebuilt.

As the formation ran past the billeting area of the Brigade's Military Police company, it was SOP to pick up the stride, yell louder, and shout insults to the MPs. This always provoked the MPs to hurl back lots of insults from the safety of their sand-bagged hooches.

The LRPs' attitude amused Hollister. He was sure that there were few in uniform who could match the spontaneous bravado of the Vietnam LRP. And his LRPs were no slouches at ex-panding the reputation.

PT gave way to breakfast and then more training. They spent the first few days after the loss of the LRP team organizing for training. Hollister came up with a list of subjects that he wanted taught, and then prioritized them, knowing that he would never get it all done.

He tapped the more experienced to act as assistant instructors and coordinated the training needs with Captain Shaw and Ser-geant Marrietta. They took care of the necessary transportation, ammunition, training aids, and aircraft that Hollister needed.

Hollister would have liked to have had more time, but there was never enough. Captain Michaelson had warned him that the training time would be short. Michaelson was able to convince Brigade to let the detachment stand down for ten days to go to a full training schedule without any combat operations or ad-ministrative details to keep the members of the detachment from attending training. He also insisted that every member of the detachment attend training every day and that the pilots and artillerymen who supported the unit do the same. And finally, he ordered that each day start and end with physical training.

While Hollister and Shaw supervised all of the training, Cap-tain Michaelson took care of the replacement problem by re-cruiting new team members from the Brigade's three infantry battalions. He was even able to root out a machine gunner from the Military Police company. His training was even tougher with the kidding he took from the LRPs about being an ex-MP.

On the third day of training Hollister was called in from the firing range to meet the two new lieutenants who had volun-teered to spend the second half of their tours with the LRPs.

Lieutenant Virgil was a former weapons platoon leader, an ROTC grad who had gone to the Citadel and was a graduate of Airborne and Ranger schools. His enthusiasm for the LRPs was enhanced by the fact that he and Lucas had been roommates back in jump school. Hollister liked him immediately.

Lieutenant Rogers had been a rifle platoon leader and, like Hollister, volunteered for the LRPs to avoid a job as the Civic Actions officer in his old battalion. He would be the only black officer in the detachment.

Captain Michaelson had already delivered his welcoming pitch, so he turned them over to Hollister to get them oriented and quickly integrated into training. Rogers would take over the first platoon, and Virgil would eventually replace Hollister.

Hollister welcomed the duo and started to run down a list of things that they still needed to do to get fully aboard. The complexities of in-processing into any unit were a necessary evil, but the nonstandard nature of the LRP Detachment made things that much more complicated. Before a man could go to the field he had to have the right equipment; his mail had to be forwarded to him; he needed to make sure Finance knew were he was; he had to fill out endless pieces of paper; and most of all, he needed a rack.

Hollister turned to Bernard, who was answering most of the questions. "Anyone put any thought into where we are going to put these folks?"

Bernard made a face; Hollister knew he wasn't going to like his answer. "Sir, all we have is your hooch. But I sent a runner over to Supply to get another cot."

"Well, that's sure gonna be tight."

Easy piped up from across the room. "Sir, we're working on scrounging some construction materials to see if we can't make your place a little larger."

"Thank you, Top. I hope we can do something before we kill each other in there."

"I'm on the case, Lieutenant," Easy said, cranking the ringer on the side of his field phone, the receiver cradled in the crook of his neck.

"I'll take 'em with me now. If you are finished with them," Hollister said to Captain Michaelson.

"There's a shitload of things to do. So take charge of these two and move 'em out. I'll catch up with you all at chow."

The three lieutenants saluted Captain Michaelson and left.

Michaelson turned around and started for his office. He caught a small expression of disapproval on Easy's face. "Problem, Top?"

"Oh, nothin', sir. Just this damn paperwork."

"I don't believe that for a minute," Michaelson said.

"No sir—I was just thinking about the day Lieutenant Lucas signed in."

Michaelson knew what Easy meant. He too was hoping that Virgil and Rogers would have a better tour than Lucas's had been. "I'm sure that you can be some help to them."

"Yessir. I'll do what I can," Easy said, shuffling paperwork—his eyes locked on to Michaelson's. "Hope I'm better at it this time."

Training picked up momentum, and the necessary assignments were made. The old-timers in the platoons were still tentative around the two new officers—feeling them out. And the replacements had been assigned to the vacancies in the shorted teams.

The entire detachment spent the few available days relearning demolitions, weapons, fire support, immediate action drills, rappeling, map reading, prisoner handling, and a healthy ration of cross-training. Each night one team went out on a mock mission with at least one extra NCO from the detachment staff and one of the experienced officers acting as evaluators.

During the patrols the evaluators simulated actions or casualties and rotated lower ranking LRPs into leadership positions. They all knew that leadership in depth might prevent the kind of disaster that had happened to the lost team.

The hours were very long for all, but Hollister seemed to be driven, getting by on very little sleep and trying to be involved in every bit of the training. Captain Michaelson watched but didn't interfere. He had been around long enough to know that Hollister could gauge the difference between pushing hard and taking on too much. He was more than satisfied with Hollister's performance and the high quality of the training that the teams were getting.

The choppers settled onto the LRP pad and disgorged two teams, one from each platoon, that had been out on heavy ambush patrol followed by a downed-chopper security simulation. Hollister and Captain Shaw had gone along as evaluators. As the teams cleared the pad for the mess hall and cold beer, the two officers compared notes.

"What do you think, sir?"

Captain Shaw dumped his rucksack onto the pad and put his rifle across the top of it. He pulled out his notes. "I've got plenty of things to cover on these two missions, but most of them I can roll into a general after-mission debriefing. I just have one that needs attention. It's Theodore. PFC, isn't he?"

"Yessir. He's in Sergeant Camacho's team. Problem?"

"Well, on the move he is pretty good. He doesn't let anything get by him. He moves well and he's a damn good map reader. I killed the team leader and the APL on one leg of the hump and made him the acting patrol leader. He was organized and knew the mission cold. The transition was smooth and his leadership skills are pretty good for a PFC."

"So? What's the problem?"

"It's nighttime. I watched him. He doesn't sleep and he's as shaky as they come. I think he's spooked. I think he's tryin' real hard to cover for it."

Hollister knew what Shaw was talking about. He had seen some of that too, but tried to convince himself that Theodore would snap out of it. He took a pack of cigarettes and noticed the spots of light brown paddy water between the pack and the cellophane wrapper. Sticking his index finger into the hole, he found the single remaining cigarette and pulled it out. It was water-stained along its full length and was still a little soggy.

Captain Shaw pulled out a pack and offered a cigarette to Hollister. "You want to cut him loose and send him back to a rifle company?"

"I don't know yet. He's a good kid. Let me have a little more time with him. I'll see if I can fix it."

Shaw slapped Hollister on the shoulder and picked up his gear. "Well, it's your call. I don't need to tell you what kinda trouble a spooked team member can be. Anyway, I'm going to get a cold one and see what my in-box looks like. My job doesn't go out in the boonies with me. It just waits back here to ambush me."

Shaw walked toward Operations. On the way he passed Bernard, who saluted then broke into a double-time till he reached Hollister. "It's official. You are now a short-timer, sir."

"What?"

Smiling, Bernard handed Hollister a piece of official-looking correspondence. "It's your alert orders, sir. You're going back to Benning. Benning School for Boys."

"Benning? No shit?" Hollister said as he read the alert message. "I'm assigned to the Ranger Department. Hot shit! I was sweating out something like recruiting duty or ROTC or some damn basic training post." He smiled and folded the page.

Bernard looked down at Hollister's rucksack and web gear lying on the pad. "Yeah, well, you better get yourself a new issue of boonie gear, sir. That old stuff of yours'll never make it through Ranger School."

The thought of endless hours of patrolling with Ranger students cooled Hollister's mood, but he had always liked Benning in spite of the demanding training. Then he wondered how Susan would like Benning. It was one hell of a long way from a BA at Amherst to Columbus, Georgia.

A shower, some coffee, and a clean uniform, and Hollister got a weak second wind. He was beginning to burn out. He had been working hard and long. And he had lost more weight, and the circles under his eyes were more pronounced, but for the few minutes he had after the shower, his major concern was getting caught up on his correspondence. He was several letters behind Susan and owed his parents and two of his cousins some news.

He sat down at his field desk and tried to start a letter to Susan, but the sight of Lucas's name tape and Ly's picture triggered thoughts of Theodore. Shaw was right, Theodore might spook and jeopardize the safety of his team. But he knew that if he sent him back to a rifle company, he was sure that the shame would never leave Theodore.

He tried to put it out of his mind long enough to get to his letter, but just couldn't get into writing. He felt guilty about it, but he just had to do something about Theodore.

He cranked his field phone to see if Davis was over at the Operations tent.

Staff Sergeant Davis met Hollister on the steps behind the mess hall. Hollister waited for Davis to get a cup of coffee before they got down to business, finalizing the new team assignments. Captain Michaelson and the first sergeant would approve the NCO assignments.

"Got one other problem."

Davis knew without waiting. "Theodore?"

"Yeah," Hollister said. "He's a hard worker and he has a

good attitude, but he's a little rattled—and that's what's worrying me. What do you think?''

''Well, sir, I think he's spooked because of One-three's losses. He's okay during the day, but at night he gets time to think about it.''

''No shit.'' Hollister laughed a little. ''That sounds like every one of us.''

''I don't want to lose him. We just oughta lay more shit on him. If he's busier, he'll get more confidence and he'll outgrow it.''

''I can't take the chance of him acting crazy and getting someone else's root in a ringer,'' Hollister said.

''Make him an RTO. He'll be close to one of us and busy all the time.''

''What if he chokes up on a team leader in the bush?''

''Make him your RTO, sir.''

The light went on for Hollister. ''Bingo. Great idea!''

Davis smiled broadly.

Three days later the officers and senior NCOs assembled in Operations for a warning order—the stand down was over.

Captain Michaelson entered and all stood. At the wobbly podium in front of the group he took out his notes and motioned to Sergeant Marrietta.

Marrietta brought over an acetate overlay and pinned it to the operations map, aligning the tick marks on the overlay with the appropriate grid coordinate intersections on the map.

Across the top of the overlay the words OPERATION MARK TWAIN had been written in grease pencil block letters. The name only served to distinguish it from previous operations.

''Let me give you all a quick-and-dirty about this operation first and then I'll go over the details of the actual warning order,'' Captain Michaelson said. He then took off his wristwatch and laid it on the podium so he could keep track of time.

Marrietta handed out a stack of tracing paper overlays to the platoon leaders, the pilots, artillery, and Air Force representatives assembled in the tent.

''Seems like the VC have been getting wise to us and are getting ambush smart. The Brigade has been saturating the entire rice bowl with so many ambushes that the VC can't move in and out at night to do their business. They can't get the rice they need and they have had to come up with a new wrinkle.''

Captain Michaelson stopped talking long enough to take some aerial photos from Marrietta and hold them up.

"The VC have decided to get off the roads and trails and start using the large streams in the valley to move. Up till now, no one has been setting ambushes along the streams because there didn't seem to be enough traffic on them at night.

"We've been making the stupid assumption that the distances were too great for the VC to make the trips from the high ground to the valley floor by water during any one night. That was wrong.

"Take a look at these. You'll see that they show small boat and sampan movement at night." Michaelson handed the stack of photos to the team leader sitting in the front row, to start them around.

"A rifle platoon found small boats turned upside down, weighted and sunk under the overhanging brush along a stream bank. Seems like the VC are moving as far as they can at night, sinking the boats in the daytime, and hiding somewhere till it's dark again. Then they refloat the boats and continue their missions.

"Pretty slick idea, but we're going to put a stop to this—right now!"

Michaelson pulled a collapsible pointer out of his shirt pocket, extended it and tapped the tip to the lime-green areas of the map. "The Brigade's mission is to saturate the roads and trails in the rice bowl with ambushes to make things look like business as usual. But we will take our teams into the foothills and set up several ambushes on the streams flowing from the high ground.

"Now, details. First, the friendly situation . . ."

Hollister took notes through the warning order, getting the information he needed to prepare for the ambush patrols. The single item in the order that disturbed him was the lack of time. Time to get ready, time to get the patrol order, and time to give his patrol order and conduct the briefbacks.

The LRP detachment AO was divided up between the two platoons. They had seventy-two hours to prep and have one team on the ground per platoon. After that, fresh teams would rotate into each platoon AO every five days.

That meant a team would spend five days on the ground, come back and stand down for two days, and then prep for three days to go back in.

Michaelson explained that the two new platoon leaders—

Virgil and Rogers—would go along as patrol members on their first two patrols, assistant patrol leaders on their third, and then would lead their own patrols on the fourth time in. They would also go with a different LRP team each time out.

Since they would be setting up on stream banks, it was generally assumed that most positions near the banks would be on low ground and unsatisfactory. So the teams adjusted their loads and their routines to set up mechanical ambushes.

Five-man patrols would go in, find the right spot on a stream bank, and install an elaborate array of demolitions under the waterline. Finishing the setup, the teams would move to a vantage point above and away from the killing zone—on higher, more defensible terrain. Then, keeping the ambush site under observation, they would remotely detonate the explosives once VC boats moved into the killing zones.

Since a water ambush was unlikely to lead to captured weapons and equipment, it was decided that there would be no sweeps of the killing zones after executing the ambushes. There was little payoff for a team to sweep the stream bank for items that were either sunk or drifting downstream.

For the time being Hollister would oversee the operations of his old platoon—the second—and Captain Shaw would supervise the first platoon.

Captain Michaelson, true to his promise to break Hollister in on some of the other duties normally handled by Captain Shaw, tasked Hollister with handling the coordination between the Americans and the South Vietnamese. That meant Hollister had to go to the Province Headquarters to explain the LRP operation and get the specific Vietnamese Rules of Engagement.

Rules of Engagement were becoming complicated sets of instructions that told the Americans when they could shoot, at what, and after what coordination or permission. They ranged from free fire zones to firing only when fired upon and when positive ID could be made of enemy forces, including the identification of the enemy weapons that were being fired. Every American pilot and ground pounder hated the complex cover-your-ass rules. But it all belonged to the Vietnamese and they called the shots.

Hollister coordinated with Sergeant Marrietta to get a chopper to go to the Province Headquarters in An Hoa city. In the meantime he had to get maps of the area, the latest intelligence reports, meteorological data, aerial photos, Signal Operating

Instructions, fire support overlays, adjacent unit information, radio frequencies . . . and the list went on.

Hollister decided that it was time to tell Theodore that he would be his new radio-telephone operator. Then he would give Theodore some of the tasks to accomplish. Hollister smiled to himself. Theodore hadn't seen busy yet.

CHAPTER 16

Hollister walked into the mess hall to get a cup of coffee to take to his hooch. While he was filling his cup he heard the distinctive, gravelly voice of First Sergeant Easy.

"Sergeant Davis tells me that you got some troubles with young Mr. Theodore, Lieutenant. Anything I can help you with?"

"Yeah, a little. But it's nothing that I can't handle."

Easy got a cup and fished a cigar out of his pocket. He pointed it at Hollister. "Would you like one?"

Hollister shook his head. "Cigarettes are bad enough. Those things'll really kill you."

"It's Vietnam'll kill you, Lieutenant. Cigars just make the dying here a little bit more dignified."

"I'd just as soon go out without any dignity. Morning runs are hard enough without smoking those things."

"Sure y'don't want me to find another job for Theodore? I got some *special* details that I can put him on. You know that motivation is a specialty of mine, if you need the service."

"No. I'm going to be floating from platoon leader to patrol leader, and from what the Old Man tells me, I'll be getting a little Operations officer experience thrown in. I need an RTO who can also act as gofer. I'll use Theodore for that. Maybe that'll give him a little more self-confidence and settle him down some."

Easy bit the end of the cigar off and spit it on the floor. Lighting the cigar with his beat-up Zippo, he exhaled a huge puff of smoke.

"Jesus, Top! That'd kill a normal person!" Hollister waved the cloud away from his face.

"You know what his problem is, don't you? He's too smart,

Lieutenant," Easy said, stuffing his lighter back into his shirt pocket.

"What? What are you talking about—Theodore?"

"Yessir. It's a theory o' mine. I noticed it first in Korea—Inchon. The smarter ones—not the slicker ones, now, but the smarter ones—they got imagination. It can be a terrible thing for an infantryman. When it gets quiet or dark or both, their little minds start goin' kinda crazy and they start realizin' how fuckin' dangerous their situation is."

Hollister took a sip of his coffee and let Easy's theory sink in a moment.

"They can conjure up all manner of evil things that them little gook fuckers could be up to," Easy said. He knocked the ash off his cigar by snapping it with his finger. "The others, that ain't so smart, don't worry so much about what's out there in the night. They tend to get everything within reach ready for a fight and hole up for the night. But the smart ones see a river in their sector of fire and start worryin' about VC frogmen. They get into a large perimeter and worry about spider holes being inside the perimeter.

"Ya see, Lieutenant, the smarter ones ain't yellow, they just let their brains work on flight idle. Gets 'em in trouble every time."

"Your theory makes lots of sense to me, Top," Hollister said.

" 'Course, if you can keep 'em from getting spooked and killin' themselves or someone else, they turn out to be pretty good NCOs later." Easy stood, put his cup back on the side sink, and pulled his hat out of his pocket. "Hell, some of us turn out to be outstandin' first sergeants."

Hollister watched as Easy put his cigar in his mouth to conceal the huge grin under his hemplike mustache. "I'll keep that in mind. Maybe I've got the makin's of a top soldier in Theodore."

"Now, that might be stretchin' it a bit, Lieutenant," Easy said, placing his hat on his head and glancing at his watch. "By your leave, sir? I've got to be getting back to that fuckin' in-box. If you think you need a fine field soldier out there—let me know. I'm losin' my mind in the paper war."

Waving in acknowledgment, Hollister smiled.

Thinking about what Easy had said about Theodore, Hollister walked back to his hooch. He decided against telling Theodore himself. He was sure that Theodore would suspect that something was up if he were to get that much personal attention from an officer. He made a mental note to let Sergeant Davis simply tell Theodore of his reassignment as a matter of course. That way Theodore would think that it was just part of the reorganization.

On his bunk Hollister found two letters from Susan, a military-looking envelope, and a bill from his bank. The bills never seemed to stop. There he was in Vietnam, and he was still making payments on the uniforms that he had bought in OCS.

He was only making about two hundred dollars a month in OCS, and still he had to buy new fatigues, boots, TWs, khakis, greens, blues, and a wide array of insignia and other items before he could pin on his lieutenant's bars. At payments of fifty-one dollars a month, it would still be another half year before he was all paid up.

He looked at his watch to see if he even had time to sit down with Susan's letters. He didn't—too many details to get done. He decided to open the official-looking one.

Its return address read: *For Official Use Only, Department of the Army, Secretary, The Infantry Center, Fort Benning, Georgia.*

Inside was a sheaf of letters and brochures to welcome him to the Infantry Center. Every piece of paper had a replica of the single-bayonet patch with a "Follow Me" slogan or a statue of an infantryman leaning forward, waving for soldiers to follow him.

The top sheet was a form letter from a colonel welcoming Hollister to Fort Benning. It suggested that he fill out all of the enclosed forms and let the housing office know his requirements.

Requirements? On-post housing? Of course, if he and Susan were going to be married, they had to get on the waiting list for available on-post housing.

He sat down. He hadn't thought about all the things that were involved in getting married and showing up at Fort Benning with a *dependent*. And how would Susan take being referred to as a "dependent wife"?

His mind started to run through the things that would be some sort of shock to her. Army words like *commissary* and *dispensary*, and all the acronyms, hundreds of them! She was a writer, but calling their car a *POV* was going to take some getting used to. He would have to teach her to recognize rank insignia, when to stop the car for retreat. She would be exposed to the world of the Officers' Wives Club. He shook his head at that thought.

Hollister started getting apprehensive. Thinking of Susan and Fort Benning at the same time was giving him some idea of the differences between her world and his. He had been to her's without too much difficulty, but she was in control there.

Now he would ask her to live in his, and he had no control over it. Everything in his world was logical, planned out, structured, regimented, based in tradition, and very static. Things didn't change. Soldiers like him would come and go, and Fort Benning would be the same as it was when George Patton and George C. Marshall were stationed there.

His mind started to spin with the volume of things that he had to do and think about. The clock was ticking and soon they would be on the ground in the foothills west of An Hoa. He had things to do. He needed a beer.

He rapped on the tent frame because it was customary, even though Captains Michaelson and Shaw could see him through the dust-clogged screen. "Sir, you got a minute?"

"Get in here, Hollister," Shaw yelled out.

He entered with the packet from Fort Benning in his hand. "Heads up!" Shaw pitched him a cold San Miguel.

Hollister caught the beer but dropped the envelope.

"Well, well . . . what have we here? 'On behalf of the commandant, let me welcome you to the Infantry School. . . .' " Captain Michaelson mocked the standard welcome. "I've received one or two of those packets myself."

"That's why I came by, sir. I'm over my head with this." Hollister picked up the envelope and raised the forms. "How much of this stuff do I actually need to fill out and send them—and how soon?"

Shaw threw a church key to Hollister. "I once worked for a colonel at Fort Bragg who used to take all the paperwork that was left over on his desk on Friday afternoons, stuff it in an envelope, mark it 'Forward to: U.S. Army Alaska,' and send it to the Message Center.

"I finally asked him what he was doing. He told me that anything that was important would find its way back to his desk at Fort Bragg. The rest would die a natural death. I asked him why he did it every Friday. He told me that he didn't want anything on his desk to make him late for Happy Hour."

Hollister laughed. "That mean I should send this stuff to Alaska?"

Michaelson took the papers from Hollister and rapidly sorted. He ended up with a large stack and a short stack. He raised the short stack. "Fill these out. These are important—housing request, checking account application, club card application, and an application for night school at American University's extension courses. That's all you need to keep you afloat. Everything else they can track you down and beat you up for."

"I don't have to fill out that application for membership to the Post Rod and Gun Club?"

Michaelson looked up. "I'll take care of your marksmanship training, and those river ambushes will give you a chance to bag your limit. So, finish that beer and get on with the business."

Back in his hooch, Hollister sat at his desk filling out the forms while Lieutenants Virgil and Rogers got ready for their first LRP patrols.

The hooch space was so cramped that Rogers finally gave up and took all his field gear outside to check everything for completeness and rerig it.

The field phone, back in working order, rang once, and Hollister retrieved the handset from under the completed forms. "Hollister, sir."

The Duty RTO in the Operations tent said, "Sir, there's a chopper inbound in zero five to pick you up to go to An Hoa city."

"Oh, shit! Okay. Thanks," Hollister said. He hung up and looked for his notebook. Getting up, he found his holstered .45. Putting on the pistol belt and finding his hat, he cranked the field phone and got the Operations RTO. "Do me a favor and call Captain Michaelson's hooch and let him know that I'm heading to An Hoa. Tell him I'll be back ASAP."

By the time he hung up, the distinctive popping of the blades of an approaching Huey chopper was audible.

"Virgil, you seen my map case?"

Lieutenant Virgil reached up on his locker and pulled down Hollister's folded map case. He handed it to Hollister. "I didn't want it to get lost under all my shit."

"Thanks. I'll be back in time to hear the patrol orders. If something holds me up—go ahead without me. I don't want to short the teams a minute of prep time if it can be avoided.

"And Virgil, this time's a free ride. Just watch and soak it up. I know you did a good job honchoing a platoon, but there are some tricks here that these NCOs can teach you. Let 'em, okay?''

Virgil smiled and nodded. "Wilco, sir."

The chopper got louder and Hollister stepped through the door. "Be back as soon as I can." He kidded, "Don't move the CP."

"Airborne, sir!" Rogers yelled to Hollister's back.

Hollister got within range of the chopper's rotor downwash, took his hat off, rolled it and stuffed it into his pocket. He stopped short of the chopper pad to allow the pilot, who was making a downwind approach, to spin around—into the wind—and nail the bird onto the pad.

It wasn't a slick. It was a clumsy-looking, overloaded, nose-low B Model Huey gunship—a hog. For all the grace and power that the Huey C and D model slicks had, the hogs were a strange cross between a chopper and a tank. Low on their noses were the barrels of miniguns or 40mm grenade launchers. On both sides of the smaller cargo compartment doors, large pods held an assortment of rockets.

The crew chief was sticking his head out of the chopper, looking at something behind the aircraft. He was also talking to the pilots over the intercom—acting as extra eyes for them.

The chopper settled, taking its weight off of the forty-four-foot-wide rotor disk. As it did, the skids seemed to spread under the strain.

The pilot's hand slipped out the side window and signaled for Hollister to cross around the front of the chopper and get into the right door.

Reaching the right side of the chopper, Hollister found that Captain Iron Mike Taylor was flying alone. A door gunner was also missing.

Hollister opened the door, leaned into the cockpit area, and slipped on the flight helmet that Taylor handed him. As he climbed over the armored seat panels and under the cyclic, it occurred to Hollister that much of the first week of flight school must have included the correct way to get into the seat of a Huey. There just seemed to be no graceful way to do it and not end up sitting on the four-point safety harness.

Flipping the microphone down to a point where it just touched his lips, Hollister wriggled his shoulders to adjust the two shoulder belts. He stuck his foot out and stepped on the floor-mounted intercom switch to test his helmet out and to talk to Taylor. "You all run out of slicks today, sir?"

Captain Taylor was looking back over his shoulder at the crew chief. Without taking his eyes off the soldier who was working on the rocket pod, he answered Hollister. "Tryin' to kill a couple of birds at one time.

"This one's been in maintenance for a new engine and some linkage replacement. They just got all the guns and pods back in working order about an hour ago. I need to take her out for a check flight, and I have to go see Colonel Minh for the Aviation battalion," Taylor added.

"Fine with me. I've never been in one of these babies—truth be known," Hollister said.

"I know. You've been avoiding my offer for months."

"I notice that you haven't taken me up on my invitation to come out on one of our patrols either, sir."

Taylor turned back around, looked at Hollister, and laughed. "Okay, smartass, I guess we're even. Hold on a sec." Taylor looked back toward the crew chief. "What d'ya say, Chief—we okay back there?"

The crew chief raised one hand from behind the pod, made a V with his fingers, and replied, "Be about zero two and we're ready to go, boss."

Taylor reached down to the collective on the left side of his armor-plated seat and slowly rolled on the rotor RPM to increase it toward takeoff speed. Taylor kept an eye on the twin needles on the tachometer.

While he was waiting, Hollister looked around the inside of the chopper. It was an older model that had seen plenty of service. There were empty holes where some of the duplicate copies of instruments were supposed to be. In the business of helicopter maintenance, they called it cannibalization. Paint was worn off all the surfaces normally handled by the pilots and crew. And even the instrument panel and the controls were worn.

The first time he had talked to Iron Mike about how complicated all the dials, switches, and instruments looked, Mike told him that it was really easy. "All you do is strap yourself in, touch all the shiny buttons and leave the dull ones alone."

Looking up, Hollister was surprised to see sets of homemade gun sights hand drawn on the windscreen of the chopper with black grease pencil. Although the chopper had an articulated, collapsing mechanical sight, the homemade sights were there should a pilot find himself with a simultaneous need to shoot, fly, and communicate—hasty sights for busy pilots.

"Okay, sir," the crew chief said from inside the chopper.

Taylor nudged the rotor RPM from flight idle to takeoff speed. "Comin' up."

The crew chief looked back out the left door again and then scooted over to the right to do the same. He replied, "Clear left, clear right, sir."

"Okay, folks, let's see if we can get this barge off the ground."

Taylor pulled some power into the collective and watched the instruments. "We are fully loaded and the damn air density is fucked today. So, hold on."

Taylor lifted more collective and pushed the left pedal to counter the torque that he was adding to the rotor shaft. The chopper got light on its skids, but they didn't come off the ground. He tried it again and it still didn't break fully from the ground.

Captain Taylor leaned forward and looked above and around him. He spotted the smoke from the burning shitters across the base camp and gave it a little right pedal while he tried again. The nose shifted to the right, putting the chopper directly into the wind, which was light and gusting.

"Hold on. I'm going to drag this pig up into the sky."

He pulled up on the collective, pushed forward on the cyclic control between his knees and pushed the spongy left pedal toward the tiny Plexiglas chin window.

The chopper started to creep forward but not up. Taylor kept trying; the skids scraped along the LRP pad and then started to bounce.

Finally the bounces got higher and farther apart. When the chopper was about three feet off the ground, it seemed to relax and started to fly.

Taylor made a quick scan of the instruments, laid the cyclic over to the left and made an ascending left turn.

"You can relax now. We call this flying. I was getting tired of the thought of having to drive this pig all the way to An Hoa," Taylor said. "I knew it would fly. It just wouldn't hover."

"How the hell is that possible?" Hollister asked, confused.

"I'll explain it to you sometime if you buy the beer."

"Okay, you've got a deal, 'cause I wouldn't believe it if I hadn't just seen it."

"The impossible is routine for us. Hell, why do you think women are so fuckin' crazy about Army aviators?"

As they made the fifteen-minute flight to An Hoa, Hollister looked out to the rice fields and beyond at the hills where the ambushes would be set up. The valley was wide and green. The area was cut into squares and rectangles that defined the centuries-old rice paddies. At the corners of the squares were the thatched huts, in clusters that made up the hundreds of hamlets.

The structures were usually placed next to the water source that flowed nearby and on the worst possible land. The good, arable land was reserved for the rice. The lumps, wrinkles, and knotted spots were where they put their homes and livestock.

Hollister thought about the rice farmers. Like his parents, they lived by the seasons and the weather. They went to bed each night hoping that the weather would not turn so sour that it would destroy the crops. And at the end of the growing season they all would worry about the market price of their harvests.

But no one was raiding the farms and confiscating the crops in Lansing, Kansas. And people weren't worried about their children being killed in battle—at least not in Kansas.

Maybe that's why he was there—to keep it from happening in his country.

"Beautiful from here. Isn't it?"

Snapping out of his reverie, Hollister heard Taylor's voice over the headset. He stepped on the intercom switch. "I was just thinking about how much this place has in common with my home back in the World."

"Difference is that these folks have never known peace, and yours have never had an air strike put in next to their sweet potatoes."

Hollister nodded. He felt saddened by it all.

While Taylor requested landing instructions, Hollister looked down at the traffic on Highway 1.

The two-lane highway stretched the length of Vietnam and had been dubbed the "Street Without Joy" by Bernard Fall. It was clogged in both directions by villagers and farmers, not one empty-handed. Some of them were already so far from their hamlets that they must have started long before he woke up that morning. Hollister knew how hard it was to live off the land, but he thought that doing it in a war zone must break a person's spirit.

While Captain Taylor finished the last entries in his logbook, Hollister twisted out of his seat, unfastened the Velcro straps holding his chicken plate, and placed it back inside the chopper.

The crew chief waited for the blades to stop turning and walked out to the end of one with a metal hook, a foot and a half long, attached to a length of red fabric strapping. The soldier snagged an eye on the very end of the wide chopper blade with the hook and let his hand slip down the strapping. Then he walked the blade parallel to the long axis of the chopper, pulled down on it and wrapped the strap around the narrow part of the tail boom. Once the crew chief was satisfied that the blades were safe from sudden winds or buffeting caused by other choppers, he stripped off his shirt and went back to his toolbox. Hollister could see the pride the soldier took in keeping his machine in shape for safe flying.

Taylor spotted Hollister watching the crew chief and smiled. "He's the best. Had to do some real slippery wheelin' and dealin' to get him away from that lift company over at Pleiku. Cost me a case of booze to get him reassigned. There ain't another crew chief in the battalion who could keep this pig running."

They started to walk across the dirt airfield that sat next to the Province Headquarters compound. "You know this guy Minh?" Taylor asked.

"I've met him once. He looks like some kind of character out of 'Terry and the Pirates.' "

"Word has it that he's a heavyweight with the Viet bigwigs in Saigon. He's got family connections and money. He's got a lot more power as a colonel province chief than he would have as a major general division commander." Taylor stopped walking, looked ahead at the compound, and laughed. "And the housing situation is better, too."

They stopped in front of the ornate and overprotected ARVN compound. The central building was French in design and had wide steps leading to a landing. The landing supported six columns that held up the overhang of the red-tiled roof. Flanking the front door to the headquarters building were two guard posts that each served as an enclosure for two ARVN soldiers in starched American-style fatigues, spit-shined boots with white laces, and patent leather Sam Brown belts with white trim. Each soldier had a brass whistle attached to a chain on his shirt pocket and wore a brightly polished helmet liner that had been squeezed to fit closer to his ears.

The building sat inside a compound within a compound, the two compounds separated by rows of barbed wire and coiled concertina wire. The only entrance into the inner compound was through a guard post manned by six ARVN soldiers who were wearing more protective combat gear, steel helmets, and oversized flak jackets. Two of them manned an M-60 machine gun, and the other four were armed with pump shotguns.

The soldiers snapped to attention and rendered rifle salutes to Taylor and Hollister, who returned them. Taylor sarcastically whispered to Hollister, "Amazing. 'Bout the only damn thing they can do without needing to take a break."

An ARVN sergeant ushered Taylor and Hollister through a cramped hallway filled with desks, soldiers, and file cabinets, to a waiting room just outside Colonel Minh's office. In broken English he asked if they wanted something while they waited. They declined and took a seat on the wooden benches, the only furnishings in the concrete-floored room.

As they waited, Hollister pulled out his map and drew a grease pencil mark around the area that they would be operating in. He had thought about doing it earlier, but the chances of losing the map case had made him wait. He was sure that he never wanted to have to send the word up the chain of command that they couldn't conduct combat operations because he had lost the map with the outline of the operational area and other tactical control measures on it.

Around them the relentless Vietnamese chattering echoed in the building. It seemed like dozens and dozens of voices were talking excitedly and yelling over phones and radios with bad connections. Taylor shook his head with contempt. "Never heard a language like this one. Sounds a lot like ducks fucking."

The doors to the colonel's office swung open. Hollister looked from the doors to Taylor and back to the doors to see if it was possible that the slur could have been overheard. Taylor didn't seem to care, so Hollister decided not to worry about it, either.

A Vietnamese aspirant—the equivalent of a third lieutenant— gestured back into the office. "Good morning. Colonel Minh will see you now, gentlemen."

Taylor looked at Hollister, surprised at the aspirant's command of the English language. "Good . . . Thank you."

Inside, Taylor and Hollister stopped in front of Colonel Minh's desk. He had his back turned to them and was speaking rapidly over the phone—in Vietnamese. He kept it up for just a moment too long. Hollister wondered if it was just to keep them standing and waiting.

Hollister looked around the room. The walls were adorned with plaques and awards and certificates. Hollister couldn't read the Vietnamese, but recognized that Minh had been to some French military schools.

Hollister's eyes wandered from one cheap, handmade Vietnamese enameled plaque to the next until he recognized a familiar document. It was a Certificate of Completion from the Infantry Officer's Advanced Course at Fort Benning. The name in Old English lettering was Captain Le Van Minh.

"Good morning. Please forgive me," Colonel Minh said as he hung up the phone and swiveled around in his chair.

Taylor saluted. "Sir, I'm Captain Mike Taylor and this is Lieutenant Hollister."

Colonel Minh returned the salute, nodded and made a sweep with the same hand to point to the two chairs flanking Taylor and Hollister. "Please sit down. Would you like some tea? Or something cold to drink?" Without waiting for a reply he spat rapid-fire instructions to the Vietnamese aspirant.

"I was told that you would be coming today. How can I be of service?" Colonel Minh asked, looking at Taylor.

Captain Taylor pulled an aviation map from his flight suit. Hollister pulled his out too. "We need your okay to operate in the western part of your province, Colonel."

Colonel Minh stood, picked up a pencil from his desk, and walked to a wall that held a large map.

Hollister disliked the man as much as he had the day he saw him drive into the compound. He was affected, and everything about him smacked of an immorality that Hollister couldn't pinpoint. He surprised himself at how the sight of Colonel Minh made him uncomfortable and angry. He wondered if it was his expensive, silly-looking uniform, or his hair—long and greased into place with some strong-smelling pomade. He did know that he felt uncomfortable about Minh's fingernails, which were long and lacquered. Hollister was embarrassed by how it made his skin crawl.

The two Americans stood and moved to the map. Taylor let Hollister take the lead.

"Colonel, we need to operate in this area," Hollister said, tracing an imaginary loop around the area that they hoped to have okayed.

"Oh, that area. That will not be a problem. It is a very bad place. There are no good Vietnamese there."

Taylor looked at Colonel Minh. "You mean that there are bad Vietnamese in there?"

"Only bad—only VC. Many times my troops have tried to

clear it. But the VC either left the area for a short time or they placed many mines and booby traps in there. My brave soldiers take many casualties.''

The aspirant entered with a tray. Colonel Minh waved the two Americans to the low table and couches in the far corner of his office. ''Ah, the tea is here. Let us sit. We can have overlays made of your AO.''

While they moved to the coffee table, Colonel Minh spoke rapidly to the aspirant. Hollister tried not to make eye contact with Taylor because he was sure he would laugh at his earlier comment about ducks fucking.

The aspirant kept nodding as the colonel spoke. As he did, he took the glasses of hot tea from the tray and placed them on the table.

Hollister looked down at the tea. It didn't look particularly appetizing. It was light brown like American tea, but had what looked like flat worms floating in the bottom. He tried to convince himself that they were only strips of tea leaves.

The aspirant placed a container of very grainy-looking sugar on the table and a ceramic vase that contained a light beige liquid that looked like heavy cream or evaporated milk.

Sitting back on the couch, the obese colonel spooned several heaping spoonfuls of sugar into his tea and then poured the thick-looking creamlike liquid in on top of it. He spoke rapidly to the aspirant and stirred his tea for a long time. Putting the spoon down, he raised his glass to the Americans in a toast. ''To our victory.''

Taylor and Hollister followed suit, raised their glasses, repeated the toast, and then brought the tea to their lips.

The aroma of the hot tea was not too unpleasant, but it was not Lipton's. Hollister pursed his lips to keep the strips of tea from slipping into his mouth and then sipped the tea. It was bitter and very hot. In all, it wasn't as bad as he had expected.

''So, does this mean that we have a free fire zone to work in, Colonel?'' Taylor asked.

''Yes . . . yes. To be sure,'' Colonel Minh replied with extra emphasis.

Hollister reinforced the question. ''So the rules of engagement for this area are unrestricted? Ah, we can fire on *any* targets? Is that right, Colonel?''

''You can shoot anything in that area. It is a dangerous area.''

''Good. I'm glad we came to talk to you. We want to take no chances,'' Hollister added.

Taylor looked at his watch. ''Well, Colonel, if you don't need any more information from us, we will let you get back to work. We are sure you must be very busy.''

The three stood. ''Thank you for the tea, Colonel,'' Hollister said. ''Our Brigade Liaison Officer will bring the exact overlay to your Operations officer this afternoon, after the final details are worked out—if that is okay with you?''

Colonel Minh nodded, then clapped his hands once. The aspirant ran in from the outer office. ''He will show you out. Thank you for coming to see me.''

Taylor and Hollister saluted Minh and left.

CHAPTER 17

"Shelton tells me that you're getting to be quite the aviator," Captain Taylor said over the intercom as they flew back toward the base camp.

Hollister spun his head around and looked at Iron Mike. "You kidding me? I have less than an hour of straight and level flight time logged."

"Well, let's work on that." Taylor took his hands and feet off the controls and said, "You got it."

Surprised, Hollister lunged for the pedals and the cyclic. The nose of the chopper shifted left then right then left again as he tried to equalize the pedal pressure with both feet. As he did, the chopper started to sink and airspeed reduced. Hollister reached down and pulled up on the collective a bit. The nose pulled to the right.

"Easy, easy, Ranger. Damn! You guys must just play hell with women," Taylor said.

Hollister nodded his head. He forced himself to make smaller corrections, to take his eyes off the instrument panel and look off to the horizon for a reference point. He had learned from Shelton to pick a point on the horizon that was on the course and fly toward that. The farther away the reference point, the easier it was to use as an aid to flying.

"Better," Taylor said. "What do ya say we find a place in the new AO where we can hurl a couple'a three-point-five rockets at the ground? S'pose you can hit Vietnam with a rocket?"

Hollister looked over at Taylor and smiled. He was excited by the thought of being able to go along on a firing run in a gunship.

They flew for several minutes and entered the near edge of

the new operational area that they had cleared with Colonel Minh. "How's this look to you?" Taylor asked.

Hollister pulled his map out and flopped it open on his knees. He cross-checked their location to be sure that they were in the free fire zone. Once he had double-checked, he answered, "Fine with me. But I think we ought to stay away from the waterways—where we'll be settin' up the ambushes."

"Okay, it's a big chunk of real estate. Shouldn't be any trouble avoiding the blue lines," Taylor said as he looked down at his own map. "Looks like there's a steep wall and a rock outcropping on that hill over there," he noted, raising his finger to point it out.

Hollister nodded and tried to make a level turn to the left. His control was good but his focus wasn't.

"Look above and behind you, below you, and where you're going. Last thing you want to do is make a textbook left turn and fly into some other dumbshit flying near you. You gotta fly inside this thing but think outside it if you want to keep from meshing rotors with some other chopper jock."

Once they reached the area that Taylor had picked out, he instructed Hollister to fly a lazy loop around it. He explained that he didn't want to start firing practice runs without making a visual search to make sure that no one was there—Rules of Engagement or not.

Finally, Taylor took control of the chopper. He spotted a small uprooted tree hanging by its roots on a slope that had eroded into a low spot between two small hilltops. "We'll start way out from the target and pretend that the friendlies are to the west, our right, of that tree," Taylor explained.

"You mean you don't start by shooting at the tree?" Hollister asked.

"Not if we can avoid it. I want to pull the impact off target in a direction I can control and walk it in toward the friendlies. Especially since I haven't bore-sighted the armament on this bucket since it came out of maintenance. And there's too much chance that the rockets can hook or slice and land on the green in some young platoon leader's back nine."

With some concern in his voice, Hollister asked, "You mean that the rockets aren't that accurate?"

"Well, there's a lot involved. You could have a fin screwed up on one, or the rocket motor could be damaged, or the wind conditions could trick us—or I could just be a shitty shot!"

"So I should worry more when I'm on the ground and I call for chopper support?" Hollister asked.

"No . . . lemme show you. It isn't as bad as you think," Taylor said to reassure Hollister.

Taylor made a hard banking turn, causing the blades to pop, and headed back toward the target. Once he was level again, he sucked the collective up under his left arm, gave it some left pedal, pushed the cyclic forward and laid the nose over—rapidly picking up airspeed. "I don't want to be over the target any longer than I have to."

Taylor picked a spot on the ground to the left of the upside-down tree, then squeezed off the trigger on his cyclic. A sudden whoosh sound filled the cockpit as a pair of rockets left the pods behind the cockpit and passed by the left and right doors only inches away from their heads.

Hollister watched the small flames coming out of the tails of the rockets as they converged in front of the chopper. Just as they were about to hit the ground a few feet apart, Taylor yanked the nose of the chopper up, dumped it over to the right, and was soon heading back to where he came from.

Hollister snapped his head to the left and followed the rockets until they impacted to the left of the tree, exploding into a thick gray-brown bubble of smoke and hurling chunks of debris into the air.

Taylor reached up and made a small tick mark on the Plexiglas window next to his shoulder to remind himself where the rockets had hit with respect to the homemade gun-sight marks. He then leveled the chopper out at the end of what became a 360-turn over the simulated friendly positions and nosed the chopper over again.

Hollister's excitement grew with the chopper's acceleration. Just short of the firing point for the first pair, Taylor fired a second pair of rockets. This time the rockets streaked closer to the upside-down tree, but about twenty meters short of it the rockets crossed over each other and started to increase the distance between them.

"Shit—too early!" Taylor mumbled over the intercom.

"But the right one was closer to the tree," Hollister said.

"Actually, it started out being the left one and became the right one. Makes a difference if you're going to make some pod adjustments."

"You sure that you want me to see all this?"

"Just you hang on, Ranger. You'll see some amazing shit as soon as I get the hang of this new equipment setup."

Taylor fired a third pair and snapped the nose up and right again. The two rockets flew straight and true to the target. Both hit exactly on the tree and obliterated it.

"See? Nothing to it."

"You expect me to be surprised?" Hollister asked.

"You aren't?"

"You gotta remember that I've been on the ground when you guys have dotted i's and crossed t's for me," Hollister said. "I was just concerned that you were going to show me it was just luck."

"Slick drivers need luck. Gun pilots are just born with hand and eye coordination that make them the envy of women worldwide. Not to mention the saviors of many an undeserving grunt."

"Sir—heads up! Over your left shoulder!" the crew chief broke in on the intercom.

Taylor snapped the chopper to the left, sliding right while doing it. "What ya got?" he asked calmly.

"I saw some movement in the tree line just on the far side of that clearing . . . the one with the trail running east-west through it. See? Down by that slash in the trees? Our ten o'clock now."

"Hot shit!" Taylor said. "We might just bag ourselves a bad guy here." He handed his map to Hollister. "Check me out, Jim. Make sure we're still inside the free fire zone."

Hollister looked out his side window and then back at the compass on the instrument panel. He reoriented the map to make sure that he had a good fix on their location. "Looks like we're easy inside the AO by over four klicks."

"Let's go huntin', then," Taylor said as he made a quick descending right turn, dumping altitude and picking up airspeed, to come back around in a wide arc that would turn the nose toward the sighting.

"Okay, keep your eyes down on the darker areas. Try not to look up at the horizon. It'll be dark in the tree line, and if your eyes aren't dilated, you won't see shit down inside the overhang there."

"Yessir," Hollister responded. He felt the motion of the chopper's descent in his stomach, and his heart was pounding with uncertainty.

"Looked like a couple of them carrying weapons on the

northwest corner of the clearing. Soon as I saw them, they were running—they just dove into the tree line," the crew chief said.

"Let's see if we can smoke 'em out." Taylor reached down to the two banks of miniswitches on the console and turned on two of the radios. "Jim, you call this in to your folks and I'll call mine. You're on the right freq.

"I want everyone to know where the fuck we are, in case one of those little fuckers gets lucky and adds a chopper to the notches on his belt," Taylor said.

It was the first time getting shot down had come to Hollister's mind.

"There they are, sir!" the crew chief yelled. "Nine o'clock . . . under the overhang."

Taylor turned the chopper toward the tree line and smoked over the treetops with all three of them searching for a glimpse of the VC.

As they cleared the tree line with no one calling out a sighting over the intercom, Taylor yanked the nose of the chopper up and did a hard pedal turn, spinning the chopper on its own vertical axis, allowing it to start back and down again without making a wide turn out of the area.

Just then Hollister yelled out, "Holy shit—trucks! There's a truck down there." He pointed over the instrument panel at a spot on his side of the chopper.

Tilting the chopper right and down, Taylor turned toward the spot and looked across Hollister's side of the chopper.

"I only got a quick look at it, but it looked like the back of it was filled with weapons and covered with a tarp. Maybe two VC crouched down next to the right front tire," Hollister added.

"You got that sixty on 'em?" Taylor asked the crew chief.

"I'm on it, sir," the crew chief said. He had already taken the free machine gun and hung it out the door by a bungee cord.

Taylor brought the chopper to a hover over the spot that Hollister had pointed out and alternately pressed the pedals gently while he moved the cyclic in a tight circle. The action caused the hovering chopper to blow the treetops around in various directions so the three Americans could see down to the ground.

As the tree cover parted they clearly saw a truck and two old Vietnamese men huddled near the front. Taylor hovered lower, knowing that the debris being blown around by the downdraft would limit the ability of the men on the ground to fire on the chopper. He knew that he was doing it right when he saw the Vietnamese shielding their eyes.

"Weapons? Anybody see any weapons?" Taylor asked hurriedly over the intercom.

"There's something under the cab, too," Hollister said.

Just then the canvas covering the load blew loose and flipped back, revealing the contents. It wasn't weapons. It was wood. Firewood. Just firewood. Nothing else. They weren't VC.

Taylor looked over at Hollister. "Shit! I'm gonna go a little lower. Look around for me. I don't want to get fixed on these two clowns and find out that a VC division is on the next hill adjusting its sights to blow our asses out of the sky."

Hollister started scanning the area around them for other threats, while the crew chief kept the muzzle of his machine gun on the two Viets. Taylor bled off a little more altitude, till the chopper was only about four feet off the ground.

The Vietnamese cowered in terror, then they suddenly acted as if no longer afraid. Hollister wondered if they recognized the chopper to be American.

They kept shielding their eyes and stood—palms to the chopper. They seemed to be trying to tell Taylor and Hollister that they had no weapons, that they were noncombatants.

Taylor spoke up. "Those aren't weapons under the truck. Just some more wood. Fuck!" He shook his head in disgust. "We could have killed these two without ever knowing they were civilians.

"Okay, let's get out of here. Let's let these two poor suckers get their firewood home. Chief? I'm coming out and back."

The crew chief put down the machine gun and looked behind the chopper. "You're clear up and back, sir."

All the way back to the LRP pad Taylor bitched about the near disaster. He was angry that he'd believed the area was clear without cross-checking it himself.

Hollister was a little confused by what had just happened. But he was happy that the firing run had not ended as badly as it could have. It would have been easy for them to shoot first and find out the mistake later. He wondered if the Vietnamese could have been VC posing as woodcutters. But from the air they wouldn't have been able to prove it, and killing them wouldn't have confirmed anything. He was sure that if they had killed the woodcutters, there would have been a picture of another new widow in one of their pockets—another Ly. He felt a little nauseous.

* * *

Inside Operations, Hollister, Michaelson, and Taylor sat in a small circle smoking and drinking cold Cokes while they listened to Sergeant Lam, the Vietnamese interpreter, talking in a high-pitched, rapid-fire whine to someone at the Province Headquarters Operations section.

No one knew what Lam was saying, but he was clearly getting very frustrated by what he was hearing. Finally, he slammed down the receiver of the field phone.

He turned to Captain Michaelson. "They say you must be wrong place," Lam said, looking at Captain Taylor.

"Whoa, cowboy! We were fuckin'-A at the coordinates I said we were at!" Taylor yelled, jumping to his feet.

"Did someone talk to Colonel Minh?" Hollister asked Sergeant Lam.

"They tell me cannot bother Colonel Minh. He very busy," Lam answered.

Michaelson rubbed his hands across his face and squeezed the bridge of his nose with his thumb and forefinger. "Okay . . . okay. Thank you, Sergeant Lam," he said. "This isn't your fault. We'll try to get this sorted out between Brigade and Province Headquarters."

Sergeant Lam executed something that was a cross between a salute and a bow, then exited as fast as he could get out of the tent. Hollister assumed that he felt badly about not being able to solve the problem, and wanted to avoid the loss of face.

Captain Michaelson turned to Taylor and Hollister. "Gentlemen, my opinion of today's goat-roping exercise is that it sucks! I've seen this kind of shit happen before, and I don't know why there aren't more damn dead South Viets than there are. They make us clear every fuckin' thing with them, but they don't seem to give a shit about their own folks!" He pulled his hat out of his pocket and slapped it across his palm. "Let's all go get some chow. We can work on this a bit more later. We're not finished with it by a long shot."

Taylor and Hollister walked across the compound toward the chopper pad.

"Well, thanks for the shooting lesson anyhow, sir," Hollister said. "Sorry it turned out like it did."

"Yeah, that's 'bout as pissed off as I've seen Michaelson in all the years I've known him."

"How long's that been?"

"We went through jump school together and he went off to

Bragg for green hat training. I went to flight school. Then we were in the advanced course together at Benning, and then I was flying outa Can Tho, down in the Delta, when he was an advisor with the zips.''

"He's a good man," Hollister said.

"More than you know. Plenty of folks on the ground can fuck you over and leave you hanging out to dry when you're flying a gunship. Michaelson never did that to any pilot that I ever heard of. He didn't call us 'less he needed us, and when he used us he didn't try to become a little king on the other end of the radio. He's a good man, all right. He ever needs anything from me, anything—he'll damn sure get it.''

The two reached the chopper, and the crew chief jumped out and started to untie the chopper blades.

Just then Bernard burst out of Operations whistling and waving his arms over his head. Once he got Taylor's and Hollister's attention, he broke into a run and skidded to a stop in the grit on the LRP pad.

"Sir," Bernard said to Taylor, "the Old Man sent me out here to get you before you lifted off. He wanted me to tell you and Lieutenant Hollister that he just got off the horn with Brigade, and the ambushes have been pushed off for twenty-four hours till they can get this Rules of Engagement flap squared away." He turned to Taylor. "Oh, ah . . . and you're supposed to call your Operations shop before you leave, sir."

Taylor motioned to his crew chief. "Whoa, tie 'er back up, we aren't going anywhere just yet."

Bernard looked to Hollister for some acknowledgment.

"Okay, thanks, Bernard. Tell the Old Man we got the message.''

"Yessir," Bernard said as he saluted, then he turned on one heel to run back to the Operations tent.

"So—buy you a cup of coffee?" Hollister asked Taylor.

"Ain't gonna be as good as aviator coffee—but it's better than swamp water 'n' Kool Aid," Taylor said, slapping Hollister on the back.

The cooks were just starting to prepare the dinner meal in the mess hall when Hollister and Taylor entered. They found the coffee and a place to sit as far away from the kitchen area and its deadly humidity as they could get.

Taylor took off his aviator sunglasses and dropped them on

the mess table. "Ya know, I just don't know who the hell is luckier—us or those gooks out there."

Hollister shook his head in silent sympathy. He was still trying to absorb the near-miss situation.

"You can bet your ass that I'll set my own fuckin' Rules of Engagement from here on out."

"Sounds okay, if it doesn't jeopardize your folks doing it."

"It's not like having friendlies on the ground. Either you're down there to tell me that you've checked their ID cards or I can just pull up, go around, and take a second look."

The door to the orderly room opened and filled with the bulk of First Sergeant Evan-Clark. "Can a man get a cup'a coffee in here, or have officers drunk it all up?" he said loud enough for Taylor and Hollister to hear.

"Okay, Top," Hollister said. "Get yourself a cup and come over and tell us one of your stories from the Crimean War."

Easy filled his cup and turned to Taylor and Hollister with a big grin under his mustache. "Okay, okay, Lieutenant. That was a low blow. I give up. I should know better than to be accusin' no junior officers of nothin'—I always end up regrettin' it."

Hollister picked up the cue. "If it weren't for officers, Top, they wouldn't make coffee, since we all know that senior NCOs operate off of ninety-proof blood and raw meat."

Easy put his cup down on the table and raised his hands in the air. "Okay, sir. I surrender. We are a sorry lot that keep the army on track and winning wars while you all are out wearing fancy uniforms and wooin' the ladies. It's a thankless job—"

". . . but somebody's got to do it," both officers chimed.

Easy's tone turned serious. "I heard about the woodcutter thing this morning. I'm happy it didn't turn out for the worst."

"Thanks, Top," Captain Taylor said. "It coulda been real bad news."

"Yessir—those guys just mighta knocked down your chopper with them sticks," Easy said, bursting into laughter.

Taylor smiled. "First Sergeant . . . I won't forget this soon. There'll be a time when you'll need something from us aviators, and we just might be too busy to help you out."

Easy picked up his coffee and smiled. "Well, sir, I can see I'm outclassed here. But it always does take at least two of you to gang up on a poor old hardworkin' first soldier like myself. Anyway, time is money, like they say out in that hippie commie civilian world, and I have to make some piasters for God and country."

Easy raised his cup as a gesture of respect, "By yer leave, sirs."

Taylor and Hollister said good-bye and watched Easy disappear back through the door to his office.

"He's really a good man to have around. Even if it means putting up with his bullshit," Hollister said.

Taylor shook his head. "We're running out of guys like him. We've lost two really good old-timers in the Aviation battalion in the last month alone. They can see that this Vietnam thing isn't going to go away soon, and they're tired of it. All of them already have a couple of wars under their belts, and they don't want to check out in this one."

"Can you blame them?"

Taylor pushed his empty cup away from him and stood up. "No, I can't."

Hollister was just stepping in the door of his hooch when he heard the strangest sound. He stopped right in the doorway and soon realized that it was his replacement, Virgil. He was lying faceup across his bunk in his olive-drab boxer shorts—sound asleep and snoring. Hollister remembered that Virgil had not slept in the hooch the night before, because he had pulled Duty Officer, which required him to be awake in Operations and to periodically make the rounds of the compound to make sure everything was in order.

Hollister had pulled many nights as Duty Officer. The dull nights when there were no teams on the ground were spent catching up on letter writing and drinking lots of coffee.

On nights when teams were out, the Duty Officer could count on having only the early part of the evening for letter writing. For the remainder of the evening the pattern was quite different. On the half hour, the teams checked in with a commo check or a sitrep. Just waiting for each team to call in provided enough tension. But it usually got more intense as the evening progressed.

Very often a team would call in that it had enemy movement around it. That was not unusual. If they even had an idea where a team was located, they would move in close after dark. Then they would lay up until the wee hours of the morning and either attack or probe for the team's exact location.

Usually, a report of movement forced the Duty Officer's first decision. Should he tell Captain Michaelson? The answer depended on if Michaelson was asleep or not. If he was in his office or just up somewhere in the compound, he would let the Duty Officer know where he was. If he had gone to bed, he usually told the Duty Officer to wake him up at the earliest indication of enemy movement.

Most of the time Hollister and the other Duty Officers waited a little bit because they didn't want to keep calling wolf, which could turn the CO into a zombie after a few nights. It was a judgment call that came from experience on the ground and a little questioning of the team leader's opinion of the threat.

In all cases, whether they woke the Old Man or not, a messenger would be sent out to the chopper crews, who were sleeping in their birds so they could inject their own preflight needs into a possible contact launch. The sleep problem wasn't as critical with the pilots and crews since they were rotated every night and only pulled standby for the LRPs every other night.

Hollister looked outside and checked out the sun. He decided that he would take some writing paper outside and get some letters written while he had a few minutes to himself. He could use the sun, and it would keep him from waking up Lieutenant Virgil.

A large bunker with a reinforced, sandbagged roof occupied the center of the compound only a few yards from Hollister's hooch. It was built to withstand the few mortar and rocket attacks that they had had since the compound was built. Hollister spread a poncho liner out on top of the soggy sandbags and stretched out.

He wore a pair of cutoff PT shorts, his shower shoes, and his floppy hat to shade his eyes. He reminded himself that he wanted to scrounge a pair of aviator sunglasses from one of the pilots. His last pair had suffered a mortal wound when he sat on them a month earlier.

The letter to Susan was both easy and difficult to write. He loved to talk to her, even if it was in a letter. The hard part was telling her that they were going to Benning—if she still wanted to marry him. He thought that he would try to prepare her for Fort Benning with a little bit of light comment about her backing out of the marriage.

He had a number of questions for her. Now that they knew where he was going to be stationed, what did she want to do? Would she quit her job in New York or was it something that she could do from Georgia? He knew how hard she had been working—trying to get a byline. He was worried that the move would cause her to lose ground. Nothing came to mind that might compensate her.

And what about the wedding? They hadn't talked about where they would get married, or how, or who was going to be invited, or a date. The more he wrote, the more questions occurred to him. He flipped over a second page and jotted down question fragments that were coming to him faster than he could form the questions in the letter.

"Loo'ten'an?"

Looking around, Hollister found Sergeant Lam standing there awkwardly—as if he did not want to be seen.

"Yeah, Lam. What is it?"

"I mus' talk."

Hollister sat up and spun around. He reached for a cigarette and offered one to Lam. Lam took it and made a little bow. "So, what is it?"

Hollister suspected that this might be a *feeling out* conversation. He had been through this with interpreters before. They tended to be scam artists who were capitalizing on their limited command of the English language. Assignment to the LRPs kept them out of direct combat, and they were close to base camps where they could scrounge or even steal. It was a much better deal than being an interpreter for a rifle company that spent most of its time in the field.

In Hollister's experience they frequently acted amiable and friendly, and then hit up the Americans for little favors—like buying them things at the PX or converting black market Military Pay Certificates into Vietnamese piasters.

Lam seemed to be uncomfortable with whatever he had on his chest. Hollister tried to get him to wind down by pointing out a spot on the bunker for him to sit.

"I talk to some friends. Oh, I cannot tell you name. They tell me som'thing you need to know. You mus' not tell ARVN soldiers or Colonel Minh that Lam tell you. Okay?" Lam said, looking at Hollister with fear.

"Okay. I promise not to tell any ARVN that you told me. But what is it?"

"Woodcutters. This mo'ning. Woodcutters. They steal wood."

"Okay. I don't understand what that means. 'They steal wood'?"

"Wood belong Colonel Minh. They much afraid Colonel Minh and ARVN soldier. Happen before, too."

Hollister thought he understood what Lam was saying but wanted to make sure there was no misunderstanding. "The wood they stole was owned by Colonel Minh? He owns the trees? He owns that land?"

"Yessir. He own."

Hollister's blood pressure spiked. He leaped to his feet and ran across the compound to the orderly room.

Inside, Hollister didn't wait for Bernard or Easy to tell the CO that he wanted to see him. He just busted in.

Unflappable, Michaelson looked up from the map at Hollister's outfit. "Is this an invitation to the beach or what?"

"The fucker's using us as his own private army, sir!"

"Whoa, whoa, whoa, mister," Michaelson said, holding his hands up to calm Hollister down. "Sit, I'll get Bernard to get you something cold to drink and some more suntan lotion."

Hollister looked down, realizing that he did look ridiculous in his shorts and shower shoes. "Sorry, sir. But I just found out that Colonel Minh owns that real estate that he cleared for us to fire up. He's using us to keep the wood poachers out of his property!"

"What?"

"Lam, who doesn't want to be quoted, told me."

"Let me get this straight. Minh gave you and Captain Taylor free fire clearance knowing that there would be poachers there? On his own land?"

"Sure looks that way. Lam said that it's happened before with ARVN troops."

"And I'm sure that the fuckers counted the bodies as VC!"

"So, what do we do now? Blow the whistle on this guy?"

"Well, we don't keep it to ourselves, but we don't print it in the *Stars and Stripes* either. It'll blow all out of proportion in the wrong direction. You haven't worked with the South Viets enough yet. It's a lot like oiling down snakes and then trying to braid them."

"But how are we going to operate in there?"

"You let me take this up the chain of command. And you get over to Province and act dumb. Tell Colonel Minh that someone sighted friendlies in the AO, so we would like him to reevaluate his Rules of Engagement."

Hollister made a face.

"Can't be helped. He'll adjust the Rules of Engagement to

incorporate some requirement like confirming weapons or
something, and we will go about our business with our own set
of rules. Just don't let on that you know about his property.''

CHAPTER 18

Word must have gotten to Province Headquarters long before Hollister did. He was met by the colonel's aspirant and told that Colonel Minh was away on an aerial reconnaissance. Hollister learned that the Rules of Engagement had been revised to account for disobedience of the Vietnamese civilians who appeared incapable of avoiding an area that had been put off limits because of the Viet Cong danger.

The aspirant also said that the LRPs and their supporting units could fire on any targets that they could identify as VC or on anyone carrying weapons or on any structures that were combat in nature—such as bunkers.

When Hollister left the Province Headquarters, he found that Colonel Minh must have left his command post without taking his gaudy jeep or his equally ornate helicopter; both were parked in the compound, and had been since Hollister's arrival.

Hollister promised to himself never to trust another ARVN or Vietnamese official again. Not when it came to the lives of his people or innocent civilians—not again.

Hollister returned to the LRP compound, met with the detachment staff and passed on the new Rules of Engagement. In a meeting of all the officers and senior NCOs, Hollister noticed that Captain Michaelson was uncharacteristically abrupt.

"Okay, this is how it's gonna be. You get fired upon—you return it. You eyeball bad guys—fire 'em up. If you're in doubt and have the time—you do what you can to develop the situation and confirm the ID before you return fire. If you can't—walk or fly away. *Don't* fuck around—walk away! There'll be other days." Captain Michaelson raised his voice even higher and asked them, "Is that *perfectly* clear?"

"Clear, sir. Airborne!" all replied in unison as they got to their feet to leave.

"I need to see Hollister, Virgil, and Rogers," the captain said.

The three lieutenants moved over to Michaelson and waited for him to speak.

"Sit," Michaelson directed. "We are going to modify our insert schedule and go about this operation a little more deliberately. We have lots of new faces and we have this raw spot with Province that we don't want to aggravate.

"I've decided that we'll pull back on the saturation in the AO. I don't want too many teams on the ground right now. So, we'll only have two teams on the ground at any one time until we get the machine working a little bit better.

"Each platoon will insert the first team on its roster tomorrow morning—Captain Shaw has the details for you. We will only stay in the AO for four days per patrol unless a team makes contact or is compromised. They'll come out and two more will be inserted in different locations on the same day.

"We'll keep this up till we put some notches on our belts or until we confirm a dry hole.

"I'll be alternating with Captain Shaw, briefing and inserting teams. So, while one of us is giving mission briefings, the other will be inserting teams. That will give us two fresh insert packages all the time if the chopper support can keep up.

"Lieutenant Hollister will be shadowing Shaw's every move, and Sergeant Davis will be the acting platoon leader of the second platoon until Lieutenant Virgil gets his cherry good and broken. Sergeant Kilmerson will do the same thing with the first platoon until Rogers gets squared away."

Michaelson looked at each of them, making solid eye contact. "Questions?"

No one spoke up.

"Okay," Michaelson said as he looked over to the Operations section. "Captain Shaw? They're all yours."

Virgil and Rogers were with their teams, getting ready for their first patrols, so Hollister was alone in his hooch for the first time in days. As he was about to lick the flap on a flimsy envelope addressed to Susan there was a knock on the door frame.

"Lieutenant? Got a minute?" Easy asked.

"Yo, come on in, Top."

Easy entered with a handful of paperwork.

Hollister looked at his watch. "Don't you ever take an evening off, First Sergeant?"

"I had to get these signed by you before all hell breaks loose tomorrow. You know, Lieutenant, it'd be a lot easier to be the first shirt in this lash-up if we didn't have to run patrols—then I could find all the junior officers when I needed them. And I could corner the dickhead troops that always seem to be out on a mission when I have to get them over to the aid station for their damn shots."

Hollister took the papers, supply forms, and requisitions that he had to okay. Since the detachment was a provisional unit, without a complete staff, the officers had to double up with additional duties. Hollister was not only a platoon leader, he was also Supply officer, Vector Control officer, Reenlistment officer, Signal Security officer, and some others that he usually forgot until the first sergeant brought him some form that had to be signed or some regulation that he had to read.

He pointed to the bottle of scotch on his desk. "How 'bout a touch, Top?"

Easy made a theatrical gesture of denial, then softened. "Well, I'm not one to touch the spirits while there's still work to be done, but I guess that I can make an exception this time. There *is* a chill in the air."

Hollister played along. "Yeah, a serious cold front might be moving in from Nepal, Top. Better help yourself."

Easy poured himself a hefty drink into a seemingly clean mess hall cup and took a sip.

Without looking up from the papers, Hollister asked, "What's the story with the Old Man? He's seems a little outa sorts, Top."

"Oh, you can be happy that you ain't him. He got his ass handed to him by that goddamn paper shufflin' brigade XO today."

Surprised, Hollister looked up at Easy. "What for?"

"Well, seems as though he went to the Brigade Commander about the province chief, and the General told Cap'n Michaelson that the XO would take care of it. When the XO got the mission, he chewed out the Old Man for going to the General with the problem and for lettin' the pilots go nosin' around out there in the first place."

"What? Well, what did he say about the province chief?"

"Seems like the brigade XO got wrapped around the wrong axle and it's now a big fuckin' flap between him and Cap'n Michaelson."

An NCO once told Hollister that being a commander is like being a tent peg for every asshole in the chain of command to pound into the ground. In leadership classes they called it *risk of command*—meaning that a commander was responsible for everything his unit did or failed to do.

"I wouldn't worry about it, Lieutenant. The Old Man isn't going to let that jerk of a colonel get to him. He'll sort this thing out one way or the other. You know Cap'n M."

Michaelson had taught Hollister a lot about *moral courage*. For him it had been all theory in leadership classes back at Benning. But Michaelson had made Hollister understand it by always fighting for what was right, even if it meant personal risk or professional loss.

Hollister knew that he could count on the Old Man.

Theodore banged on Hollister's door frame. "Sir, it's 0430. You wanted me to come get you up."

With some difficulty, Hollister came out of a black void. He rubbed his eyes, threw his poncho liner back, and swung his legs over to the floor. The smothering pressure of sleep tried to keep him in the black, but he knew that he had to get up.

"Sir . . . did you hear me?" Theodore yelled.

"Yeah . . . I heard you. Go over to the Ops tent and find out where we are. You know? Choppers, weather—the whole nine yards."

"Yessir. Where will you be when I get it?" Theodore asked.

"Somewhere in Vietnam—I think you'll be able to find me."

As Theodore ran off, Hollister opened his eyes for the first time. The only light he could see was coming from the mess hall. He found his cigarettes on the top of his footlocker and lit one. The smoke cut into his lungs while satisfying some urge that was greater than the discomfort. Exhaling, he reached over and turned on the light in the hooch.

He realized that Virgil and Rogers were already up and gone. He smiled to himself—he remembered his first cherry patrol with the detachment. He didn't sleep a wink the night before either.

There were lots of indignities in Vietnam, but the shitters were way up on the top of the list. Even having to take a crap in the field was more pleasant than having to use a two-holer.

Cautiously, Hollister sat down on the rough plywood box that covered the half drums used to burn off the human waste they collected. It occurred to him that he had never sat on any shitter in Vietnam where his feet actually touched the floor or the ground.

The door swung open with a squeak. "Mornin', Lieutenant," Easy said as he dropped his trousers and took the hole next to Hollister.

Hollister grunted in acknowledgment without looking at Easy. He just looked out of the screened-in upper half of the GI outhouse at the figures moving silently in the darkness. "They're awful quiet."

"I been in outfits like this my whole life in the army. An' I found out one thing about volunteers in dangerous jobs," Easy said.

"What's that, Top?"

"If they could leave and go back to a safer job—and no one would know that they'd quit—they'd all up and disappear.

"Ya see, after they get in an outfit like this and find out how fuckin' terrible it is, they stay because they don't want to be called quitters and they don't want to let each other down. I may give 'em hell because they sometimes play crazy. But they are 'bout the best soldiers I've ever served with."

Hollister thought Easy might be right. It was funny. He wasn't sure why *he* stayed. He was just sure about some reasons why he didn't leave.

"Lieutenant? You in there?" Theodore yelled, rushing up to the shitter.

"Yes, Theodore. What is it?"

"I got that info you wanted, sir."

"Can it wait a few minutes till the first sergeant and I finish our little meeting in here?"

Hollister had rerigged his web gear for the command-and-control chopper. He might need some items to survive if the chopper went down, but he certainly didn't need all the combat gear that he normally took on a patrol.

The extra frag grenades were replaced by smoke grenades. And an ammo pouch holding an URC-10 replaced a canteen. The pouches and the pockets in his uniform held survival gear and eleven magazines of M-16 ammo—all tracers. The tracers would allow him to mark targets from the chopper.

The magazines only held seventeen rounds each. It was a safety measure that came from stories of soldiers who had filled their magazines with twenty rounds only to find that the com-

pression caused the spring to lose its ability to push a round into
the receiver of the rifle to be chambered by the bolt—resulting
in a stoppage. That could mean disaster. Hollister had never
actually seen it happen, but didn't want to take the chance.

Suddenly, Lieutenant Virgil ran into the hooch to lock a packet
of letters into his footlocker. Their eyes met. Virgil took a deep
breath. "I don't mind tellin' you that you couldn't drive a greased
hat pin up my ass with a sledgehammer."

Hollister smiled. "Let me tell you something—every minute
you spend with NCOs like Davis and Camacho is like life in-
surance. They're the best. You just try not to make noise, follow
their lead, and soak up everything they do. You'll be okay."

"I hope you're right. Well, guess I better get out there."

Virgil started for the door.

"Hey, Virgil," Hollister said. "Don't worry. When we put
you in today—we'll be gentle."

The coffee was sour in Hollister's stomach as he strapped into
the left-hand seat on the nylon bench in the cargo compartment
of the C&C helicopter. He picked that seat because it would
give him the best vantage point for what was happening on the
ground, while allowing him to talk face-to-face with Captain
Shaw, who sat in the jump seat that was installed just behind the
aircraft commander. Unlike the bench seat, the jump seat faced
perpendicular to the direction of flight.

Shaw pressed the transmit button that was part of the cable
running from his helmet-mounted mike to the avionics system
of the chopper. "How do you hear me, folks?" The noise of
the chopper vibration and the swishing sounds of the blades
spooling up could be heard over the helmet mikes when any
crew member keyed his mike.

"I got you wide, loud, and ugly," Shelton said.

"Thanks," Shaw replied with a faint hint of playful sarcasm.
He looked over at Hollister and raised a questioning thumb in
order not to tie up the intercom while other cross talk was going
on between crew members.

Hollister gave a thumbs-up.

Shaw reached up to the recessed box that held a bank of
miniswitches. He tripped all the other switches off, turned the
operations frequency on and called Operations radio. "Quarterback, this is Three. How do you hear this station?" Hollister
could hear both sides of the conversation.

The RTO's voice was strong and clear—transmitting over a

tall antenna that was erected just behind Operations. "This is Quarterback Base, I hear you five by five. Over."

Shaw thanked the RTO for the commo check and spun around as much as he could with his seat belt fastened to look over his shoulder. He looked out the right door at the insert ship that had Team 2-3 in it, led by Sergeant Davis.

Vinson raised his radio handset to signal that he had heard the commo check, and keyed the handset twice to let Shaw and Hollister hear that his radio was transmitting.

Shaw gave Vinson a thumbs-up.

Virgil thought that it was meant as a good luck gesture and returned the thumbs-up.

Hollister had been in and out of the hills west of An Hoa so many times that he could almost tell the time of day by the cloud cover or absence of it. That morning, wispy white thready clouds rose from the dark green trees that covered the foothills.

The clouds were typical. Hollister always hated the cloud cover when he was on the ground. It kept the cold damp morning air close to the ground and kept the sunrise from warming him up quickly. And sometimes it was so thick and so low that it prevented the gunships and the Forward Air Controllers from doing their jobs—because they wouldn't fire into areas where they couldn't clearly identify the friendly positions and enemy targets.

Cloud cover was one of the reasons that they put teams in early and then extracted teams later. Inserting didn't present much of an identification problem. Until the team was on the ground, the pilots were not so skittish—anyone shooting at them from the ground was fair game.

If supporting fires were needed after a team was inserted, their location was rarely in question since the air crews had just put them in and had seen the terrain from skid level.

They had just finished a false insert on the first LZ and were going to insert Team 2-3 on the second LZ. The level of tension in the slicks, C&C and the gunships hung over every message. The closer they got to the LZ, the less laughing and joking there seemed to be on the radios and intercoms. Each man was privately making deals with his own God to just let him through that insert without the worst happening. Plenty of sacrifices were promised—going to church, quitting bad habits—the list was endless.

Hollister watched Shaw closely. Too soon, Hollister knew, Captain Michaelson would expect him to take over putting teams in and taking them out. That would put him in the jump seat calling the shots. He would be responsible for the teams and the air crews and the choppers. The thought made his sour stomach tighten in anticipation.

Just as hard to face was the responsibility for the coordination of the supporting fires and the Air Force aircraft. Even though the pilots of at least half of the aircraft outranked him, he would be in operational control of their employment. He would decide when to execute all of the steps of the operation plans and, more important, what adjustments to make when things went sour.

He looked at Captain Shelton and out and across at Iron Mike Taylor in the lead gunship. He was happy to have experienced pilots like them. At least he would be able to count on them to steer him out of harm's way.

"You watch the tree line for me. I'm going to try to keep my eye on all the aircraft and the team," Captain Shaw said over the intercom while making eye contact with Hollister.

Hollister nodded in acknowledgment.

"And keep that list of preplanned fires in your fist. If I need to call for arty, I don't want to have to go looking for it."

"We're ready—on final," Gladiator said over the intercom.

Hollister thought that Shelton must have transmitted the same message over the radio because the gunships peeled off and started to circle the LZ in opposing directions—screaming across the treetops.

Hollister looked out and below. The insert ship was just breaking over the leading edge of the LZ and starting its flare to slow and touch down. As it did, the chase ship continued to fly straight across the LZ a hundred feet above the insert ship. Reaching the far end of the LZ the pilot of the empty ship kicked it up and laid it over—hard right to double back and keep an eye on the insert ship which was down and skidding forward through the wet grass.

"They're down," someone said over the intercom.

Shaw reached up to throw the switch. Immediately Hollister and Shaw could hear the chopper cross talk.

Spotting the movement on either side of the insert chopper, Shaw announced, "They're out."

The C&C had reached a point at the far end of the LZ, but over five hundred feet above it. Captain Shelton made a wide, slipping left turn to put the C&C into a gentle left orbit which would allow him, Shaw, and Hollister to watch everything on the LZ.

Below them, the grasses on the LZ were blowing and swirling violently under the downwash of the insert chopper blades. The team spread out as each man ran for the nearest point on the tree line to minimize his time in the open.

"Comin' up," the insert pilot announced over the radio.

Hollister watched the chase ship fall in several rotor disks behind the insert ship, to be in the best position to snatch any survivors if the insert ship took ground fire on the way out and had to put it into the trees.

As the two slicks pulled out and up they gained airspeed and altitude to join the C&C in a long, lazy orbit around the LZ.

The two gunships continued to orbit the landing zone, but widened their circle to see if they could spot any movement or draw any enemy fire from any VC outside the immediate perimeter of the clearing.

Everyone was silent while they waited for Sergeant Davis to report the situation on the ground.

While it looked pretty tame from the back of a Huey, there could be a small war going on and no one would know unless one of the LRPs called contact over the tactical frequency.

"Three, this is Two-three. We are cold. I say again—cold insert. Over," Davis said in hushed and labored breaths.

Shaw turned to Hollister and smiled at the news, then responded to Davis's message. "Okay, Two-three. We're going on to the next LZ. We will be a holler away if you need us. Over."

"Roger that," Davis said, still hushed.

"Good hunting. Out."

Shaw reached up and switched the transmit switch off. "We ready to go to the next one?" he asked the pilots.

Hollister heard Shelton click the mike button twice—a yes.

Shaw switched the Operations radio back on and transmitted. "Quarterback, this is Three. Over."

A small voice answered. "This is Quarterback. Over."

"Three, Two-three is down and cold. We are going on to the next touch-and-go and then will be returning to your location to pick up One-two. Over."

The radio operator rogered Shaw's transmission, and the chopper made a hard right as the five-ship flight got back into formation to make a fake insert on the third landing zone of the day.

As they flew away, Hollister kept his eyes on the spot on the ground where he assumed Davis and Team 2-3 to be. He caught himself thinking about how they were doing and what they were starting to hear now that the chopper noises were fading.

It was nearing noon when Hollister and Captain Shaw stepped out of the C&C chopper back at the LRP pad. They had inserted two teams, been back to refuel once, made four false inserts, and had reconned two possible landing zones for future inserts.

Hollister's legs felt rubbery and his throat was dry. The two powder-dry biscuits that he had for breakfast were just not adequate to keep him going all day. But it would be a while before he would get to eat. There was still plenty for him to do back in Operations.

His own map in hand, Hollister cross-checked the locations of the inserted teams on the Operations map. It would prove very embarrassing for Operations to have the locations marked incorrectly when clearances for H&I fires were plotted or when a team called in a contact and the choppers flew out to the wrong location.

Captain Shaw handed Hollister a fistful of papers. "Here, you need to go over all this and fill out the ones that need input." They were intelligence updates, intelligence summaries, feeder reports for information collected throughout the Brigade, requests for map changes, and after-action report forms. Hollister looked back up at Shaw—puzzled and a little overwhelmed.

Shaw smiled. "You thought maybe my job was all caviar, champagne, and riding to the rescue? You'll soon find out that this ain't all sex and battle streamers."

The paperwork was followed by a quick cup of coffee, and then back in the chopper. That sortie was an aerial recon of landing zones and ambush sites with the leaders of the two teams that would be inserted next.

All the while, Hollister kept his radio on the detachment tactical frequency to monitor the two teams already on the ground, which had both moved to lay-up points away from their LZs to wait for dark. After dark they would move to their ambush sites and set up. Hollister knew there were plenty of chances for them to get ambushed or compromised before they settled in for the evening. They wouldn't leave his mind for a moment.

Somehow, the day had gotten away from Hollister, a fact he realized when he watched the sun setting in the mountains.

Back in Operations, he went over the list of notes he had taken. He could see that if he were going to keep flying the C&C, he would need more notebooks or at least a larger one. He decided that he would look for more rather than larger. His rationale was that if he lost a notebook, it would be best that it had the least amount of information in it.

Two team leaders and Hollister then sat around a map of the AO and discussed the LZs that they had reconned, and routes to and from them. He let them describe how they wanted to get to and from their ambush sites. Both sergeants picked routes that were bounded by easily distinguishable terrain features, a great aid to night movement. Routes through distinctive terrain were easier than walking on a football field in the dark. And unique terrain allowed pilots to more quickly identify targets and friendly locations.

Listening to the two team leaders, Hollister became comfortable with their terrain analysis and their selection of routes. They made good choices, which would minimize their exposure and reduce movement time.

Hollister released the team leaders to go back to their hooches, where they would complete their patrol orders. Before they left, he made sure that he knew what time they would be giving their patrol orders to their teams. Hollister, one gun pilot, one slick pilot, and the Operations officer or NCO would sit in on the orders.

Having everyone present for the patrol orders and the briefbacks helped to clear up the details that could easily get screwed up out in the bush. It also gave the pilots a chance to see the faces of the troops they would be lifting, get used to the voices they would hear over the radios, and generally be able to form a mental picture of just who was who and what jobs they had.

"Hey, you gonna eat or are you just operating off of last night's beer ration?"

Hollister turned around. Captain Shaw was standing there, hands on his hips and a cheap cigar in the corner of his mouth. "Yessir. Food sounds good, even if it is Kendrick's."

As they walked to the door, Shaw patted Hollister on the shoulder. "You're going to have to pace yourself and get some food in you or you'll find yourself coming up short out there in the dark some night."

As they sat in the corner of the mess hall, Shaw critiqued Hollister's actions. He was generally satisfied that Hollister was on top of everything. That was ninety percent of the job. "If you don't know what the hell is going on every minute, you can't make the right decisions. If you get behind the power curve, you'll get somebody killed.

"This is no different than what you've been doing for the better part of a year. You ground-guided forty grunts all over Hell and back as a platoon leader, and as a platoon and team leader here you've made the tough decisions that make the difference."

Hollister pushed his tray away and lit a cigarette. "Yessir, but it seems different up there. It seems so easy to screw up."

"It's a matter of confidence. The more you do it, the better you'll get and the more comfortable you'll feel. And I don't have to tell you that those folks on the ground want to hear lots of *comfortable* in your voice.

"If you sound like you got your head up your ass, you'll get them rattled on the ground and they won't help you do your job. So, even if you're having trouble—*don't* sound like it. There are plenty of folks up there with you that have a lot of experience. Need some advice—ask. They won't let you down."

Theodore shook Hollister's shoulder. "Sir? Lieutenant?"

Hollister looked around and realized that he had fallen asleep on the desk in his hooch. "What is it, Theodore?"

"Sir, Two-three's got movement. Sergeant Marrietta sent me over to get you."

Hollister was still lacing his boots up as Sergeant Marrietta finished briefing him on the details. "They've been reporting movement on the east side of their position." Marrietta grabbed a look at his watch. "And that makes it 'bout an hour and half now."

"Where's Captain Shaw?"

"Sir, he's up at Brigade S-2 for a briefing. I sent the runner to get Captain Michaelson, too."

"Choppers?"

"They're on five minute standby. The crews are in the mess hall giving a hand-off briefing to the replacement crews. But they're going to stay here until things quiet down or a pickup out at Two-three's location."

Theodore burst through the tent doorway. "Sarge, Cap'n Michaelson's over at the shower point. He'll be here soon as he can get dried off."

Hollister turned back to Sergeant Marrietta. "What's been happening—details?"

Marrietta picked up the radio log clipboard from the RTO, flipped back to an earlier entry, and read, "Team Two-three reported that they were moving to their ambush site at 1945 hours."

Hollister looked at the situation map next to the radios. On the acetate overlay, bits of information had been added in grease pencil. Someone had marked the frequencies, call signs, the challenge and password, and the time for EENT—End Evening Nautical Twilight. It read 1841 hours—it was plenty dark down in the low spots along the stream banks where 2-3 was moving.

Marrietta waited for Hollister to look back, and then continued, "At 2050 they reported reaching their objective area. At 2105 they reported site recon complete and that they were moving into their ambush position."

Marrietta flipped the page on the clipboard. "They reported closing on the ambush site at 2155."

He traced his finger down the page until he found the next entry. "And at 2200 they sent their first sitrep. At that time it was negative.

"Then at 2210 they reported movement two hundred meters west of their killing zone. It was along the trail on the near bank of the stream—closer to them."

"Was it coming from the direction they had just come from?"

Marrietta shook his head. "No, sir. They moved into position from the northeast."

"Any more?"

"Yessir. They have reported unidentified noise approaching them twice since then. And that whoever it was was not at all concerned about how much noise they were making."

"If they are making lots of noise, they must be deaf. How could anyone be working in that area and not know that we put someone down there this morning?"

The squelch on the table-mounted radio broke. "Quarterback, this is Two-three," a hushed but excited voice said.

Hollister picked up the pork-chop mike. "This is Two-six. What you got? Over."

"Movement getting closer. My guess is that they'll come up on the stream bank. It'll put 'em between me and my demo. We've got Claymores covering the area, but no real fields of fire."

Hollister closed his eyes and thought over the options. They couldn't trigger an ambush on an unknown force outside the killing zone. If they had to cut out, it would be bad to leave the demolitions that were in place along the waterline. He would have to make the call before Michaelson or Shaw returned.

He pressed the button on the mike. "It gets too flaky, you blow it all and head for your PZ." Then he had a thought. "Stand by one. Break. One-two this is Two-six. Are you moving? Press two for yes, one for no."

Hollister let up on the transmit button, and the aggravating hissing noise of the radio spilled from the small speaker. After what seemed too long, there was a break in the squelch and not a second.

That ruled out a map error where one of the teams might be moving near the other. Hollister continued, "Thanks, One-two. Hang tough. Out. Break. Two-three, this is Two-six. Just give me two for yes . . . you got any more movement?"

The squelch broke twice.

"Okay, partner. You suck it up. We're going to launch an extraction ship. I'll be in the air in five. Do what you have to."

The squelch broke two more times, letting everyone in the Operations tent know that Davis agreed and understood. Hollister turned around and almost ran over Captain Michaelson, who had been standing behind him during the entire radio traffic.

Michaelson adjusted his web gear and pointed to the doorway. "What are we waiting for, Ranger?"

CHAPTER 19

It felt like they were slicing through cooler layers of air as the chopper gained altitude on the way to 2-3's location. Knowing that it was only going to get colder before the evening ended, Hollister rolled down his sleeves and buttoned the top button on his fatigue shirt.

Looking out into the black outside the chopper, he felt the muscles in his gut start to tighten. It was unusually quiet in his headset, so he leaned back to look up into the overhead switch box to see what channels Captain Michaelson was monitoring.

Just then Michaelson leaned forward and transmitted a message as if he could see Davis's men out in the inky night. "Two-three, this is Six. We are en route to your location. Give me two breaks if you can hear me. One if negative. Over."

The squelch broke twice.

"You still got movement?"

Twice again.

"Can you talk?"

Once.

"Okay. You get your shit together. We're zero—" Michaelson looked over his shoulder at the peter pilot, who raised his left hand and four fingers. "We are zero four out of your location. I want to yank you out of your primary PZ. You copy? Over."

Two breaks.

"If you need to blow your Claymores, do it. If you don't, wait. But blow everything on the way to the PZ. Don't try to disarm anything. Hold on tight, Ranger. We're inbound."

Two breaks.

Hollister stared out into the darkness, looking for the small river. Finally he picked up the white slate color of the water and followed it to a tributary junction that identified a precise point on the ground. He snapped on his red filtered flashlight and oriented his map to the terrain.

The team was just inside the wooded foothills on the margin of the rice fields. Hollister tapped Michaelson on the sleeve and pointed at the area.

Michaelson had not been on the recons or the insert, so it was the first time he had seen the area. He looked closely at his own map to burn the control measures marked on his map into his head.

Without warning, the night chopper sounds were broken by Sergeant Davis yelling over the handset. Everyone stiffened at the sound of the first syllable. If he was speaking above a whisper, it was because they were under fire.

"Six, this is Two-three. We're being probed. We are taking no fire, but we've popped two Claymores." His voice transmission stopped abruptly and they heard the distinctive sounds of more Claymores detonating, and automatic weapons fire. Everyone in the chopper listened as the squelch broke once more, but only firing and grenade and Claymore detonations could be heard—no voice.

Hollister hit Michaelson on the arm and pointed out into the black where small fireballs and red tracers lit up the stream bank.

"Base, this is Six. Contact! I say again, Two-three has contact!" Michaelson said into the helmet mike. "Break, Two-three—okay now, tell me what you need."

The firing stopped and for a long moment the radio was too silent.

Nothing. In the C&C they all strained for any sounds over the radio while they watched the spot on the ground for more shooting. No radio transmission usually meant the worst. Hollister's stomach cramped up as he tried to push the thought of another wiped-out team from his mind.

It was Davis's voice that broke the silence. He was out of breath, but talking rapidly. "Six, this is Two-three. We have three seriously injured. I need an immediate medevac right now! Over."

"What is your situation? Are you under fire? Do you have contact or not?" Michaelson asked.

"Negative, Six." But the rest of the transmission was garbled, and Davis had let up on the transmit button on his handset.

Michaelson turned to look at Hollister to see if he had understood what was going on down on the ground. But Hollister wasn't sure and shrugged his shoulders.

"You're broken. Say again, Two-three. What happened?"

"You ain't gonna believe this. We spooked two water buffalo. They charged us!"

Michaelson turned to Hollister. "Oh, shit!" He pressed the mike button. "Two-three, Six. Okay. Let's go through this by the numbers. I don't want to get anyone else hurt. Are you clear of your ambush site? Are you moving?"

"Negative on the moving. We are still at the same location. Can't take a chance. I've got a back and a possible head injury that I don't think should move. I'm working on blowing a couple of trees for a one-ship LZ just east of my position. Too far to move to my primary PZ. Let me know and I'll mark. Over."

"Stand by."

Michaelson turned and talked to the back of Captain Shelton's flight helmet. "What d'ya think up there, front seat? You game?"

Shelton lifted a gloved hand, his thumb pointing skyward.

"Okay, Two-three. We'll bring in a slick to get your injured out. Give me a mark, now. Over."

"Stand by," Davis replied, still out of breath.

Hollister pointed down at the strobe light just east of the stream fifteen hundred feet below them.

Shelton flashed the chin light for Sergeant Davis to let him know that they had him.

"I think we are going to need a little help. You okay with some flares?" Michaelson asked.

"Rog on the flares. I could use the light," Davis replied.

Michaelson called Operations and laid on artillery flares to light up the area.

While Michaelson adjusted the flares, Shelton coordinated the upcoming actions with the other pilots on another frequency. Shelton then pulled the chopper out of its orbit.

The C&C quickly descended to treetop level to take a look at the new PZ that Davis was preparing. It was very tight, but enlarging it to a more comfortable size would take several more hours and cause other problems. Michaelson and the pilots decided to send in one slick to take out the wounded, and use the chase to extract the remainder of the patrol. That way each chopper would carry a light load, which was better than having one chopper pick up the entire team and then try to maneuver out of the tight PZ. Michaelson decided to take the risk of exposing both slicks to get them out.

After Michaelson announced the plan, the slicks and the C&C circled the team while the gunships prowled the treetops in a lower, wider orbit, trolling for ground fire.

Finally, Davis announced that they were ready for the first pickup—the injured.

Captain Michaelson directed the pilot's course and speed since the C&C had a better view of the small hole in the trees than the approaching chopper did.

Hollister held his breath as the slick slipped over the near edge of the LZ and settled into the center of a hole only slightly larger than its rotor disk.

No one spoke—listening and watching the area around the pickup chopper for any indication of trouble or enemy activity.

Then the radios crackled. "Coming up," the slick pilot announced.

The crews of the orbiting choppers watched as the slick pilot expertly brought his chopper to a high and dangerous hover and then rolled forward over the trees. As he gained speed and altitude, he called his progress. "Six, Two-three. WIAs are out. We are ready for the next lift," Davis announced.

Michaelson took a breath. "Okay, stand by. Gladiator One-nine, the chase ship is a minute out."

"Negative! Negative!" the chase ship yelled over the headsets. "I'm aborting. I got a chip light and a master caution. I might have to put it down. Lemme check this shit out."

Shelton's voice took over the radio cross talk. "Wave off. You got that clearing to your three o'clock?"

"Affirm. I'm going on over there and see what's wrong with this pig. If I have to park it—that's where I'll be."

"Guns?"

Iron Mike Taylor didn't even hesitate. "Gladiator, I'm going to widen my orbit to include the team and your busted slick. If you go down, we got you covered."

Shelton switched to the intercom to give Michaelson the setup. "Okay, the chase hasn't figured out what the problem is yet, but he doesn't want to be hovering over those kids and lose it all. We can go in and get the three remaining on the ground. We just gotta hope that the slick doesn't lose it while we're going in, but I can't wait. I don't want to leave them on the ground while we are fucking with a maintenance problem."

Michaelson clicked the transmit button twice and then

switched his radio back on. "Quarterback, this is Six. You copy our situation? Over."

"Good copy, Six. We've alerted the necessary stations. Over," Marrietta said from the base camp radio.

"Rog. Break. Two-three, we are coming in with the C and C to get you. We are zero two out. Dump what you can—we can use the weight break. Over."

"Wilco, Six. We're ready."

It went silent again as Shelton dumped the collective on the C&C, causing it to fall rapidly from its orbiting altitude to one more suited to approach the hole in the trees.

Hollister fingered his rifle on the seat next to him while Michaelson pulled out his Browning 9mm pistol, chambered a round, checked the safety and reholstered it, leaving the flap unfastened.

The door gunner reached up, grabbed the handles on the back of the M-60 and pulled the weapon down into firing position. He then took off his gloves and stuffed them into the neck of his flight suit to get a better feel for the weapon and the ammo he would have to handle. That done, he wrapped his fingers around the handgrips, his thumbs resting on the twin triggers.

Hollister looked down. The trees were barely feet below the skids as the chopper slowed to a crawl, pulling its nose high. After several seconds Shelton pulled the chopper to a full hover over the hole.

There was no room to make a normal landing—a gentle, controlled glide. Instead Shelton leveled out the chopper and dropped into the hole by letting the chopper settle into it.

The trees rose in front of Hollister's face. In the seconds before the skids touched the ground, the exterior of the chopper was a blur of activity. As the trees whipped around, Davis's remaining team members scrambled over the deadfall on the PZ and crawled toward the chopper.

"Fuck! Look!" the door gunner yelled over the intercom.

Hollister looked toward the margin of the landing zone. There, only a few yards away, was a huge water buffalo, bleeding from a large wound on his left side. In the flashing of the chopper lights and the white wash of the artillery flares, he looked terrified, threatening and unpredictable. He was disoriented by the lights and noise and it was clear that it wouldn't take much for him to charge the chopper while it squatted in the tiny clearing.

Hollister knew that they had to do something, but couldn't

until everyone was accounted for. He spun around to Davis. "You got 'em all in?"

Davis bobbed his head up and down.

Hollister relayed the word to Michaelson, who couldn't turn far enough to make eye contact with Davis. He registered Hollister's message and leaned over, slapping the door gunner on the shoulder. "Fire. Shoot him. Don't wait!"

As the door gunner opened up on the water buffalo, Michaelson gave the word to Shelton, "Outa here. Go! Go!"

The stumbling, terrified water buffalo took hit after hit from the machine gun. Its eyes flashed the whites in a show of panic. Every fifth round was a tracer that streaked from the weapon to the animal's flesh in a flash of red only extinguished by the animal's bulk.

The chopper strained under the nine-man load and slowly rose till they had nearly cleared the treetops.

Shelton leaned the cyclic forward to pick up some airspeed. As he did, the chopper sank and the blades cut into the trees with disturbing chopping sounds. In a few seconds the chopper started forward with even more of a sinking sensation.

He looked back. Crazed with pain and confusion, the wounded water buffalo thrashed wildly around the small clearing.

"He's still alive, sir."

"Shit! Poor fucker." Michaelson looked out. "Iron Mike, Six. Can you put that animal out of its misery for us?"

"If you got everyone up."

"Yeah, we're clear."

Remembering the other chopper, Hollister looked out several hundred yards at the troubled chase ship. The pilot had fallen into an orbit above the emergency landing zone that he had picked out, but he was still flying.

By then the C&C was picking up altitude and airspeed. As Shelton started a lazy left turn to head back, the gunships rolled in on the water buffalo, firing 40mm grenades at him.

After the second pass the animal lay on his side in the center of the small LZ with steam coming from his nostrils. Soon even that stopped.

It was well after midnight when everyone assembled in the mess hall. Michaelson had decided to hold the debriefing there in order not to distract the duty NCO and officer in the Operations tent. There was still a team on the ground, and it deserved the attention. Michaelson also wanted to allow those involved in the extraction to get something to eat or a cup of coffee during the debriefing.

Hollister found a chair in the corner of the room where he could listen and take notes on the table next to it.

Michaelson looked at the silent group of LRPs and pilots, focusing on the three survivors of the stampede. "Let me take a minute to tell you what I know about the rest of Two-three. But let me start by saying this was nobody's fault. Just a fluke. One I hope we don't see again.

"Clearing tells me that Doc Norris has a broken collarbone and a handful of broken ribs. He'll be okay, but he's short, so they are sending him back to the World as soon as they can.

"Vinson has a banged-up leg and a fractured wrist. He'll be back here for light duty in ten days.

"Lieutenant Virgil wasn't so lucky. He has a broken back and neck. They're pretty sure he won't walk again."

The silent room got even quieter.

Finally Michaelson said, "He would have made a real fine platoon leader. I'll make sure to tell him how you all feel."

Michaelson picked up his cigar from the edge of a mess table and relit it. He blew the smoke upward, as if to avoid someone in front of him. "Those fuckin' water buffalo cost us a lot tonight. Can somebody tell me how it happened? I'd like to try not to get in a fix like that again."

"I can, sir," Sergeant Davis said.

Michaelson looked at Davis, who was pretty beaten up—like he had been in a good fistfight. He stood up and turned to the larger part of the group to speak.

"If this hadn't been so serious, it would be funny. How they got to us is anybody's guess. Anyhow, we started gettin' movement on the trail between us and the stream we had rigged for ambush. We had no reason to believe that it wasn't folks—good or bad guys. We couldn't see 'em, but we could damn sure hear 'em."

Davis shifted his weight on what seemed to be a sore leg and continued. "Whoever they were, they were in a bad place for us to consider firing on them. So, I passed the word to let 'em go by if we could and blow 'em away if they came for us.

"It went okay for a while. It seemed like whoever was below us was just sorta milling around. I figured it must have been someone who didn't know we were in the area—and that they just might pass on by. Suddenly Vinson felt a jerk on his Claymore wire and he punched it off. He thought somebody was either trying to disarm it or turn it around. He didn't want to give them a chance to do either.

"That's when all hell broke loose. The water buffalo spooked and ran our way, hitting us like a couple'a buses. As fast as they were there—they were gone. And they were as close to bein' in a shit panic as I've ever seen any animal.

"I realized how bad the casualties were and passed the word to blow the ambush. I figured it would spook 'em some more and maybe keep 'em moving away from the water and away from us.

"I guess you know the rest."

Hollister entered the darkened, musty tent and stripped his shirt off. He didn't even want to know what time it was. He could tell by how he ached. His feet hurt from wearing his boots too long, and his waistline was sore from the constant rubbing of the rough fatigues against his hipbones. His eyes were burned from the cold night air in the chopper and the smoke-filled mess hall during the lengthy debriefing.

As he sat on his bunk, he inventoried the detachment's losses for the night. In addition to the loss of two good men, Captain Shelton had announced in the debriefing that the C&C would have to go in to maintenance to fix three bullet holes that the chopper took sometime during the extraction of Davis's team.

No one had ever been aware that they were being shot at, much less hit. It was an unnerving thought to Hollister—that he could be shot at and not know about it.

As Hollister unlaced his boots, he cradled the field phone in the crook of his neck and cranked the handle on the side of the case.

"Operations, Specialist Bernard, sir."

"Hey, Bernard—Lieutenant Hollister. Can you roll me out at 0530?"

"I can handle that for you, sir. But do you know what time it is now?"

"I don't want to know."

"Yessir. Airborne."

Hollister hung up and stood to drop his trousers. He dropped back on his bunk in his shorts and T-shirt. No one wore underwear in the field. It was sign of a REMF. He laughed halfheartedly. Him, an REMF! How many REMFs had nights like he had just had?

He dropped off into a black void.

* * *

Hollister was angry when the runner woke him up. He had promised himself to get a letter started to Susan the night before. It had been three days since he had written her or anyone. As he dressed he realized why: he just didn't want to write until he had something positive to say. He didn't want to tell her about the team being trampled or the lost team from first platoon or so many of the little tragedies that seemed to happen, one right after the other.

He tried to remind himself to take some stationery with him and work on a letter to her during the few moments he might be able to steal out of the day. He could even tell her what he was doing during the day. It would be something that wouldn't tell her anything more than how busy things were for him without alarming her.

The letter didn't come along well. Hollister lost the morning to patrol briefings and briefbacks. After that he was saddled with the lengthy accident report on the water buffalo stampede, which had to be forwarded to the Brigade Safety officer.

Hollister's initial reaction was that it was just so much chickenshit to have to write up multiple-copy reports on water buffalo. But he knew that it just might come back down the chain of command in the form of recommendations for units to warn their people about the likelihood of such an accident. If Davis's people had any idea that water buffalo might have been the cause of the noise outside their tiny perimeter, things could have turned out better.

Hollister found an out-of-the-way corner of the orderly room to finish his tasks. Easy helped him with the myriad of Brigade Safety regulations that he had to read and respond to.

As he was finishing the paperwork, Easy gave him another task. "Lieutenant, the Old Man told me to ask you to handle the inventory on Lieutenant Virgil's gear."

"I'm not surprised. With Rogers out on ambush, I'm back to being the low man on the pole." He made a note and nodded. "Okay, Top. I'll take care of it."

Easy smiled and pulled another piece of paper out of the stack in his hand. "How about some good news for a change?"

"I wouldn't know how to handle it. What's the catch?" Hollister asked.

Easy read from a column of names. "Take your pick. You

are up for R and R, and you can have Bangkok or Honolulu—
but you have to make up your mind yesterday.''

''Yesterday?''

''Sorry. The paperwork got lost somewhere between Brigade
and my in-box.''

Hollister took the R&R allocation notification from Easy and
stared at it. *Honolulu,* he thought—Susan! God, was it possible?
Could he get her to meet him there? He read down the page—
he would have to leave the next morning or lose the allocation.

''Shit—I've got to get moving!'' He handed Easy the accident
report. ''Can you get this stuff typed and forwarded? I've got to
get to the MARS station.''

Without waiting for an answer, Hollister shot out the door.
Easy laughed. ''Bernard, lad, ain't it wonderful what love does
to the heart of a warrior?''

Without bothering to look up from the Morning Report Feeder
that he was trying to type, Bernard replied dutifully, ''Whatever
you say, First Sergeant.''

The MARS station was filled with soldiers from the Brigade, all
trying to make phone calls home by radio.

Hollister checked in with the NCOIC and got a number indicating his priority—first come, first served, with a catch. He
would have to wait behind all the troops who were making emergency calls, and the ambulatory patients from the hospital who
were letting their families know they were okay.

Finding a dry spot on a sandbag parapet outside the tent,
Hollister sat down to wait his turn. He pulled the letter out of
his pocket and then realized that he would probably be seeing
Susan before she got the letter, if he finished it. He decided not
to take the time to finish it. Instead he started a letter to his
parents.

He had the same problem with his folks—tell them the truth,
and it would worry them. Tell them anything else, and he would
be lying by omission. He split the difference and told them a
much diluted version of the water buffalo patrol. Then he told
them about getting alerted for Fort Benning. That would make
his mother happy.

Watching the stream of wounded soldiers being wheeled into
the MARS tent made home seem millions of miles away. Since
he had just seen it, it was a bigger tug on his heart than it had
been before.

''Hollister?'' He heard his name called. He was up.

Inside, the tent was filled with the sounds of soldiers yelling over poor connections to the States. Conversations were complicated by the fact that only one party could talk at a time—like on a radio. So, each time a sentence or phrase was finished, the soldier had to say "over," so the person on the other end could transmit. That tended to take the romance and the spontaneity out of the conversations.

After several tries, Hollister got a connection to the MARS station at Fort Hamilton in New York. He strained to hear the phone in Susan's apartment ring over the static and strange atmospheric interference.

Hollister didn't have to say anything when he returned to the orderly room. It was obvious to Easy that something had not gone well for him at the MARS station.

"Couldn't find her, Top. I must have missed her at home. I tried where she works, and they said that she was somewhere in Manhattan at a conference. I better wave off on this. Who's next up for R and R?"

"Sir, you can still go to Bangkok and find some terrific substitute companionship. If you know what I mean."

Hollister gave Easy a slightly disapproving look. "I just don't think that would cut it for me right now, Top."

"Okay, I understand. Well, the next up is second platoon—Theodore, I believe. Let me check." He handed Hollister the typed paperwork for his signature and stepped toward the mess hall.

Hollister proofed the pages and signed the copies of the accident report while Easy located Sergeant Davis.

Easy came back from the mess hall with two cups of coffee in hand. He put one down on the field desk in front of Hollister.

"Thanks, Top. Find Davis?" Hollister asked.

"He's still in the mess hall feeding his face. Not doin' too good at it. Y'know he's got a broken tooth? Anyway, Theodore *is* next up."

"Perfect. That'll be it, then. Can you make the arrangements to put him on my allocation?"

"Sure can." Easy turned to Bernard. "Bernard, get on over to second platoon and round up Theodore. Tell him I want a large piece of his hide—and right now."

Bernard smiled and ran out the door.

Hollister gathered up the supply forms to inventory Lieutenant Virgil's effects. He then found the essential data on him—

service number, full name, all of the information that was required on the form.

Theodore exploded through the door and skidded into the orderly room. He snatched off his floppy LRP hat as he came to a stop in front of the first sergeant's desk. "You wanted to see me, First Sergeant?"

"Of course I wanted to see you, dickhead! Why would I send young Mr. Bernard out in the hot sun after you if I didn't want to see you?"

"Well, I, ah . . . I, ah . . ." Theodore stammered.

"You are, Mr. Theodore, the worst fucking excuse I have ever seen for an Airborne soldier, much less a LRP. Look at yourself!

"Your boots look like you shined them with a Hershey bar, your shirt pocket is unbuttoned, and your gig line is off."

Theodore looked down. He had misbuttoned his fatigue shirt, the bottom edge of the skirt was staggered, and the entire shirt looked twisted.

"Ah . . . First Sergeant, I, ah . . ."

"Shut up! I got all the stripes—I'm doin' the talking here."

Theodore stood more rigidly at attention. His eyes were riveted on the wall behind and above the seated first sergeant.

Hollister, seated behind Theodore, tried to suppress his laughter.

"Would a week in Bangkok help you get your head out of your ass, young soldier?" Easy asked, getting to his feet and leaning over the desk to get his face closer to Theodore's.

Theodore was nonplussed. He let the question sink in for a minute before breaking out in a huge grin. "Yessir! I mean, yes, First Sergeant! I think that will make me a candidate for soldier of the month."

Easy stuffed the R&R allocation paperwork into Theodore's hand and told him he had forty-five minutes to get his shit together and get packed.

Theodore sailed out of the orderly room.

Easy and Hollister shared a smile at the semispastic Theodore's reaction to the news.

CHAPTER 20

Hollister tacked one of Virgil's name tapes on the hooch wall under the one that had belonged to Lucas. He sat back and looked at it for the longest time. Would Rogers return from his fifth, tenth, or twenty-fifth patrol and nail Hollister's up below the others? An uneasy feeling started to come over him again. It was kind of a cross between being tired and being worried. He felt heavy and tense.

He picked up the almost empty bottle, drank what was left in it, and went to his locker to see if there was another.

He stripped the metal seal, twisted the cork out of the bottle, and smiled. Lucas used to pull the cork out of a bottle, throw it across the room, and announce that some serious drinking was about to begin by saying, "We won't need that anymore."

Hollister poured himself a conservative shot and then thought about what might lay ahead. There was only one team out—but it was in Rogers's platoon, and Captain Michaelson was available if they made contact. Lieutenant Perry—the Intelligence officer—was Duty Officer and would be there if things needed tending, to gear up an extraction.

So, Hollister rationalized, he had nothing really pressing until the following morning, when he would go along on the insert of two more teams. He poured half again what he had already poured into the cup and then took a long drink.

The scotch burned just as much as the short sip he had taken from the dead soldier. He took still another.

Susan! He had to write her about the R&R. Or maybe not. After all, he hadn't been able to reach her. She would never know what she was missing. So why should he upset her with a missed opportunity? He'd have to tell her something, but at that moment he wasn't sure what or how much.

He pulled the three new letters from her out of his pocket. He hadn't had a chance to read them yet, and it had been days since he had received her last—but not as long as it had been since he had sent her one.

He was angry for promising himself to write her and not following through; for having things he wanted to share with her, yet not being able to; for loving her so much, and being so afraid to let her into the world that surrounded him.

He had some more scotch and opened her first letter. She had just received his note about Benning. He prepared himself for what she had to say. They had never really talked about the future, not in any detail. The scotch was starting to taste bearable.

She was actually excited about Fort Benning. She started to ramble on about how much time she had spent in the East and that she wanted to see the rest of the country and meet new people.

Hollister laughed. *New people*—wait till she got her first glimpse of the hundreds of characters like Easy at Fort Benning. They were wonderful people, but they weren't her people. They weren't educated the way she was, and they didn't have her sense of the world, of politics and culture. They weren't soft like she was. They didn't smell like she did. They were nothing like her. God, how he missed her.

He was getting drunk. But he just didn't care. He wanted whatever was hurting to stop just for that night. Just for a little while. Just a minute of relief. That was all he wanted. Just a minute.

Hollister's head pounded as he swung his feet over and onto the floor. He sat still for several moments while he rested his face in his hands. The taste of cigarettes and scotch had soured his mouth in the few hours of sleep he got. The sounds of a misfiring generator near Operations wasn't much help.

He flipped open the lid of his footlocker and rummaged around in the top tray for a small bottle of GI APCs. He found a paperback copy of *Stranger in a Strange Land* that he hadn't had the chance to crack open. Another pleasure postponed.

He found the bottle and tried to shake two out. Nothing happened—they were all stuck together and crumbly from moisture. The broken aspirin wasn't a surprise. Army-issue aspirins always started disintegrating as soon as the army bought them. By the time they were in a pill container and were shipped somewhere, the inside of the container became coated with a white powder that was once the sharp edges of the pills.

With the tip of his ballpoint pen he fished around inside the bottle and pulled out enough bits of aspirin to equal two tablets.

His web gear hung on the hook on the wall and held a canteen. Unsnapping the canvas cover, he pulled the green plastic canteen out of the carrier and shook it, checking for water.

He popped the aspirin into his mouth and hurried to wash it down with the water before the taste made him gag.

Hollister's attempt to avoid the unpleasantness failed. One of the chunks of aspirin dissolved into a small puddle of paste on the back of his tongue. He tried to suppress his gag reflex, which only made his head pound worse.

While he rinsed the bitter taste from his mouth, he looked at his watch. He had about half an hour before he had to report to Operations. He could go to breakfast or take a shower, but not both.

The thought of Kendrick's breakfast convinced Hollister that a shower would probably help him get by the hangover better than eggs would.

Hollister knew that the water would be incredibly cold. He reached for the spigot and slowly turned the water on while he tried to arch his body out and away from the flow. He missed most of it, but some of the water ran to his wrist, down his arm to his armpit and right side—sending an icy shock through his body.

There was just no option, he had to get used to it or go without a shower. He cupped his hands under the stream and splashed the water onto himself until he was over the initial shock. The smell of the soap was the first positive thing that he had experienced that morning. It smelled clean. It smelled like America. It smelled like Susan.

As he lathered up his close-cropped hair, Hollister looked over toward the chopper pad. Two teams had lined up their rucksacks and gear in straight rows with their rifles resting, muzzle up, against the tops of the rucksacks.

Hollister knew what they were thinking of while they all sat in the mess hall having some breakfast, looking out the window at their gear and the waiting choppers. It was a gut-gripping sensation. If they were like he was, they would be thinking about the insert—not the bacon.

LRPs were rarely concerned about the patrol or their actions at the objective or immediate actions in the event of contact. They had all that under control. They had rehearsed and rehearsed and knew that they could handle contact on the ground. It made no difference that they had a high casualty rate—ground operations didn't bother them as much as the thought of being inserted.

It was during those moments of loss of control that they were most frightened. They didn't talk much about it. Rather, they told jokes about choppers and aviators and door gunners when what they really meant was that they hated the exposure, the vulnerability and the risk.

It was about not being able to meet the enemy on a level playing field. The fact that the enemy was always hidden on the ground while they were sitting in the slow-moving and vulnerable chopper was their worry. That filled their thoughts while they ate a breakfast they would not even remember.

Hollister collected all of the last minute data he needed for the insert. He read over the duty log from the night before and saw that the team on the ground had nothing to report, was still at the same coordinates, would be laying up that day and moving to another ambush site after dark.

The weather was iffy, even though he had just walked in from a hot and humid sunrise. He made a quick check of the forecast and then a short inventory of what he had collected . . . frequencies, call signs, maps, Signal Operating Instructions, and fire support changes. He folded the scraps of paper and stuffed them into his pocket as he left Operations.

His head hadn't cleared much as he approached the left side of the C&C. Captain Michaelson was already standing there, facing the ship, his web gear stretched out on the floor of the cargo compartment.

"Am I late?" Hollister asked, yelling over the noise of the turning rotor blades.

Michaelson turned around and cupped his hand to his mouth. "Anytime a lieutenant shows up after a captain—he's late. Even if the captain's early."

Hollister looked at Michaelson to see if he was serious. Michaelson put the stub of an unlit cigar in the corner of his mouth and smiled at Hollister. He was kidding.

Hollister laughed, placed his rifle on the bench seat, and got ready to crawl in.

Michaelson looked at him and shook his head from side to

side in an exaggerated motion. "Nope. You ride the jump seat today."

Hollister looked at him, to make sure that he understood. Realizing that Michaelson was not kidding, Hollister stepped up on the cargo deck and sat in the jump seat, putting on the helmet that had been resting on it.

Michaelson took the bench seat and put his flight helmet on.

"I don't understand, sir," Hollister said over the intercom.

"You are honchoing these inserts today, young Ranger."

"Me?" Hollister said in surprise.

"Yep. I just can't wait around for a slow movin' boy from Kansas to catch on. We just gotta get your feet good and wet—firsthand, right away and right now."

Hollister let it sink in for a moment and then nodded. "Okay, you're the boss."

"Wrong!" Shelton said from the left pilot's seat. "Today *you're* the boss. Don't fuck it up." He smiled.

"I'll do my best." Hollister looked across at the first of two lift ships that held one team, and back behind it at the second ship with the second team. He then gave and received a thumbs-up from the team leaders.

"Cap'n Shelton, I think we're ready when you are," Hollister said.

"Roger that. Comin' up."

Hollister had a little talk with himself while the choppers were crossing the wire marking the base camp perimeter. He was trying to run down the list of things that he had to do and in what order. He was also very angry with himself for being so out of sorts because of his hangover.

The flight to the AO was smooth and too short for Hollister. He wished he had more time to calm down inside, clear the cobwebs out of his head and get comfortable with the complicated tasks before him.

He pushed the transmit button on his mike. "Quarterback, this is Quarterback Two-six. Over."

"Quarterback. Over," Sergeant Marrietta replied.

"This is Two-six. I'll be honchoing the inserts today. Over."

"Roger that. We'll be here. Piece of cake. Over."

"Thanks. Out," Hollister said, appreciating the vote of confidence in Marrietta's cryptic transmission.

Hollister switched the radio to monitor and turned to Michaelson. "Anything special, sir?"

"What d'ya mean?"

"Any special instructions?"

"Yes—follow the plan."

In his head he knew what was expected of him—*take charge*—that was his task.

As they flew, the LRPs in the two slicks out Hollister's left door looked over and surveyed the C&C. It only took them a few minutes to realize that Hollister was at the controls. Sergeant Burke, team leader of 2-2, gave Hollister an encouraging clenched fist and a smile, while Sergeant Jackson, team leader of 1-1, in the second slick, gave Hollister a simple wave.

He felt confidence and pressure. He wanted not to focus on the fact that their lives could well rest in one of the many decisions he was about to make. Still, he didn't want to forget it.

He quietly said a little prayer—nothing personal. It wasn't for him; it was for them. He didn't use the word God in his thoughts. He just asked for help. The words in his head were simple: *Please don't let me screw this up. Please.*

"About the plan . . ." Hollister said to Captain Michaelson. "I'd like to do *two* instead of one false insert first. That goin' to be a problem, sir?"

Michaelson raised his hand and pointed at Captain Shelton's seat—he was okaying the idea provided that Shelton didn't have any problems.

"What do you think up front?"

"Can do easy, GI," Shelton said.

"Okay, we'll do it, then," Hollister announced over the intercom just before he switched on the radio to tell the other choppers and the teams where and when.

After the fake inserts, the first real one went off without a flaw. The timing was perfect, the LZ was cold, and all of the communications worked perfectly.

Hollister reported Team 2-2 "down and in—cold" to Marrietta, and directed the flight to move on to the second insert area.

"Wooly Bully" came over the intercom as Captain Shelton tuned the ADF to American Forces radio for the chopper crew.

Sam the Sham was just the right thing. Hollister appreciated the break in the tension. He knew that it was just Shelton's way of telling him that he did a good job on the first one, without having to say so in so many words.

Hollister looked around the chopper at Shelton, Michaelson,

de Shazo—the door gunner—and Chief Warrant Officer Patterson, the peter pilot. He wondered how many other junior officers ever got a chance to do such dangerous stuff with the help of guys like them. He felt pretty lucky. No less nervous, but lucky.

He looked across the open space to the insert ship filled with Team 1-1—barely a hundred feet away. He felt a little guilty that he wasn't going in with them. He knew what was ahead of them. They would either spend three miserable nights of boredom and hair-trigger readiness, and four days of worrying about being discovered, or come out early because of some moment of stark terror that would feel like an eternity.

Hollister became aware of the reducing volume on the music. They were approaching the first fake insert LZ for the second team's insert.

In—out. No problems, no ground fire. Hollister took a deep breath and got ready for a second feint. It went the same as the first.

The actual LZ was coming up too fast for him. He didn't feel like he had it all together, even though he had done one successful insert already. The gunships prowled the margins of the LZ while the insert ship reared back like a horse—nose up. A second before the ship touched down in the tall grass, the troops started jumping off the skids—something was wrong. The insert ship was rocking erratically. It touched down hard and skidded with a jerky right torque.

The silence in the headsets was broken by the voice of the pilot in the insert ship. "Fuck! I hit a goddamn stump! Think I'm spilling fuel. Watch me. Comin' up!"

"Roger—we are on you," Shelton said as he dumped the collective to unscrew out of the sky, and spun the nose of the C&C around to get a better view of the insert chopper.

Hollister looked at the back of Shelton's helmet for some sign or hand signal that might give him a clue of what his next move should be. He didn't want to start issuing conflicting instructions to the team or the choppers while an uncertain situation was in progress.

But he got nothing. No sign from Shelton and no report from the insert chopper. Hollister looked back down at the chopper coming out and the LRPs who were still about five long strides from the tree line they were racing for. He had to remind himself to keep his eye on the troops—Shelton would monitor the crippled ship.

Hollister grabbed a quick look around, at the chase ship and the two guns. He looked out on the horizon to the east for the forward air controller, who was shadowing them if they needed him.

If the damaged slick had to belly in, Hollister would need to have the FAC line up close air support to protect the downed crew and chopper while the risky changeover of out-of-fuel choppers took place.

"Two-six," the team leader's voice whispered. "We are down and cold. Out."

"Roger. Good hunting."

Hollister pressed the button on his drop cord and spoke. "Everybody got that?"

The door gunner gave Hollister a hand signal that they all got it.

"How's the insert ship?"

"He split the belly open and he's losing fuel, but I think we can get him across the valley if not all the way to the base camp," Shelton answered.

"If he can't make it?"

"If he has to put it down, we've got lots of places. I'm gonna kick this fucker in the ass and try to get in front of him to help look for good LZs. Chase will follow him, and I'm going to let the guns orbit a big one back over the teams till things quiet down on the LZ. Okay with you, chief?" Shelton asked Hollister.

"Okay. You got it from here, sir. Unless we get a contact call from one of the teams."

"Rog."

Hollister turned to Michaelson. He had forgotten that the Old Man was even in the aircraft. He was sitting back with his arms across his chest. He nodded at Hollister. "Not bad for your first day on the job. Not bad."

Hollister smiled. He wondered how many more of those kinds of mornings he would have. How many more could he handle? He searched his pockets for his cigarettes. As he lit one, he alternately watched the crippled ship and the tree line where the LRPs had disappeared.

As they got within sight of the base camp, Shelton tuned in The Beach Boys' "Fun, Fun, Fun" and brought a smile to everyone's face in the chopper.

"Hell, he's okay," Captain Shelton said as the damaged slick broke left from the formation and headed for the Aviation company maintenance area.

Shelton broke right with the other slick and headed for the LRP pad.

Hollister looked down at the pad. From the margin, Easy held his hand up to shade his eyes as he watched Shelton jockey the C&C onto the mark. Off to one side a three-quarter-ton truck stood by with a soldier sitting in the cab.

Shelton let the chopper settle onto the skids and rolled off the throttle. As the lift disappeared, the skids spread and creaked under the weight of the load.

Hollister unbuckled his seat belt, pressed the transmit button before the others took off their helmets, and said, "Thanks, everyone. You sure made it look easy out there."

Shelton raised his fist and gave a railroad engineer's pumping motion.

While Shelton shut down the chopper and got loose from his harness and chicken plate, Michaelson folded his map and slowly moved to get out of the aircraft.

When the entire insert crew had crossed the pad, heading toward the mess hall, the canvas drop in the back of the truck flipped open and the entire detachment headquarters leaped out yelling and squirting beer cans at Hollister.

Captain Shaw had a can in each hand, which he simply held inverted over Hollister's head. With the spray they were directing from their cans, Lieutenant Perry and Easy were trying to outdo each other for distance. Sergeants Marrietta and Tillotson applauded and whistled.

"Hey! Wait a minute. What's all this?" Hollister asked while trying to dodge the beer.

"Just tradition, Ranger. This marks your busting your cherry on your first insert," Captain Michaelson said.

Dripping with cold beer, Hollister looked at Michaelson to see if he was serious. "What tradition?"

"Just started it. It's a *new* tradition," Easy said.

Hollister had to go to the CP to take the phone call. It was coming in on a line not patched to his field phone in the hooch. A friend who was working in Personnel at IFFV Headquarters in Nha Trang had called to say he had just seen a casualty feeder report on Kerry French—Hollister's old OCS roommate.

French had been critically wounded and was in the Division hospital at An Khe. The description of the damage was not complete, but it appeared from the skimpy information that the odds were against Kerry.

Michaelson overheard the conversation, stepped out into the outer office, and relit his cigar. "You got forty-eight hours. That's as long as I can do without you," he said without looking up from his Zippo.

Hollister was surprised at the gesture. "Thank you, sir. I'll be back as soon as I can."

"Don't thank me. Being a wonderful commander and an inspiration to my troops just comes natural," Michaelson said, tilting his head back to avoid the smoke coming from the cigar. Then he smiled and took the cigar from his mouth. "Seriously, go on up there and see if you can make him feel a little better."

Hollister paced up and down on the dirt runway at the Dong Tre Special Forces camp northwest of An Hoa. He was impatient to get going again. But he had to wait for the Montagnard soldiers to unload the resupply cargo the twin engine Caribou brought to their remote outpost.

The flight started early that morning in An Hoa—the milk run to all of the Special Forces camps from the South China Sea to the Laotian border. The plane would have to stop at An Khe for fuel. That's where Hollister would get off.

As he waited he thought about Michaelson's generosity. He realized what a complex man Michaelson was. The same Michaelson who had seemed so cold in Ranger School and so controlled in combat knew how important it would be for him to see Kerry.

Hollister hadn't spent much time in Caribous. But they had a good reputation with the troops. They were solid-looking, army olive-drab instead of air force gray, and also had a throaty sound from the exhaust ports on their wing-mounted engines. They sounded healthy—like a tuned, overpowered hot rod.

The cargo compartment was like a scaled-down C-130. The length of the compartment was lined with red nylon webbed seats for passengers, and the center of the floor had rows of rollers that allowed cargo to be moved in and out easily.

Riding in a Caribou had a less intimidating feel to it than a C-130. Gone was the feel of the very powerful machine and greater engine noises. The more compact Caribou felt like a sports car of the cargo planes.

Hollister had picked a seat at the far end of the cargo compartment, near the open ramp. He watched the beautiful and changing landscape scroll by.

The rice paddies gave way to the gently rolling foothills that would become the Central Highlands. As the terrain changed, so did the population. It was most dense nearer the coastline and Highway 1.

As the Caribou flew deeper into the mountainous terrain, the vegetation changed to wild tropical rain forest with taller and taller hardwood trees.

The ethnic shift toward the interior was away from Vietnamese nationals to the tribal Montagnards—mountain people. In the area that the Caribou crossed, the tribes were the Rhade, Jarai, and the Mnong.

Hollister knew a little about the Montagnards—that they were nomadic farmers who cleared small plots by burning them first. From the few he had met, he knew that he liked their independence, sense of dignity, and total self-reliance. They were not far from the Stone Age man that must have inhabited the same mountains. What they lacked in sophistication they more than made up for with their mastery of nature and things unwritten.

The terrain kept climbing. As it did, the vegetation got thicker and darker. Eventually there was no sign of the floor of the forests that densely covered the highlands. The only glimpse of the ground was the thin red-orange ribbon of roadways that had been cut through the mountain passes.

After two more stops, the Caribou took off for An Khe, the base camp of the First Air Cavalry Division.

As they approached An Khe, Hollister got his first glimpse of the sprawling combat base. An Khe was not like any other division base—it took up much more real estate. They needed the extra space for the area known as the golf course, large fields cleared to park the division's 418 helicopters.

Each chopper was spaced a safe distance from any other chopper to prevent their being bunched up and making a good target for VC mortars or rockets.

In addition to the golf course and the general size of the base camp, there was another distinctive terrain feature right in the middle of the camp. It was the small hill that Kerry French had told Hollister about back at Camp Zama, in Japan—Hong Kong mountain.

On the side of the hill, the division engineers had poured a massive slab of concrete in the shape of the division's shoulder patch, often called the horse blanket. The slab was painted in the black and yellow colors of the division, complete with the diagonal slash and the horse's head.

The base camp was a hub of activities. All of the dirt roads were clogged with vehicles, soldiers, and Vietnamese civilians—all in a hurry to get somewhere else inside the perimeter. Everyone was covered with a layer of the fine dust that was constantly kicked up by the endless stream of vehicles and nonstop helicopter traffic.

As Hollister rode across the base camp in the back of a deuce-and-a-half, he looked up at the top of the hill for any evidence of Kerry French's countermortar effort and saw nothing.

The Staff Sergeant in the orderly room of the Admin company started off on the wrong foot with Hollister, who had asked for directions to the Division hospital and a suggestion on where he might find somewhere to flop for the night.

"You mean that you don't have orders assigning you TDY or PCS to this division?"

"Sergeant, I asked for directions to the hospital and a place to lay up tonight," Hollister said. "I am here on a VOCO pass from my unit. Not everyone in this damn war is either *in* the Cav or trying to get in the Cav." Hollister was immediately irritated by the aloof attitude of the smug NCO wearing a clean, starched set of fatigues which showed that he did not go to the field.

"Well, Lieutenant, I think you are going to have a problem because it is Division policy that all persons arriving are expected to report to—"

Overcoming his urge to grab the soldier by the shirt and pop him with his fist, Hollister turned and walked back out of the tent.

As he walked down a path flanked with dusty whitewashed rocks, Hollister tried to talk himself down. He had never had a temper, at least not before Vietnam, and he had again surprised himself at how angry he got at the NCO's attitude.

Hollister squared his hat away on his head and looked up; a crackerbox ambulance was coming down the road. He stepped out into its path and flagged it down.

The baby-faced shirtless black soldier driving the ambulance had a large and engaging grin. His wire-rimmed glasses had their own film of what Hollister was already thinking of as Cavalry dust.

During the ride to the medical battalion area, Hollister and the PFC got acquainted. The driver told Hollister how he wanted to get a job with a combat battalion—even LRPs would be better than driving an ambulance. He was tired of being called out for sprained ankles, sunburns, and barbed-wire cuts. Even worse than the routine duty was the fact that he had to wash the crackerbox after each low-priority emergency.

Hollister looked around the inside of the ambulance. The interior was spotless, and all of its painted surfaces seemed to have a coat of wax.

Reaching a major intersection in the center of the base camp, the MP directing traffic gave a confusing and somewhat stylized flip of the wrist that made no sense to the medic.

"What's that mean?"

The MP whistled at the ambulance and put his hands on his hips. "Hey, dumbfuck! You gonna move that thing or park it?"

The medic stuck his head out the window and yelled back, "Hey, man, who died and left you in charge of Vietnam?"

The furious MP walked to the driver's side of the ambulance. He pulled out his pad and glared at the driver. "Let me see your operator's permit and your trip ticket, wiseass."

"What do you want it for?" the medic asked. "You gonna give me a DR for not bein' able to read sign language, man?"

"You're out of uniform."

"*Out of uniform?*" the medic said, mocking the MP. "This is fuckin' Vietnam, man. I been in this sweatbox since I got up this morning."

The MP started filling out the delinquency report form.

Hollister had already had his fill of rear-echelon attitude. He leaned toward the driver's side. "Something bothering you, Specialist?"

The MP squatted and peered into the cab. He could only see the Infantry officer's branch insignia on the left collar of Hollister's fatigue shirt—not his rank. So he safe-sided his response. "Oh, good day, sir. This soldier is out of uniform. It's against Division policy to operate a vehicle without a shirt or headgear on unless it interferes with the safe operation of the vehicle."

"I instructed this soldier to take his shirt off. He looked like he was going to suffer a heat injury if he didn't. Now, we are on our way to the dispensary. If you hold us up any longer, it might not be so good for him."

The MP knew that he was being outranked, and didn't want the trouble it would take to match authority with the officer in the ambulance. ''In that case, sir, I think y'all ought to be on your way.''

The MP stepped back from the vehicle and saluted.

The medic smiled broadly, jammed it in gear and drove off.

CHAPTER 21

Like everything else, the Division hospital was covered with dust. A clerk at the Admissions and Disposition desk directed Hollister back outside the hospital headquarters tent to the ward that held Kerry French.

Kerry's ward was made up of four tents that had been butted together in a cross. As he approached it, Hollister felt a tightening in his chest.

Inside, a medic pointed Hollister to the nursing station at the intersection of the four tents. There, a seated nurse flanked by two piles of medical records pointed the blunt end of a pencil toward a bed at the near end of a tent. Hollister had been in enough army hospitals to know that the beds closest to the nurse's stations were reserved for patients who needed the most care.

As he walked around the nursing station and into the other wing, Hollister didn't recognize Kerry. Still, it was the right bed.

Kerry was facing away from him, so Hollister had a moment to take it all in. Kerry was on a real hospital bed; others in the ward were on simple army cots.

His body was contorted into an extremely uncomfortable-looking position. Cables drew tension against his legs, and a plastic corset braced his torso from hips to armpits. In a cast, one arm was raised at an awkward angle, supported by a brace. Tubes led from under the sheet that covered him to plastic bags hung below, from the frame of the bed. One held urine with evidence of blood in it; the other seemed to be a drain of mostly blood. Kerry's head was bandaged, and one eye was completely covered with dressings. Hanging from a stand, containers of saline solution and other medications were dripping through tubes to his free forearm.

Hollister walked around the bed to be in his friend's field of vision. "Kerry?" he said tentatively. "It's me, man. Jim Hollister."

Kerry turned his head with much difficulty. He smiled.

Hollister tried not to wince. A stomach tube was stuck out of Kerry's nose. Several teeth were missing and others were chipped off at the gum line. He leaned over and touched Kerry's hand. "How ya doing?"

"Oh . . . I guess I'm okay. Won't be dancing anytime soon. But what are you doing here?"

Hollister suddenly realized that his visit might alarm Kerry. He decided to tell a white lie. "Had to come up here to find out about the Cav's Aerial Rocket Artillery. I asked around and was told that you were here."

Kerry smiled again. "That's great. I'm glad I didn't miss you. They're sending me home soon." His voice was thick from the painkillers.

"That's good. But how did this happen? You in a firefight or what?"

Kerry formed another crooked smile and uttered what sounded like a laugh modulated to keep from hurting himself. "Wish it were something that heroic. Damn chopper crash. I was on a recon in a Huey with my CO and the Artillery FO and we lost it. All of a sudden we were falling out of the sky."

"Is there something I can do for you?" Hollister asked.

"Yeah. I'm pretty dry. Could you get me some ice?"

The plastic container on the tray next to Kerry's bed had a bent straw sticking out of it. Hollister picked it up and shook it. Empty.

"Sure. I'll be right back." Hollister grabbed the container and walked back to the nurse's station.

"Can someone point me to the ice, Lieutenant?"

Her last name, Boyer, was hardly visible on the faded name tape she wore. She stood and took the cup from Hollister. Her pretty face was a pleasant surprise in the drab and gloomy hospital. "Sure can. But how 'bout you? You thirsty?"

Hollister thought about it. He was thirsty but he really wanted some coffee.

"You got coffee?"

Lieutenant Boyer motioned for him to follow her. As he did, Hollister got his first good look at her. She was tall, maybe five feet seven. She had her hair up with some kind of a barrette, but very feminine wisps fell loose from the clip and curled at her collar. She had a tiny waist and a very pleasant-looking ass, even covered by some pretty unattractive women's fatigues.

He was amazed at how small her jungle boots were. But best of all, she trailed a sweet scent of woman—nothing more elaborate than that. She just smelled like a freshly scrubbed American female. Hollister thought of what a joy it was in a country that smelled like a dirty sweat sock.

She led him to a small kitchen area, stopped, and turned around—catching him admiring her from behind. She said nothing.

The little mess area held an ice machine, a GI coffee urn, and lots of utensils and containers that had obviously been scrounged from the supply system. There were also two chairs. She pointed to them.

Hollister made a gesture back toward Kerry. "But he—"

"He's so doped up that nothing bothers him except being strapped down in that rack. Most of the time he sucks on the ice to have something to do. We're pouring so much IV fluids into him that he can't be thirsty, just bored."

The nurse poured two cups of coffee and handed Hollister one. "Cream, sugar?"

"Oh . . . no, thanks. Just black is fine for me, please."

She shook her head, stirred a clump of sugar into her coffee, and smiled knowingly. "Tough guys drink it black, huh?"

Hollister knew that she was teasing him. "No, it's not that. I just can't take that GI reconstituted milk."

Lieutenant Boyer laughed. She had a pretty laugh that transformed her serious nurse face to that of a lovely woman.

But Hollister couldn't play with her anymore. "So, what's the verdict on Kerry French?"

She lifted her cup to her lips, blew across the surface of the coffee, and took a sip. Putting it down, she took the container to the ice machine and flipped the damaged lid up. Holding it with one hand, she scooped up a cupful of ice. "He's in very, very bad shape. His pelvis is broken in several places. Both his legs are broken, he has lost his spleen, and they are talking about going in again—he's still bleeding. He's got some pretty banged-up internal organs. His left arm and shoulder blade are broken, and he's lost one eye. If he knew what kind of shape he was in, he'd die right now."

Hollister felt a sinking sensation in his stomach. Something triggered the memory of the day at Benning when they were commissioned. They went to the Post Exchange with silver dollars to find their first salutes. It was a tradition that newly commissioned second lieutenants gave a dollar to the first soldier who saluted them.

Kerry gave his to a bear of a sergeant from the Airborne Committee. Hollister gave his to a newly promoted Specialist 4 who still had tailor's chalk above and below his new sleeve insignia.

The nurse's voice interrupted his thoughts. "It's good that you came to see him. It'll improve his mood."

Hollister played with his cup while he was still trying to absorb the extent of Kerry's injuries. "I had no idea how bad it was."

"And I just gave you the highlights. I don't know how he is alive at all. The rest of the guys in that chopper were burned to a crisp."

"Why didn't Kerry?"

"Story I got from the Dust-Off medics was that the chopper crashed and rolled down the side of the hill. They aren't sure if it took ground fire or what. He was thrown out of the chopper before it burst into flame. They found him three hundred feet below the chopper ashes in a rocky streambed. The attending physician said that he was lucky to end up in the stream. The cold running water kept him from going into deep shock."

"I can tell you he was in really bad shape when he arrived."

"Why is he still here? Why isn't he in intensive care or something?"

"This *is* intensive care. Anyway, we can't move him till he is stabilized—maybe a couple of more days."

Hollister took the ice container out of her hand. "Can I spend some time with him?"

"Sure. If you get in the way, I'll let you know. It'll take his mind off things—must be pretty screwed up anyhow. He's pretty much in and out of it most of the time."

Hollister spent the rest of the afternoon with Kerry. Their conversations were spotty, interrupted by short periods when Kerry drifted off to sleep. Periodically Lieutenant Boyer came over to check on Kerry, replace bags of fluids, and make notations in his chart. While she did, Hollister stepped outside the tent to grab a smoke.

He felt a little guilty when he jumped at the chance to leave for an hour while they bathed Kerry and fed him through the tube in his nose. Hungry, Hollister walked over to the mess hall, and after a little negotiation with the headcount, he was able to get a meal—also covered with a light layer of Cavalry dust.

It had been dark for about an hour when Lieutenant Boyer came to Kerry's bed for a last check. Satisfied that the sleeping lieutenant was okay, she looked at her watch and then at Hollister. "He's out of it for the night. He won't know if you're here."

Hollister got to his feet and folded the chair he had scrounged earlier. "Well, I hope he's comfortable." He stretched and looked from Kerry to the nurse. "Hey, where can a guy get a drink around here without dust in it?"

"You can get one over at the Officers Club, but you have to take the dust with the drink. It's a Cav tradition."

"So where's that?"

"Follow me. I've been on duty forever and I could use a cold dusty one, too. You buying with all that big-time jump pay?"

Hollister realized that she had inventoried his uniform and recognized that he was in a parachute outfit.

He liked the thought of having a drink with her. After waiting for her to pass a few slips of paper to her shift replacement, he motioned toward the exit. "Okay, I'm buying. Lead the way."

The Officers Club was a sorry excuse for a place to drink. It was half a Quonset hut and four tables. Against the plywood end wall, a counter served as a bar, tended by a Vietnamese bartender.

Two other nurses were seated at one table. A male Medical Service Corps officer sat by himself at another, sipping a beer and writing a letter.

"Where is everybody?"

Boyer looked up on the wall. A blackboard had an announcement on it that read: MOVIE TONIGHT. She pointed to a window in the side wall of the hut.

Through the opening Hollister saw an outdoor theater. A plywood screen was attached to the trees, and rows of planks had been nailed to tree stumps in front of it for seats. All of the benches were filled with off-duty medical personnel, beers in hand, waiting for the movie to start.

Hollister and Lieutenant Boyer mounted stools at the end of the bar. They ordered, drank, talked, and ordered some more. They wouldn't get to know each other. They didn't want any soul searching, and they would only talk about totally unimportant things. Hollister didn't want to bring up Kerry French. He knew enough about his friend's condition.

The drinks flowed and they laughed. He liked her. There was plenty of her that he wouldn't get to discover, but he liked what he saw and heard—mostly her laugh. It was rare, but genuine, and she seemed to be genuine, too. Too soon for both of them it got late.

"You suppose there's an empty rack somewhere in the hospital where I could get some sleep?"

The nurse's eyebrows rose while she was taking a drink of her bourbon. "Hmmmm," she mumbled through the drink. She put it down, reached in her pocket, pulled out a folded piece of paper and handed it to Hollister. "Sorry, I forgot. Brownie left this for you."

"*Brownie?*" Hollister opened up the note. It was from the ambulance driver—if Hollister needed to, he could sleep in the ambulance. The note included directions to the medical battalion motor pool and the bumper number of the vehicle. It also thanked Hollister for bailing him out with the MP. It was signed, PFC Clarence P. Brown.

Hollister found the ambulance. Inside, Brownie had made a bed on one of the padded platforms in the back of the ambulance. Clean hospital sheets were topped with a clean army blanket, a pillow, and a pillowcase. On the other platform the medic had left a pair of clean socks and a Red Cross sundry packet. It held a toothbrush, toothpaste, soap, a razor, two blades, a comb, and a small bottle of mouthwash.

Hollister smiled. Something from his Kansas upbringing made him quick to do things for others, and they always seemed to come back to him when he needed them.

He undressed, brushed his teeth, crawled into the ambulance bed quickly, and said a few words of prayer for Kerry. The thought of his buddy so badly injured made him think of the terrible word *maim* once again.

Hollister was still wiping the sleep out of his eyes when he entered the ward. He wouldn't be able to spend much time with Kerry because he had to start thumbing a ride back to An Hoa. He thought about what he wanted to say. It might be the last time he saw him. He had never had a chance to say some things to Lucas.

"Hey, stranger."

He looked up and saw Lieutenant Boyer. She was heading toward the kitchen area, an empty cup in her hand.

"Cup of coffee?"

"Yeah . . . sure. My head feels like I put it in a vise last night."

"Cav booze is not the best," she said. He turned around and followed her to the coffee. She found a cup and looked in it. She poured some hot coffee into it, swished it around, and then poured it out under the tent flap. She then filled it and handed it to Hollister. When he looked up from the cup, she said, "Don't know any easy way to tell you. Your friend didn't make it through the night."

"What?" Hollister said. "He was okay when he went to sleep last night."

She reached out and gently touched the back of Hollister's hand. "It happens sometimes. He threw a blood clot and it killed him."

Hollister dropped his head. He didn't want her to see his eyes flood with tears.

She reached over and touched him lightly on the shoulder.

Less than an hour later Hollister caught a chopper leaving An Khe. The inside of the slick was a wreck. Hollister had never seen a Cav chopper before. None of the insulation material was still in place, the decks were scarred and discolored, and paint was worn off the chopper everywhere he looked. He hoped that the engine was in better shape than the bodywork.

But the beaten-up chopper fit his mood. He had lost two good friends in a matter of months, and there was no reason for him to believe that the losses would end anytime soon.

The next morning he was crossing the compound, on the way to let Captain Michaelson know he was back. Just as he looked up, Michaelson was coming out of the orderly room.

"Hollister! Just the man I'm looking for."

Hollister saluted.

Michaelson quickly picked up on Hollister's mood. "Bad?"

"Yessir. He died—chopper crash. He hung on for a few days, but then he just . . . well, he just went in his sleep."

"Sorry. Listen, grab a beer and meet me in Operations. We have to talk about a few things."

Thinking he might look like he was feeling sorry for himself, Hollister straightened up. "Yessir, be there in zero two."

Michaelson took two steps then stopped. "Hollister."

"Yessir."

"Glad you're back, Ranger. We need you."

Captain Michaelson, Hollister, and Lieutenant Perry huddled over a map spread out on a field table in the Operations tent.

Michaelson tapped the blue line on the map with the end of his pencil. "We've got a whole shitpot of intel that sampan convoys are using this major stream coming out of the high ground west of the valley."

"What have you turned up on the other ambushes?" Hollister asked.

"We blew away one small boat the day you left. But we had to wave off on one last night because the team leader couldn't be sure that he didn't have a boatload of civilians," Captain Michaelson said.

"So what's the story on this route?"

"It comes out of a part of the hills that has a lot of caves," Lieutenant Perry answered. "The Vietnamese tell us that these caves have been used to cache supplies since the French were here."

Michaelson relit his cigar and leaned back in the creaky folding chair. "We wanna try something different. The area has just too damn many LZ watchers.

"The ambush the other night was just a fluke, and I'm suspicious that the one last night might have been a setup. I think they sent civilians downstream to get us to waste 'em and then spend forever trying to explain the accident."

"Okay—how do we get around it?" Hollister asked.

"We need to walk in a heavy patrol from way the hell up above the ambush site and throw a bunch of diversion inserts about ten klicks to the north and east of there to make them think we're moving the area of saturation ambushes."

Hollister looked up at Michaelson. "Okay, sir. When do I leave?"

"I want you to do a detailed map recon and then make a good aerial recon of the area before we nail down any of the details. The longer we take to get this one off the ground, the more confident they'll get out there."

"Can I pick the teams today to give the team leaders time to get prepped?" Hollister asked.

"Do it," Michaelson said, gently breaking the ash off his cigar on the edge of his jungle boot sole.

"How soon and how long?"

Michaelson handed Hollister a message from the Air Force Meteorological Section at Tan San Nhut Air Base. It contained weather forecasts for the upcoming two weeks. "Roll your own. If they're using that stream and those caves as their supply and backhaul route, they're just as likely to be there in a week as tomorrow.

"So it's up to you. I'm more interested in this one going good than going fast. We've been taking too many lumps, and I think that we need to work on our batting average," Michaelson said.

"Yessir. How are we doin' on replacements?"

"I think we're doing okay on team members, but I haven't found a turtle for you yet. I still want to get you ready to fill in for Cap'n Shaw, but I also have to replace you."

Hollister stood up, assuming that the meeting was over.

"Jim."

"Yessir."

"Let's do this one by the numbers. It can have an impact on everything from troop morale to the future of the detachment."

There were officers and NCOs in the Brigade who didn't like the idea of the detachment and its mission. Many of them were jealous of the elite status of the unit and were looking for reasons to badmouth it. Hollister hadn't even left the tent and he could feel the pressure growing.

At the far end of the mess hall, Hollister, Allard, Davis, and Camacho had maps spread out. Allard and Davis were selecting possible ambush sites while Camacho and Hollister were searching for landing zones, routes, and pickup zones.

They kept it up through the morning until the mess sergeant threatened to run them out so he could serve lunch, so Hollister and his NCOs put their maps away and bellied up to the long tables to eat. After a typically heavy meal—pork roast, mashed potatoes, and Parker House rolls—designed by food service people in the basement of the Pentagon, Hollister was pleased that they would be going out on a recon. At least in the chopper he wasn't likely to fall asleep.

"How we look for fleshing out Two-three?" Hollister asked.

"Well, sir, I think we'll be okay," Davis said. "I got Theodore to replace Vinson on the radio, and we got a medic from the first platoon. They were one over on witch doctors."

"I think I want to leave Sergeant Davis back here to work on training and refitting the platoon while we go out heavy with

Allard and Camacho as assistant patrol leaders. What do you all think?''

Davis smiled. "I'm sure Allard wants to go out to get another notch on his belt, and Camacho needs the field experience. I am old enough and wise enough to know that I should be back here sharing my fabulous combat experience with the FNGs.''

Camacho and Allard booed Davis.

After they all had a good laugh, Davis got serious and answered Hollister's question. "Yessir, I actually think that's a good plan—best people in the right places.''

"Okay, then, let's go round up a chopper and take a look.''

Hollister, Davis, Camacho, Allard, and Captain Shaw sat in the back of the chopper with maps in hand.

In order not to give away their intentions, the recon took place while one of the first platoon teams was being extracted from a completed, but unsuccessful, ambush patrol.

This allowed the recon ship to take up a large lazy orbit a couple miles from the cluttered air over the extraction. From the ground it looked as if the recon ship was just a backup chopper holding high and wide for the nearby extraction.

Inside the chopper Allard and Davis tried to confirm the viability of the ambush sites they had selected in the mess hall, while Camacho, Hollister, Shaw, and the pilots scrutinized the few holes in the canopy for possible landing zones. All had to yell over the turbine noise and buffeting since there were not enough headsets for them to use the intercom system in the aircraft.

While they reconned the objective area, Captain Shaw photographed the terrain using a tiny Pen EE half-frame 35mm camera, a new toy issued to the LRPs. The vibration of the chopper made it difficult to take the pictures, but even blurred ones would be useful.

On the way back to the LRP pad, the chopper flew over an ARVN unit that was stopped on Highway 1. The troops were stretched out for a good mile, all lounging around on their trucks, playing cards and smoking. From the air it was obvious to Hollister that there was absolutely no sense of vulnerability to enemy fire. None of their commanders had put out security to protect the main body of the convoy, and the troops were unconcerned about any possible enemy threat.

At one point, forward of the center of the column, a tight knot of Vietnamese officers and two American advisors huddled around a map spread out on the hood of a jeep. One of the Americans was waving his arms and pointing in a direction away from the apparent direction of march.

A slight shiver went through Hollister as he thought of what an awful job it must be to work as an advisor to the Vietnamese army.

After deciding on the general area for the river ambush patrol and selecting several LZs and alternates, Captain Shaw drew up a map overlay containing all of the control measures to be coordinated with adjacent units. He took the plan to the American units and the ARVNs while Hollister got stuck taking a copy to Province Headquarters to coordinate with Vietnamese units under the control of the province chief.

At Province Headquarters, Hollister learned that Colonel Minh was in Nha Trang with his American advisor, Colonel Baird. In the Province Tactical Operations Center, Hollister eventually found an American sergeant.

While the American NCO couldn't make any promises for what the Vietnamese would or wouldn't do with the overlay, he did say that he would make sure that it got to the province chief and his operations officer.

Hollister explained that the overlay was firm even though it didn't display all of the specific locations of the proposed ambushes. The details of the specific patrols, locations, and such would be sent over when they had been worked out. He also noted that they would be operating in the area starting two days hence and would notify Province when they cleared the AO.

Leaving out the details of the ambush locations was no accident. Hollister and Michaelson had decided not to give the Vietnamese any more information than they absolutely had to. So, Hollister just wanted to make sure that the Vietnamese knew that the Americans were in that area, and to confirm that no Vietnamese ground forces operations were scheduled there.

The sergeant spoke with the Vietnamese Plans officer and cleared the area of any Vietnamese units. He assured Hollister that he would see that everyone got the word.

Hollister then got the frequencies and call signs of all adjacent Vietnamese units and outposts. He asked specific questions about fire support available, and then, with little confidence in the answers, about any restrictions on fires in the AO.

Hollister left Province Headquarters only partially satisfied with his coordination with the American advisor. He knew that he could not completely count on the Vietnamese, but had to go through the motions. He was just as happy not to have bumped into Colonel Minh. At least with the advisor he felt that they were understanding each other and there wasn't any other agenda going on.

On the way back in a jeep he made notes on who he talked to and what they talked about. Something told him that if anything went wrong, Province Headquarters would try to blame it on the Americans. He wanted to be ready with dates, times, and bumper numbers.

Even if things went smoothly, he would need the details for the After Action Report. And if anything needed to be changed, he could more easily get things done starting with the sergeant he had actually talked to.

Captain Shaw's aerial photos came back from Brigade, printed and marked with a few key grid coordinates. It was the first time they'd used photographs that were not several years old.

Shaw brought the key players into the Ops tent to look over the photos and make the final decisions about the LZs and routes. The ambush sites had already been decided upon.

The enlarged black and white photos gave a panoramic view of the AO, but they were low-angle photos and the distortion didn't allow the exact transfer of map data like grid lines, distances, elevation, and relief. Grid coordinates of key terrain features had been accurately marked on the map by Sergeant Marrietta in white correction fluid.

They had just concluded that there was a severe shortage of optimum distance LZs in the area of Hollister's primary ambush site when Captain Michaelson entered.

"What's the problem?"

"We're having trouble finding a good LZ. If we use the better ones, we'll have to go to a secondary ambush site. If we stick with our best ambush site, we're stuck with one very tight, very marginal LZ," Hollister said.

Michaelson pulled his cigar out of his mouth, leaned over and looked at the photos. Everyone waited while he examined the photos of the landing zones and the primary ambush site. "You feel good about that location for an ambush?"

Hollister and Davis both nodded yes.

"So how 'bout this?" Michaelson pointed to a bare ledge, an eroded piece of ground that was barely the size of a car.

"Too small, isn't it?" Hollister asked.

"You can go in on a rope . . . . It's on the side of a hill, nothing much above you. Won't be silhouetted. And your trip from there to the ambush site is all downhill along that skinny finger that runs away from it," Michaelson said, stuffing the cigar back into his mouth.

"Is it level?" Davis asked.

They looked at another photo for a different angle.

"I've gone in on a rope, only to lose it trying to stand up under my ruck with the rotor wash kicking my ass," Davis added.

"Yep. Look at this," Hollister said. He passed around a photo that showed the spot to be very close to level.

Everyone looked at the details with a small magnifying glass. No one had any other objections.

"What's the moon phase gonna be?" Camacho asked.

Marrietta consulted a chart on the tent wall next to the radios. "Three-quarter."

"Why?" Hollister asked.

"I'd rather go down a rope at night," Camacho said. "If we don't get a cloud layer and we wait till the moon is full up, we got a better chance at seeing the spot on the ground without being sitting ducks for some gook with a decent rifle. We don't want to be hoverin' around with the lights on looking for that spot in the trees. The moon'll be a help."

"Yeah, but can the pilots find that dot at night just usin' the moonlight?" Allard asked.

"I'll go look tonight," Hollister said, looking up at Michaelson.

"Those are your choices," Michaelson said, tapping another point on the map. "It's either go in by rope or you got a very long walk from the closest decent LZ."

They decided to plan on rappeling in unless the night recon or the weather data was discouraging.

"We ought to get the troops up on the wall this afternoon," Davis said.

"Right," Hollister said. "But with full gear, weapons and blindfolds. If we get time, we'll try some rappeling later tonight too. Okay?"

"Roger that," Davis said.

Captain Shelton screwed up his face as he leaned over the map and aerial photos on the table in Operations. "From the looks of that, we'll need a seeing eye dog with a strobe light stickin'

out his ass to find that twelve-digit grid coordinate at night.''
He shook his head and laughed. ''You guys are just trying to
test our aviation excellence, now, aren't you?''

Hollister waited until he was sure that Shelton was kidding,
and then picked up on the teasing. ''If this is too much—we can
get some of those *real* combat pilots from the First Cav down
here—''

''Whoa! Whoa! I'd rather you say something bad about my
mother, youngster, than be talkin' about my flying skills.''

''That mean you want to give it a shot, sir?'' Hollister asked.

Polishing his fingernails on his flight suit, Shelton announced, ''I'm a senior aviator. I got the control touch of a
surgeon. The VC applaud my flying.'' He then reached in his
sleeve pocket on his flight suit and pulled out his sunglasses.
''And, I got me a new pair of gen-u-wine, bullet-proof aviator
sunglasses today. So—no problem.''

Hollister threw his hands up in the air as if to signal that all
was perfect. ''So what are we waiting for?''

''You're right. Let's go out to that chopper, kick the tires and
light the fire, youngster.''

''Think we ought to wait till it gets dark first, sir?'' Hollister
asked.

''Maybe we ought to stop by the mess hall for a cup of coffee
first. It'll be dark in another half hour.''

Shelton had let his co-pilot go see Sergeant Tillotson, the LRP
senior medic, about a bout of diarrhea that doubled him up on
the flight to the LRP pad. Still, he didn't want to wait for a
replacement pilot to arrive before he and Hollister took off for
the night recon.

The recon time was critical, so Hollister strapped himself into
the right seat next to Shelton and they lifted off without a second
pilot.

The moon was high and behind them as they moved toward
the insert location, and they had a clear view of the ground
below. If they inserted the team at exactly the same time of
night, it would be a little more difficult for someone on the high
ground above them to make out features on the chopper with
the large moon behind it.

As they flew along at fifteen hundred feet, they saw specks
of light in thatched huts, even though everyone was supposed to
be out of the valley each day at sundown.

Hollister knew that it didn't mean they were VC. Lots of the older farmers couldn't make the trip in and out of the valley each day to tend their rice fields. And there were no young men to do the hard work—only old men, old women, and young women with children. So, many of them hid or bribed the ARVNs to let them hole up in their homes for the night.

Hollister looked up from the valley to the hills in front of the chopper. They were flat black in contrast to the monochrome shades and water reflections of the rice fields. There were also sparkles of light from lanterns and cook fires on the hillsides, and it was fairly certain that those lights were VC hiding in the caves that dotted the slopes of the foothills.

"How 'bout some music?" Shelton asked.

Hollister stepped on the floor button. "I could go for that. It's not Mantovani, is it?"

Shelton gave Hollister a look and screwed up his face while he twisted the frequency dial on the ADF radio in the console between them.

The Moody Blues were just finishing the chorus of "Go Now." It was one of Susan's favorite songs. Hollister looked out at a formation of birds that was heading south below them. He felt very far away from her at that moment.

CHAPTER 22

The visibility in the objective area was not as good as it was over the rice paddies. Shelton and Hollister strained, looking out the open side windows in their chopper doors to find terrain features and landmarks on the ground.

By looking out the open windows instead of through the windscreen, they could eliminate the little bit of glare and distortion that came from the reflected red cockpit lights and the tiny scratches that were all over the Plexiglas windows and the windscreen.

"There it is," the crew chief said. " 'Bout nine o'clock and almost right under us."

Shelton let the chopper drift out past the spot a respectable distance, did a quick right turn and then a long lazy left that put the spot out their left door again on the return trip.

"Yeah, I think we have it. The world's smallest LZ," Shelton said.

Hollister tried to stretch and look over Shelton to see out his side of the chopper.

"Hold on a sec. Let me come around again and let you have a look." As the chopper crossed back over the spot on the ground, Hollister saw it out his door. "Jesus! That's gonna be tough!"

"Naw, going in ain't gonna be so hard. It's coming back up the ropes once they start shooting at your ass—now, that's really gonna be tough!" Shelton said.

Hollister flipped his map open, dropped it onto his lap, and looked for reference points that he could identify on the ground. He found a couple and circled them with his grease pencil.

At the same time, Shelton looked in vain for places to put a chopper down if they ran into trouble during the insert.

There were too few breaks in the canopy. The insertion would be a whole lot hairier than his humor indicated. If Shelton had to put the insert chopper down, it would be into the trees or into the water below a break in the canopy over the wide part of the streambed.

Shelton let Hollister have the controls on the way back to the LRP pad. Flying at night felt different. Hollister seemed to project his awareness farther out, perhaps because he was trying harder to distinguish the horizon and pick out distant landmarks to use as navigational aids along his compass heading. He was getting used to the feel of the large chopper being under his control and kind of liked it.

"So? How 'bout putting in the paperwork?" Shelton asked.

"Paperwork? Paperwork for what?"

"Flight school. Don't you want to be an Army aviator like every other red-blooded, God-fearing, skirt-chasing American male?"

"Oh, no. I don't think so. I think that this is just about all the flying that I want to do."

Suddenly the headset in Hollister's helmet filled up with a low and rising chant from Shelton, the crew chief, and the door gunner: *"Grunt, grunt, grunt, grunt, grunt."*

Hollister laughed.

"I think what we have here is a little fence riding," Shelton said. "A little more stick time and you'll be dreaming about the wonders of flight and the joys of the brotherhood of aviation."

"And the painful results of excessive alcohol consumption, sleep deprivation, and social diseases," the crew chief added.

Shelton and Hollister walked toward the mess hall from the chopper. Hollister took out a pack of cigarettes and offered one to Shelton, who waved his hand. "Thanks, no. I've had too many of those things today. I feel like I'm still wearing a chicken plate when I'm not."

Hollister lit one and slipped the pack and lighter back into his pocket. "What do you really think about that hole in the canopy out there?"

"You mean that divot in the rough?" Shelton asked.

They both stopped to watch team members silently rappeling down the side of the tower. They made no noise except for the zipping sounds of the rope flying through the snap links on their Swiss seats, and the soles of their jungle boots tapping the wood face on the way down.

"I can get the choppers in there if you can get these kids off those strings in a hurry," Shelton added.

Hollister didn't reply. He watched as Camacho, Davis, and Allard put the LRPs down the rappeling wall over and over again. It was hard to climb to the top of the tower with all of their gear on, but not one LRP complained. They knew that the success of the insert hinged on their ability to get down, touch the ground, and get unhooked from the rope rapidly.

They would practice until well after midnight. Three of them would even go through a pair of rappeling gloves.

In Operations, Hollister and Shelton were drinking coffee and comparing notes on their maps when Michaelson walked in. He was fresh from the showers, wearing PT shorts and a T-shirt with a large set of master parachute wings on the front. He carried an envelope in one hand and a beer in the other. "So? What do you two think?"

"We can hover over the insert point long enough to get'em in," Shelton said. "But if they run into a welcoming party— we're fucked."

Michaelson looked to Hollister.

"I agree. We can get on the ground. As long as we're the only ones there, it'll be no problem."

"How would you feel about taking a reaction force with us?"

Hollister looked back at the map and tapped a light green spot. "If we put in troops here and they weren't too worried about security on the move, they could be to us in about thirty minutes on a flat-out run."

"Well, we're going to have a full-strength infantry platoon in choppers in the air to back us up. I was able to talk Brigade into it. I'll put them in the air near that LZ—in a high orbit.

"If you take one round of ground fire, we can put them on the ground before the last man is off the rope," Michaelson said.

Hollister looked at Michaelson, puzzled. "Something about this mission we don't know, sir?"

Michaelson dropped the envelope on the table.

Hollister reached in and pulled out ten large black and white photos. They had been taken the night before by an infrared reconnaissance camera from a much higher altitude than Shaw's snapshots.

At the bend in the river that was to be the ambush site, there were four sampans loaded with boxes and containers. They were headed downstream—toward the west side of the valley.

Hollister shuffled through the photos and laid them all out on the table. In two other prints sampans were moving upstream with huge baskets on board. "Rice?" Hollister asked.

"That's their guess," Michaelson said. "Field Force G-2 is pretty sure that it's weapons and gear going into the valley and rice and fruit coming out. Anybody on that river at night is up to no good."

Hollister made a disapproving face. "Can this be another case of poachers? I'd hate to fire up some poor fucker and his family trying to make a buck."

Michaelson reached into his trousers pocket and pulled out a small magnifying glass. He dropped it on a spot circled on one of the photos. "Poachers don't carry those."

Hollister picked up the photo and looked through the loupe. "Shit! RPGs. Take a look." He handed the loupe to Captain Shelton. "At least one of 'em is carrying a loaded ChiCom grenade launcher," Hollister said, pointing to a standing man on the bow of one of the boats.

"And it's good enough for me," Michaelson said.

"Let's see—hovering over a spot where one of those fuckers can lay an RPG sight on me," Shelton said. "And you want us to do it at night. *And* you want to take along a spooky grunt platoon. Yeah, that's just about right for us. Lesser men would be worried. But then, lesser men aren't real aviators."

Michaelson smiled at him. "You guys are so full of shit."

Hollister nursed a drink as he wrote to Susan. At least now that he had orders to Fort Benning, he could write about something that was forward-looking, hopeful, and concrete.

It filled the void of pages that had remained unwritten about the ugliness of his days, and he didn't feel as deceitful about avoiding the details of the carnage for the little things that he and Susan had to discuss about their future.

Wedding plans. She had asked questions in a letter he had received earlier in the week. What did he want to do? Big family wedding? Just the two of them slipping away? Hollister tried to explain that he really wanted to get on to their lives together as fast as they could.

He told her that he was reluctant to suggest plans that would delay the time it would take them to get married, get to Fort Benning and set up housekeeping, but he knew that there were very few options. Susan's father had died just before they met, and her mother was the only family she had left. A big family wedding would be a problem because his family was so large and her mother couldn't leave New York because of her poor health.

Hollister left the decision up to Susan but suggested that they just get married in a simple civil ceremony and get to Benning. They could take some time off later and visit Kansas for her to get to know his family better.

Housing—he thought that they ought to apply for on-post housing. His hours would be brutal at the Ranger Department, and he wanted her to be surrounded with other Army wives rather than being isolated in some neighborhood in Columbus that might not offer the kind of support that living in Army quarters might.

Work—it was his turn to ask. What did she want to do about her job? They hadn't talked about it. He hoped that there was something she could find to do that she would enjoy. He told her that at the current rate, he could probably expect to make captain in their first year at Benning. That would mean a sixty-seven dollar a month pay raise—before taxes.

Dispensing with some of the details and coordination that he could discuss with her, he spent a page telling her how much he missed her and how excited he was becoming over the nearness of his departure date. He had grown comfortable with the thought of being married to her, and that made him even more eager to get home to her.

As the LRP column of fours came running down the road past the MP company area, they chanted as loud as they could. A couple of the MP's coming back from the showers gave the LRPs the finger. They were met with boos and catcalls from the LRPs.

Hollister's stomach was sour and his head dull from the scotch he had drunk the night before. He tried to convince himself that the evils he had done to his body the night before could be cured by a hard morning run.

He hoped that he would start feeling better soon. He had a very long day ahead, which would end with him leading the ambush patrol into the AO.

As they ran, his mind started to reel at the endless list of things he still had to do before they were skids up.

When the column turned back into the LRP compound, Captain Michaelson, who led the run, brought them to quick-time, halted the detachment, and instructed them to fall out.

The thirty soldiers who had made it to the PT formation that morning collapsed onto the ground or wandered around bent over at the waist, hands on their hips, trying to get their wind back. Many pulled cigarettes out of their pockets and lit up even though they were in pain and still coughing from the run.

Theodore started talking about his recent visit to Bangkok, but his first words were met with a barrage of groans and complaints from the others.

Bernard coughed up something disgusting and spat it out. "Theodore, if I hear one more story about you and the hookers on Pat Pong Road, I'm really gonna puke." He turned to some of the others standing around, heads thrown back, gasping for air. "Why is it the cherry boys who come back from R and R spend all their time talking about getting laid like they invented it?"

There was some laughter at Theodore's expense, but he just shrugged it off. "Okay, okay. I won't tell y'all, then. Just fuck you guys!"

Hollister tried to watch Theodore without being noticed. He was hoping that Theodore was getting along better with the others. The fact that they were teasing him without crossing the line was a good sign.

After breakfast there was plenty still to do. Hollister pulled out his notebook while he lingered over a cup of coffee. He checked the list and looked at his watch. Not all of the items were absolutely essential—they were rechecks of things he had already checked.

He decided to leave through the orderly room. Inside he found Bernard at the typewriter and Easy hunched over a four-drawer file cabinet.

Captain Michaelson was in his office talking on the land line to Brigade. He was still in his PT uniform, unshaven, smoking a cigar, with his dusty jungle boots up on his desk.

"First Sergeant, I'm going out tonight and won't be back for four days if we don't get lucky. Are we square?" Hollister asked.

Easy looked around, his hand holding a place in the files in the second drawer. "About what, Lieutenant?"

"Do I owe you anything? I hate getting back from the bush only to find out that I've missed some fucking suspense date on some form that I didn't even know existed. Like last time—

Vector Control Officer's Quarterly Report? You know I was really thinking about it, clutching a Claymore detonator in one hand and a bottle of bug juice in the other.''

"You go on out there and smite the wily Cong and I'll cover for you, Lieutenant. Can't have my young warriors worryin' about the paperwork. That's why God invented first sergeants. Anyhow, I'm getting pretty good at finding your signature when I need it.''

"Hope you're not forging my signature, First Sergeant."

"No! Never! I just put the paperwork in Bernard's in-box with a note that it needs your signature and," Easy snapped his fingers, "that fast, I have 'em back—signed."

Hollister looked at Bernard, who had stopped typing. Realizing that Hollister was looking at the back of his neck, Bernard quickly started typing again—rapidly.

"Well, I feel a lot better then, Top. Glad to know that the wheels of administration won't come to a halt while I'm gone.''

Michaelson stepped out of his office and waited for Hollister and Easy to quit talking. "Once you two have solved all of our problems, may I have a word with the first sergeant?"

"Oh," Hollister said, "yessir. Don't let me hold you up." He pointed toward the door. "I have plenty to do anyway. So, if you'll excuse me, sir. I have to check out the chopper rigging.''

Hollister waited for Michaelson to make some kind of response, but he only smiled and rolled his eyes. Clearly, the captain thought they might find something better to do than bullshit about the paperwork.

Hollister fingered the cable used to create the anchor ring on the chopper floor. Two loops of three-eighth-inch steel cable were connected to the chopper by double climber's snap links hooked to the cargo tie-down rings on the decking.

The snap links were set in opposing bites, their gates opening in different directions. He followed the cabling with his eyes and his fingers until he was sure that there were no crimps or burrs in the spiral wires that made up the cable.

Satisfied with the cable ring, he inspected the double snap-link connectors that held the rappeling ropes to the ring. Again they were reversed for opposite bites. He snapped each spring-loaded gate to make sure that the springs would hold them closed.

Attached to the snap links were the rappeling ropes, bent double and hooked to them in the center point on the ropes. The ropes' free ends were coiled loosely into sandbags. Standing near the open doorways were five ropes, five sandbags.

Hollister spread the twisted coils of each rope, looking in between the coils for dirt, grit, or signs of damage that might weaken the ropes.

Allard and Camacho stood by, watching Hollister inspect the rigging. They were happy to have him double-check their work. No one wanted to step off the skids of the chopper and fall sixty feet to near certain death.

Hollister was walking back to his hooch, flipping through his notebook, when he heard a jeep approaching. It was driven by an American, but he couldn't see through the dusty windshield. The front bumper markings identified the jeep as one belonging to the Advisory Team in An Hoa.

The driver swerved over to Hollister and came to a jerky halt. It was then that Hollister finally recognized Colonel Baird—Colonel Minh's U.S. advisor.

Hollister raised his hand to salute, but before he could say anything the colonel was out of his jeep and had his face pushed into Hollister's.

"You are just the man I am looking for! Just who in the fuck do you think you are fucking with?!" the colonel yelled.

Hollister started to ask just what Baird's problem was but was cut off.

"Shut up! I'll do the talking here. And you can stand there with your goddamn heels locked together until *I* tell you to stand at ease. You got that, Lieutenant?"

The blood was pulsing in Hollister's temples. Again he tried to reply and was cut off.

"I want to know just what made you think you could come over to *my* Province Headquarters and decide just how much information you were going to coordinate with *my* people. You don't tell us what the hell you are doing, what kind of units you are moving into *our* area, and you don't even leave a complete overlay of your control measures! You running your own goddamn war here, Lieutenant? Huh?"

The colonel waved his finger in Hollister's face, only a fraction of an inch from his nose, and screamed even louder. "Let me remind you that this is not *your* country—you got that?"

Hollister didn't know what the colonel's problem was, but he was a second away from knocking him on his ass.

"Colonel!"

Hollister and Colonel Baird looked around at Captain Michaelson running toward them from the orderly room. He stopped very close to the colonel and pushed his chin out. "Colonel, if you have a problem—take it up with me. I command this unit, not Lieutenant Hollister. And he works for me—not you!"

The colonel raised his hand to point at Hollister. "I've been told that this man—"

Michaelson cut him off. "Let's take this into my office . . . *now*, Colonel."

The colonel looked at Michaelson, offended by the captain's insubordinate tone, but decided to go with him to his office.

Hollister watched them walk toward the orderly room. He knew that all hell was going to break loose once they got inside. Michaelson was known for not letting people mess with his troops, and he was a bulldog when it did happen.

Hollister finished cleaning his rifle and set it down across the half-filled laundry bag on the floor. Nothing in his hooch was cleaner than the bag.

He had decided to tear down his field gear completely for the forthcoming patrol. He made the decision because he was concerned about not carrying any more weight than he needed down the rappeling rope, because they would be crossing at least one fast-moving stream, and because a bottle of insect repellent had burst in a side pocket and seeped into the contents of the rucksack.

The leak meant that some gear inside might be contaminated and that the smell might be a little too much for the field to absorb. He didn't want to get sick from eating something poisoned by the repellent or get shot by a VC who had homed in on his bug juice.

Hollister had dumped everything out of his rucksack and spread it out on his cot, field table, and the top of his footlocker. Just as he started to inspect the stack of thirty loaded M-16 magazines, he heard loud talking from the direction of the orderly room. He looked out the door of his hooch.

Colonel Baird came flying out the orderly room door in a rage. He was threatening Captain Michaelson with going to Michaelson's commanding general about unprofessional and insubordinate conduct and something about setting an embarrassing example for Vietnamese officers.

Michaelson stood in the doorway of the orderly room with

his hands on his hips and a cigar clenched tightly in his jaw. Michaelson was about as angry as Hollister had ever seen him.

Colonel Baird got in his jeep and searched in vain for the starter switch up under the dash—above the clutch. Finally finding it, he started the jeep and ground the gears getting it into low.

Michaelson sarcastically came to attention, cigar still in his mouth, and gave Baird a salute that dripped with disgust, yelling, "Have a very nice day, Colonel," over the sounds of the racing jeep engine.

The colonel made a jerky U-turn in the center of the compound and accelerated. But just as he hit second gear, his baseball cap flew off his head and into the backseat of the jeep.

That broke Michaelson up. He stood on the steps of the orderly room laughing as Easy stepped out.

Easy broke into a huge grin. "He's right, you know, Cap'n?"

Michaelson's head snapped around to look at Easy. "Right? Right, First Sergeant? That pissant doesn't have a clue about coordination and behavior. He'd be hard pressed to find his ass with a map and a flashlight!"

"Not what I meant. He's right that you ain't heard the last of this. He's the type of officer, if the cap'n doesn't mind me saying so, that'll spend mosta the rest of his tour over here tryin' to fuck the cap'n up."

Michaelson dropped his chin and looked down at the ground, thinking for a minute. "Well, he better bring his fucking lunch bucket if he's gonna fuck with me."

"I'da told him that, if I'd been asked," Easy added.

Michaelson met Easy's eyes and they both broke up.

Hollister agreed with Easy. That wasn't the end of it. He remembered that he had a magazine in his hand, walked back to the cot, sat back down in the folding chair facing it, and began to check the magazines.

He stripped the first few rounds out of the magazine and looked down inside. The rounds were oily and clean. No sign of dirt. He pressed down on the top round to test the strength and travel of the spring. It worked smoothly and had plenty of upward pressure. He then raised the magazine to his face and smelled it, looking for any sign of insect repellent. He didn't know what the bug juice might do to the ammo or the magazine, but he knew he didn't want to find out on the upcoming patrol.

Theodore knocked on the frame of Hollister's hooch. "Sir, Sergeant Davis sent me over with some stuff for you."

''Get in here, Theodore,'' Hollister answered without stopping his inspection.

Theodore entered with a case of C rations, a Claymore bag full of det cord, and a second bag with a complete Claymore in it, and a third on his shoulder. He put the first two bags on the field table and dropped the rations on the floor.

''Chow and demo for you. And wait till you see what else I got, sir.''

Hollister turned to look. Theodore was proudly holding the M-79 that Hollister had recovered after Lucas was wounded. ''Just got it back from Brigade. Bernard told me to tell you that your contact up there said that this is boocoup *unauthorized*.''

Hollister took the weapon and looked it over. ''Thanks, Theodore.''

He had always been bothered by the fact that as a platoon leader he was often called upon to mark targets for gunships and tactical air support only to find that he had to either identify a terrain feature for the pilots or give them directions from however far he could throw a smoke grenade. Both systems were too iffy for Hollister.

His solution was to use the training rounds that were supplied to M-79 grenadiers. On impact they gave off a small amount of yellow smoke. It would give a platoon leader or team leader the reach beyond his throwing ability. The only problem was, the size and length of the M-79 was a little too much for the occasional use it would get.

The idea came to him when he saw Lucas's damaged M-79 at the Clearing Station. He thought that chopping it down might solve the bulk problem. The modifications cost him a bottle of bourbon.

Hollister turned it over and then held it for balance. The barrel was cut off at the end of the hand grip, the sight was removed, and the stock was cut off just behind the trigger housing. It was short enough to slip into a primitive holster that Hollister had made in the local village.

For balance, it wasn't bad. He broke open the shotgunlike chamber and looked down the shortened barrel. It looked okay to him. Closing the barrel, he slipped the weapon into the clumsy-looking holster. It fit snugly and creaked as the new leather swelled to accept the weapon.

Hollister smiled. ''It won't be as accurate as a regular M-79 is. But it'll be hell for marking targets.''

Theodore slipped a third Claymore bag off his shoulder. ''Sir, this is filled with practice rounds. Sergeant Davis got 'em from a buddy in Saigon.''

"Good deal," Hollister said, looking at Theodore. "You ready to go?''

Theodore looked up at Hollister as if there was something wrong. "Yessir, why?''

"Why? Because if you aren't ready to go, it's going to be a rough trip," Hollister said, and then gave Theodore a smile.

Theodore realized that he wasn't in trouble and relaxed a bit. "Yessir. I'm ready. Got my shit, ah . . . I mean my gear, packed already. The radio's working five by five and I'm ready.''

"Okay, then do me a favor and help me show the newbies how it's done out there. I'll need all the help I can get.''

Theodore straightened up and pushed his chest out a little. "Yes, sir. You can count on me. I'm on the job.''

"Okay, then. Thanks for bringing all that gear over.''

"Oh, no problem, sir. You want me to fill your canteens for you?''

"No. I'll take care of it. Thanks again.''

"Anytime, sir. I, ah . . . I, ah, better get back to the team hooch.''

"Okay, Theodore, I'll see you at chow.''

Theodore saluted and stepped out the door. As he did, Hollister could hear the lift in his voice as he forcefully said, "Airborne, sir!''

Hollister smiled at Theodore and went back to systematically checking the other twenty-nine magazines. He found that he had only one with a sign of corrosion and one with a spring that dragged. He replaced them, took eight magazines and started to put them into the two ammo pouches on his pistol belt. The others he'd load into the rucksack when he repacked it.

When he got to the second ammo pouch, he realized that he had replaced it on his last patrol and still had to cut down the upper corners, as he'd been taught by Davis. He pulled out his demo knife and opened it. Lifting the top on the new pouch, he cut the forward corners down about three-quarters of an inch to relieve the tight grip that the well-sewn edge had on the magazines. He then reloaded the pouch and checked the ease of removal of the magazines.

Then Hollister lifted his shoulder harness and pistol belt and turned it around to face him. It was all just about ready to be replaced, except for the new ammo pouch, which was dark green against the faded and stained colors of the other items.

The smaller straps on the bottom of the harness were thread-bare and would certainly not make two more patrols. He started at the top—jumpmaster style. On the left side of his harness was a first aid packet that held his compass. The compass was at-tached to the harness by a length of parachute suspension line—a dummy cord.

The term came from Ranger School, where students were so semiconscious most of the time that they often left things behind when patrols moved out. So, an enterprising instructor who was tired of having to double back to look for lost equipment made it SOP that all students would tie a full bootlace on important items, such as weapons, and the other end to themselves, so they wouldn't get misplaced.

The line on Hollister's compass was long enough for him to hold it at waist level, but not so long that he could sit on it if it were hanging by the line.

He pulled out the compass, opened the cover, and pulled the sight away from the dial. He let the compass lie flat in the palm of his hand. The dial spun rapidly at first, overshot north, then reversed itself and sought out magnetic north again.

The spin was free and the face was clear and unbroken. He grabbed the bezel ring and turned it. It was good. He checked the knot on the cord, folded the compass, loosely wrapped the length of parachute suspension line around it, and dropped it back into the first aid pouch.

An L-shaped flashlight was hooked into the small squared metal ring attached to the right side of the shoulder harness. Hollister took the flashlight off the harness and untied the har-ness end of the dummy cord. Free from the web gear, he flicked the flashlight on and off twice. It worked. He then pressed the small button above the on-off switch to see if it would work as a quick signal without making noise. It did. He quickly un-screwed the base of the flashlight and dumped the batteries out into the palm of his hand. He rolled them around for a second to see if there was any leakage or corrosion. Satisfied, he re-placed the batteries and replaced the end. He untied the cord from around the harness and tossed the flashlight onto the pile of other items that would go into the rucksack.

He decided that the flashlight was too likely to come loose while he was rappeling, and get fouled in the gate of his snap link on the ride down from the chopper. He couldn't take the chance. Anyway, he was sure that he wouldn't be needing the flashlight on the trip down.

He passed up the ammo pouch in the left side of his pistol belt since he had checked it out when he put the magazines in it. Next to it was a first aid pouch that held a combat dressing. He pulled it out and inspected it for damage or moisture.

Next to that was a one-quart canteen cover. It was empty. The canteens were all in a pile on the floor. He would fill them later. He flipped the belt over and checked the attaching clips on the back of the canteen cover. Because they took so much abuse from the frame of the rucksack bumping and rubbing up against them, they tended to go first. One was good and the other had come open. He bent the clip and slid it into a locked position.

Hollister ran his hands around the open part of the belt and checked the four hooks that held the harness to the pistol belt. It was the harness that held up the pistol belt, not the tension around the waist. They were okay.

The canteen cover on the right-hand side had a large hole worn in the bottom, but the back clips were okay.

Next to the second canteen cover was a square nylon survival packet that was closed with a large patch of Velcro. He had scrounged it off a Special Forces lieutenant he had met earlier in his tour. It was full of aspirin, iodine, fishing line, and water purification tablets, and very difficult to repack once opened.

The next item was the C rations that Theodore had brought over. The case had been opened on the bottom, and all but Hollister's rations had been taken out by the others.

Picking rations from the bottom was a custom in infantry units. Rations were pulled out of the case with the markings down so that everyone had a fair chance at the good and the bad rations.

Left in the case were ten boxes. Ten complete meals. He would never eat that much. He always lost his appetite in the bush, and would rather hump the weight in water.

He flipped the boxes over. From the selection, he pulled the beans with franks; the beefsteak, potatoes and gravy; and the beans with meatballs. He cannibalized all ten of the boxes to get the pound cake, peaches, fruit cocktail, crackers, peanut butter, and cheese cans.

He pulled open three of the sundry packets for the tiny salt packets he would use to brush his teeth, and the chewing gum, to keep his mouth moist.

He grabbed two pairs of rolled-up woolen boot socks from the top tray of his footlocker and busted the first one open. He put a main meal can and a couple of fruit or cracker cans in each of three socks and tied the socks onto the frame of his rucksack.

Rations down—he looked around at clothing. He would wear his tiger fatigues in and carry a second set of trousers. The shirts usually made it in the field, but the trousers got torn up the back. He rolled a spare pair of beaten-up trousers very tightly and placed it back on the cot.

He made sure that he had his floppy bonnie hat, a medical cravat, a spare pair of bootlaces, an olive-drab towel that had been cut in half lengthwise, and a poncho liner.

Hollister set the items aside and started on the odds and ends.

He reinventoried and reinspected his sealed film can of matches and a small signal mirror with a bootlace tied to it so he could slip it around his neck and drop it inside his shirt.

That done, he surveyed the pile and found the three metal tubes of camouflage stick—black, loam, and green. In his locker he found another plastic bottle of insect repellent and threw that on the pile.

The field phone rang.

"Lieutenant Hollister. This is Marrietta. We just got some new met data in."

"Not any bad news, is it?"

"No sir. Not unless you're a dink."

"Thanks. I'll be over."

Hollister hung up and tried to remember where he had left off. The survival packet. He moved on to the next item, a lumpy canteen cover that held four fragmentation grenades. He pulled out each grenade, checked that the pins were folded over, and then looked closely at the condition of the spoons, searching for any cracks.

The next was a first aid packet that contained a pencil flare gun and six small flares. He dumped them out into his palm and looked them over. They were a little chipped, but everything else looked okay.

He dumped the flare gun and flares back into the pouch, snapped the flap and moved on to his knife.

A field knife was every LRP's essential tool. It was usually some type of civilian hunting knife—larger than a folding knife and more useful than the useless GI bayonet.

He unsnapped the leather retaining strap that secured his Marine Corps K-bar knife. He ran his thumb across the blade to feel for sharpness. It needed a little work.

The sheath had a small sharpening stone attached to it, in a pouch that Hollister had had a shoe shop stitch onto it back at Fort Benning.

He spit on the stone and ran the blade across it a few times. He thumbed it a second time and was satisfied. He put it back and swung the harness over the back of the chair next to the bunk.

Hollister looked around the room. Canteens! He had to fill his canteens. He picked up the four one-quart canteens and the single two-quart canteen off the floor and started out the door.

Hollister held the water trailer nozzle open to fill his canteen. Looking at the top of the canteen, he could tell that the small bottle of water purification tablets taped to the canteen was filled with water. That meant the tablets were bad. He'd have to get some more before he left, or risk any number of bugs in the water out in the AO—not to mention what was already growing in the water trailer.

CHAPTER 23

Hollister returned to his hooch only to discover that he had not yet checked out the Claymore mine that Theodore had brought him. Few things could be as useless as humping a Claymore that had something missing. Or more dangerous than leaving one in the bush because it was incomplete or inoperable.

Even an inoperable Claymore was a useful item for the VC. It could be disassembled and rebuilt into small booby traps, and contained the makings for command-detonated mines and fragmentation that could even be used in a homemade shotgun. If he was going to take a Claymore to the bush, it was going to be in working shape.

He dropped his canteens on the floor next to his rucksack and grabbed the Claymore bag. Flipping open the flap, he squatted and spilled the contents onto the floor. The Claymore in the bag had been taken out on a patrol at least once before. The firing wire had been rewound around the body of the mine itself.

It was a convenient way to wrap up the wire, but it made it very difficult to unwind the wire without getting it fouled in the folded scissor legs on the bottom of the mine. It was sloppy fieldwork.

As he unwound the wire, he checked it out for breaks or cuts. He next inspected the body of the mine itself. The Claymore was designed to be placed on the ground, facing out from a perimeter or near the edge of an ambush killing zone. Once detonated, the mine would hurl seven hundred ball bearings out into a sixty-degree fan less than six feet high. It was lethal out to as much as fifty meters. In addition to the knockdown power of the Claymore, there was a shock effect that could be relied upon to stun those caught close to the killing area of the mine.

The arched body of the mine, which looked like a book with

a curve in it, was none the worse for wear from having been humped to the bush and back. The shipping plug was missing, and the well for the blasting cap that attached to the end of the firing cord had a little dirt and debris in it. Hollister blew it out and flipped the mine over. The two pairs of folding legs on the bottom were dirty where they had been stabbed into the ground, but were otherwise undamaged.

Hollister put the mine down and picked up the firing device. It was a simple handheld pulse generator that provided enough electrical current down the firing wire to detonate the blasting cap and ultimately detonate the directional mine.

When the firing device was unconnected, he turned it over in the palm of his hand a couple of times and then gripped it for firing. Squeezing the handle, he felt the resistance that was part of the mechanism. If the device had no resistance or wouldn't move at all, he would replace it.

Last item—the electric blasting cap. There was little Hollister could check except the condition of the metal body of the cap and the connector to the firing wire.

Satisfied that the entire Claymore was intact and likely to work properly, he put all of the items back into the carrying bag except the wire, then looked around the hooch for something to wrap the wire around to keep it from getting tangled. The cardboard box that had held the C rations was just what he needed. Tearing off a piece and folding it to make a core, Hollister wrapped the wire around the cardboard and then put it into the bag.

The last items he checked were his snap link, gloves, and sling rope. He opened the gate on the snap link to separate his worn rappeling gloves from the metal mountain climber's connector and ran his fingers over the surface of the solid aluminum oval, looking for any burrs in the metal that might cause the rappeling rope to snag or tear. He had been using the same snap link since arriving in Vietnam, and it was discolored from the weather but still smooth. He thought for a moment about replacing it, but gave in to a sentimental hunch that it was his lucky snap link.

He snapped the gate several times to check the action. It was essential that the spring hold the gate closed while he was hooked onto the rappeling rope. If the spring failed, it could be fatal.

His sling rope, a ten-foot length of nylon climbing rope, was new. Hollister had replaced it when he discovered the insect repellent bottle leak. Some of it had soaked a section of his old sling rope, and he didn't want to take the chance that it would weaken the nylon.

The rope was so new that it was still a shiny dark green color. He stretched it out and looked at it for kinks or loosening of the twisted coils. Satisfied, he held a lighter to the cut ends of the rope, then checked the condition of the melted nylon stubs. Once melted, the ends wouldn't unravel into the hundreds of small nylon threads that made up the rope. He ran his finger over one melted end and then did the same to the other end.

He folded the rope twice and placed it next to his rifle. There was no need to coil it since he would have to fashion it into a Swiss seat before he got into the chopper. The Swiss seat would be the hasty field harness that he would tie around his hips to hold him onto the rappeling rope by the snap link.

Hollister completed the inspection of the rappeling apparatus by checking out his own sling rope. He had examined the tie-down ring in the chopper, the rappeling ropes, his snap link, and his sling rope. It wouldn't be the last time he would inspect it all.

He looked at his watch, considered going to the mess hall for some lunch but decided against it. He still had too much to do. Anyway, he could live without a heavy lunch.

He finished packing his gear into his rucksack, stuffing the canteens into their carriers, and found a new bottle of water purification tablets.

Hollister put on his web gear and slipped the rucksack over his shoulders. The load was heavy. He jumped up and down several times to check for clanking, banging, or rattling. He discovered that the handle of his knife was making a noise against his rucksack frame. With a tightening of the shoulder strap, the rucksack frame rode higher and stopped the noise.

He dropped his ruck and harness back onto his cot and stood in the center of his hooch trying to decide what to do next. Maps, SOIs, notes? All that was in one pile on his desk.

Trying to write just before a patrol was almost impossible. Davis came by the hooch with some last minute coordination. After five minutes Theodore came back with some changes in the radio frequencies, then Bernard called to ask about an item on Virgil's inventory.

Hollister gritted his teeth and promised himself that he wasn't going to give up. He had made up his mind to get the letters written and he was going to do it.

Three more interruptions followed the others, but he still got two short letters written. He addressed them and made one final check to see that he had the letters in the right envelopes. He closed the self-sealing flaps, flipped the envelopes back over, wrote FREE in the corner where stamps usually went, and smiled. He could only imagine what a mess postage stamps would be in the humidity of Vietnam. Free postage was one of the very few good deals that the troops got in country.

Michaelson, Hollister, Davis, Allard, and Camacho from the LRPs, and pilots Iron Mike Taylor and Shelton, sat together while they ate supper. The other patrol members and the aircraft crews clustered at another table. Because of their schedule, Sergeant Kendrick had prepared their meal early and they had the mess hall to themselves.

At Hollister's table they did some eating, some kidding around, and some final coordination for the insert. At the other table the conversation was mostly centered on women.

There wasn't much anxiety about making enemy contact on the insert, but they were all a little more skittish about going in on ropes.

Hollister ate some of the gluelike mashed potatoes and flipped the page on his notebook with his free hand. The infiltration of two chopper loads of LRPs by rope required a higher degree of coordination, timing and luck than the more routine inserts. He wanted to make sure that he hadn't forgotten something.

He looked up from his notes to Davis and Allard. "You go over the emergency commands with the chopper crews?"

Davis put down his coffee. "Yessir. We're gonna go over it one more time with the crews and the teams chopperside—after the inspection."

"Without the choppers cranking?"

Captain Shelton raised his hands in surrender. "Okay, we'll keep 'em shut down till y'all are ready. Whew, what prima donnas," he added.

Captain Michaelson cleared his throat and wiped the corner of his mouth with the back of his hand. He looked at his watch and then over toward Hollister and Shelton. "Well, as much as I hate to eat and fly—we got to go sink the VC navy."

The talking stopped. Hollister felt his gut tighten. He tried to convince himself it was a natural response that would keep him sharp. It was better than admitting how anxious he was. Unconnected scenes flashed through his mind. He thought of Lucas' family at graveside. He thought of Susan.

"You coming, Lieutenant?" someone said.

Hollister looked around, realizing that he was the only one still seated.

"Yeah, sure. Wouldn't miss it."

Standing in front of Theodore, Hollister started the inspection at his head and worked down. No one was wearing head gear for fear that it would be blown off during the insert. Theodore's camouflage job left a quarter-inch line of white skin above the dark, mottled grease and below his hairline. Hollister pointed out the white ribbon on Theodore's face to Sergeant Davis, who was standing next to Hollister.

Continuing, Hollister traced his eyes and fingers down the front of Theodore's web gear, checking out his grenades, the homemade wire hook on the back of the radio handset, the plastic battery bag that covered the handset to keep it dry, ammo pouches, and finally his rifle.

He lightly punched Theodore in the stomach. "Bend over."

Theodore bent at the waist and supported his weight by resting his rifle across the tops of both thighs. Hollister looked over the top of Theodore's shoulders at the PRC-25 radio that was strapped into place on the frame above Theodore's rucksack.

Hollister asked Theodore the primary frequency. Theodore gave it to him. Hollister checked the preset stops on the radio. He then flipped the frequency dial to the second preset stops and read the frequency. He asked Theodore the alternate freq. Theodore's answer matched the numbers on the dial. Hollister flipped the dial back to the primary frequency and reached for the connector that attached the handset cord to the radio. He looked for breaks or wear.

Satisfied with the connector, he checked the base connector for the small antenna and then ran his hand out to the tip of the flat, flexible antenna.

"Okay, get your face fixed up and go sit down till we're ready to go."

"Yessir," Theodore said, exhaling nervously.

Hollister moved on to the next man.

As the chopper blades spun up, Hollister found himself fingering his rifle and checking the seating of its magazine.

He looked around the inside of the darkened chopper. He

eally hated the thought of rappeling in at night, because of the greater possibility of error.

He stretched his neck and looked out and above the chopper for the moon. It was every bit as large and bright as it had been he night before, and he couldn't see any cloud cover. But the sky out over the South China Sea was totally black, and he knew that it could conceal a weather front that might move in on them n minutes.

The trip to the landing zone was much more charged with feelings for Hollister than the same trip just a day earlier. He could feel his pulse pounding and taste the dryness that came to his mouth whenever he started to pump adrenaline.

Sergeant Davis got up on his knees in the center of the chopper. He started with the soldiers in the trailing edge of both doors and touched each one on the back, working his way to the front of the chopper. Every man turned around and made eye contact with Davis to let him know that they understood his hand signal—to hook up.

Hollister leaned over and tapped Theodore on the shoulder. "You got commo with Allard?"

Theodore bobbed his head up and down to make sure that Hollister could see his answer.

"Check it again. I gotta be able to talk to him if things get fucked up while we're going in."

Theodore took the handset off his harness and held it to his face. "Two-one, this is Two-six Romeo. Commo check. Over."

Hollister watched as Theodore listened to the handset, holding his finger in his other ear. He must have had good commo with Allard or his RTO because he replied, "Roger. Good copy. Have you same. Out."

Theodore hung the handset back on the canvas tab on his harness and looked back at Hollister. "Yessir!" he yelled over the chopper noises.

To reduce the number of loose items that could get fouled in the rappeling rope, Hollister reached over, took the handset from Theodore's harness, and pulled open the neck of Theodore's shirt. He dropped the handset down the front of the shirt and stuffed as much of the coiled handset cord down after it as he could.

Pushing Theodore forward, he folded the short antenna and tucked it down between Theodore's rucksack and his back.

"Get ready!" Davis yelled.

One at a time Davis had each man step out onto a skid of the chopper while Davis held him firmly by his Swiss seat. This allowed each soldier to straighten up and thread his individual rappeling rope through his snap link without having to use one hand to hold on.

Once each man was set outside the chopper with his feet on the skid and his weight pulling against the anchored climbing rope, Davis checked the bight of the rope through the gate of the snap link and then reached over to check that the soldier's slung weapon was on safe. Satisfied, he pointed at the soldier, looked him directly in the eyes, and yelled, "Okay."

Quickly, all five LRPs, including Hollister, were outside the chopper, looking out and down over their shoulders at the ground.

The co-pilot signaled Davis as the pilot killed off some airspeed and altitude.

Starting with the rearmost rope-filled bag, Davis kicked them out.

One after another the bags fell, stretching the coiled ropes down and slightly to the rear of the chopper. Each man looked down to see that his line played out smoothly.

Davis flattened out on the floor of the chopper and stuck his head out on the side that only had two rappelers on the skid. He watched as the ground got closer and closer. He held up his hand for the rappelers to see him count down his fingers—five, four, three, two, and one.

He got to his knees just as the chopper stopped its forward motion and came to a high hover more than forty feet above the trees. Davis pointed to the last man on the right of the chopper and yelled, "Go!" He then turned to the last man on the left of the chopper and did the same. He continued ordering each man off the skids until he reached Hollister.

Hollister gave a large nod and was gone.

Davis watched the last two men fly down the rope. The first three were already on the ground and pulling the free ends of their ropes through their snap links. As soon as they were free, they held their arms out to their sides to let Davis know they were clear.

The fourth man hit the ground and lost his footing. Then Hollister stopped dead in the air, about eight feet above the ground. His line was fouled and he couldn't get to the ground or off the rope.

Hollister let loose with his guide hand as he spun out of con-

rol on the rope. He kept his right hand on the braking end of
the rope in case whatever was fouled came loose, to be able to
control his rate of descent. Even an eight to ten foot fall could
put him out of commission.

His free hand found the problem. A small branch blown loose
by the violent downwash of the chopper had found its way into
the snap link just below his waist. He knew he couldn't free the
snag, so he looked back up the rope to the chopper and searched
for Davis.

Davis was squatting in the door—a step ahead of Hollister,
he already had his knife out and was holding it so Hollister could
see it.

They couldn't land the helicopter, and it would jeopardize the
crew if they tried to gain enough altitude to take off with Hollister dangling underneath the chopper. Hollister had no choice.
He took his left hand and patted himself on the top of the head,
the standard Airborne signal that a hung jumper gives to let the
jumpmaster know that he is conscious and ready to be cut loose.

Davis recognized the signal and slashed the taut rope, cutting
Hollister free without delay.

Hollister fell to the ground, landing on his back. The rucksack broke his fall, but it knocked much of the wind out of him.

Davis reached for the handset to the radio he had lashed to
the leg on the door gunner's seat. "Two-six Romeo this is Two-
six Alpha. What's Two-six's condition? Over."

Hollister rolled over and looked at the edge of the small scar
in the trees. Theodore had the handset to his face. Hollister gave
him an okay sign to pass to Davis. Time was critical. They had
to get the second chopper to and away from the landing zone as
fast as possible.

Even though Hollister couldn't hear what Theodore said to
Davis, he assumed that the message got passed because the
chopper nosed over from its high hover and slipped down the
side of the hill to gain airspeed. As Hollister watched the chopper fall away, he could see Davis in the door, pulling in the
trailing ropes.

Allard's chopper quickly came to a hover directly over Hollister, who rolled off his rucksack and tried to get to his feet to
make room for Allard's team members. His back hurt like hell.
He had overextended it and the pain was sharp and hot at the
same time.

Allard's team flew down their ropes in record time, cleared

them, and stepped out from under the chopper—just the way it was supposed to be done.

The chopper nosed over and did a descending left turn, kissing the trees on the way down the slope.

Then it was silent time. The LRPs listened for movement—any movement that would tell them someone was nearby. As the chopper noises faded off to the east, the night sounds returned. That was a good sign.

At Hollister's instruction, Theodore called the *in-and-cold* message to Captain Michaelson, who was orbiting a few miles east of the patrol's position.

The patrol then took up their march order and moved out. The going was tough at first; loose rock and gravel made the footing unreliable. Hollister heard the crunch of boots against gravel and the occasional misstep.

After two hundred meters the rock and gravel gave way to the moist, decaying, layered ground cover that blanketed most of the wooded areas in the Central Highlands. The going then got quiet.

Hollister let the patrol move another ten minutes and then held them up.

He called Allard and Camacho to his location—fourth man back in the file. He had them take up hasty security positions so they could have a few minutes to catch their breath and adjust their loads.

Hollister dropped his rucksack to reach around and feel for any damage to his back. There was no doubt that he was going to know about landing on his back for the remainder of the patrol.

For a moment he considered asking the medic to look at it, but decided against it as he thought of the message it would send to the others. He decided just to tough it out.

He pulled out his compass and turned to face down the hill. His compass heading was what it should be, and the small knoll, where they would hole up, was only about a half hour's hump away. He hoped that it was unoccupied.

The night sounds were a little muted by the wind. Hollister looked out through a break in the trees toward the ocean. The stars filled the sky, and he stole a second to enjoy them. Vietnam's night skies were beautiful on a clear night. The black was deeper and the stars were crisper and seemed closer.

Then the wind stopped for a brief time, the trees stopped

rustling, and Hollister could hear the water running in the fast-moving stream below them that was their objective.

Hollister found Camacho, motioned him over, and leaned forward to speak softly in Camacho's ear. "I figure that we got the right route. Oughta be at the ambush position on schedule. Everything else okay?"

Camacho gave an exaggerated nod. Everyone was ready to move.

Hollister gave him a pat on the shoulder, indicating he, too, was ready to get on with it.

The closer they got to the streambed, the thicker the vegetation got. They made more noise moving, but much of it was covered by the growing noise of the gurgling water.

Allard was walking point when they reached the knoll where the patrol would hold up. It was too early for them to go down to the stream and emplace the demolitions, so they would establish a perimeter and then send a recon party to the stream to take a quick look at the ambush site.

Camacho, Allard, and Hollister met in the center of the hastily established perimeter. Keeping his web gear on, Hollister dropped his rucksack next to Theodore, squatted down, and took the handset. Cupping his free hand around the mouthpiece, he exhaled and then spoke. "Quarterback. We have closed on the hotel. Over."

The base radio operator rogered the transmission, and Hollister gave the handset back to Theodore. He pointed down the hill and said, "Twenty minutes."

Theodore was to start worrying if his boss and the recon party weren't back by then.

Camacho reached the spot where the stream, which had been running parallel to their path, turned and crossed their line of march. He held up the file and waited for the others to move forward.

They all found a spot to lie down and watch the stream flow by. They were in the bend in the stream, which flowed on three sides of them, and each man had his own needs on the recon.

Allard was trying to locate spots to place his half of the patrol to provide security while Camacho's demo team placed the explosives along the far bank just under the waterline.

Camacho strained to see the details of the far bank. He looked for the strongest part of the bank, laden with roots and a sharp-

cut wall with growth on it. He didn't want the patrol to collapse
parts of the stream bank trying to get in or out of the water. It
would be too hard to repair the damage or to conceal it from
sampans coming down the stream into the turn.

Hollister looked for a place to cross the stream that wouldn't
give them away while they were doing it.

They each got what they wanted, and Hollister turned the
recon party around to head back to the knoll.

The trip back was uneventful until they got out of sight of the
stream itself. Fifty meters up from the bank Camacho tapped
Hollister on the shoulder and motioned for him to stop and listen.

They froze in place and listened.

Down the hill they heard the sounds of paddles and some
talking. They couldn't make out what was being said, but it was
clearly Vietnamese.

Hollister decided to take no action. With the patrol split, no
understanding of the enemy threat, and no way to coordinate
fires, he decided to let them go by.

While they passed, he looked at his watch and tried to figure
out how many boats were involved and how many people were
on them. He would have to include the information in a sitrep
he would send once he reached the nighttime position.

It didn't take long for the moon to set. Hollister could see the
stars through the small trees on top of the knoll, but the mottled
pattern of shadows that the moon threw had disappeared.

He rolled his fatigue shirt cuff back and looked at the luminous hands on the dial of his watch. It was almost one A.M. It
was getting cold, and the night sounds had quieted considerably
since the moon was at its highest.

He knew that he had half an hour before he needed to wake
Theodore, and an hour before they all had to get ready to move.

Hollister thought about the move. He was concerned that they
might run into some VC activity at the streambed just before
sunrise. His theory was that whoever used the stream to go down
into the valley after dark would want to get back up into the
foothills before daylight. That hardly gave him a clear window
of time to feel more secure about putting the demolitions in. He
had picked a time three hours before dawn as a guess that those
coming down into the valley had already passed and the ones
returning hadn't started back yet. He hoped he had guessed

right. He didn't want to get caught with half his patrol in the water attaching demolitions to the stream bank.

His gut gurgled. He was anxious about putting the demo in. They had to get the job done in the shortest time possible to reduce their exposure and get the hell out of the killing zone— the bend in the stream.

If the VC came up on them in their sampans before the demo team could scramble out of the water, it could be a nightmare. He was glad that they had rehearsed every move before leaving the base camp. It would pay off in time saved, and cut down on the need to talk while putting the explosives in place.

As always, he just had to trust that his LRPs would do their job—fast.

Reaching the near bank of the stream, the patrol stopped to put out security. Allard's team broke into two elements and set up firing positions that alternately looked up and down the stream.

While they moved into position, Camacho and Cullen, from Allard's team, took off their gear, shirts, trousers, and boots. Naked, they placed all of the gear in the center of two ponchos they had spread out on the ground. Using leaves and four empty canteens for bulk and buoyancy, they wrapped up everything but their rifles and tied the bundle together with parachute suspension line. That done, Camacho clipped a flashlight to the line and helped Cullen lift the fabricated raft to the water without dragging it.

Once the security was in place and the two swimmers were ready, Hollister called the Operations RTO and reported that they were crossing the blue line. Hollister then gave the signal, and Camacho and Cullen slipped off the bank and into the ice-cold stream. Every other man on the patrol felt for them, anticipating his own trip across the cold water.

Because the bank was sloped on the inside of the turn, the stream got deeper as they waded out into it. It would be deepest on the far side, where the water moved the fastest and cut the bank and bottom away during the monsoon season.

Cullen held on to the two running ends of a 120-foot climbing rope as he swam to the other side. The doubled rope would just reach the far side. On the near bank it was wrapped loosely around the base of a tree so that it could be pulled through to the far side once they were finished using it as a safety line.

Camacho slipped the poncho raft into the water and held his rifle over his head with his free hand.

Hollister stayed with the others on the near bank, covering Cullen's and Camacho's movements in the water. He checked over his shoulders to make sure that the security, up- and down-stream, was paying attention to the sectors assigned to them and not watching the swimmers try to get to the far side. He knew from experience that it was human nature to want to know what you were about to get yourself into, and watching the two in the water would do that.

Hollister couldn't tell who, but one of the heads on the down-stream side turned to look back. Just as he did, Sergeant Allard reached out and popped him on the back of the neck to discipline and correct the man.

Camacho and Cullen were just reaching the far bank as Hollister turned back toward them. They had drifted more than forty-five degrees downstream from what would have been a straight line across to the far bank. It told Hollister a lot about how strong the current was. He had selected Camacho and Cullen to cross first because they were the strongest swimmers in the entire platoon.

The black ribbon of the tree line on the far bank quickly gobbled up the naked swimmers as fast as they got out of the water. The only way that Hollister knew they were okay was by watching the slack come out of the safety line.

In a few seconds Cullen had taken in all the slack he could and tied the rope off to a tree trunk on the far bank. Slack in the rope would only make it more difficult for the others to cross the stream. Once they reached the middle, where the slack was greatest, they would then have to fight against the current to make the other half of the crossing—going back upstream.

The rope stopped moving. Hollister waited several long sec-onds for Camacho to signal. Even though Hollister couldn't see them, he knew that both men were shaking violently from the cold.

Finally, Hollister saw it. It was only a sliver of red light that Camacho allowed to slip between his fingers, which covered most of the lens of the flashlight. First one, then a second rapid flashlight blink.

It was time for Hollister to take the rest of the patrol across. He reached for his top shirt button.

CHAPTER 24

As Hollister stepped into the cold mountain stream, he was reminded of the first time he had experienced the discomfort of crossing water at night—as a soldier. He was in Advanced Infantry Training at Fort Benning—they had to cross the Chattahoochee River.

At first it didn't look like it would be a problem, except the expected—getting wet. It was only when Hollister felt the cold brown water of the Chattahoochee rising on his legs that he discovered it might be a bigger problem. The moment of truth came when the water level reached his crotch. Then he became painfully aware of just how cold it was.

Hollister knew that the stream in the foothills was not going to be any more comfortable than that crossing in Georgia.

As he crossed the stream he looked up to check the visibility from above—should he need to call for air support. The trees overhung the banks enough to create a narrow slot that offered a clear view of anything that might be in the center of the stream. It didn't please Hollister. It meant that anyone on the stream could easily use the overhangs on either side to conceal themselves from aerial detection or fires from above.

He then looked up- and downstream. Crossing at the center of the turn, both the up- and downstream legs were over his shoulders. Turning, he saw that the runs to and away from him were long and straight. That was good. It would give them plenty of time to get ready to execute their ambush by having early warning of the approach of any enemy sampans.

The water finally reached Hollister's crotch. He took a sharp, deep breath and gritted his teeth to avoid crying out.

As he looked back to the front, he could see Camacho helping the lead element onto the far bank. Camacho was still barefoot and naked to the waist. Suddenly, Hollister felt a little foolis worrying about the cold he was experiencing. He knew on thing for sure. It would be a cold, wet night, and dawn couldn happen soon enough for anyone on the patrol.

As Hollister got past the halfway point in the stream, th bottom fell off rapidly. He wasn't surprised by the drop-off, bu still had a little difficulty holding his rifle and his sawed-o M-79 over his head.

Nearing the far bank, he could barely touch bottom, and th force of the current made it very difficult for him to keep hi footing. He was glad he had decided to stretch the safety rop across the stream. As he felt himself getting more buoyant, hi snap link—connected to the sling rope around his chest and th safety line—kept him from being swept downstream.

Camacho had found a point where a large root was expose on the face of the bank. It made it fairly easy for each man t crawl up and get to solid ground without having to rely on grab bing for the slick bank. Camacho was not only smart enough t use the root as a ladder, but to use it to keep the patrol fror beating up the vegetation along the bank. A disturbed strear bank would surely give them away to the VC.

Once he was on the far bank, Hollister got up from his knee and looked around for a place to move the troops completin the crossing. Under the overhang there was plenty of space o the bank to stretch out the patrol for the time it would take ther to get ready to move up the shallow slope overlooking the stream

Standing on the bank, Hollister waited for the water to drai out of his trousers before he took the first step. As he did, h watched the remainder of the patrol crossing the stream. He wa concerned that the patrol had been in the water several minutes and each additional minute increased the possibility of a V sampan coming along and compromising them.

Camacho was pointing out places away from the stream fo each soldier to move to once he got out of the water. They wer silent, save the noise of the water and their labored breathing.

The last man to cross was Sergeant Allard. As he reached th center of the stream, there was a clunking sound coming fror upstream. Everyone heard it. It sounded like an oar bangin rhythmically against the side of a waterlogged boat hull.

Hollister signaled for everyone to freeze and not to shoot i they weren't fired upon. They had gone over this in the briefbac and rehearsals back at the base camp. But he wanted to mak

sure no one got jumpy. They were just in too compromising a
position to take on a sampan at that moment. Everyone flattened
out on the stream bank.

But Allard was still in the water, and the rope was still
stretched across the stream. If Camacho pulled the rope in with
Allard hooked to it, it would take too long. Whoever was coming down the stream would be there before Allard could be
pulled out of the water.

Not quite at the middle of the stream, Allard realized what
was going on and took action on his own. He pulled out his
knife and cut one strand of the double rope. The free end quickly
slipped back toward its anchor point on the bank they had just
left; it came loose from the tree and then slipped into the water.

Allard held on to the short end of the rope as it drifted downstream—still connected to the bank where Camacho, Hollister,
and the others were.

Hollister watched as Allard drifted about forty feet downstream, holding on to the rope. The force of the current and the
anchored rope caused Allard to be pushed up against the stream
bank on Hollister's side. With a little silent paddling, Allard was
able to move to a point next to the bank and under the drooping
branches of a large tree.

Hollister waited anxiously as the thumping and thudding
sound got louder and closer. He thumbed his rifle selector switch
off safe to full-automatic.

Every man in the patrol held his breath as they waited for the
source of the noise to get closer and become visible.

Hollister raised his hand to his brow to shade his eyes from
the slight glow of the sky as he strained to see.

Then he spotted something floating in the water, though he
couldn't clearly make it out, but he was sure that something was
there. To his right he heard one of the soldiers groan in release.
He had seen it, too.

Then Hollister could see it clearly. It was not a VC sampan.
It was a large piece of a long-dead hardwood tree trunk floating
down the stream. The noise was coming from a broken branch
that had snagged the trunk and was banging against it as it floated
along.

Hollister dropped his head, breathed, and took his rifle off
automatic. He quickly remembered Allard, who was still holding on to the safety line. He reached over and tapped Camacho.
They were both thinking the same thing. They had to pull Allard
upstream to keep him from having to fight the current himself

or get out of the water and have to weave through the overgrowth on the bank to get to the patrol. And if they didn't act fast, there was a slim chance that the large log floating his way might hit him.

Allard, Camacho, and Hollister stood on the bank watching while another soldier pulled the remaining safety line from the water and coiled it up.

Time was pressing them. Allard was ready to take his team up the hill, to provide security, while Hollister and Camacho's people stayed behind to rig the demolitions.

Hollister huddled with Allard and Camacho. "Okay, let's get this done. We've already lost too much time." He looked directly at Allard. "You let me know when you're in position. And Allard—be careful."

Allard gave Hollister a nod and watched as Hollister turned his attention to Camacho.

"Soon as they clear this area—you get cracking. I want to get that demo in fast but right," Hollister said.

Hollister knew that he could count on Camacho. He thought, for a minute, what a luxury it would be to have a whole platoon of Camachos. He realized that it was his job to encourage the Camachos, and it was his job to develop and train the Camachos. He just didn't know how you put the heart into them; a heart like Camacho's.

Hollister cross-checked the firing wires that led under the deadfall near the streambed to a spool fifteen feet away. He looked for any sign of exposed wires. In the dark it was hard to see if the wires were completely covered, but it would also be hard for the VC to see. He would send a party back down in the daylight to make a final check.

Hollister signaled for two soldiers standing near him to finish spreading the dead leaves they had collected. It would be the final layer of camouflage to conceal their presence and the wires leading to the demolitions under the waterline.

The patrol was just settling into their new perimeter as the sun broke the horizon. Hollister stopped checking the individual positions just long enough to enjoy the shafts of red-yellow light that were coming through the trees. He could almost hear the groans of pleasure from the others, each of them having suffered the cold for the few hours after crossing the stream.

Hollister ended up at the key position that looked back down the hill toward the streambed and the watery killing zone. He got down to see what it offered for visibility.

He could see the upstream leg and the killing zone. His worse view was of the downstream leg. He shook his head at the luck. He knew it would be a little much to expect to have an observation point that would give him concealment but would also give him an unobstructed view of the killing zone and both approaches.

The lack of visibility on the downstream leg would mean that the position to his left might have to be adjusted to pick up that responsibility. Hollister looked over at Allard, who was in the position. He understood what Hollister was doing and pointed down toward the downstream leg and then back to his own eyes to let Hollister know he had a good shot at the approach.

Two wires, threaded from the demolitions placed under the waterline, wound up the hill to their position and the two hand detonators. Getting back up into a squat, Hollister checked out the detonators. Either one of them would set off the ambush.

Done, Hollister could go sit down for a while. He moved to a position that was just off the crest of the small hill, so that he couldn't be seen from the killing zone. Even though he couldn't see the killing zone, he was satisfied that he was just a few feet away from a position that could.

Unable to fully detach from his duties and take a break, Hollister scanned the patrol perimeter to make a check of the layout in the daylight. Theodore had just finished calling in a negative sitrep, and the others were quietly rearranging their gear.

Hollister spun his rucksack around to get to one of the canteens attached to it. As he drank the water, flavored by the plastic canteen that held it, he watched the sun move higher on the horizon, and felt the air getting warmer as it filtered through the thinner branches of the young trees that covered the hilltop. He pulled the canteen away from his face and poured a little into his hand to wipe across his eyes, which burned from the long hours without sleep.

As he did, he noticed that his hands had lost all of their camouflage. He knew that if the greasy coloring was gone on his hands and arms, it would be the same for his face and neck.

Putting the canteen away, Hollister pulled the camouflage stick out of his rucksack and reached inside his shirt for his signal mirror. Before touching up his camouflage, he raised the stick in the air and waved to get everyone's attention. They all knew

the message he was sending. They, too, had to work on their
camouflage.

Hunching over his signal mirror, carefully shading it in order
not to wildly play the sun's reflection around the area, he looked
at his face. He looked terrible. The cold, the dirt, the lack of
sleep, and the traces of camouflage around his nose, ears, and
eyes made him look old, dirty, and tired. There were dark circles
under his eyes, and his skin looked pale and a little on the puffy
side.

He didn't want to see any of it. He wanted to see himself as
strong, refreshed, confident, and ready. But it wasn't there. Instead there was a face belonging to a soldier in his mid-twenties
who looked at least ten years older. He didn't want to think that
the effect was permanent. He preferred to rationalize his look
as the result of the long hours and the work, rather than the
strain of the job, too many cigarettes, too much booze and pain.
Pain that had been in his chest since the first day he had seen
the first soldier die in his rifle platoon. He could clean up his
look. But he wasn't sure about the pain. Something told him
that it would be with him forever.

He knew that the only way to stuff the pain into the corner of
his mind was to get busy. At that moment he could do it with
the camouflage touch-up.

The cold morning air had made the camouflage stick stiff and
crumbly. He tried to wipe the color on his face from the push-
up tube, and could feel the skin being stretched as the stick
dragged on it. It was no use. He had to do something to make
it go on and stay on.

Hollister finally gave in and rummaged around in the outside
pocket of his rucksack. He pulled out the new bottle of insect
repellent and squirted a few drops of it on the end of the camouflage stick. The fluid softened the stick, allowing him to smear
it on his face more easily—but at some added cost. The insect
repellent made the mixture burn as he ground it into his skin.

Finishing, Hollister pulled out his notebook and slipped the
plastic bag off of it. He opened the book and checked it for
water damage. He was lucky. The book was spared the damage
that he had done to so many others. He was pleased that he had
made a point of scrounging the bag. It wasn't a normal plastic
bag. It had been wrapped around a new .45-caliber pistol for
packing and shipping. Whoever made the bag used thick, flexible plastic that was very durable and stuck to itself like Saran
Wrap—only many times thicker.

Flipping through the book, Hollister refreshed his memory of the call signs, the target numbers of the plotted artillery, and the new coordinates of the hilltop.

Running down his own checklist, he came to a note to re-check the wiring in the daylight. That was it—his next move.

Down below, Hollister was satisfied with the condition of the stream bank and the concealment of the emplaced demolitions and wire. Knowing that it was all done right pleased him, but he didn't want to waste a minute near the stream. He was eager to get the demo party back up the hill to reduce the likelihood of being seen by anyone on or near the stream.

Once in the perimeter, Hollister decided that he had to get some sleep. The toll of the night before, and the anticipation of the night or even nights to come, weighed him down. He checked with Theodore to see if they were current on sitreps, and then told Camacho and Allard that he was going to crap out for a while.

Hollister found a shady spot and moved his rucksack to a position where he could get comfortable. He was not bothered by the dampness of the ground or the discomfort that the roots and rocks caused him. He simply made little adjustments to his sleeping position until he found the right spot.

Sleep came over him almost immediately. It was punctuated with hurried dreams. In one of his dream patrols, he was very late. There were so many things to do, and he felt sure he was not getting them done in time. He dreamed that he was getting radio messages from Captain Michaelson chewing him out for being too slow. Too slow moving, too slow getting into position, too slow at reporting.

He also felt heavy during the dream. He was surrounded by some force that slowed his movement as if he were in mud or syrup. Still, he slept.

The heat from the sun beat down on his face. He could feel it, but didn't want to give in to it and move to the shade again. He knew that if he moved at all, it would break the veil of sleep and he would never drop off again.

He suffered the sun for several more minutes and then was assaulted by a fly. It wasn't just a regular fly. It was one of the large ones that everyone considered to be the Vietnamese equivalent of a horsefly. It was large, persistent, and very noisy. The fly kept buzzing around his face and would bump into him every now and then.

Again, Hollister tried not to move more than he had to or open his eyes as he reached down and unbuttoned the flap on his trouser leg pocket. Once open, he reached in and pulled out his wet floppy hat. He quickly unrolled the hat and dropped it loosely over his face.

The hat seemed to take care of most of the fly problem. The fly was still buzzing his face, but it wasn't landing on it. The new problem was with the sun. The dark tiger-striped pattern on the hat soaked up that much more heat, and the lack of circulation under the hat was about all the discomfort that Hollister could stand.

He sat up straight. There was no denying it. His nap was over.

As soon as he opened his eyes he realized how hot and sweaty he really was. The front of his shirt was drenched with sweat, and the back was wet from sweat and the dampness of the ground. For a fraction of a second he remembered the luxury of the bed he shared with Susan back in New York, and even the crisp BOQ room in Japan. He started to ask himself just what possessed him to be with that patrol, that day on that hill. But he didn't want to finish the question because he didn't want to get to the answer.

Hollister stood up and dropped his hat onto the top of his rucksack. He picked up his rifle and made the rounds of the positions—just to check on who was asleep, who was awake, and who was alert. He knew how the birds and the breeze in the treetops could lull his people into a complacency that could be deadly.

He hated laying up waiting for nightfall. It was an unavoidable part of ambushes. He was hungry, but the thought of C rations didn't perk him up. It would be something he would have to do after checking the perimeter and calling in a sitrep.

The cheese with caraway was beginning to run from the heat. Hollister didn't care one way or the other. It was something to satisfy the hunger pangs and required no serious preparation to eat.

He was careful not to put too much pressure on the fragile C-ration cracker as he scooped some of the cheese onto it. He had gotten pretty good at eating the crackers in such a way as to end up with a pointed wedge of cracker which he could use to get the cheese out of the right angles at the bottom of the small cans.

A bug landed in the last bit of cheese and became helplessly mired in the yellow goo. It was enough to end Hollister's meal. He collected the cans and put them aside to take with him when he answered a call to nature. Using the single entrenching tool that the patrol carried, he would bury everything at the same time.

The afternoon dragged on. Hollister took turns on the radio, spelling Theodore, allowing him to get some food, sleep, and a trip outside the perimeter to relieve himself. Bored, he re-checked the firing wires that led from the perimeter to a point nearly level with it on the lazy finger that led away from their perimeter, to a Claymore. It was part of the protection that they had laid in along with other Claymores, independent of the demolitions in the stream.

Satisfied with the Claymore, Hollister sat back in a small column of shade and tried to occupy his mind to kill the time. He decided that he would try to compose a letter to Susan in his head.

He went over the recent events since his last letter to find items he could share with her. He watched Theodore stirring cocoa powder in cool water from his canteen. He knew without looking that Theodore had a mixture of brown liquid and lumps. The lumps would take a long time to dissolve, and many of them would never dissolve.

Ultimately, Theodore would tire of stirring and wipe the caked powder off the plastic spoon. He would then drink the lumpy liquid and then try to get the clumps out of the canteen cup with his fingers. If he didn't get the caked cocoa out of the cup right away, it would be like chipping cement off the inside of the cup once they got back to the base camp.

A sound snapped the heads of every man in the perimeter. It was a single-engine airplane. The droning engine brought fear to all. They knew that there was no bird dog laid on to provide radio relay or tactical air support to the patrol.

It meant that whoever was flying the plane was not part of their operation and could stumble on them and then either circle them to try to figure out who they were or assume they were bad guys and fire on them. Hollister remembered how the province chief gave out free fire instructions for that part of the Province. He knew that they were in as much jeopardy from the bird dog as the wood poachers had been when he and Iron Mike had spotted them.

He quickly motioned for Theodore to get out the fluorescent marker panels. He took the handset while Theodore and Cullen spread the marker panels out in the pool of sunlight spilling through the hole in the canopy.

Before he spoke into the handset, Hollister stood up and looked out through the treetops toward the source of sound. It was an olive-drab L-19, rather than a gray one like the Air Force used. It meant that the airplane belonged to the Army or even one of the allies—like the Koreans. It had also changed its direction from straight and level flight to a large, lazy circle over their position.

He had a sinking feeling that it was a failure in coordination that had allowed the plane to wander into his position. It was certain that someone had not warned the pilot of the bird dog that friendlies were on the ground, so he had to assume that the pilot would think that any movement on the ground was hostile.

Cupping the mouthpiece, Hollister pressed the button on the side of the handset. "Quarterback, this is Two-six. I've got an Oscar one circling my location. Can you help get him off my back? Over."

Captain Shaw answered the call and asked for a tail number.

"Can't read it yet. It's an Oscar delta colored aircraft, though. Over."

"Rog. Let me get on it. Call me if you can catch the number. Out."

His response was enough for Hollister. If Captain Shaw said so, Hollister could be sure that he would take care of it.

Every man in the perimeter knew what Hollister was doing and held his breath to see if there was any change in the flight path of the small airplane. It made one more lazy circle that put the LRP position off center but still inside the circle.

Hollister pulled out his SOI and looked up the air-to-ground frequency to attempt to make a direct call to the aircraft. It was a last resort effort that he didn't want to have to take. Making contact with a stranger meant too much conversation on the radio—adding to the risk of being overheard on the ground. But it looked like he was going to have to make the call, when it suddenly turned out from its orbit and made an exaggerated wag of its wings.

The signal was a universal statement of understanding. It was the pilot's way of telling those on the ground that he got the word and would not be a threat to them. He continued to make a new orbit on the hilltop south of the perimeter, as if it was of equal importance to him as the last orbit.

Hollister raised the handset to his face and called in the situation. "Quarterback, this is Two-six. You did it. He's gone hunting somewhere else. Thanks. Out."

The base answered with a double break in the squelch.

Happy that was behind him, Hollister passed the handset back to Theodore, but suddenly a distressed look crossed his face. He quickly looked around the perimeter and spotted the lone entrenching tool. Snatching it with one hand and his rifle with the other, he signaled to Theodore that he was stepping out of the perimeter—in a hurry.

Hollister didn't know if the diarrhea was from his generally skittish stomach or the malaria tablets that he had to take early that morning. Mondays were always the worst for him.

It was the one day of the week that each man in Vietnam had to take the daily *and* the weekly pill at the same time. As he squatted over the small hole he had made with the entrenching tool, he thought of Easy. Hollister was also the detachment Malaria-Control officer and was responsible for making sure that the medics administered the daily and the weekly antimalaria pills.

He made one last check of the perimeter before the sun slipped beyond the horizon. Settling into his position for the night, Hollister began to lay out things he needed to reach for in the dark. Everything else was tied down and ready for a quick scramble out of the perimeter.

After dark the mosquito factor went up dramatically. Hollister tried to tough out the constant buzzing and the bites without moving around to swat at them. Most of it was just bearable, except the mosquitoes that hovered around his eyes and his ears. He took the cravat from around his neck and squirted more bug repellent into it. After putting the bottle back into his pocket, he dabbed the wet spot on the cravat around his eyes and on his ears. A small drop of the liquid mixed with the sweat on his eyebrow and slid into his eye.

The burning sensation was enough to cause his eyelid to quiver in convulsive muscle contractions. He hated mosquitoes! He hated the night.

* * *

It was almost nine P.M. when he checked his watch for the third time that hour. The night was dragging on. Everyone was awake and anxious about the ambush. Still, nothing was happening. There was no movement, no unusual sounds from the stream below, and the time just continued to drag on.

Hollister decided to try to finish his letter in his head. He felt the twinge of desire for Susan. He let himself get sucked into thinking about his last night with her, and forgot where he was or what he was waiting for. He knew better, but decided to compromise and allow himself just a few special seconds to relive the moments with her in his mind and then get back to work.

For a moment the damp night, the mosquitoes, and the hardness of the ground were gone and he was back in New York at Susan's apartment with her. He tried to remember how she smelled. It was a delicious memory.

An explosion went off in the hills to the north of them—artillery, H&I fire. Hollister's blood raced in anger. He knew that the ARVNs were shooting the harassing fire into the area owned by Colonel Minh, in spite of the fact that he and Michaelson had made a point up the chain of command that there were friendly wood poachers in the area. He was angry, but the perimeter overlooking the stream ambush was hardly the place to sustain it.

He tried to calm himself and get back to the mental letter writing. His reverie of Susan was shattered again by the 105 round hitting in some trees along a trail several miles from their location.

Shifting his position to get off of a spot on his hip growing numb from inactivity, Hollister's stomach started to rumble a little. He decided to take a chance on overcorrecting the problem by taking another one of the antidiarrhea pills that Doc Briskin gave him earlier.

The night droned on with the chorus of night creatures, but still nothing happened on the stream. By the time midnight came and went, Hollister was starting to wonder if there would be any traffic at all. He hoped that even though they hadn't seen any sampans going downstream, it didn't mean there weren't any that had been hidden downstream that would be coming back up.

His hopes started to fade around four in the morning when the dark was the blackest and the time moved at a painfully slow pace. He tried to keep himself awake by convincing himself that if he started to drift off, there was a chance that the VC could slip by without being seen.

He tried all of his usual tricks to keep his eyes open. The effort was agonizing and he was failing, miserably. He found a rock with several edges on it and slipped it under his left hip. As he put his weight back on the hip, the pain that the small rock caused woke him up—a little.

Dawn came and bones begged for sunlight. The first priority was warm up, then recheck everything, then sitreps, then something to eat, then touch up the personal and position camouflage, send out a small party to check around their perimeter for security, check the Claymores and the wires down to the ambush demo—then wait for another night.

For Hollister and the others, the day followed the previous one—an almost identical copy. The only difference was that their whiskers were longer, they had less food in their rucksacks, their eyes were redder, their patience was diminished, and their anxieties grew larger. No LRP liked to stay anywhere in the bush any longer than he had to. The longer they stayed in position the more likely they were to be discovered by the VC.

Hollister tried to figure out why they had sampan traffic on the stream the night they were inserted but none since. Had they been discovered going in? He was sure that they had picked a good insert point and created enough diversions on a nearby hilltop to telegraph their intentions to a completely different area. Maybe it was just a fluke.

Hollister checked his watch—another midnight. He was tired of waiting. Nothing again. No movement on the stream, no sign or sound of any kind of enemy activity in the foothills or the valley below. He wondered what had gone wrong. He decided to kill the time by going over everything from the moment that he got the warning order. He might find something there.

It was over an hour later when he mentally relived the coordination of the Operations plan. He remembered the argument between Captain Michaelson and Colonel Baird over providing incomplete overlays to Province Operations and their Fire Support Coordinator. He knew that Baird's bitch was that they were being given a large piece of real estate and only told that operations would be conducted there. No specifics.

It had been Michaelson's decision to not inform the Vietnamese where and when the team was going in until the choppers were in the air.

Hollister sat bolt upright. That meant that no one on the Vietnamese side could have known about his ambush patrol early enough to tip off the VC what they had heard on the stream. But right after the ARVNs knew the patrol's position, the stream traffic had stopped. He let it all cook in his head while he watched the stream below and the unmoving hands on his watch.

The faces looked even grimmer by the next morning. The humor was gone. The smiles were missing. The patrol was bone tired.

Hollister looked up for the shafts of sunlight. There were none. Low-hanging clouds were hugging the treetops. The dampness was chilling. He stretched and drafted a message in his notebook. He had lots to say and wanted to do it in the fewest words possible. He rewrote the words several times. Then it started raining.

A couple of groans were just barely audible. Hollister was the only one who was pleased that it was raining. The noise from the rain patting, plopping, and hissing on the leaves would cover his voice a little and reduce its travel. He moved over to Theodore and picked up the handset.

Theodore stopped him. He held up a finger to let Hollister know to wait one, then took off his floppy hat and placed it tightly over the tension clasp on one side of the battery case. Silently, Theodore unfastened it and then did the same on the other side, muffling the clasp. He slipped the battery out of the bottom of the PRC-25 and quickly replaced it with a fresh one. After he reclosed the clasps with the same attention to noise discipline, he sat back and smiled at Hollister. The radio was ready.

Smiling back at Theodore, Hollister cupped his hat and his hand around the mouthpiece of the handset and balanced his notebook on his knee. "Quarterback Six, this is Two-six. Over."

He waited for a radio operator to reply. But Michaelson's voice came back to him first try.

"Six, Two-six. Important you do the following. Will explain later. One: Execute fake extraction at a nearby alternate PZ today. Two: Send word to the little people that we are out of AO. Do not do same for their fire support. Will stay one more night. Convinced we have been compromised and are being avoided. How copy? Over."

There was a long pause, then Michaelson's voice replied, "Two-six, this is Six. Good copy. I agree. Understand your request. Stay close to the horn. Will try it your way. Good hunting, Ranger. Out."

Hollister put down the handset and looked around the perimeter. Every man in the circle knew what was going on and was angry. No one said a word. They were with Hollister.

CHAPTER 25

They all wondered if the rain was ever going to stop. Not a single man on the patrol was able to escape the drenching rain that had started just after sunrise. By noon the freak storm was still producing a steady downpour.

While they were all miserable from the rain, their minds were not on their discomfort. Their concern focused on the impact the rain could have on the demolitions below their position. If the runoff swelled the stream enough, it would also fill it with more deadfall and debris that could dislodge the explosives under the waterline or pull part of the det cord loose and simply render the entire ambush worthless.

Ignoring the rain, Hollister shifted over to the vantage point overlooking the stream and tried to gauge the impact of the swelling stream on the hidden demolitions.

It was too early for him to see much. It would all depend on how long it rained. He turned around and looked up through the hole in the canopy for some indication of the weather. The low-hanging cloud layer didn't seem to be moving and there were no breaks in any direction that he could see. He rolled over and waved across the perimeter to get Theodore's attention.

Theodore looked up.

Hollister pointed at the sky, shrugged his shoulders in a questioning manner, and pantomimed making a radio call.

Theodore understood. He grabbed the handset and called back to Operations for a weather check. They were able to tell him that the forecast was for the weather to break in mid-afternoon.

He turned back to Hollister, gave a slicing motion across his throat and then tapped his watch before holding up enough fingers to indicate fifteen hundred hours. Then he flipped his open palm over twice to indicate "more or less."

The news didn't encourage Hollister. He knew that he would have to check the demo before dark. He got up and crossed the perimeter to assemble a detail to go to the stream bank later in the day. Reaching Camacho's position, he was amused to find the sergeant's water-catching contraption working well.

Camacho had taken several large leaves and set them up in the bushes to catch rainwater and funnel it down, from leaf to leaf, until it finally dripped into his canteen.

Both Camacho and Hollister knew the value of avoiding any more moves out of the perimeter than were absolutely necessary. Water was one of those necessities that justified the contraption that Camacho had put up.

Using a scrap of soggy notebook paper, they wrote notes to each other about the demo below and the need for a recheck. There was no need to discuss Hollister's suspicion that someone had let the word slip out of Province Headquarters that they were in the area.

Around four the rain let up and the sounds of a fake helicopter pickup could be heard from the perimeter. Hollister grabbed the handset and listened to the radio traffic.

Somewhere on the other side of the hill mass, Captain Shaw was making false transmissions while someone else was answering as Hollister's patrol. As soon as the fake extraction was over, Shaw called back to Operations and announced that 2-6's team was out and bound for the base camp.

Hollister knew that in a matter of minutes someone from Operations would drive an updated overlay over to the Province Headquarters that would show that his team had been extracted.

It was iffy, and could increase the danger of them being hit by ARVN troops or fire support because they weren't there—at least not on paper. But Hollister was confident that the ARVNs would not mount any operation in the area during the time they had remaining on the ground. That left artillery as the major threat. Since he had suggested Michaelson not send the changes to the fire support staff of the Province Headquarters, he was equally confident that the Operations staffers wouldn't be in any hurry to coordinate the changes they had received with the Fire Support staff. So every artillery unit responsive to Province would still think there were friendlies on the ground.

It was dusk when the demo team came back into the perimeter. Camacho simply gave Hollister a nod and moved the three others back to their positions with the minimum of noise and motion.

Camacho dropped his gear and moved over to the position that was the observation point for the ambush. He was the only one who would connect the firing wires to the detonators. While he and the others were down near the explosives, the wires were disconnected and tied to tree branches a foot apart, while the detonators themselves were slipped into an empty Claymore bag to keep them clean, dry, and away from the wires—and hands.

The humidity rising from the ground and the trees changed the quality of the sounds and affected their travel. And the lack of a breeze made everything seem much louder, crisper, and closer.

Just after sundown Hollister moved to the observation point overlooking the stream. He was very aware that there was a lot at stake. He was risking the lives of his patrol by manipulating the situation.

He had stuck his neck way out and asked his boss to intentionally deceive the ARVNs. If they were caught and not vindicated by the return of the VC sampans, it could mean some disciplinary action against them. The more he thought about it, the more he started to get angry about having to mislead and deceive to do his job.

Dark came quickly. But the moon rose just as fast. The crickets were much louder then the previous nights. Conscious of the difference, Hollister assumed that they were trying to make up for lost feeding time.

He took the Starlight scope out of its case and propped it up in the crotch of a small tree to look through it without having to steady its weight. Pressing his right eye to the rubber eyepiece, he quickly scanned the area below. He could see some things very clearly. Those few things that were unclear were blurred because of the branches and leaves in his line of sight.

The ambient light level from the moon made visibility with the Starlight scope worth the trouble of getting it out of its case. Hollister slowly scanned the upstream leg, then worked down to the killing zone in the bend in the stream, then the downstream leg. Finding no boats or anything unusual, he started at the upstream leg again and made a more detailed inspection of the stream.

His first concern was the debris floating in the water. It was much worse than before nightfall. He knew that the smaller tributaries, swollen from the earlier rain, were flushing deadfall down to the stream and clogging choke points below the ambush site. Because of the damming, the water level had risen a foot over the bank. That meant that the debris floating over the swollen stream bank could pose a danger to the firing wires that led back up to Hollister's position. The only thing he could do was to try and trust Camacho's work—and hope for a little luck.

The hands on Hollister's watch were straight up. Midnight and nothing. More debris, more muddy water, and still no sampans. He was starting to wonder if he had made the right decision.

He wondered if he should wake up Theodore and get some sleep himself or hang in for another hour or so. The ground cold and the wetness of his uniform started to make him shiver uncontrollably. He hated it when he started to shiver. It was a sign that he was reaching a point of exhaustion.

A small pebble hit him on the shoulder. He spun around and looked over at Sergeant Allard, who had taken the Starlight to spell Hollister for a while.

Allard was pointing down the hill to something on the upstream leg. Hollister flipped back onto his stomach and looked.

Bingo!

A sampan was approaching. His heart started to race as he ran through what he had to do. He reached over, put his hand over Theodore's mouth and woke him. He then reached out to touch the detonators. He then raised the Starlight and made a check of the progress of the sampan. It was roughly a minute away from the killing zone, moving slowly down the center of the upstream channel.

Hollister rolled over on his back and threw a small stick across the perimeter at the moonlight-blotched outline of Camacho, who was sleeping against a tree trunk. He made a large pointing gesture for Camacho, letting him know that there was someone approaching the killing zone.

Camacho started getting everyone ready to move. If it went sour, they would either need to defend in place, run, or wait and then leave after blowing the ambush. They had rehearsed all of the possibilities.

Hollister looked back to Allard, who had alerted all of his people and was looking back through the Starlight. Suddenly he raised his hand and waved at Hollister.

Hollister looked back down at the sampan. He could see what Allard was watching through the Starlight—a second sampan. Shit! Hollister thought. If they got too far apart, he would have the problem of either blowing the ambush on the lead boat, the trailing boat, or neither. He wouldn't be able to get both of them if they drifted farther apart than the width of the killing zone.

He looked across the stream at two distinctive trees that were the reference points marking the left and right limits of the blast area. He knew that he would have to get the targeted boat into the space bracketed by those trees and then trigger the demolitions. He could feel the blood pounding in his neck and the restriction in his breathing. Time was passing too fast.

The lead sampan changed its direction to avoid a large bush that was floating in front of it and had become fouled by something under the water. As it did, the following sampan closed a little on the lead.

Hollister was pleased to see them close up, even though he had decided to blow the demo on the lead, hoping to get some of the second with the blast and fragmentation.

As the sampans got even closer he could make out the boatmen. The first sampan was an open fifteen-footer with some cargo stacked in the middle. At the bow a single soldier squatted with an AK-47 on his lap. At the aft end of the boat a second VC handled the tiller, his rifle slung across his back.

In the second boat, only slightly longer, a soldier sat on the cargo holding a loaded RPG grenade launcher. Hollister couldn't tell if the man on the tiller of the second boat had a weapon.

Time finally reversed itself for Hollister and came to a crawl as the nose of the lead boat slowly entered the killing zone. He put the detonator in the palm of his left hand and grabbed the T-handle with his right. He let the boat drift deeper into the killing zone and wondered if there would be even a second's delay in the detonation once he twisted the handle of the pulse generator.

He decided to wait long enough for the second boat to get at least half of its length into the killing zone before triggering the demo. But as he did, the front of the first boat was reaching the limit of the killing zone. He could wait no longer. He swallowed hard, closed his eyes, and forcefully twisted the handle.

As soon as the explosions started to go off, he grabbed the second detonator and did the same with it—just in case. He kept his eyes closed and ducked his head to keep from losing his night vision.

The near bank of the stream exploded up and out, throwing a wall of water, fragmentation, and mud at and under the sampans. A split second later Hollister heard the distinctive whoosh of the RPG launching a rocket-propelled grenade. It ended with an explosion that went off to Hollister's right—near the hilltop. Then, before the noise of the RPG faded, an explosion twice the size of the ambush went off—a secondary! They had hit some explosives on one of the sampans. The night lit up for a moment from the red and yellow ball of fire the secondary produced.

The flash, blast, and heat subsided as fast as it happened, but debris rained down in the trees for what seemed like several seconds.

Cautious to still protect his night vision, Hollister opened one eye and looked down the hill toward the killing zone. It wasn't the same. It was as if a bomb had hit the bend in the stream. The near bank was gone—moved back about a foot. The small trees on it were completely blown away, and the ones on the edge of the far bank were mowed down.

The water was filled with pieces of unidentifiable debris. Most of it was already floating out of sight—downstream. Realizing that there was no longer a threat to his night vision, Hollister opened his other eye and started a methodical search of the hill sloping away from them, then the bank, then the water, then the far bank.

There was no movement. He could find no bodies, no threat, and no sign of life. Suddenly he remembered that they might not have been the only sampans on the water. He quickly looked back upstream.

There was nothing but black. And, though his ears were ringing, he could only hear silence. Hollister was overcome by a sense of relief and dread. He didn't know exactly what the feelings were. He just knew that he didn't have time for either. He had plenty to do. Everyone for miles around would know that there was probably a U.S. element in the hills responsible for the ambush. They would know that only one of two options was available. Either the Americans would stay put or move to one of the obvious pickup zones to be extracted. The limited number of options favored the VC.

Security was his next thought. Hollister knew that he had to focus on that and nothing else. He looked back over his shoulder to get a signal from Camacho and Allard about the condition of the patrol. Camacho caught Hollister's eye and gave him an "okay" sign.

Hollister could see that Allard was still moving from man to man to check them out. He had stopped at Prather's position.

Allard was crouched over him. It looked to Hollister that Allard was speaking to Prather—into his ear.

Hollister reached for the handset to call in the ambush as soon as Allard gave him an up on his half of the patrol.

Allard seemed to be taking a long time with Prather. Hollister thought it might be related to Prather's inexperience. He had only been with the detachment for a few weeks.

Instead of turning around to look at Hollister and give him a sign, Allard got up and moved to Hollister's side. He had some bad news. The VC with the RPG got a shot off and hit the trees above the perimeter. It detonated near Prather—killing him. Allard couldn't find the wound, but Prather was definitely dead.

Suddenly Hollister felt nauseous. He could only nod his head in acknowledgment. He was sure that the cost wasn't worth the enemy body count.

Wrapping his hand around the handset, Hollister spoke softly into it. He reported the successful execution of the ambush and the one friendly KIA. He requested an extraction at the primary PZ an hour after first light. He didn't want to stay in the AO for any longer than he had to.

They moved out of the perimeter just as the sky was taking on a pale purple glow. As they started down the eastern side of the hill mass that they had occupied, the sun broke the horizon and began warming them. But there were no signs of welcome on the faces of the patrol members. The loss of a LRP had dampened each man's spirit—especially Hollister, who kept looking at the body being carried by two of the others.

In order to reduce the chance of being ambushed, Hollister took a roundabout path to the southeast to get to a PZ that was almost due east of the perimeter. It made it difficult, but was understood by the patrol members.

The loss of a man was also the loss of an important function on the patrol. Prather had been one of the two medics they had. If they ran into trouble on the way to the pickup, there could be more wounded than the remaining medic could handle. Hollister had decided to carry Prather's medical kit himself. It wasn't smart. He had enough to do and enough to carry. He knew it, but he just wanted to have the gear close at hand.

Halfway to the PZ Hollister changed the direction of march back to the northeast, to approach the PZ from a direction that was not only a dogleg, but took them down a long gentle finger to the clearing.

The patrol started to move without their usual caution. They were exhausted, eager to get back, and didn't want to stay out in the AO a minute more than necessary. Hollister had to grab a couple of them by the arm and point out their sloppiness. He could see the resentment in their eyes.

He knew how beat they were and how bad they felt about Prather's death. But he had to keep reminding himself that being a patrol leader wasn't a popularity contest. He had to not care if they were pissed at him, Allard, and Camacho. He knew that it would be easy to kill them with kindness. They had to move. He had to kick ass. He knew it and they knew it. They didn't like it.

After leaving the patrol near the PZ, Hollister and Camacho reconned the clearing. It appeared to be big enough to get two choppers in at once.

Hollister took the handset from the radio that Camacho had brought and called in for Operations to launch the pickup ships. They told him to expect a twenty-minute ETA.

On the way back to the patrol, Camacho suddenly stopped and dropped to his knee. Hollister hugged up behind him to see what had spooked him.

Camacho pointed to a small twig on the ground. It was the size of a cigarette and was laying next to an impression in the ground that was identical to its shape. It had been kicked out of its place in the hard ground by someone or something.

The alarming thing was that the side of the twig facing up was still moist from the dirt. It meant that the sun had not had time to dry it out. The twig had been turned over within the past several minutes. Everything around it had been dried by the sun. And it couldn't have been them. They were heading back using a new route. They realized that they were not alone.

Back with the patrol, Hollister, Camacho, and Allard put their heads together in the center. The fact that they had seen some indication that there was someone near the PZ did not guarantee that it was VC or that it had been done by someone still in the area. Hollister's decision was to alert everyone and continue the mission—and get them out.

Only a few minutes passed before they could hear the approach of the flight of choppers coming to pick them up. Hollister didn't wait until he could see them to let Michaelson know the situation. He grabbed for the handset. "Quarterback Six, this is Two-six. Over."

"Six, go."

"This is Two-six. We've got what might be fresh tracks near the southwest corner of the PZ. Twenty meters into the tree line. Very fresh. But no sighting, no hostile fire. Request victor romeo of that location or recon by fire if you feel necessary. We are clear up to two hundred meters back from tree line. Over."

"Roger, Two-six. I'll send guns in to prowl. Stand by."

"Roger that. Out," Hollister said, and passed the handset back to Theodore. He then turned around and told the man standing behind him to spread the word that the guns might be making a firing run to flush out any VC.

Everyone realized the risk and squatted down to reduce the chances of being hit by rounds skipping through the trees.

They could see the first gunship approaching the PZ. He was almost down into the treetops. His wingman was to his left and behind him, but at a greater altitude. They were sticking their necks out to try to draw fire on the low ship to allow the high ship to spot the shooter and blow him away. Hollister had to shake his head at the guts of the gun pilots. He made himself a promise to buy them a beer.

Wanting to hear what was going on, he took the handset from Theodore. The choppers kept prowling without any cross talk over the tactical freq. Finally the lead chopper came to a hover over a spot not too far from where Hollister and Camacho had discovered the wet twig. It then started to crab sideways.

The squelch finally broke. It was Iron Mike. "Folks, put your heads down. We're gonna hose this area down. We got a pair of Ho Chi Minh prints in a muddy spot and the grass is a little beaten down."

Hollister squeezed the press-to-talk button. "This is Two-six. Roger that. We copy friendly fire."

The low gunship broke right and pulled around and up to a firing-run altitude while his wingman rolled in with miniguns blasting. The snapping of the rounds and the zipping of the occasional skipping round kept everyone's heads down.

While they were crouched down they scanned their respective sectors for any sign of enemy ground fire directed at them or the choppers. There was none.

The lead gunship rolled into position and nosed over into a run that would begin just as soon as the other ship broke off.

They tried to cover each other's tails and bellies on the pullout by keeping the fire on the target area without interruption.

The lead—Iron Mike's chopper—started belching a stream of 40mm grenades that thumped a section of tree line, splintering trees and throwing up small fans of dirt. He took no fire that anyone could see.

Michaelson asked each chopper and Hollister if anyone saw any ground fire. All the way around the answer was the same—no enemy fire sighted. He told the guns to resume their normal search-and-cover pattern so that the extraction could begin.

Not waiting for the word, Hollister signaled the patrol to get up and move toward the PZ. They had taken about three good steps when Michaelson gave the pickup the go.

The team took a little longer to get to the tree line because of the extra weight of Prather's body and the extra caution about the possibility of unfriendlies in the area.

They were out of breath when they finally reached the choppers. Hollister held back while the others climbed onto the two pickup ships. The team getting into the second slick was having trouble loading Prather's body. But once Hollister was sure that they were all inside, he jumped into the lead slick, slapped the peter pilot on the helmet, and yelled, "Go! Go! Go!"

The choppers rolled forward and started up and out of the landing zone. Every man in the two choppers watched the tree line for any sign of enemy fire.

The choppers rose to thirty feet and started picking up airspeed when the lead slick took three enemy rounds through the cockpit. Mr. Patterson, the co-pilot, simply slumped forward and then a little to his left over the console between the seats.

Hollister just happened to be looking down at the point in the tree line where the VC fire came from—catching a glimpse of a tracer. Without thinking, he pulled out his sawed-off M-79 and lobbed a marker round in the direction of the enemy rifleman.

He was way long with the shot, having not allowed for the forward throw of the chopper's motion. Still, the training round made a puff of yellow smoke on impact.

Hollister grabbed the handset of his radio and yelled into the mouthpiece, "Heads up! I just marked the location with yellow smoke. Anybody got it? The fire came from a point two-five meters north of the marker. Over."

At the same moment the inside of the chopper became a cacophony of noise as the door gunners opened up with all they had on the ground north of the yellow smoke. And Iron Mike's gunships abruptly changed their direction.

Mike spoke up. "Roger, Two-six. We're gonna make a grease spot out of the target area."

Hollister remembered that they had been hit, and looked around the inside of the chopper for any damage. The air was still filled with the sounds of machine-gun fire and LRPs firing at the spot on the ground that was quickly getting behind them.

He looked up to see how the co-pilot was. He didn't need to check. The young warrant officer's helmet had an exit hole about the size of a tennis ball behind the left ear. Hollister fought the urge to vomit. It was Patterson, the warrant officer who had flown right seat on the first insert that Hollister had honchoed.

Everyone in the chopper stopped shooting as soon as they realized that they were too far away from the smoke marker and that their rounds might jeopardize the gunships rolling in behind and below them.

The door gunner nearest Hollister locked off his machine gun, reached over and tapped Hollister on the shoulder. Since Hollister didn't have a helmet or headset on, the door gunner stuck his finger up inside his helmet and pulled the foam ear piece away from his ear in order to hear Hollister's reply, and yelled, "Sir, we're going to the Clearing Station first."

Hollister knew that Patterson was dead, but understood that no one wanted to fly a chopper around with a dead man in the front seat. It was best that they take the co-pilot's remains to Clearing first.

"Sure, don't worry about us. I'll get some ground transportation sent over," Hollister yelled back. He knew that the crew would want to take Patterson in themselves and stay as long as was necessary to make sure that his remains were taken care of.

Sergeants Marrietta and Easy were waiting at the medevac pad with a deuce-and-a-half when the chopper landed. The medic ran up and helped the door gunner unstrap the dead pilot and get him onto a gurney. No one was willing to assume that he was really dead until they had him inside and a doctor made it official.

Hollister and the other LRPs waited until the pilot was through the door of the hospital Clearing Station before anyone moved to get in the truck. And no one spoke.

Hollister motioned to Camacho to load up the truck as he walked back around to the pilot, who was still shutting down

the chopper. The pilot was Lieutenant Reitz. Hollister had rid-
den in his slick several times.

"Man, I'm sorry about your peter pilot. We were sure that
the tracks were probably nothing." The pain shot through Hollister's stomach as his gut made one last grip against itself. "I
guess I was wrong."

Reitz opened the door, stepped out on the skid, and put his
hand on Hollister's shoulder. "Hey, we were wrong. It ain't your
fault. Okay? It happens. You know?"

As Hollister turned around, the second chopper, with the
other half of his patrol and Prather's body, landed on a second
medevac pad marker. As the team gently lifted Prather's body
out onto the stretcher a medic had brought, Hollister and Easy
headed toward the Clearing Station to take care of their fallen
member.

Back in his hooch, Hollister dropped his gear, cleared his weapons, and poured himself a serious drink. The first taste of the
scotch made his mouth burn, tightened his throat, and hit his
stomach with a jolt. He didn't care. He just wanted to take some
of the feeling of despair out of his head.

He picked up the field phone and called Operations to see
what time the debriefing would be held. Captain Michaelson
was still out inserting and extracting teams and had sent back
word to hold on Hollister's debriefing until he returned.

Given the time, Hollister opted to have a second drink and
get a shower in before Michaelson returned. He poured the drink
on top of the remains of the first one and turned to his locker
for a towel. He spotted the four letters on his cot.

Reaching to pick them up, he quickly saw that three of them
were from Susan and one was from his mother. He felt guilty
for being so far behind in his letter writing and for knowing that
again he would not discuss the painful things like the deaths of
Prather and the young warrant officer. He would think of some
other way to fill the pages of his replies. But he resented having
to do it.

Taking another long sip of his scotch, he felt the sudden alarm
of his bowels revolting. The unmistakable urgency of diarrhea
gave him only seconds to get to the latrine.

After the debriefing, Michaelson asked Hollister to come see
him in his office. They had not discussed the issue with the
Province Headquarters during the debriefing. Without saying

so, both Michaelson and Hollister thought that any discussion would be a negative morale factor for the troops. They had enough problems without hearing that their officers had no confidence in the South Vietnamese's ability to safeguard classified information.

"Here, you could use this," Michaelson said as he handed Hollister a beer from the cooler in the orderly room.

Reaching for his demo knife, Hollister took the bottle of San Miguel and held it between his knees while he unfolded the bottle opener. He popped the top, snapped the knife closed and slipped it back into the webbed nylon carrier that was attached to the belt above his back pocket.

Captain Michaelson silently raised his beer in a mute toast. He put the bottle down on his desk and shuffled through some handwritten notes in front of him. "I need your input on this thing with Province. I want to lodge an official complaint about the poacher incident and the ambush last night. This shit is fuckin' criminal!"

"Yessir. Where do you want me to start?"

"I want you to write up everything from the first coordination visit before the wood poaching thing through today," Michaelson said as he shoved his pages toward Hollister. "Look over my notes and make sure I got my shit together.

"This is not going to go over well at Brigade, and I don't want to give them any reason to buck it back—like errors in dates or times or names or whatever the fuck they can find."

Hollister took the pages and tapped the bottom edges on his knee, straightening them up. He was uncharacteristically silent.

"Get it off your chest," Michaelson said.

"I'm so pissed. I also feel like I'm the last one to get the picture. I've been in country for almost a goddamn year and I just now realized that I haven't been involved in one damn operation where I felt we had the upper hand.

"Is it me? I feel like there's a script being passed around the Vietnamese—on both sides—that we never get to see. It's a loose plan for when they let us win a little, and lots of days when they fuck over us!" He took a long sip of his beer. On top of the scotch, he was feeling a little fortified in his indignation. "Tell me something, sir. Do we really have any fucking idea what's going on?" He suddenly realized that it sounded as if he were accusing Michaelson of something, and started to soften the question. "I didn't mean that you—"

Captain Michaelson raised the palm of his hand to stop Hollister from apologizing. "I got a couple of years here. We *aren't* running this show. In my opinion there are too damn many folks involved. Sure, we have a pretty good idea what's going on out in Indian country. The problem is that everything we know, the ARVNs know, and that's where it starts to come apart. It's one of the reasons that I stay in outfits like this."

Hollister looked at him, somewhat puzzled at the remark.

"You've been a platoon leader. Every step you took in the bush was leaked to every zipperhead from Hanoi to the U Minh Forest. Ever wonder why it was so long between contacts? Your best ones were chance contacts when some chopper pilot would catch the zips and Brigade would dump maneuver units on them. That's when the game wasn't stacked against you," Michaelson said, a note of anger in his voice.

"That's why staying out of the line units gives you a better chance of protecting your own and having a little more control," Michaelson added.

Hollister looked at Michaelson and realized the futility of it all. He shook his head slightly as it sank in.

"It's not what they teach at the War College or Leavenworth or Benning," Michaelson said, "but you got to give away information over here like it has serial numbers on it. If you don't watch your own ass, nobody else will."

"But look at the hell it caused with that leg colonel from Province."

"Don't worry about him. If an ass chewing now and then is all it costs to keep from publishing our Op plans in the Saigon newspaper, then he can just bring a fuckin' bib," Michaelson said.

"But we can't prove anything on this ambush. They'll just claim that it was a coincidence or something," Hollister said.

"Well, I'm not as interested in catching someone doing something wrong as I am stopping it from happening again. There's a difference," Michaelson said.

Hollister smiled and nodded his head. He remembered why he liked Michaelson. He was always putting the troops and the mission before personal wars or ego or revenge. He knew that he had to get his own emotions under control if he wanted to be half the soldier that Michaelson was.

He looked at the stack of envelopes sitting on his footlocker. He had written his parents, Susan, and Prather's parents. And he had told half-truths to all of them.

Hollister took a long drink of scotch and lit another cigarette. He leaned back in his cot and let the smoke fill his lungs. It still felt like his first smoke since leaving for the ambush patrol, but the C-ration can filled with butts said otherwise. It made his head swim for a brief second.

He threw his cigarette lighter on the stack of letters and tried to rationalize all the lies in his head. How could he explain Prather's death? The head shot on the pilot? The sampans blown into shreds of splintered wood? The ARVNs he couldn't trust? None of it would make their lives any easier back in the World, and he couldn't change what was happening in Vietnam. He swallowed the emotion with more scotch.

He considered having still another, but then looked at the notes Captain Michaelson had given him. He had put that off till last.

Reaching for the scotch bottle, Hollister got up from the cot and stepped toward the notes.

"Anybody home?"

He turned to find Easy standing outside his hooch.

"Come on in, First Sergeant. Pull up a drink and take a load off."

Easy entered and waved a handful of papers at Hollister. In his other hand he held his personalized coffee cup with a splash of coffee still in the bottom. "It never stops. Now we have to submit friggin' forms for press releases."

"Press releases?"

"Each man has to fill out a form sayin' yes or no to allowing his assignment here in Vietnam to be published in his hometown newspaper. Now ain't that a crock? Even if the guy *doesn't* want it in his hometown rag, he still has to sign a form saying so."

Putting down the bottle, Hollister took the forms out of Easy's hand and looked at them. "What does this have to do with me?"

Easy put his cup down and picked up the scotch bottle. He examined the label as if what it said would make any difference. "You got to fill one out on yerself and sign all the others for each man in the detachment."

Hollister thumbed the stack of forms for size and groaned.

Easy unscrewed the top of the scotch bottle. "I'm sure the lieutenant understands that I'm only drinking this inferior brand of spirits to be hospitable. I'm partial to a more aged brand."

Finding a pen, Hollister began signing the forms on his footlocker lid as Easy poured a couple of fingers of scotch into his mug.

"Please, sit down, Top. I'll only be a minute with these."

Easy pulled the chair out from the desk with his foot and straddled it. Crossing his arms over the back of the chair, he sat and sipped his scotch.

He watched Hollister rapidly scrawl his signature on form after form and laughed. "I'd like to have a buck for every lieutenant whose handwriting I've seen go to shit before he made captain. That's what does it, you know. You sign your name enough times without a break and pretty soon you can't even read whose it is. Guess that has its blessings, too."

Signing the last one with an exaggerated flair, Hollister picked up the stack and handed it to Easy. "There you go, First Sergeant. Service with an Airborne smile."

Easy took the pages and got to his feet. He killed the last of his scotch and looked down into the empty coffee mug.

"Why don't you fix another one for the road, Top?" Hollister said, looking out the screen door toward the orderly room across the small compound. "Looks like it might be bad weather between here and there."

Easy crouched down, looked out across the compound, and grunted in agreement. "Sure does look bad. Maybe the lieutenant's right. Maybe a touch will steel me from the storm." He poured another three fingers into the cup and raised one of his bushy eyebrows. "Hmmmm, I might have to revise my opinion of this brand."

Hollister laughed. "I might have to find another bottle of that brand."

Easy put the bottle down and spotted the addressed envelopes on the desk. "Would the lieutenant like me to take these over to the orderly room?"

"Yeah, that'd be great, Top. I'd appreciate it."

The address on the top was one Hollister had gotten from Bernard earlier. It was the dead LRP's family. "Prather's people will appreciate the thought," Easy remarked. "Hope it wasn't too hard to write."

"Never wrote one that wasn't hard to write. I'd rather eat rocks," Hollister said.

He watched Easy walk across the compound trying not to spill the scotch in his mug. The same ground fog that had closed in on the ambush site was crawling across the compound.

Hollister lit another cigarette and crushed the empty pack. As he spit a shred of tobacco from his mouth, he could see that the troop hooches were subdued. The normal marathon drinking and card playing sessions had been watered down by the two deaths. Hollister could see the outlines of clumps of soldiers sitting in the lights of the hooches drinking and talking quietly. He could hear the sounds of a portable radio over the distant sounds of artillery, choppers, and the ever-present drone of the generators spotted around the base camp.

Less than an hour later there was another knock at the door. Hollister looked up from the report. "Come."

A new man from the first platoon entered carrying a hand grenade crate. "Ah, sir, I'm the CQ runner. The first sergeant sent me over with this."

Not knowing what it was about, Hollister pointed the top of his ballpoint toward the corner. "Just put it down over there."

The soldier straightened up, nodded, said good-night, and left before Hollister could thank him.

He tried to get back to the report, but the amount of drinking he had been doing fogged his thoughts, and curiosity about the grenade crate got to him.

He stepped over to the box and opened the lid. Inside, the box was filled with a few rolled-up sandbags that were cushioning a quart bottle of Johnnie Walker scotch. There was a note written on a DA 1049 Disposition Form. It read: *Was able to find resupply for your foul weather elixir. This might help any other NCOs visiting your hooch and will also ease some of the headaches that lieutenants get. Airborne!*

It was unsigned.

Hollister had to shake his head at how far he and Easy had come since that first day on the airfield road. He certainly had changed his opinion of the crusty first soldier. He was a rock that Hollister could always count on—rough edges and all.

The pounding of his jungle boots against the roadway sent shock waves to Hollister's aching head. The sun was too bright and the sound of the chanting soldiers around him was painful. To top off all the misery, the column of fours was returning from a three-mile run and he still hadn't gotten his wind. He made himself another promise to cut down on his drinking and smoking. It was getting to be a regular thing with him—promising to get on some kind of health kick.

Michaelson and Hollister bumped into each other as they tried to catch their breath while walking around half bent over at the waist.

"Your people were excused from training. What's it take to get you to sleep in?" Michaelson asked.

Hollister started to quote an old infantry adage. "More sweat on the training field—"

Michaelson raised his hand. "Spare me. But now that I look at you, you look like you could use a little heavy PT to get that rat piss out of your system. What'd you do last night—play too much poker with the troops?"

"I wish I had. It took me too many scotches to finish all the writing. I better just stay in the Infantry," Hollister said.

"I won't have time to look at it till midday. I've got a shitpot of things to do first. Why don't you drop what you got off around lunchtime? And get some sleep."

"Yessir—I got to square away my field gear first."

"Go to it, Ranger," Michaelson said.

Hollister saluted and picked up a double-time on the way back to his hooch.

Michaelson stood there watching him run away. Easy stepped up behind Michaelson. "He's a good man, boss. He's gonna be a good CO if he doesn't wear himself out first."

Michaelson looked over his shoulder at Easy. "He never lets up, does he?"

"No, sir. Reminds me of a young lieutenant I remember back at Bragg. You mighta known him—I think his name was Michaelson."

Michaelson smiled at Easy. "You know, I can't remember the last time I gave push-ups to a first sergeant."

Not to be bested, Easy countered, "Maybe not, but I can remember when you did it to a dashing young three-striper back at Bragg."

CHAPTER 26

The chaplain's words were not registering on Hollister. He stood there with his head bowed, hands loosely clasped in front of him, and said his own prayer for the dead soldiers.

The memorial ceremony had been put off once—long enough to add the two recent deaths to the list of the soldiers being remembered.

The chaplain's prayer ended and Captain Michaelson called the detachment to attention and barked out the command to present arms. Unarmed, each man saluted. On a nearby berm a firing squad raised their rifles to their shoulders and fired the first volley of blanks to salute the lost warriors.

Standing out in front of his platoon, Hollister looked at the rifles, stuck bayonet down into the dirt. In front of each rifle was a pair of shined, laced-up jungle boots. And on the tops of the rifle butts were floppy hats—all except one. It had a flight helmet in place of the LRP headgear.

Each rifle represented a soldier lost since the last memorial ceremony. Hollister thought it was a nice gesture to include the death of Mr. Patterson in the ceremony and to invite the chopper crews.

After the last volley, Michaelson ended the salute and dismissed the detachment. Hollister didn't leave for his hooch. He was drawn by the emotion of the ceremony to remember the faces of the men he had lost. He could picture every one of them—including those from his rifle platoon before he came to the LRPs. But he remembered them alive, not in the moments after their deaths. The dark mood, a feeling of helplessness, came over him and brought him down even lower than the ceremony had.

He turned and started to his hooch, unable to get the deaths out of his mind. He wondered if this was temporary or if it was going to dog him for the rest of his tour. He was very aware of the fact that he was getting short, and it was normal for everyone around him to watch him for any signs of a short-timer's attitude. He had seen his share of soldiers, NCOs, and officers who had reached that point in their tours where they started to get distracted by the nearness to their departure date.

They would get spooky, nervous, overly cautious, gun-shy, and even stupid. That often led to mistakes that got people killed.

Sure, he wanted to go home. He wanted it all to go away. But he knew that he had to keep his feelings to himself. If his troops picked up what he was feeling, they would suffer. Hollister knew that one of the fastest ways to bottom out the combat effectiveness of a unit was to let them start to feel sorry for themselves. He knew that there was no such thing as a good platoon with a platoon leader who was short and showing it. He also knew that he didn't want to be a cartoonlike cheerleader, but it was his job to keep his fingers on the attitude pulse of his platoon. He clenched his jaw, put it out of his mind and cautioned himself to suck it up and stay tough.

Hollister amended his running list of resolutions to include not getting crazy about getting short.

Weeks went by with a good mix of successful ambush patrols and dry holes. For Hollister the best part about it was that there were no more losses, with the exception of a sergeant from Team 2-2. He was evacuated as a nonbattle casualty when a smoke grenade hanging on his rucksack accidentally ignited and burned his neck and shoulder blade. They got word that he was evacuated to the States for some skin grafting work, but that he would be okay.

During those weeks, Hollister had stolen every minute that wasn't devoted to actual patrols to conduct team training. He had convinced himself that many of the ills of the unit and problems in the field could be overcome by hard training.

He went back over every After Action Report and all of the debriefing notes since the detachment was activated to find problems—that could be fixed by training.

The troops were not happy to lose the time off, but to a man they understood that every hour they spent sharpening their skills would increase the chances of coming back from patrols—alive.

Still, there were other losses. Malaria, dengue fever, boils, jungle rot, and dysentery took their toll. New faces came from somewhere. There never seemed to be a shortage of volunteers to join the detachment. But every new face meant a step back in the overall training level in the detachment.

It just seemed like a never-ending cycle for Hollister. But it also meant crowded hours—hours that he spent getting the job done and getting the training done. It meant less time to think about how he felt, what he feared, and what it all meant to him. It was a kind of escape for him.

So, although Hollister lost more weight and began to look exhausted, he felt like he was doing the right thing. To him, working harder to prepare the troops for the field was proof that he was not stacking arms.

With less than sixty days to go, Hollister was smothered in the last minute details of getting ready to return to the States. He and Susan had finally decided upon a civil ceremony in New York followed by some leave time in Kansas. And Hollister was given the additional task of training his second replacement— Lieutenant Matthews.

Matthews came to the LRPs after finishing five months in the 4.2-inch mortar platoon in Hollister's old battalion. Matthews was a Citadel graduate, a Ranger and Jungle Warfare School graduate.

Hollister liked Matthews, but was concerned that his field skills might need some polishing since he had spent his time in battalion fire bases and reinforced company perimeters. Matthews agreed with Hollister, and they laid out a plan for Matthews to go on every mission that the second platoon sent out until just before Hollister's departure.

After three weeks of letting Matthews hump with the teams, Sergeant Davis let it slip to Hollister that Matthews was getting high marks from the troops.

It was met with mixed emotions by Hollister. He was pleased to find out that Matthews was measuring up. Inside he knew that he would be angry if he turned the platoon over to someone who they didn't accept or who might get them killed. Still, he would like to think that he couldn't be replaced. He wrote it off to ego and kept it to himself.

During those same weeks, the problems with the province chief had still not been resolved. Michaelson had been given some lip service by the Brigade Executive officer that the entire matter was under investigation and that the LRPs had better toe the line. If it turned out that they were even the slightest bit at fault, or if their claims were wrong, it could reflect poorly on the Brigade.

It sounded to Michaelson and Hollister like the whole thing was being swept under the rug to avoid a confrontation and to keep from creating more friction with the Vietnamese.

Hollister was asleep when the phone rang in his hooch. He fumbled through the darkness and pressed the receiver to his face. "Hollister, sir."

"Sir, this is Sergeant Marrietta. The Old Man wanted me to get you over to the mess hall ASAP. He's mounting a mission on an agent report. Your folks have to be ready to go in an hour."

"An hour?! What time is it?"

"Sir, it's 0240."

Hollister sat up and reached for his cigarettes. "Okay. Give me a minute to find my trousers."

One of the new soldiers poured coffee from a stainless steel pitcher into the cups in front of Hollister, Sergeant Marrietta, Captain Shaw, Lieutenant Perry, and Sergeant Davis. Just as the heat from the coffee reached Hollister's face, someone yelled, "A'tench-hut!"

They all stood and saluted as Captain Michaelson and the first sergeant entered the mess hall. Michaelson returned the salutes, took a cup of coffee, and motioned for everyone to take their seats.

The captain waited till the scraping of the chairs stopped, took a sip of his coffee, looked at his watch, and lit one of his cigars. "Sorry about the hour. I know this is going to be particularly bad on the first sergeant's beauty sleep."

Everyone laughed as the first sergeant blustered in protest to the humor at his expense.

"We got a mission that Brigade wants to mount right now. Lieutenant Hollister, your platoon has the standby team. Right?"

"Yessir. Sergeant Camacho's team is locked and loaded," Hollister said, looking over at Davis, who nodded his head in confirmation.

"Well then, he's gonna be it," Michaelson said. "Is he at full strength?"

"Yessir," Davis said. "Camacho, Sergeant Gerhart, Vinson,

Wyman, and Doc Briskin. Wyman is still pretty cherry, but he'll be okay.''

"The Provincial Recon Unit grabbed a VC messenger last night who they say puked his guts up all over their S-2 shop about his unit's operations.''

"Bet he wet his pants first,'' Marrietta said under his breath.

Michaelson ignored the comment on the Vietnamese interrogation techniques and looked at the slip of paper in his hand. "According to the VC, there's a paymaster coming to his unit tonight to pay the VC guerrillas operating in the western part of the valley.''

Michaelson took a drag off his cigar and then blew the smoke skyward. "If this is true, and we can snatch this guy—we can get the name of every friggin VC in the province. On the other hand, if it ain't true, we can run a dry hole and risk a team.''

No one in the room commented on Michaelson's assessment. They knew that he was right on the mark. Getting a pay roster of the VC infrastructure would go a long way toward upsetting the Communist control of the An Hoa area. Not to mention the negative morale impact of the pay not coming through.

"I don't know if the intel is good or just bullshit. But we're going to send a team in as a stay-behind, with the mission of snatching this gook if possible,'' Michaelson added.

There was a collective groan at the words "stay-behind.'' Every man in the room knew that it usually meant meeting up with a maneuver unit and walking into the area in question only to be left behind. They all hated working with regular units because they were clumsy, loud, and, in the minds of some, more dangerous.

Michaelson raised his hand. "Hold on. Hold on. I know how you feel. Our problem is time and method of infiltration. If we don't do it as a stay-behind, we'll be forced to insert the team much too close to the snatch location to make it workable.''

They all knew he was right. They trusted him to be right.

Michaelson smiled as if he knew a private joke and continued. "The snatch team will depart here by chopper as soon as we can get them ready, and fly to the southern end of the valley, where they'll link up with C Company, First of the 511th.''

Hearing the unit, Hollister perked up. "All right! My old company!''

"Right,'' Michaelson said. "Make you feel any better about this?''

"Yessir. Cobra Company is the only infantry company in Vietnam I'd trust with our people," Hollister said, smiling.

"Okay then, the deal is that C Company will sweep through the snatch area as if they're doin' a routine search-and-destroy operation. But they aren't gonna stay long. They'll keep on going till they're well north of the area we're interested in and then be choppered out by late afternoon. And they'll make sure that everyone knows they're gone.

"As they pass through our objective area, they'll simply drop off the snatch team." Michaelson paused. "Everybody with me?"

They all nodded.

"Okay. This will be a one-night operation for our folks. If Mr. Big Piasters doesn't show by daylight tomorrow, we'll go ahead and plan on pulling the team out by noon."

Taking the pen from the corner of his mouth, Hollister interrupted. "And if they do get the guy?"

"We'll pull 'em at first flyable light," Michaelson replied. "Your folks can just hold on to him until the sun comes up. I don't want to send in a chopper in the dark just to pull a pay officer.

"I don't have all the details yet. I'll feed 'em to you as I get them. I think that you want to get that team cranking right now. Captain Shaw will issue the op order in an hour and we'll try to get a briefback from Sergeant Camacho an hour after that. That a problem for anyone?" Michaelson asked.

Several hands went up.

"Hold it! Hold it. I know. I mean *real* problems."

The hands went down.

Michaelson called Davis, Hollister, and Camacho into the Operations tent to sit in on a surprise visit from Colonel Baird, the angry province senior advisor. He told Michaelson that he wanted to come to the LRPs to make sure they had all the facts straight on the upcoming snatch operation. He felt that they should know the details of the prisoner interrogation that had generated the snatch mission.

It was a crock. Hollister watched the charade that Baird put on. It was obvious to him that Baird had been on the receiving end of some ass chewings because of the flap between the LRPs and the province chief. The visit was all for show. Baird could care less if the LRPs knew anything. It was Hollister's guess that Baird just feared losing his soft job at Province.

* * *

The rifle company was in a perimeter just a little smaller than a
football field. Every man was rigged to move out, but relaxing
till the LRP link-up happened.

Davis and Hollister came in the C&C, and Camacho's team
landed in a second slick. They waited till the choppers cleared,
and walked toward the company command post in the center of
the squared perimeter that encompassed a tiny hamlet and several rice paddies.

A voice rang out. "Hollister, you rear echelon motherfucker,
you!"

Looking up, Hollister spotted First Lieutenant Andy Martinson. He was company commander of C Company. When Hollister had last seen him, they were both platoon leaders. "Well,
you old boonie rat!" Hollister said, exchanging salutes and
shaking hands with Martinson. The sight of his old friend was
reassuring. Hollister knew that Martinson was a good man and
could be trusted not to screw over his LRPs.

They sat and talked a little business and did a little catching
up. Martinson called Sergeant Lawrence, Hollister's old platoon
sergeant, to the CP to say hello. It was good for Hollister to see
him, but Lawrence had plenty of bad news about losses of good
troops after Hollister left the platoon. Even Hollister's replacement had been killed.

The information took the joy out of seeing a few of the friendly
faces that were still in Cobra Company.

The sweep went well. Hollister took a little pride in the way his
old company moved through the area. The hump took him back
to the days when he honchoed a rifle platoon with Sergeant
Lawrence.

Lawrence had taught him much in six months with a platoon
about leading troops. Hollister was glad that Lawrence was running his old platoon.

The sweep itself was nothing new for Hollister. He had done
it many times when he was with C Company. For a platoon
leader, sweeping an area looked very casual, but was really a
walking nightmare. He worried about booby traps, mines, snip-
ers. He had to make the decisions about where to sweep—trails
were dangerous, paddy dikes were trouble, but walking through
the paddies slowed them down and put people into the most
open areas.

And once they got into the villages and hamlets, it was a

whole new list of problems on top of the others. The structures made it difficult to cover the movements of all the troops with effective fire. Worries about the safety of the villagers were tempered by the suspicion that they might be VC or VC sympathizers. And the treatment of the villagers was always a concern for the platoon leader.

Hollister remembered the first time he walked a platoon into a hamlet and searched it for VC, weapons, food caches, and other contraband. He was amazed at the living conditions of the villagers and the total lack of young men.

They went from thatched hut to thatched hut, invading the homes of the frightened children and old people. The fear in the villagers' eyes was something Hollister would never forget. He never spent a day in a village where he was comfortable with his decisions.

After an hour on the march, the company swept through a wooded area that flanked the trail the VC paymaster was supposed to use later that night. Lieutenant Martinson gave the word to drop off the LRP team and continue to move, as if nothing had changed.

Hollister wished Camacho and the team a quick good luck before he and Davis moved on with the rifle company. As they walked away, the last man in the patrol was Theodore. He had volunteered to go out as tail gunner for Camacho when it was decided that the snatch would go with a six-man team. Hollister thought that it was Theodore's way of proving to himself and everyone else that he had gotten over his spookiness. He had been making a big deal out of how many patrols he'd been racking up.

Everyone at the LRP compound was at supper when the truck dropped Hollister and Davis off. They had spent the rest of the day walking in the hot sun with C Company and watching huge billowing clouds gather to the north.

Hollister sent Davis to check out the orderly room for any messages for the platoon, while he went to Operations to see if there had been any activity with Team 2-3.

In Operations, Hollister found that the team had been laying up without any problems in a thick stand of bamboo two hundred yards from the trail they hoped the VC paymaster might use. But they were concerned by their proximity to the hamlets in the area. The trail was getting plenty of foot traffic, as the

farmers used it to get to the nearby roadway leading to the mar
ket in An Hoa city.

Hollister left Operations with instructions to find him the min
ute the team called in any activity.

The coffee in the bottom of Hollister's cup started to taste bitter
He finished it and decided to walk over to the mess hall to get a
refill and some fresh air. He had been sitting by the radios in
Operations since sundown, and the clock was showing that it
was just about quarter after nine.

"I'll be back in a few minutes," Hollister said to Sergeant
Tillotson.

"Take your time, sir. I don't think we're going to get very
lucky tonight." Tillotson laughed. "S'pose the guy went AWOL
with the money and he's in the ville spending it on good-time
girls and booze?"

Reaching the door, Hollister stopped, thought about it for a
second, and turned to Tillotson. "What'd you do?"

Tillotson laughed again. "You gotta ask?"

Hollister raised his empty cup. "You want some?"

"No, sir. If I had one more cup of coffee, I might not get to
sleep when I get back to the World."

The Operations tent was stale from cigarettes and the smell of
dirty canvas. Hollister finished his letter to Susan. It was the
easiest one he had written in weeks. He was able to tell her how
great it was to see some of the faces from his old company
There was also plenty to talk to her about concerning their plans
And it was easier to tell her how much he missed her and how
eager he was to see her. Somehow, the personal, romantic, and
sexual emotions were hard to talk about in letters when the
possibility of seeing her had been so far out of reach.

It was almost torture to tell her how much he wanted her and
how he missed being with her when he had to seal the envelope
and know that she was so far away in both time and distance.

Much of what he had put in his letter to Susan was news to
his parents. So Hollister explained some of the details of the
plans that he and Susan were firming up. He was happy that his
parents were excited about his marriage to Susan, and pleased
that she had found the time to write to his mother often. They
collaborated on sending Hollister small care packages and silly
greeting cards.

Before he could finish the letter to his folks, Captain Michael son walked in to check on the night's events. Hollister was surprised to find that it was almost six A.M.

"Anything?" Michaelson asked, not waiting for any formalities. He picked up the Staff Duty Journal, which held summaries of all the radio traffic, and checked the time of the last sitrep.

"Dry hole, sir," Hollister replied. "They had movement just at dark, but you knew that. Most of the night was lights in the nearby villages and some foot traffic. None of it was near them. Looks like the intelligence from Province was worthless."

The captain put his hands on his hips and thought for a second. "Okay. Enough of this. I've got teams to brief and debrief. Captain Shaw already has a team to put in and one to come out this morning. I don't want to screw all that up with this unscheduled mission. So, I want you to take the C and C and pull your snatch team after Shaw gets back.

"But before you tell them that you're going to pull them, check with Brigade on the weather forecast." Michaelson pointed his thumb toward the tent doorway. "There's a mean-looking front boiling up out there. Could screw us up."

Once they were in the air, the pickup ship, the chase, and the two gunships fell into formation with the C&C. The flight was only a seventeen-minute hop to a large paddy area near the snatch site. It was the primary PZ that had been selected before the mission and confirmed on the sweep through the area.

On the flight, the pilots and Hollister kept an eye on the storm clouds building over the hills to the north. They all knew that the weather between the monsoon and the dry season was erratic and could change very quickly.

The pickup was preceded by a wide aerial sweep of the area around the pickup zone. Because the PZ was close to populated villages, Hollister wanted to make sure that they all knew where any civilians were before the choppers dipped into the paddies to scoop up Camacho's team. If they had to start shooting to protect themselves, Hollister wanted to make sure that they weren't accidentally firing toward civilians.

Satisfied that the nearest civilians were more than a thousand meters away, Hollister gave the word to start the pickup sequence.

Ready to be pulled, Camacho's team held up short in the trees.

The guns made their sweeps of the clearing just as the rain

started to fall. Hollister leaned out the door in the C&C and
watched the slick make a long slow descent into the PZ.

Estimating the touchdown point, the team burst from the tree
line and ran toward the pickup ship. But before the first man
reached the side of the slowing chopper, the pickup went sour.

As Hollister saw the first man fall, a small reddish cloud of
flesh, bone, and fatigue shirt was blown out of the man's lower
rib cage.

"Contact! Contact! Contact!" overlapping voices of the two
pilots and Vinson, Camacho's radio operator, screamed into
their radios.

Searching the tree line below him, Hollister quickly spotted
the source of the fire. From a dense cluster of bushes on the
opposite tree line, repeated bursts of automatic weapons fire
crossed the PZ, hitting the chopper and chewing up ground
around it.

At a point on the margin of the clearing ninety degrees out
from the first VC position, a second firing position lit up with
green tracers that lashed out across the landing zone. The enemy
fire trapped the LRPs between the chopper and the tree line.

Shit! Hollister thought. "Guns?" he yelled into his mike.

"We're on 'em," the lead gun pilot replied as he reversed his
direction and stood his gunship up on its nose to pick up air
speed and get into position to pour minigun fire onto the target.

The pilot of the C&C came up on the intercom and filled
Hollister in. "The pickup's down. I've told the chase to go in.
don't think he can pick up the team *and* the crew, though."

"Then we go in and get the leftovers!" Hollister announced
without hesitation.

"Okay here," the C&C pilot replied.

Hollister switched back to transmit. "Quarterback—Contact!
Contact! Do you copy?"

Michaelson's voice was the first up from the base camp.
"Good copy. Contact. What do you need first, Jim?"

"Don't know just yet. Got one man down on the LZ and a
crippled ship. Going in with chase and C and C to pick up
everyone we can. Guns are waxing the firing positions, but the
weather is fucked. Gonna need troops to secure the downed
chopper till we can get it out. And I might need more guns. I'll
keep you advised. Out," Hollister replied as they fell in behind
the chase ship and started to slip into the PZ.

"Break. Two-three. Can you put your people into the chase

and we'll get the crew of the pickup with C and C—the trail ship?''

Camacho's voice came on, broken up by the fierce small arms fire and chopper noise in the background. "Rog. We've got one WIA. I think there's a wounded man in the chopper.''

"Okay, hold on, partner. We're coming in now!''

As the chase ship slammed into the ground, bounced and slid forward to the right rear of the crippled chopper, the C&C started his flare—heading for the left rear of the downed chopper.

Hollister got out of the jump seat on the left side of the C&C and moved into the right door to see and be able to help pull people in.

As he reached the other side of the chopper, he saw two more LRPs fall from a third VC firing position at another point on the tree line behind them. "Fuck!" Hollister yelled. He knew that it was not a chance meeting engagement. The VC had plotted every inch of the clearing and picked the best firing positions to crisscross the landing zone with intense knee-high fire.

As the crew from the downed chopper broke free from their ship and ran to the C&C, Hollister kept his eye on the LRP team trying to get their wounded to the chase ship.

The enemy fire was intense. Hollister heard the C&C take hit after hit, while he helped the two warrant officers pull a wounded door gunner into the C&C. As they tried to get back in, one of the pilots took a hit and fell backward—out of the chopper.

Hollister looked down at him. He was on the ground with his legs folded back underneath him. His eyes were wide and searching while his lids fluttered from the downwash of rain off the chopper blades.

Hollister tried to step out to help the pilot when he was snatched up short by the inadequate length of the drop cord that tied his headset to the chopper. Holding on to the wounded pilot, Hollister jerked his head away from the headset, letting it clatter onto the floor of the chopper. He then helped the other warrant officer lift his co-pilot up and slide him into the chopper.

Still outside the chopper, Hollister looked up to see how Camacho's team was making out. As he did, he was surprised to find the hand of the co-pilot of the C&C flapping out the small window right in front of his face—trying to get his attention. The co-pilot pointed to his helmet to let Hollister know he was needed on the radio.

Jumping onto his knees on the cargo bay of the chopper, Hollister repositioned his headset and ran his hand down the drop cord till he found the transmit button. "This is Two-six. Go."

"We're in a trick bag! Need help here!" Camacho's voice rasped into the headset.

Hollister looked over his shoulder at the team. Three soldiers were down. Camacho was on his knees next to one of them, and two others were trying to drag a second wounded soldier toward the chase ship. A lone body was lying lifeless on the paddy a few yards from the chase ship.

The door gunner on the LRP's side of the chase was firing rapid bursts over the heads of Camacho's team—at the tree line fifty meters behind them, which concealed a VC light machine gun that was churning up mud all around the LRPs.

The original pickup ship started to burn, belching dark smoke from the turbine engine that was eating itself up with pieces of fragmentation rattling around inside it.

Hollister knew that the success of any recovery from the ambush would rest in the length of time it would take for the three surviving LRPs to load the three wounded LRPs into the chase ship. Until that happened, the chase couldn't take off. And Hollister knew that the Gladiator pilots wouldn't take off and leave the surviving LRPs on the ground.

He made a decision, jumped out of the C&C, and ran toward Camacho's team. He took no more than three steps before he realized that he had left his rifle in the C&C. He decided that he couldn't stop. He ran as fast as he could in the direction of the LRPs, trying to use the burning chopper as cover from some of the VC fire. Two of the other positions were still able to fire on him. One continued to pour fire into the choppers, and the other sprayed Camacho's team and Hollister.

He skidded to a stop on his knees, sliding into the downed body of Doc Briskin. Theodore was trying to drag him to the chopper while hunching over to avoid the enemy fire.

The pale appearance of Briskin's muddy skin worried Hollister, but the lack of time to check him out prompted Hollister to just assume that he was alive. He reached for a handful of Briskin's slippery uniform to help Theodore drag him to the chopper.

Once they had Briskin in the chase ship, Hollister turned to see what the situation was with the others. Wyman and Gerhart were wounded, but with help from Vinson and Camacho, they were able to get into the chopper.

Hollister looked up and saw that the door gunners were doing their best to keep the fire up while the gunships were obliterating the tree lines around the south and west sides of the landing zone. Their job was complicated by the increasing downpour and the seriously reduced visibility. To compensate, Iron Mike kept making his gun runs lower and lower—so low that he was in danger of taking frags from his own rockets and grenades.

Hollister assumed that the fact that any of them were still alive at all was because the weather had turned so shitty, making it more difficult for the VC to see their targets.

That, coupled with the suppressive fire of the gunships and door gunners, continued to degrade the accuracy of the enemy fire. Still, Hollister was surprised that there weren't more dead LRPs and crippled choppers.

The unflagging enemy fire kept translating itself to the words *Go! Go! Go!* in his mind. He pushed Theodore up and into the chopper. At the same moment, out of the corner of his eye, he saw Vinson flinch. He looked over Theodore's shoulder and saw Vinson clutching his neck. Blood was streaming out between his fingers from a wound just under the collar of his shirt. Vinson shrugged his shoulders and flicked his rucksack off to get his hands up to his neck.

Hollister knew that he had to get the choppers off the ground—fast. He was the only one left still standing in the mud. He looked back to the C&C waiting for him. He would have to dash back to the ship, causing them to stay on the ground for those extra few seconds. But he might be able to get into the chase and get both ships off the ground faster.

Hollister stepped back from the side of the chase ship to signal the C&C to go without him. He then climbed into the chase ship and yelled, "Go! Go! Go!"

Looking out and behind, Hollister saw the C&C pull in some pitch on the blades, causing the chopper to rise up as the pilot took the weight off the skids in preparation for takeoff. But he seemed to be waiting for the chase to start up and forward.

After a long pause the chase chopper still had not lifted. The pilot swiveled his head around, looked at Hollister, and shook his head to let Hollister know that it wasn't going to get off the ground. Immediately Hollister realized what a stupid stunt he'd pulled, leaving the C&C and ending up in the chase ship. He was angry with himself for making such a stupid, grandstanding move to help Camacho.

The problem with the chase ship was that it had been topped off with fuel, as had the other choppers, before they left to make the pickup. With Hollister's extra weight and an almost full fuel load, they couldn't lift off.

The options spun through Hollister's head. He could get out and run the forty yards back to the C&C, but that would mean the C&C would have to stay put for several extra seconds while he slogged through the paddies. If he did that, he just might get someone killed in the C&C.

There was really only one option. He knew that Michaelson was inbound with more choppers, so he grabbed one of the rifles off the floor of the chopper and jumped out. He spun around, crouching to reduce his size as a target, and waved for the pilots of both ships to go. They looked at him like he was crazy. Enemy fire was snapping up spouts of muddy water near his feet while he stood there in the downpour waving them off. Neither chopper pilot made a move to leave. He could even see the pilot of the chase ship waving at him to get back in the chopper.

Hollister knew he had to do something to get them off the ground without him. He looked over his shoulder at the tree line. He knew that if he took the option away from the pilots, they would leave. If they saw him run for the tree line, they would know he was serious and that they couldn't do anything.

He calculated the shortest route to the tree line and started for it. He ran as fast as he could through the knee-deep mud— the wet air making him gasp for each breath. The footing was treacherous. After several long strides Hollister slipped and fell, face first, both hands going out in front of him to break his fall.

He waited for a VC bullet to hit him, but the enemy fire seemed to be behind him. He thought that the VC must not have been able to see him through the rain, and that they were still shooting at the choppers.

He lifted his head and realized that he had lost his M-16— somewhere under the muddy runoff flowing from the slightly higher ground in the tree line.

He searched the six-inch-deep water in front of him and found the upturned magazine of the rifle. As he crawled forward to get a grip on it, he heard the choppers lift off behind him. He turned to look over his shoulder to see if they were making it only to be met with a face full of muddy spray being blown into his eyes by the chopper blades. He cradled the rifle in the crook of one arm while he tried to wipe the muddy water out of his eyes with the sleeve of the other.

"Lieutenant!"

He heard someone calling out and thought he was imagining it. Wiping the water from his eyes, he tried to shield them with his forearm while he looked at the rising choppers. Only a few feet from his face he saw the stumbling form of a soldier, a rifle in one hand and a rucksack in the other. He ran toward Hollister, lost his footing, and fell.

Hollister reached out to help break the man's fall and caught sight of the face—Theodore! What the hell was he doing?

Theodore raised his face out of the mud and tried to speak, winded and coughing, with bits of rice straw stuck to his muddied face.

Hollister knew that they had to get out of the open—and fast. He grabbed the neck of Theodore's shirt and lifted him. Theodore scrambled up and the two ran the ten long strides to the tree line.

Reaching the small clump of trees, Hollister and Theodore dove over the brush clustered at the base of the trees and bellied into the ground behind them. Hollister spun around on his stomach and looked up—able to catch sight of the navigation lights of the C&C pulling out and away from the far side of the PZ in a left turn. He looked around the clearing for any sign of the chase ship. He couldn't see it in front of or above the C&C, and was afraid it might have been shot down or lost power on takeoff. The only thing on the ground was the half-burned hulk of the original pickup ship.

Hollister turned to Theodore, who was on his hands and knees, vomiting. Hollister tried to speak but couldn't get his wind. So he tried to calm himself as he gasped for air. They were in serious trouble. And no one knew it better than he did.

CHAPTER 27

The enemy fire had stopped, even though the rain hadn't. As the distant sounds of the climbing choppers diminished, Hollister became conscious of a hissing sound behind him. He looked around and found the source of the noise.

Theodore had brought Vinson's rucksack and radio with him when he jumped out of the chopper. The radio handset was stretched from the radio to a bush behind him.

Theodore looked up, saw that Hollister was looking at the handset, and reached up to pull it toward him. Getting a grip on it, Theodore swiveled into a seated position and pressed the mud-caked handset to his face. "This is Two-six Romeo. Over."

He listened for a second and his face showed concern.

"Roger, Six. Stand by one." He poked the handset toward Hollister. "The Old Man—they're still at the LRP pad!"

Expecting him to already be airborne—en route to their location—Hollister winced at the news. He was hoping that after his last transmission to Michaelson, they had been able to mount and launch a reaction force and pickup choppers. He pressed the handset to his face and spoke into the mouthpiece. "This is Two-six. Over."

"What the hell are you doing? Gladiator One-five told me you are on the ground! Is that correct? You stayed on the ground?!"

"Affirmative. And I've got line number—" He looked over to Theodore for his unit roster ID. Theodore mouthed the numbers. "Ah, line number Bravo three three with me. Over."

In a calming tone, Michaelson responded. "Okay, okay. Here's the problem. We are down—weather unflyable. It should lift within the hour. Can you hang on?"

"This is Two-six. I think so. Haven't got much of a choice.

Over.'' He hoped against hope that when his hand reached his trouser pocket, his map case would still be there.

It was! He flipped the mud-soaked map open on his knee and looked up to orient himself and then his map while Michaelson continued.

''Okay—I've got a FAC waiting to take off. Guns will be back ASAP. You hole up till we can get you out. You still taking fire?''

''Negative. The visibility is zero zero. I don't think they even know I'm here. Will lay low. Might need help coordinating some fires. I'm going to call redleg on enemy positions. Over,'' Hollister whispered into the handset.

''Okay, partner. We'll be there just as fast as we can get there. It'll be okay. Out.''

Finding his mud-soaked notebook in his shirt pocket, Hollister flipped open the cover and thumbed the pages to the artillery frequency and call sign for the Fire Direction Center that controlled the American artillery batteries at the north end of the valley. As he closed the notebook, the green dye from the cardboard cover ran over his fingers. He wiped the dye on his trousers and reached out for the radio on the upright rucksack frame.

After switching the dial to the correct frequency, Hollister called in a request for artillery fires on two of the enemy positions he could identify on the map. He requested that they fire a smoke round first to alert him, since he would be on another frequency. That would allow him to come back up on their frequency and adjust the fires.

They told him to wait while they plotted and cleared the mission.

Trying not to let his voice rise out of control, Hollister leaned over and stuck his face into Theodore's. ''Just what the hell are you doing? Why didn't you stay in that fucking chopper?''

''Something I learned. A lieutenant without a radio is just a lieutenant. And a lieutenant with a radio is a commander—sir.''

Hollister couldn't help but laugh. This was a far cry from the timid Theodore he had been worried about many weeks earlier. All he could think of doing was to reach out with his green-stained fingers and shake Theodore's hand. ''Thanks. You were right. But we *are* in a very bad spot.''

''No sweat, sir. You'll get us out,'' Theodore said with his hopeful grin. ''And you're buying the beer.''

The rain was still coming down hard after an hour. Hollister and Theodore were shivering from the cold as they sat back to back,

each watching half of the two-man perimeter they created. Hol
lister spun the radio dials again and called the artillery. "This
is Quarterback Two-six. What the fuck is the holdup on the
artillery?"

The weak and broken reply came back. "Look, we aren't the
problem. We do not have clearance yet. I say again—we do *not*
have clearance. Are you taking fire now? Over."

"Negative. Must fire on those targets to bring in extraction
choppers. Please try to clear. Over," Hollister replied.

"We're working as fast as we can. Stand by. Out."

Hollister looked down at the water pooling on either side of
his legs. The bottom half of each outstretched leg was hidden
under the cold and muddy water. He could feel Theodore's back
shaking from the cold. Readjusting the frequency, he passed the
handset over his shoulder till it came to rest on Theodore's.

The two continued to watch their half of the trees around them
for any sign of the VC. Both were hoping that the VC had cut
and run, figuring that they had done all the damage they could
do and trying to avoid the certain artillery fires that would be
called on their firing positions.

Then Hollister remembered the downed chopper in the paddies. He was sure that the VC would keep an eye on it and set
up some kind of a trap for whoever would come to extract the
carcass. Or they might even send a party out to strip anything
useful off the chopper—like the machine guns and the ammo.

The only hope was that the VC might lose interest if the
chopper had completely burned, leaving nothing to salvage. But
Hollister didn't know what condition it was in. He last remembered the chopper burning slowly, hindered by the downpour.
And from his position inside the tree line, he couldn't see the
chopper on the LZ.

After a second hour there was still no artillery fire. Hollister
was furious. There was just no excuse for not being able to fire
and adjust artillery on known enemy positions. But he continued
to get the same answer—*not cleared to fire*. And the rain continued to pour down with no break in sight.

The squelch broke on the radio. Theodore passed the handset
to Hollister.

"Two-six, Six. We are lifting off. Clearing here. Over," Michaelson's voice announced over the radio.

"This is Two-six. Roger. Still no letup on the rain here. No enemy fire or sightings. And still no artillery! We're ready. Call us zero five out. Over."

"The ceiling's very bad, but we'll get there if we have to hover the whole way. Just stand by. Out."

Theodore reached for his gear. He tried to snug down the radio.

Hollister knew that if Theodore carried the radio and all of the gear that was with the rucksack, he would slow the two of them down. And they would need all the speed they could get to cross the paddies and get into a pickup ship.

Hollister reached over, unbuckled the top flap on the rucksack and zipped the nylon drawstring open. Inside he found a spare pair of trousers and pulled them out. He tied the bottoms of each trouser leg in a knot and buttoned up the fly. Having created a bag, of sorts, he rummaged through the rucksack and the side pouches, pulling out items that he didn't want to leave behind for the VC. He tossed out the other items, which couldn't be used against the Americans. After the rucksack was empty, he lifted the trousers with one hand to test for weight.

The squelch broke on the radio and Theodore answered. It was Michaelson. They were trying to find a break in the weather that would allow them to get to Hollister and Theodore.

Theodore passed the information to Hollister. They both looked up at the cloud cover. It was still fairly heavy over their heads.

"Call the arty folks and tell them to cancel the fire mission. Be our luck that they'll clear and fire the targets when the choppers are trying to pick us up. Make sure they know that the cancellation is to allow aircraft into the target area," Hollister said.

Theodore nodded and sent the message. While he was taking care of that, Hollister rechecked the action on his M-16 and got up into a squat. He made a complete 360 check of the area immediately around them.

The rain had slowed and the visibility had improved. He knew that wasn't all good news. The lifting of the cloud cover allowed the VC to see better, too. They were also smart enough to know that someone would be coming to check out the condition of the downed chopper—even if they didn't know there were Americans still on the ground.

As soon as Theodore switched back to the tactical frequency, he heard Michaelson's voice calling for Hollister. Without answering, he quickly passed the handset.

"This is Two-six. Go," Hollister said, without taking his eyes off the widening circle he was scanning.

"We think we have this licked. We should be at your location in zero five. What's the weather?" Michaelson asked.

Looking up, Hollister answered, "Ceiling is about two hundred feet and the visibility is almost a half mile. Still raining and zero winds. Over."

"Stand by One," Michaelson said, switching to intercom to talk to the pilot.

Hollister turned to Theodore. "Get it on. They're inbound." He reached into the first aid pouch on his pistol belt and pulled out his pen flare and a couple of loose flares and handed them to Theodore.

"This is Six. Okay. We are inbound. What's your ETA to the PZ, and can you mark?"

"This is Two-six. We can be in position in zero two. We can mark with a Paper Mate. Over," Hollister said, referring to the pen flare.

"Okay, partner. Start moving. You should be hearin' us any time now. We'll call for a mark if we need it. Gladiator seems to think he knows enough about the PZ to find you without much trouble. We're on final."

Hollister and Theodore spun their heads, reacting to the chopper sounds. Without saying anything, Hollister threw the trouser bag around his neck and got up to lead the way back to the PZ. Theodore followed, half walking backward to cover their rear.

The PZ was covered with calf-deep water. The downed chopper was nothing but muddy ashes and a few chunky pieces of the carcass sticking up out of the water.

The gunships were the first to break over the trees at the end of the PZ. They came across with one chopper on each side of the PZ—flying low and fast.

"Two-six, Iron Mike. How 'bout givin' me a mark?" Mike Taylor said over the radio.

Theodore had the pen flare in his hand, waiting for Hollister's signal.

From the cockpit of the gunship, Captain Taylor saw the red balls of fire leap from the tree line and arc out over the PZ like a Roman candle.

"Got you. I want to light up the area before we come in. That a problem, Two-six?" Taylor asked.

"No problem. Wish you would. If you have us—anything else is bad guys. Over."

"Okay, put your heads down. We're just going to try to fuck up their aim before we bring in the slicks."

The gunships nosed over, picked up airspeed, lost a little altitude, and started to rain rockets, miniguns, and 40mm grenades on both sides of the PZ.

Taylor's wingman started his run along the tree line that concealed Hollister and Theodore. They watched as the gunship belched 40mm grenades from the snoutlike pod on the chin of the chopper. The exploding grenades got closer and closer, and Hollister began to worry if the pilot really knew where they were. When it looked like the next few grenades would hit close enough to shower them with fragmentation, the gunner let up on the trigger and the pilot kicked out into a hard ascending left turn, almost stalling out over their heads.

"Short final," Michaelson announced over the radio.

"Roger. We're ready, Six," Hollister replied as he reached over to get Theodore into a track star's starting position.

The pickup slick appeared over the tree line, the C&C above and behind it, and the chase below and behind the C&C. Hollister gauged the speed and touchdown point and started to count out loud, over the clamor of choppers and gun runs. "One . . . Two . . . Three . . . Go!"

Hollister and Theodore burst from the margin of the PZ throwing up chin-high splashes of muddy water as they ran for the chopper.

The burning in Hollister's chest and the muddy water in his eyes were only minor problems compared to his concern for enemy fire. *Were they there? Would they fire? Were they already firing and he just couldn't hear it?*

Getting closer, he could see Easy kneeling in the middle of the open doorway of the chopper. Hollister might have known that Easy would insist on being belly man on the pickup.

It was going too well for Hollister. He had a momentary flash of panic at the thought of getting into the chopper and not getting Theodore in. He slowed his pace to allow Theodore to come abreast of him and then get in front of him. He wanted to make sure that Theodore got into the chopper before he did.

As Theodore's bulk crossed in front of him, Hollister turned half around to cover their backs. The chopper was on the ground, and he knew that they only had about four more long strides to get to it.

Without warning, a line of green tracers crossed Hollister's field of vision, coming from behind them, somewhere in the tree line they had just left. Hollister's heart sank. "No," he yelled. "Not again. Not again!"

An RPG came whooshing out of the tree line, headed for the pickup ship. But it somehow went wild, spiraled and augered itself into the ground halfway to the chopper. The warhead detonated, throwing Hollister backward, as if he had been hit by a car.

Turning around just inside the chopper, Theodore was stunned by the sight of his boss down only yards away. He dug his mud-covered heels into the corrugated deck and scooted himself back to the edge. He lost his balance and fell out of the chopper. Getting to his feet, he ran at a crouch to Hollister's side.

By then the enemy fire crossed the PZ from four different positions. Two of them were within meters of where Theodore and Hollister had hidden, waiting for the pickup.

As Theodore reached Hollister, he dropped to his side as if sliding into base. As he was falling in a long, diagonal stretch, a burst of enemy fire found his torso and spun him over—ripping large chunks of his side and hip away.

Easy was out of the chopper the second he saw the tracers slice through Theodore's body. He bounded across the paddies yelling, "Hold on. Just hold on!"

Even though he was a larger, slower target, Easy reached Hollister and Theodore without getting hit. The noise and confusion went up considerably as Michaelson and Iron Mike had adjusted the gunship firing runs into tight circles around the three LRPs and the pickup chopper waiting courageously on the ground.

Easy found Hollister very dazed and Theodore critically wounded. He hoisted Theodore over his shoulder and grabbed Hollister under the arm to lift him to his feet, and then started for the chopper.

As they moved clumsily toward the waiting chopper, the door gunner unhooked his drop cord and jumped out to help.

As the clumsy trio reached the chopper, the door gunner helped Easy hoist Theodore into the cargo compartment. Easy then turned to help the disoriented Hollister. As he did, a burst of enemy machine-gun fire stitched across the paddies, splashing water, and bounced off something beneath the surface—popping up and hitting Easy in the leg.

Easy simply collapsed without recoil from the impact of the distorted enemy machine-gun bullet.

Hollister wasn't sure if he was seeing or dreaming the night-care. He didn't care. He mustered all the strength he could find, reached down and grabbed for Easy.

From somewhere, the hands of the door gunner reached down, too. Between them they were able to get Easy into the hopper.

Hollister tried to crawl into the chopper but found that he was totally drained of strength. His fingers found the cargo tie-down rings and he pulled against them, hoping to let the chopper pull him up and out of the paddy. He summoned up what breath he had and instinctively whispered, "Go! Go! Go!"

He had no idea just how much time had passed. But Hollister suddenly became aware of being in the chopper at flight altitude. He was not sure where they were or even if it was the same hopper that had rescued them from the muddy pickup zone; not until he realized that he was freezing from the wind evaporating the paddy water from his uniform.

Though his vision was still blurred from the concussion of the RPG that had knocked him off his feet, he looked around and saw one of the door gunners trying to hold pressure on the side of Theodore's body.

Nearby, Easy leaned against the back of the pilot's seat, attempting to tie his cravat around his thigh to stop his own bleeding.

Responding to some reflexive urge to help, Hollister crawled across the floor of the chopper toward Easy and simply blacked out again.

Sometime the next morning, Hollister coughed to clear his throat. The sudden pain woke him from a deep sleep. Opening his eyes slightly, he felt his head pounding and sharp pains at the points where each rib connected to his breastbone. He tried to open his eyes and clear his vision, which was still blurred, but it caused him pain when even the slightest amount of light entered his eyes.

He tried a few more times, but each time the pain was too much and he quickly shut his eyes before he could focus on anything. He decided to wait a few seconds before he tried again.

Slowly he began to realize where he was. The crisp sheets, the feel of a real pillow coupled with the medicinal odors that filled his nostrils, convinced him that he was in a hospital bed. He knew that he was still in Vietnam because of the humidity. It would have been drier in Japan. Then he remembered that he

could be in Guam or Hawaii. No, they wouldn't be using th
large generator that he could hear chugging somewhere outsic
the ward. But what difference did it make? Was he maimec
Was he whole?

He tried to make himself concentrate on limbs. He moved h
legs slightly and grimaced at the soreness in the big muscles i
his thighs. That was enough to convince him that he wasn
paralyzed.

He raised one hand to his face to cover his eyes. It only ge
about six inches off the bed before it was stopped by the I
needle that went into a vein on the back of his hand.

He tried with the other hand and was able to shade his ey
while he opened them. It felt like the worst hangover of his lif
without the nausea. He could see that he was in a ward in th
Brigade hospital. There were nine other beds in the tent. Ha
of them were empty. *Theodore? Easy? Camacho's people
Where were they?*

He tried to lift his head, and immediately got dizzy and fe
like he was going to throw up. He lowered it back onto th
pillow—slowly. He was sure that if he just tried to lie there, stil
for just a minute, he would be able to try again. The waves
nausea began to wane and he steeled himself to try once mor

He heard someone's boots making a grating noise against th
flooring as they walked to the side of his bed and stopped. I
decided not to try to open his eyes, lift his head, and talk at th
same time. He settled for just trying to speak softly—so as no
to hurt his pounding head. "Who's there?"

"How you feeling, Ranger?"

"Cap'n M—I, uh . . . actually, I don't know. How are you?
Hollister asked.

"Well, I'm okay. But you look like you got into a rock fig
and came in second. But the docs say you're gonna be okay.'

Raising his hand in a questioning, palm-up gesture, Hollist
took a shallow breath to avoid the pain, and spoke again. "Wh
happened? Where's Easy and Theodore and the others?"

"You remember the pickup?"

"All I remember is busting out of the trees. Then the ligh
went out—like someone kicked me in the head."

"You were knocked on your ass by an RPG," Michaelso
said. "You have a concussion and lots of bruises. Lemme te
you, I've seen people hit by trucks not get knocked as hard
as far as you were!"

"Musta landed on my head! But how 'bout the others?"

"Theodore is in another ward. They have a bunch of tubes in the kid. He took a couple of rounds in his chest and hip. He's hanging in there for now. The others on Camacho's team—well, Briskin was killed, Vinson and Gerhart were wounded and are going home. They're gonna be okay. Wyman was slightly wounded and returned to light duty."

"And Easy?" Hollister asked.

"They evac'd him to Japan last night."

"That it?"

"He lost his leg, Jim. He's gonna live, but they just couldn't do anything with his leg. I saw him before they wheeled him out. He said for me to tell you that you'll have to get your own scotch from now on."

Hollister let the casualties sink in for a few seconds as he opened his eyes. Tears welled up as he spoke—almost inaudibly. "You know, this sucks. It really sucks."

Michaelson reached over, grasped Hollister's arm and gave it a firm squeeze. "I know, Jim. I know how you feel."

Hollister just stared up in the direction of the ridge pole holding up the tent. He was motionless and speechless for the longest time as he thought of Easy and Theodore and the others. He then painfully turned his head and looked at Michaelson. "What do we do now?"

"You remember that day in the swamps? The lightning?"

"Yessir."

"We do the same thing. We drive on, Ranger," Michaelson said.

Hollister dropped his eyes, not eager to hear that. "Yessir. Guess there's nothing else we can do."

The next day, Michaelson came back to see Hollister.

"Am I glad to see you, boss!" Hollister said with more energy than before. "I'm on somebody's shit list here. I've been trying to find out where they're keeping Theodore, and all they keep telling me is that I shouldn't get out of bed and he can't have visitors right now."

"Well—" Michaelson started to reply.

"Shit, I'm not a visitor. I'm his platoon leader. He's my RTO, for Chrissakes!"

Michaelson took his floppy hat off, put his hands on his hips and looked down at the floor. "Jim—Theodore died last night."

Hollister felt like someone had hit him in the chest with a shovel. *Not Theodore, too.* He mustered up the strength, then threw the covers back. Pushing his feet over the side of the bed, he clenched his teeth and made a muffled sound as he overcame the pain. "I gotta get out of here!"

"No! There's not a thing you can do. Now, lay your ass back down and give it time. You've got a head injury and God knows what else," Michaelson said, reaching out as much to stop Hollister as to catch him.

"I have to get up. I got to go strangle some artillery fuck!"

"Now hold on!"

"If I'd been able to adjust fire on those gook positions, there might have been no one to shoot our asses up on the PZ!"

"It wasn't Brigade arty's fault. They couldn't get clearance from the ARVNs. They were complaining that you were too close to friendly villages to clear the fire mission."

Hollister's face went red with anger. "ARVNs? It was that goddamn Colonel Minh? Wasn't it?" He tried to straighten up to stand on the floor, and had to reach out for the bed frame as his knees buckled.

"Whoa! Just a minute! You *will* stay in that rack! Now, lay down and quit running your mouth," Michaelson said forcefully. "You let me handle this. It's my job. Your job is to get better and get back to duty as soon as you can."

Drained by the effort, Hollister slumped back onto the bed and dropped his head—despondent over the developments. "Yessir," he said weakly.

Michaelson squeezed Hollister's shoulder. "I need you, Jim. We're in a world of hurt back at the detachment. We've got to look forward and get it back together or we won't have a detachment.

"I can't do it alone. I've got to have you back. But I don't want you for duty pissed and hurt. Get well, get over it, and get back in the saddle."

By the end of the third day in the hospital, Hollister was getting anxious. He wanted out of bed and out of the hospital. Still, he knew that it was a chance to rest, collect his thoughts, go over what had happened and think about what he had to do.

He dozed fitfully and drifted in and out of sleep. He had muddled dreams that seemed real but couldn't be. He awoke from one of them around nine at night and found Sergeant Davis sitting in a chair next to his bed.

"How ya doin', sir?"

Still foggy, Hollister reached out to touch Davis, making sure that he was real. He then sat up and reached for the cup of water next to his bed. His pajama top was wet with sweat from the neck to the hem. "Been better. You?"

"I'm overworked, underpaid, and unloved. The Old Man moved Marrietta to Easy's job, and I'm doubling as Ops NCO till we can get some more bodies in."

"Good. That's good. You need the experience. It'll help get you some E-7 stripes."

Davis laughed. "C'mon, Lieutenant. I'm a boonie rat, not headquarters material."

Thinking of the flap over the artillery, Hollister replied, "But that's what we need—more boonie rats in more headquarters slots." The bitterness was unmistakable in his tone.

"You got that shit right."

Watching the expression on Davis's face, Hollister realized that he was just bumming both of them out and tried to change the mood. He lowered his voice and leaned toward Davis. "How can we get me out of this place?"

Davis looked around to make sure no one was listening. "You want, we can bust you out of here tomorrow. Give me a chance to get back to the platoon and get some firepower."

They both laughed at Davis's suggestion that they blast Hollister out.

In spite of the fact that it hurt his chest to laugh, Hollister loved to see Davis laugh. He did it so rarely that Hollister knew it was genuine when he did.

Holding his ribs with one arm, Hollister shuffled to the latrine outside the ward, just barely managing to keep the poorly designed paper hospital slippers on his feet.

The latrine was a semipermanent structure; the toilets were holes cut into plywood boxes, and the sink was a sheet-metal trough with garden spigots—cold only. The portable army showers were made of a pole topped with heads pointing down in four directions. The sinks and showers were fed by a large hose that snaked into the latrine from a water truck outside.

The one item of sophistication in the latrine was the row of metal mirrors mounted over the sink trough. They were very scratched and reflected the viewer as more like a fun-house image than reality.

Scuffing to one, Hollister leaned over the sink to the mirror and ran his hand over the stubble on his face. At first he thought he saw streaks of camouflage paint, but as he got closer to the mirror he could tell that his face had multiple lacerations that must have happened when the RPG upended him. He examined them for a moment and decided that they would probably heal without much scarring.

While he shaved, two other patients entered the latrine and took showers. Both reacted with a start at the shock of the first spray of cold water.

He had to laugh at himself. The cold shower, the dull razor blade, and the distorted mirror were all symbols of a level of luxury that he had often craved while sitting in his own filth on the floor of the Vietnamese rain forest.

"While I reorganize the detachment, I have to accomplish several things," Michaelson said to the assembled LRPs. "I've got to find more replacements while freeing up enough of you to do a good job training them and still continuing operations.

"The fact that we racked up some VC bodies and a few weapons on that fucked-up snatch mission will not compensate for the losses we took. It means that many of you will double up on duties, and I'm expecting a lot out of you. I just want you to know that I have confidence in you and I want you to put your efforts into getting us back to fighting shape and not on licking wounds."

There were approving comments from the crowd. The only intelligible one was the repeated use of the word "Airborne" as a sign of support for Michaelson's goals.

Sitting in the back of the room, Hollister was amazed at the stamina of the detachment and the faith they had in themselves and in Captain Michaelson. He shared their feeling for Michaelson, but was still a little shaky about his own capabilities. The soreness in his chest was still with him, and it reminded him of his vulnerability.

Susan's letter was filled with excited anticipation. They were under sixty days. And she was counting every one of them until she could be with him again. Her enthusiasm made it easy for Hollister to write a reply.

As he did, he found himself getting used to the idea of going home and starting a real life with Susan. It had seemed so far off before. They had been dating for three years, but he was never in one place long enough for them to set any real goals.

He finished his letter and raised the envelope to lick it. As he did, he spotted the picture of Phuc's wife, Ly, still tacked over his desk. There was something different about looking at Ly's photo—different than before.

He had spent months chasing an enemy that was so effective and so unpredictable, only to realize that he could only recognize one face as that of a Communist—Ly's. A twinge of frustration went through his body as he remembered the glimpse of Theodore and Easy in the chopper when they were extracted. Men who wouldn't be going home would still be laying in wait for Easy's, Theodore's, and his own replacements. He clenched his fist and reminded himself that he could do something about that—more than Michaelson expected of him.

"Got a minute?" Michaelson's voice interrupted Hollister's thoughts as he stepped into the hooch.

Hollister stood. "Yessir. C'mon in."

Michaelson spun the chair around and put his foot up on it. He pulled out a cigar and unwrapped it.

"What's that?" Michaelson asked.

"A photo we took off a VC sometime back," Hollister answered.

Leaning over to take a long look at it, Michaelson lit his cigar and spoke. "They're funny people. They may not have a pot to piss in, but they can find the money to have their picture taken. If they closed all the photo shops in Vietnam, the economy would go under."

"I look at her picture when I get really fuckin' pissed. It helps me remember that they're people. I really don't want to think of them as animals. 'Cause I'm afraid of what I'd do if I—"

"Jim, you've had a pretty tough year. I've been here a little longer than you and I understand what you're thinking and how you're feeling. My recommendation is that you do more work and less thinking. It'll help the days go by, and you'll see the results of good, hard training. You know I'm right, don't you?"

"Yessir, but I was in that rack at the hospital thinking about Easy and Theodore and the others. I feel kinda funny about packing up soon and just getting on a 707."

"Don't do it. You think too hard about the guys that we lost, and the next thing I know you'll be bustin' into my office wanting to extend your tour over here."

Hollister looked up, surprised, as if Michaelson was reading his mind.

"No. Disapproved! You're going home. What you're feeling is *the* wrong way to extend—it's called revenge. No one wants to work with someone who has it out for the gooks. And I don't want anyone in this outfit with that kind of shark in their gut.''

Michaelson had to relight his cigar. He took a few short puffs to get it going and changed his tone. ''The reason I came over here is to talk to you about this thing with Province and Colonel Minh. I've done some pretty loud yelling up at Brigade and I feel bad weather coming. It could solve itself, but my guess is that a shit storm is brewing. I want you to just lay low and stay out of it. Whatever can be done—I'll do. You got that?''

A flush of anger gripped Hollister and he started to protest.

Michaelson raised his palm to stop him. ''You just get on with the business of reorganizing and retraining your teams. We don't need to discuss this with anyone else. I'll make sure we don't have to rely on zip artillery clearance in the future, and we'll let Brigade follow up on my bitching. Otherwise, it stays with us. Wouldn't do the troops any good to know that they can't trust the ARVNs. I know they've got wind of all this, but let's not feed it.'' He stood, not waiting for any more discussion.

Hollister stood, moving slowly.

''You feeling better?''

''Yessir.''

''Good—take the rest of the day off, and I'll see you at PT in the morning.'' With that, Michaelson kicked the door open and stepped out of the hooch.

The training went on for two weeks, with only light missions outside the wire. They were used as shakedown patrols. Hollister's hours were longer than ever before and his mood was darker. Everyone around him missed his sense of humor, but no one gave him low marks in training.

He tested and retested each man in the platoon in immediate actions drills, marksmanship, patrolling, movement, and a list of other techniques that made the difference between a failed patrol and a successful one.

After the last class in terrain navigation ended, Hollister stood on the perimeter berm, drinking a beer and looking out into the night. Tracers were silently arcing across the sky. It was hard for him to tell who was doing the shooting. From the direction, it could have been the ARVN outpost along Highway 1, the Regional Force compound, or some maneuver unit that was temporarily in the area.

He wasn't sure if he was even interested in knowing the answer. He only knew that he had never felt the way he was feel-

ng. His energy was down, he was sullen, and he had an angry
mass inside him that kept a slow fire burning in his belly. He
wasn't happy with who he was. He didn't like being short-fused
and testy all the time. On top of all that, he knew he couldn't
tell anyone how he felt. It would certainly be taken as a sign of
weakness.

It was still important to him how people felt about him as a
leader. He had no idea if he would stay in the army or not. But
he did know that he didn't want to get a reputation for being a
weak sister or a complainer. He would tough it out. It was how
things were done. He needed another beer.

"Lieutenant?"

Hollister turned around and found Sergeant Camacho standing behind the berm.

"The Old Man told me to tell you he has a warning order to
issue in an hour. He wants you in Operations."

"Thanks, Sergeant Camacho. I'll be there."

Camacho began to turn, and then remembered something.
"Oh, I forgot." He reached into his trouser side pocket and
pulled out an envelope. "There was some late mail that just
came in. There's one for you."

The announcement shot a small guilt pang through Hollister.
He knew he was way behind in his letter writing again. He
reached out for the envelope.

"It's from Easy, sir."

The return address was Camp Drake in Japan. Drake was one
of the army hospitals that served as way stations for the wounded
on their way back to the States. From the postmark, it had taken
over a week for it to get to An Hoa.

Easy wrote the letter with a blunt handwriting style that was
a perfect match for his personality. In it he complained about
the rear echelon types who were running the hospital and the
skating they were doing. He had little use for soldiers who
punched a clock and spent the evenings and weekends on the
Ginza while there were Airborne soldiers in Vietnam picking
leeches off their testicles and eating canned lima beans.

He told Hollister that he was scheduled to leave Japan the
next day for Fitzsimmons Army Hospital in Denver.

Another pang of guilt shot through Hollister as he realized
that he didn't even know where Easy's hometown was. He wondered if Fitzsimmons was the nearest hospital to his home or if

he was being sent there because they had some medical specialt
that Easy needed. He hoped that Easy was from Denver.

Easy spent the rest of the letter asking how everyone was bac
at An Hoa and who was doing what. His mood sounded positiv
and optimistic. It was better than Hollister's. It made Holliste
feel guilty about his own sullenness after what Easy had bee
through.

Easy included the Denver address for Hollister and hinte
that he could use some mail from some real soldiers after bein
surrounded by hospital pukes and other patients who were com
plaining with hemorrhoids and hernias.

What was missing from his letter was any personal com
plaints—real ones. He said nothing about the loss of his leg o
about any prognosis. He was most concerned with the men i
the detachment, and made a strong point of asking Hollister t
look out for Captain Michaelson.

Easy had risked his life to save Theodore and Hollister, an
it cost him a leg. Yet nowhere in the letter was there any mentio
of his pain or his sacrifice.

Hollister folded the letter to keep it.

In the Operations tent, Hollister found some paper and starte
a reply with the time he had before meeting with Michaelson
It was effortless. He could talk to Easy about what he was feelin
and what was going on in the detachment. He didn't have t
protect him from anything. He was happy to have the opportu
nity.

CHAPTER 28

The sun beat down on the group assembled outside the large tent that had been erected for the investigation. There were soldiers and officers from Brigade Artillery, LRPs, and even some of the pilots.

The small cluster from the Artillery Fire Direction Center stayed together and avoided anything more than polite conversation with the LRPs and their pilots.

One at a time, each man was called into the tent to be questioned. The LRPs blew the whole morning waiting for the artillerymen to finish.

The battery commander of the supporting battery stepped out of the tent and gave the LRPs a confident smile, got into his jeep and rode off. He was followed by a starched and spit-shined lieutenant from Brigade Headquarters who announced that they would break for lunch. The LRPs and pilots could eat in the headquarters mess a few hundred yards away.

Michaelson gave a cautionary look to his charges, which warned them not to make a fuss or act like country bumpkins at the sight of the sparkling clean and well-appointed dining facility. They all got the message. They would be on their best behavior—well, as good as they could be.

Inside the mess hall they found a real steam table with a large array of offerings for lunch. The tables had individual chairs and plastic tablecloths. Each chair had a vinyl covering on its back imprinted with the Brigade insignia and slogan.

Hollister caught Davis's eye as he was about to make some remark and shook his head to dissuade him. Davis frowned at being stifled.

Everyone inside was drinking iced tea from real glasses, and their trays were topped with real plates, saucers, and bowls. As

fast as a diner sat down, a dining room orderly would take the
tray away to allow the diner to place his heaping plates on the
covered tabletops.

Hollister could tell that the LRPs and pilots were on the verge
of making a scene over the relative grandeur of the dining facility. It got so bad that he and Davis wouldn't look at one another
for fear that they would break out laughing at the phony elegance
that permeated the place.

The group of outsiders found a large table away from the
headquarters rats.

"What d'ya suppose the redlegs told them?" Hollister asked.

Captain Shaw tried to wind spaghetti around his fork. "I'd
guess they simply gave them a rundown on the delays and gook
double-talk they got from Province."

"They sure couldn't tell 'em about firing anything. Maybe
they talked about the spiderweb problems in their howitzers,"
Davis said sarcastically, tearing apart a roll.

"Cut 'em some slack," Captain Michaelson said. "You and
I both know that they tried to fire that mission."

Davis moved the awful-tasting cold beets to the side of his
plate, looked at Captain Michaelson and changed his tone to
something more tolerant. "Yessir. I know you're right. I can't
fault them. But things sure mighta turned out a lot different if
they'da stuck their necks out a little."

"My guess is that they would have fired without the clearance
from Province Headquarters if our people hadn't been so close
to friendly villages," Hollister said.

"Friendly?" Captain Shelton said. "Friendly villagers don't
splatter choppers across their front yards!"

Poking his thumb back toward the investigation tent, Hollister
spoke up. "How come there's no one from Province Headquarters waiting to be questioned?"

Michaelson looked at Hollister as if he were gazing over the
top of bifocals. "You won't live to be old enough to understand
the complexities of Vietnamese political moves, or absence of
moves."

Each man mumbled some snide remark about the Vietnamese, drawing attention to themselves from the adjacent tables.

It was the first time Hollister had even spoken to Colonel Lanham, the Brigade Executive Officer. Lanham was seated in the
center of the long table flanked by two lieutenant colonels, a
major, and a master sergeant. Hollister discovered that he didn't

like Lanham from the moment that he walked into the tent for his turn to be questioned.

Lanham explained to Hollister that he was presiding over an investigation to determine if there was any wrongdoing in the matter of the fire missions called by Hollister.

The first words out of the colonel's mouth pissed Hollister off. The colonel got through his entire canned speech about the purpose of the investigation without ever using the words Province or Vietnamese Army. Hollister could feel his anger growing as Lanham questioned him. He was impatient with the questions, which were so simple and designed to discover nothing troubling. *What were the weather conditions? Could you positively identify enemy targets? Were you taking fire at the time?*

Hollister thought that when the questions and answers were strung together, it made the situation sound as if he didn't really need any supporting artillery fire at all—as if it were a hysterical whim on his part to even call for it.

It also angered him that he wasn't given a chance to go into any detail about how threatening he thought the situation was. The questions were posed to get the desired answers—and to discover nothing. When he tried to expand on his answers, the colonel cut him off. In short order he was dismissed without so much as a thank-you.

Outside, Hollister tried to calm down. He was angry at the tone of the investigation and the obvious attempt to distance anyone in the Brigade from any charges of wrongdoing.

As he stood there field stripping a cigarette, a jeep rolled up with two familiar faces in it—Wasco and Elliott. Hollister had remembered them fondly as being fair and seemingly hardworking in their investigation of the hamlet leveled many months before.

"How y'doing, Hollister?" Wasco asked.

"Fine, sir. What brings you two here from Nha Trang?"

Wasco pointed toward the tent where Michaelson was still inside being questioned. "We're a little involved in the investigation."

"Whatever happened to the one you were doing on that hamlet that got wasted?" Hollister asked.

Wasco patted Hollister on the back in a slightly patronizing manner. "Still working on it, son. But we're closing in on the bad guys on that one."

"Well, I hope you can work some of your magic on this one.

There's a Viet colonel that needs someone looking over his shoulder.''

Wasco and Elliott exchanged knowing looks.

"Guess we got some bad news for you, partner. That colonel you're talking about just got himself promoted to brigadier general the other day. He's in Nha Trang right now, picking out furniture for his new office.''

"What?! Are you shitting me?" Hollister asked, incredulous. "That fat asshole got promoted? He belongs in jail!''

"Sorry, but he's the new Chief of Operations for Military Region Two," Elliott said.

"Why him? Why did *he* get promoted?"

"He's got family in high places in Saigon—so the story goes,'' Wasco speculated.

Baffled, Hollister shook his head at the news. He couldn't believe the turn of events. He thought of Easy and Theodore and the others and what it cost them. He could feel the heat rising and knew his face was flushing.

"Don't worry. We're on the case. He can't escape an investigation just because he has a new address," Elliott said.

There was more that Hollister wanted to know, but the conversation with Wasco and Elliott was interrupted by the yelling coming from inside the tent. Hollister was unable to tell exactly what was being said inside, but was sure that Michaelson was very angry and letting the colonel know it. His tone of voice was way up on the high end of what might be considered insubordinate and disrespectful.

Everyone outside the tent stopped talking to listen to the noisy discussion going on inside.

Wasco patted his pockets, looking for a cigar, realized that he must have left them in the jeep and walked back to it.

Hollister looked at Elliott for some sign. He had a feeling that there was lots more to it than Elliott or Wasco had said.

"This guy a double agent, a VC in an ARVN uniform?" Hollister asked.

" 'Tween us? I don't even think he's that principled. My gut tells me that he has just figured out several ways to make money off the war, and he spends what he has to to keep making money and stay in a position where he can turn another piaster," Elliott said, so only Hollister could hear him.

"Can you prove enough of this to get to him?"

"I think so, but no time soon."

"Why? What the hell's the holdup?" Hollister asked.

Elliott jabbed a thumb toward the tent. "That colonel in there's going to make sure that the American skirts are squeaky clean before he even thinks of making some rash charge that could blow up in his face." He leaned even closer to Hollister and continued, "Ya see, in their country an investigation is like an indictment. You try to pin something on a high-ranking Viet and you better have a damn good pin, pal."

Wasco returned. Elliott gave Hollister a look that suggested he not reveal the details of what he'd just been told. Hollister gave him an almost imperceptible nod.

"So how long before you all get somewhere with what you're investigating?" Hollister asked.

Wasco lit his cigar, took a drag and picked a bit of loose tobacco off the end of it. "What? You wanna be around when we start putting out the wanted posters?"

Hollister straightened up. "I sure as hell do!"

"You better extend, then."

All the way back to the LRP compound, Michaelson was uncharacteristically quiet. Hollister could tell how angry he was by the way he kept clenching and unclenching his jaw. He decided not to interrupt Michaelson's thoughts with questions.

Hollister busied himself with the view. He realized how little time he had spent in any other part of the base camp other than the LRP compound and trips to the hospital complex. Everywhere he looked there was construction going on. New tropical hooches, new roads, pole climbers stringing commo wire, Vietnamese laborers filling sandbags, and rocks—white-painted rocks.

In true rear-echelon fashion, the rocks outlined the paths from the roadways to the entrances of the tents. Every rock had been whitewashed by hand and placed in straight lines. Hollister thought what a distance there was from the headquarters area to the LRP hooches. The actual distance of a half mile was dwarfed by the distance in understanding and appreciation for the risks and the devotion to duty that the kids in his platoon demonstrated every day.

The letters from Susan and Easy quickly perked Hollister up back at his hooch. The first half of Susan's letter was filled with little details of what she had accomplished and what she wanted him to know about her preparations for his return. She then filled the second half with plans and questions about Fort Benning and quarters and the little things in life like driver's licenses, state income-tax filing, and voting registration. Hollister couldn't believe how her letters were creating a tunnel for him to pass through from warrior to husband. It intimidated him a bit.

Easy's letter was like a conversation with him in the hooch. He made recommendations to Hollister on who he ought to move to what slots in his platoon. He discussed strengths and weaknesses of members of the platoon and some others in the detachment. Hollister was amazed at his awareness of the past performance and the potential of each man. Easy couldn't possibly have any records to help him; still, he knew the time remaining in country for every man still in Hollister's platoon.

Hollister put the letter down and thought about Easy, and how every day that he had known him he had learned something new from Easy, about himself and about being a platoon leader. He was sorry that he hadn't been able to tell Easy that before he got evac'd. He made himself a promise that he would find a way to do it.

Letters to and from Easy became a common event, but the tone in some of Hollister's letters must have reflected his confused frame of mind because Easy picked up on it and gently cautioned him, as Michaelson had, against letting revenge be the fuel that stoked his furnace. He did it in a way that didn't directly accuse Hollister of being vindictive. Instead, he told Hollister a story about a friend of his who had made life miserable for himself and those in his charge over the relentless goal he had set for himself to get back at a drunken radio operator who was asleep on duty one night, costing his unit some casualties. The story was perfectly timed to help Hollister put things into perspective and get on with the business of rebuilding his platoon.

Hollister put himself into the days he had left and took a sense of accomplishment out of the successes that the teams were having. He had decided to give up any further efforts to push about the investigation. He was convinced that even if the conclusions couldn't blame the deaths and wounded on Minh, that it would clear everyone on the American side of any wrongdoing.

Just less than a month before Hollister was due to leave, there was a cease-fire scheduled for a Vietnamese holiday. He went to bed early after having spent the afternoon packing some of his personal effects to ship home by surface.

Not able to sleep, Hollister got up and tried to write a letter to Susan. He was losing his enthusiasm to write because he knew that very soon he would probably beat a letter home. He had a few drinks and was angry with himself for using the scotch as a sleeping pill. He thought that he would cut back on his drinking when he got back to the States, but for right then, it was the only way to reward himself or to relax. The States would be different.

He wrote the letter as if it might beat him home, and enjoyed telling Susan that. He also told her how he was trying to make arrangements with the travel section at headquarters to route him through Denver so that he could stop off and see Easy. He hoped that she would understand. He was pretty sure that she would.

Quickly, the scotch made him drowsy and he went back to bed.

A soldier shook Hollister vigorously to wake him from the soundest sleep he had had in months. "Lieutenant, the captain wants to see you right away. He said ASAP!"

Hollister was still half asleep as he crossed the compound trying to tuck his T-shirt into his trousers. He looked around and thought it was strange that there was no noise coming from the team hooches. He looked at his watch to see what time it was and realized that he had left it on the desk next to his cot. He assumed that it was late, and continued to the orderly room, where he found Bernard drinking a cup of coffee in his shorts and shower shoes.

"Old Man's in the mess hall, sir."

Hollister entered through the connecting door and found the room completely dark. He had never seen the mess hall dark.

Suddenly the lights came on and he was being showered with the spray of shaken-up beer cans and bottles. The platoon had taken advantage of the stand down to throw a surprise going-away party for Hollister. Every member of the detachment had jammed himself into the small room to pull it off.

To no one's surprise, the party turned into a regular Airborne drunken brawl. Hollister knew that the noise level of the party was not just to celebrate his departure—that was just an excuse. They were really celebrating a feeling of competence that came from the hard work they had put in after rebuilding the detachment.

Somewhere around midnight Sergeant Marrietta walked over

to Hollister and leaned in close to him to be heard over t singing. "Somethin's up and I don't like it."

"What are you talking about?" Hollister asked.

Marrietta turned around and looked toward the doorway. was just coming back from the pisser and somebody from B gade just showed up. They wanna see the Ol' Man up at hea quarters."

"Could be some new mission."

"No, sir. It's not anyone I recognize from the S-3 shop."

Letting Marrietta's hunch sink in, Hollister looked at the be in his hand and decided to slow down just in case somethi was in the wind. He then looked at the troops getting very dru "Well, let's not spoil the party for them."

His head pounded and his mouth felt like it was stuffed w cotton as Hollister entered the orderly room, happy to get of the morning sun.

Marrietta looked up from Easy's old desk and responded Hollister's questioning look. "Yessir, he's waiting for you. I me tell him that you're here." He got up and walked to the op doorway to Michaelson's office. "Sir, Lieutenant Hollister here." Marrietta turned back to Hollister and pointed into t open doorway. "Go on in, sir."

Hollister started for the doorway and looked at Marriett expression for some clue as to the purpose of the meeting.

Marrietta was stone-faced serious. He spoke very quietly. " ain't good."

Standing at attention in front of Michaelson's desk, Hollis saluted. "Good morning, sir. You wanted to see me?"

"Sit."

The tone in Michaelson's voice was flat. Hollister could read anything into it, but could exclude any discussion abo upcoming operations. That topic usually provoked a distinct tone of excitement and enthusiasm in Michaelson. Hollis looked for some other clues—something to tell him if the su ject of the meeting was him or his performance or something should brace himself for.

The top of Michaelson's desk was cleared. The only thir on it were the two field phones. Hollister didn't know what th meant, but like Marrietta said, it couldn't be good.

"Jim, I'll give it to you straight out. I've been relieved command of the detachment. Effective today."

Unconsciously, Hollister bolted upright out of his chair. "What? No goddamn way!"

Expecting the response, Michaelson gestured for Hollister to calm down and sit down. "The deal is that I was not happy with the investigation on the Minh thing. I said so. And it got to the wrong people. *General* Minh went to his three-star boss and raised hell that I had impugned his honor and insulted him and undermined his authority and charged him falsely, and on and on. Bottom line is that he has insisted that I be punished. So, I'm gone as of today."

"But sir—they can't—what kind of shit is this?" Hollister stammered.

"You're wrong there. *They* can do whatever the hell they want. According to the Brigade XO, I have caused considerable embarrassment for the Americans, and this is their solution. They're offering my head to the new general. I guess I've fallen on my own sword by opening my mouth and not allowing the system to work."

There was a sinking feeling in Hollister's chest that felt cold and heavy. The thought of losing Michaelson so soon after losing Easy was overwhelming for him.

"Jesus, sir—I'm so sorry. I didn't mean to cause all this—"

"Wasn't you, Jim. It's a symptom of a much bigger problem. I saw it on my last tour with the Viets, and something told me then that sooner or later it was going to come around and bite me in the ass. Anybody who stays here long enough gets eaten up."

"What now? What are you going to do?" Hollister asked.

"I was on an extension. It's been pulled, and I'm on my way to the States for reassignment this afternoon."

"This afternoon?!" Hollister said.

"Captain Shaw will assume command of the detachment, and he wants you to be the new Operations officer."

"But what about my platoon?"

"Shaw wants to make Sergeant Davis the acting platoon leader for now. Lieutenant Matthews is only a couple of patrols away from being able to honcho that bunch. But for now, Davis can fill the gap. And I talked to the Brigade Sergeant Major this morning. Davis is going to make E-7 next month. He'll be all right."

"That's 'bout the only good news." Hollister hung his head, absorbing it all.

Michaelson came around the front of his desk and leaned up

against it. "Jim, I know you're short, but these kids need for
you and Shaw to keep it going without a moment's interruption
to the routine. Don't let them or any of the officers go wandering
around draggin' ass. Lead, set the example, and move on. I'll
be okay. Hell, I never planned on being a general anyhow. I'm
not qualified. My parents are married."

Hollister looked up to see one of Michaelson's rare smiles.
He was holding his hand out for Hollister to shake. He took
Michaelson's hand and shook it firmly. As he searched for words,
he felt an embarrassing and uncomfortable lump in his throat.

He felt like he was losing another friend to the war—a nonbattle casualty, but a casualty. "Boss, it isn't going to be the
same. I'm not sure that I want to be here with you and Easy
gone."

"You have to stick it out. If we all disappear, we'll be aban-
doning about the best troops I've ever worked with," Michaelson said.

"I understand, sir."

"Finish your tour standing tall. Get your ass back to Benning
and marry that girl. Have a good time back there, and remember
all this. But don't let it eat you up. You hear me?"

"Yessir. Will do."

The battle to keep up his own morale and not infect the troops
with the anger he felt over the screwing Michaelson got was
difficult for Hollister. The troops demanded a lot from him, and
he didn't want to let anybody down. He worked long hours as
Operations officer, but also spent time training his replacement
and helping Davis with his old platoon. He was sleeping less,
drinking more—to ease some of the pain—and becoming more
confused about things.

For the first time he had to start thinking about the future. In
his letters to Susan he explained that he didn't know what he
wanted to do about the army. He was angry over the decision to
relieve Michaelson, but knew that was not the whole army.

The thought of getting out felt to him like a pressure release
and a cop-out all at the same time. He told her that he didn't
want to make the decision right away. He wanted to spend some
time with her, back in the World first.

He even wondered if his decision would be affected by Vietnam's future. A year into the war, how long could it go on?
Waiting to make the decision was his best guess at how to handle
it, and he hoped that Susan would agree.

* * *

The few remaining weeks flew by for Hollister. One morning Bernard pulled Captain Shaw's jeep up to Hollister's hooch to drive him to the airfield for his flight to Cam Ranh Bay to meet the plane that would take him home.

Saying good-bye was tough and fast. Lots of promises were made all around to stay in touch and to write.

He was very disappointed that there had been no more progress in the investigation of General Minh's conduct. He decided that he couldn't let it eat him up. But he promised himself never to get in a situation like it again.

The stewardess woke Hollister just before they began their descent into Stapleton Airport in Denver. For a moment he didn't know where he was. He had slept the entire trip from Cam Ranh Bay, except for the few hours they spent on the ground in Guam to refuel. He almost felt embarrassed by how much and how deeply he had slept.

He had thanked the stewardess for waking him in time to get to the lavatory to clean up. As he stared at himself in the mirror, he realized how long it had been since he had actually seen himself in a decent mirror. He looked much older and very tired.

He took his shirt off to wash his face and shave. He surprised himself at how much weight he had lost. He had never been heavy. But under the harsh overhead light, he could see every rib and his collarbones poking through his pasty white skin. He thought of food. He decided to find a decent steak while he was in Denver, but first he had to see Easy and call Susan.

The light came in sideways through the bottoms of the three-quarter-shaded windows on each side of the huge ward and reflected off the checkerboard asphalt tile. It made the patients visible only in backlit outlines.

A medic had directed Hollister to a bed on the far end of the ward. He didn't know what to expect when he got to Easy. The last time Hollister had seen him, Easy was a fog of mud, blood, and torn flesh.

Long before Hollister could see Easy, he could hear him. His voice carried from the far end of the ward and out into the hallway. "You tell those fuckers that they're gonna be down here anyway. So will I! You hear me?"

Hollister came up behind Easy, who was sitting up on the

edge of his hospital bed yelling at the Specialist 7 medic wh was trying to deal with him.

"First Sergeant, you have a specific number of appointmen in therapy. They have been prescribed by a surgeon and are mor than adequate for your needs. More trips to physical therapy wi *not* earn you any extra points with the doctors."

"I don't give a flying fuck about any goddamn peacenik puss college-boy doctors! I want to get the fuck out of this goddam monument to fuck-offs! Do you understand me, Specialist? Easy asked, leaning forward for emphasis.

The medic was glad to see another face approaching ove Easy's shoulder.

"First Sergeant, I'm so glad to see that your vocabulary ha improved," Hollister said.

Easy spun around. His face lit up at the sound of Hollister voice. "Well, I'll be goddamned."

"No doubt about that," the medic said under his breath a he took the opportunity to get away from Easy.

As Hollister walked around the end of the bed to reach ou for Easy's hand, he caught sight of the bandaged stump stickir out from under the sheet.

Easy caught Hollister. "Ain't this a bitch? Is there anythin more ridiculous than a one-legged paratroop NCO?" He laughe at his own remark, to take the awkwardness out of the reunio with Hollister.

"Top, I could have found you in this hospital even withou having to stop and ask."

Easy made a disapproving face. "Don't get me started abou this fucking place. It's something out of the Dark Ages. I'≀ getting out just as soon as I can call in a few favors from som staff pukes back at the Pentagon."

"Getting out of the army?"

"I'm getting out of this place. They're not going to keep m here any longer without a serious fistfight."

Hollister didn't want to get into an argument with Easy ove the chances of the army allowing him to stay on active duty onc he did get out of the hospital. Hollister was sure that the arm would discharge him as soon as they could. It provoked th painful thought of Easy being treated at a Veterans Hospit somewhere.

Easy's tone quickly changed, and he changed the subject fro himself to Hollister. "Sit, tell me how you are. Going to Be ning, huh? Getting married, too? Damn!"

"Yeah, all that. I gotta tell you that we missed you after they evac'd you, and I just don't know how I'm ever going to thank you for what you did for me—and Theodore."

There was an awkward moment while they both remembered, but decided not to speak about Theodore's death.

Easy made a wide wave of his hand and tried to laugh it off. "Aw, hell. You think I was going to let my star lieutenant drown out there in a puddle of water buffalo shit?"

"Well, if you hadn't jumped out of that chopper—I wouldn't be here today."

"Forget about it. If *you* hadn't jumped out of your chopper, there might have been more dead LRPs and chopper jocks on that landing zone. But I do think there's a bottle of the spirits in it. Don't you think I have that much coming?"

"You got it. You name the brand, and I'll see that you're swimming in it," Hollister said, feeling more comfortable with Easy's efforts to lighten up the conversation.

"I understand you guys did some good stuff after I left. How the hell did that happen without me?"

"We muddled by without you, and you know that Captain Michaelson got—"

"Relieved! Yeah, I know. He was through here on the way home. Good man, that Michaelson. He'll be okay. He's the kind that you can't hurt with a hammer."

"It just wasn't the same in the detachment after you two left."

"You know that Michaelson sure thought a lot of you?" Easy asked.

"Me? I always felt like I was a day late and a dollar short around him."

"Not so. He did a lot of braggin' on you when he was here."

"Well, damn him. He pretty much kept it to himself around me."

"You didn't want him to give a lieutenant a swelled head, did you?" Easy asked, joking.

They both laughed at Easy's constant attempts at light disrespect folded into his backhanded compliments.

Easy found a pack of cigarettes on his nightstand and lit one. "So, what are your plans, sir?"

"Well, you know that I'm going to Benning, gettin' married—"

"Yeah, I know all that. You sticking with it or what?"

"Staying in?"

"Are you?" Easy asked.

"I don't know, First Sergeant. I don't know if I'm cut out for this. The past year was nothing like I expected it to be. I don't feel too good about the way I handled things. Too much of it got to me. And I'm not too sure if I ever want to be responsible for someone else's life again."

Easy tapped the ashes from his cigarette into a flimsy ashtray that kept spinning on a high spot on the nightstand. He leaned forward and lowered his voice, as not to be heard by the others in the ward. "Let me tell you something, Lieutenant. I been in this Army, man and boy, for longer than you been alive. I've seen officers come and go.

"There are a lot of pompous assholes, plenty of jerks that shouldn't have ever been commissioned, dangerous ones, selfish ones, and some that haven't got a clue what the hell is going on. But you ain't in that list. This is something I know about. And I'd be lying if I told you that I'm only concerned for you.

"You can bail out. Sure, just go on with your life and never look back. But chances are you'll be replaced by one of those assholes I'm talking about. Those kids need officers like you to worry about them, to fight for them, to hurt for them, to kick their little lazy butts when they need it, and to bust their asses in training. If you don't stay and do what you do—there'll be more dead Theodores.

"I think you ought to go back to Benning, enjoy that little girl you're gonna marry, get some time to breathe Stateside air, and then get on with the job. Your job.

"For you the job is training. If you let up on those kids back there—might as well write 'em off. You're in this now. Don't walk away. Don't forget the Theodores and the others.

"They need what you know and who you are. You're going to be a terrific company commander someday, and God only knows what after that.

"Makes no difference if this fuckin' war is right or wrong as two left feet. So long as they're sendin' troops over there—they need honchos like you.

"Give it some thought. None of us can just stack arms."

Easy's words sliced through Hollister's belly like a shard of glass. "I'll promise you that I'll give it lots of thought. That all I can do right now," Hollister said.

"Then that's good enough for me."

The next few weeks were a whirlwind for Hollister. His reunion with Susan was wonderful. She was everything he had thought about, prayed for, and waited for. Every day started with her smile and ended with her arms around him. They laughed and played while they packed and moved to Benning. The wedding ceremony happened somewhere in the middle of all the travels.

Nothing slowed the pace, not even the visit to Hollister's folks in Kansas. Friends and family kept their visit packed with things to do and plenty of well-wishing. Hollister was thrilled that everyone in his family fell in love with his Susan as quickly as he had. They took her into the clan as if she had grown up on the Kansas plains.

Moving into Army quarters was a mystery and an amazement for Susan. She had never seen a place as spotlessly clean as the small two-bedroom duplex that they were assigned in the officers' housing area called Custer Terrace. It was her first real appreciation for the family feeling that characterized Fort Benning in the sixties.

That some couple would spend so much time cleaning the quarters for another couple they would probably never meet was a very pleasant surprise for Susan.

She spent the first few weeks at Benning trying to make a home for the two of them. She had forgotten how she had practiced homemaking as a little girl with her friends. It was not a popular notion among her grown friends in New York, but she was at Benning and it was nothing like New York.

Hollister went to work early and came home late. Every night was filled with plenty of homework. He had to attend the Instructor Training Course, affectionately known as Charm School. In it, every move he made and every teaching technique was scrutinized and critiqued by instructors who were masters of military instruction and public speaking.

It was tough for Hollister, and he appreciated the help that Susan gave him. Many nights he would rehearse classes in front of her before he presented them to his classmates and the instructors for a grade.

Finally, he graduated from ITC and was classified as a qualified platform instructor—up to Benning's standards.

He still hadn't caught his breath from leaving Vietnam the morning he left the house to teach his first class at Harmony Church—the home of the Army's Ranger School.

He was worried that he might not be up to it. He had rehearsed his pitch over and over at home and had given it to other Ranger instructors in a brutal critique session known as a Murder Board.

But that morning was different. He was on his own. He wou[ ]
give the orientation to a new class of anxious Ranger students[ ]

Susan was careful not to smudge his brass as she kissed hi[ ]
good-bye at their front door. She could tell just how importa[ ]
that day was to him.

Two hundred fifty new, eager Ranger students filed into th[ ]
bleachers surrounding the sawdust-filled, hand-to-hand comb[ ]
pit at the Ranger School.

Lieutenant Hollister, dressed in starched and tailored f[ ]
tigues, entered the pit.

As he did, the student company commander called the clas[ ]
to attention and reported the class ready for instruction.

Hollister looked the young Ranger student directly in the eye[ ]
sharply returned his salute, and calmly told him to have the[ ]
take their seats.

As they sat down, Hollister stood ramrod straight in the cente[ ]
of the huge circle. The creases on his shirt and trousers we[ ]
sharp and unbroken. His patrolling cap, topped with a gold an[ ]
black Ranger tab over his lieutenant's insignia, was tilted dow[ ]
over his eyes. He took a long pause before speaking.

There was not a sound as all eyes were fixed on him. Th[ ]
students took in every detail of his appearance from his spi[ ]
shined paratrooper boots to the Airborne patch on his rig[ ]
shoulder and the parachute wings sewn on his shirt just belo[ ]
the coveted Combat Infantryman's Badge.

Every man in the bleachers knew that what Hollister wa[ ]
about to say couldn't be more important—it would be abou[ ]
Vietnam, it would be about their chances of living through wha[ ]
lay before them. Each student knew where he was going afte[ ]
Ranger School—Vietnam. They wanted Hollister to tell the[ ]
what to do, what to avoid, and how to survive.

Hollister began his class on the importance of Ranger Schoo[ ]
to them and the men who would be in their charge on the ba[ ]
tlefield. They hung on every word.

They believed every word.

He had been there.

And he would return.

GLOSSARY

A1-E—Single engine, prop-driven fighter bomber. Originally carrier aircraft adapted to land based operations in Vietnam. Flown by the VNAF.

ADF—Automatic direction finder—navigational aid that uses AM radio frequencies.

AO—Area of Operations. That geographical area assigned to a unit by specific boundaries.

APL—Assistant patrol leader

Arty—Shorthand for artillery. Indirect fires provided by howitzers and cannons

ARVN—Army of the Republic of Vietnam

ASAP—As soon as possible

AWOL bag—A small, soft-sided bag with two loop handles and a zipper top that soldiers often took on weekend passes to carry changes of underwear and shaving gear.

BDA—Bomb damage assessment

Briefback—Having received an order, subordinate leaders analyze the mission and give the order back to higher headquarters to ensure understanding

Camp Alpha—The replacement detachment in Saigon that in-processed the new arrivals from the States

CID—Criminal Investigation Division

Claymore—Directional, command detonated antipersonnel mine. Normally set up above the ground.

CONUS—Continental United States

CQ—Charge of Quarters. That NCO on duty during the night, standing in for the detachment headquarters personnel.

Cyclo—A three-wheeled bicycle that carries one or two passengers

Daily Dozen—Standard Army calisthenics

DEROS—Date of estimated return from overseas

Det cord—Explosive cord used in demolitions

DR—Delinquency report

Dust-Off—Original call sign for all medevac choppers

FAC—Air Force Forward Air Controller—who directs tactical air support

FNGs—Fucking new guys

FO—Forward observer—who adjusts indirect fires

G-2—Intelligence section of division and higher level headquarters

GP Medium—Rectangular squad tent

H&I—Harassing and interdicting fires

HE—High explosive ordnance

Headcount—NCO who checks for authorization to use mess hall facilities and keeps count of diners

Hogs—Overburdened, early model Huey gunships

IFFV—First Field Force, Vietnam

Jumpmaster—NCO or officer in charge of parachutists and the execution of a parachute jump

Klicks—Kilometers—map/ground measurement

Leg—Derogatory term used by parachute-qualified soldiers to refer to non-qualified ones

Lima-Lima—Phonetic alphabet for LL, land line—telephone wire

LZ—Helicopter landing zone

MACV—Military Assistance Command, Vietnam

McGuire rig—Anchor rigging and lines in a chopper to carry troops below on climbing ropes

MARS—Military Affiliate Radio Station

Medevac—Term usually meant the chopper evacuation of a casualty for medical attention. Sometimes applied liberally to any mode of transportation to medical facilities.

Mikes—Meters or minutes, depending on the context

NCOIC—Noncommissioned officer in charge

OCS—Officer Candidate School

Old Man—Affectionate term used to refer to the commanding officer. Never used in his presence.

Operations—That staff/headquarters section responsible for the tactical employment and planning of maneuver units (S-3, G-3)

PCS—Permanent change of station

Peter pilot—Helicopter co-pilot

Point—The lead man in a combat patrol was called the point man, and the position in the file was known as point

Papa Zulu—Phonetic alphabet for PZ, Pickup Zone

POV—Privately owned vehicle

PSP—Pierced steel planking—used to make runways

PT—Physical Training

PZ—Helicopter pickup zone

Redleg—Nickname for the artillery

REMF—Rear echelon motherfucker

RON—Remain overnight

RTO—Radio Telephone Operator

S-2—Staff section at battalion or brigade that handles all battlefield intelligence

Slicks—Troop and cargo carrying helicopters

SOI—Signal operating instructions, code words, call signs, and frequencies—classified information

SOP—Standard Operating Procedure

Sortie—One aircraft flight of a takeoff and return

Spoons—Cooks

Starlight—Night vision scope that uses ambient light

TDY—Temporary duty

The Cav—The First Cavalry Division (Airmobile)

The World—The United States—evolved from the term ''the real world''

Tokarev—A Communist 9mm automatic pistol

Trung-Uy—Vietnamese for First Lieutenant

Turtle—A soldier's replacement—because he takes so long to get there

TWs—Tropical worsted uniforms

URC-10—Small survival radio that emits a signal and can be used for voice transmission

victor romeo—Phonetic for visual reconnaissance

VNAF—(South) Vietnamese Air Force

VOCO—Verbal orders of the commanding officer—to identify instructions without paperwork

Warning Order—Early operations order issued, minus the details, so planning and preparation can start

WD-1—Double strand communications wire

web gear—Load-bearing harness for troops to carry their equipment

XO—Executive officer

Zoomies—Slang for Air Force(s)

The media was screaming for withdrawal
but the LRPs stood strong.

TAKE BACK THE NIGHT
A Novel of Vietnam

by Dennis Foley

During his third tour of Vietnam,
Captain Jim Hollister returned to Juliet
Company LRPs, this time as its commanding officer. Whether gassing tun-
nels, snatching prisoners, or rescuing
downed comrades under fire, these
LRPs never forgot that theirs was a sav-
age, desperate war of courage, honor,
and sudden death.

SPECIAL MEN
A LRP's Recollections
by Dennis Foley

After a lackluster high school career, Dennis Foley enlisted in the army. By the time he completed basic training, Foley had decided to become an officer. In six short but eventful years, he would move up from private in New Jersey to sergeant in Germany to LRP officer in Vietnam. Foley eventually retired a lieutenant colonel, a Ranger, a Special Forces soldier, and a hero.

This is his story of the uncommon, valorous men with whom he worked and of whom he was one. A tale of heroic achievement in combat, SPECIAL MEN is also a magnificent introduction to the art and science of leading men who are prepared to battle valiantly and die hard to fulfill their mission and protect their own.

Published by Ivy Books.
Available in bookstores everywhere.

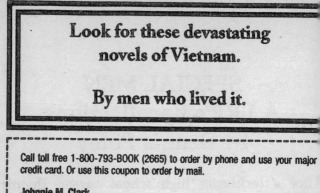